THAT SWEET AND SAVAGE LAND

Also by Emma Drummond:

Some Far Elusive Dawn
A Captive Freedom
The Bridge of a Hundred Dragons
Forget the Glory
Beyond All Frontiers
The Gathering Wolves
The Jade Alliance
Dragon of Destiny
The Burning Land
Scarlet Shadows

THAT SWEET AND SAVAGE LAND

Emma Drummond

St. Martin's Press
New York

Library of Congress Cataloging-in-Publication Data

Drummond, Emma.
    That sweet and savage land / Emma Drummond.
        p.   cm.
    ISBN 0-312-05973-6
    1. India—History—British occupation, 1765-1947—Fiction.
I. Title.
PR6054.R785T4   1991
823'.914—dc20   90-28539
                                                                CIP

First published in Great Britain by Victor Gollancz Limited.

First U.S. Edition: August 1991
10 9 8 7 6 5 4 3 2 1

THAT SWEET AND SAVAGE LAND

Chapter One

The insistent glorious call of a song thrush outside the cottage window woke Elizabeth at an early hour. In the stillness of dawn the echoing chorus of other birds was sweet music to the ears of a young woman more used to the strident sounds of the city. The inner restless yearning which had driven her down to this Sussex village now set her on her feet in the determination to ease it with action. Washing swiftly, she then donned a blue riding-habit and soft kid boots. The sophisticated matching hat she left in the wardrobe. A morning such as this was no time for restrictions. She wanted to ride with the wind in her hair and the chill of dawn flushing her cheeks. Freedom hung tantalizingly before her in this rustic environment. She would snatch it greedily while it was available.

Her unexpected appearance made Thompkins jump nervously as he turned with a mug of hot tea in his cupped hands. Unlike the grooms in city stables, he was a simple country man, inexperienced in hiding his private thoughts beneath an appearance of smooth urbanity. His ruddy face registered disapproval of her clear intention to go riding at such an hour.

'Oh, marm, you did fair give me a start,' he scolded. 'What be you doing up already? Miss Mount did say you was come fer a rest and this don't seem like no rest to me. Does she know you be up and about?'

Elizabeth gave her most persuasive smile. 'Don't preach at me, Thompkins. The rest I have come for is from people set on preventing me from doing anything I enjoy. Saddle up Marny for me, if you will. I'll be back in London soon enough. I can't afford to miss opportunities such as this.'

Thompkins had no choice but to do as he was bid, muttering darkly about city ways being unsuitable for the country and telling himself that this former charge of Miss Mount's behaved as she did because she was half French. That terrible revolution was behind it all. Thompkins did not hold with killing off the aristocracy and letting people do just as they pleased. He believed in social order, with every man knowing and keeping his place in it. So he sighed and tut-tutted as he clothed the mare in a blanket, then a ladies' saddle. When he then began preparing a grey gelding, Elizabeth guessed his intention and spoke swiftly.

'There is no need for you to accompany me, Thompkins. You have your tasks to do.'

The groom looked at her aghast across the dim stable filled with the aroma of fresh straw. 'You can't go riding alone, marm. It be too dangerous.'

She dismissed his concern lightly. 'I would never dream of setting foot in the streets unaccompanied before ten in the morning in London, but whatever danger could I encounter in a sleepy place like Wellford?'

'That's just it, marm,' warned the groom, shrugging into his old cloth coat. 'You'd be out there all alone.'

'Then no possible harm can come to me, for who is to administer it?' Elizabeth declared, leading Marny to the mounting-block and settling on the saddle with her long skirt draped gracefully over her legs. 'I'll be away for an hour. Tell Miss Mount that I shall be ravenous when I return.'

Before the sturdy middle-aged man could force his company on her she was out of the yard and trotting the mare through the winding main street of the village. Her destination lay beyond the huddle of stone cottages and through the small copse at the eastern boundary of Wellford. Marny's hoofbeats rang on the cobbles as they passed between little homes whose owners took competitive pride in their gardens. Elizabeth loved the tiny rectangles filled with forget-me-nots, honeysuckle, wild daffodils and a rainbow of lupins amid neat rows of feathery carrot-tops, flowering potato plants and dark red beetroot leaves. This morning she took particular pleasure in all she saw, for only last evening had she arrived here feeling desperate for escape. Already that caged sensation was fading. Yet desperation was present in another form now that she was relatively free, because she knew it could never be more than an illusion.

Her father's forebears had escaped from the Terror, abandoning their title along with their lands in the bid to reach England. They had brought with them money and jewels enough to enable them to live in extreme comfort, until Elizabeth's father, René de Rioches, had been obliged to accept a post on the board of a respectable trading company in order to support his wife and daughter. Miss Mount had been employed as governess to the only child of middle-aged parents. She had remained as a genteel companion when the adolescent Elizabeth had been placed in the charge of an aged bachelor related by marriage to Madame de Rioches on her death a year after her husband's. Uncle Matthew had leapt at the chance to rid himself of his unwanted ward when William Delacourt, a young army officer from a respectable family, had asked permission to marry Elizabeth.

A faint sigh escaped the unhappy Mrs Delacourt as she guided Marny along the path cutting through the copse. How could William have been so blind? How could she? They had known nothing of each other's true character before the wedding, it seemed. At seventeen and filled with a yearning for affection, she had been dazzled by the large blond handsome fellow in a scarlet jacket whose youth had called to her own after a lifetime spent with ageing parents and an octogenarian guardian. Yet she should have seen the warning signs in his over-protectiveness and she had been naïve in the extreme to have ignored the style of his mother and four sisters. Emily Delacourt and the Misses Delacourt were gentle biddable creatures, concerned only with their stitching and uninspired water-colours. They occupied their days with such pastimes as choosing new ribbons for their bonnets, paying morning calls on other genteel females, or taking short walks in the park when the weather was just right. Why had it never dawned on Elizabeth that William would expect a wife in that same mould? Why had he imagined that the lively well-read girl who had caught his bachelor fancy would turn overnight into a copy of his colourless sisters? The heedlessness of youth had deceived them both and led them into a union which had failed after the first few months. The charming, ardent beau had become an intolerant, domineering husband making no attempt to hide the fact that he continued to chase excitement in the company of females willing to please any man for a few shillings.

Their quarrels had grown more and more frequent. William had been outraged, not so much by what his wife said to him in anger, but by the fact that she said anything at all. When Austin Delacourt spoke, William's mother and sisters listened then obeyed. Not once had they ever answered back. Elizabeth's French flair for colour and style in her dress had been dubbed by William as too daring for the wife of an ambitious young officer. She had flatly refused to become a dowd at eighteen. Even her paintings, which also expressed her love of vibrant colour, had been likened to the daubings of an untutored child. The greatest cause of discord between them, however, had been Elizabeth's insatiable appetite for learning. Being bilingual she read the works of the most distinguished British and Continental travellers, scholars and intellectuals. In conversation she would probe and question anyone with interesting things to say; she saw nothing wrong in having conversations with gentlemen on subjects rarely broached by females. A man of few convictions, William bitterly condemned her free manner which he claimed made her the subject of raised eyebrows and whispers of disapproval. She had asked him why intelligence in a young woman should be considered undesirable.

'I fail to see why you are ashamed to have a wife who can amuse and entertain your guests more comprehensively than those of most of your friends.'

'My guests require from you an excellent meal, solicitous attention to their comfort, and skill enough to guide the conversation throughout the evening.'

'And I fail in those three?'

'Only in the third, Elizabeth. You do not guide the conversation, you dominate it. If it becomes known that Delacourt's wife is a precocious chatterbox it will do untold harm to my career. No commanding-officer cares to have his officers embarrassed by their ladies.'

Only then had it dawned on her that she had committed the sin of continuing to be a person in her own style instead of becoming the silent, submissive partner who valued social status above intellect. The qualities which had amused and stimulated him during their carefree courtship now rebounded, causing him to feel inadequate in her presence; consequently he was telling her that she must subdue her own natural personality, which outshone his in public. It was an intolerable proposal and she protested.

'I am the same girl you first met. Why did you take me as a wife?'

'I have asked myself that a hundred times over.'

'Well it is done now, William, and I must tell you that I cannot play the docile simpering miss and neither can I be silent in conversations unless I cut out my tongue.'

'It may come to that,' he had said darkly, walking from the room.

Such had been the situation between them when the regiment was warned for India eight months after their wedding. The news had thrilled Elizabeth and filled her with fresh hope. Away from the Delacourt drabs, in an exotic country where colour and ethnic culture thrived, they could surely recapture a modicum of their former delight in each other. She had offered up a prayer of thanks. Then William had shattered her with the information that he intended to leave his wilful wife with his family, who had kindly agreed to have her, during an absence which could last as long as ten years. Elizabeth had been frantic. She had begged and implored him to change his mind, promised to be all he wished if he would take her to India. He had clearly anticipated such extravagant promises for he had then stated that India was no place for a well-bred female. In vain she had spoken of the very many instances, even among his own friends, where ladies of higher birth than herself had lived there for many years with their husbands. He had claimed that she was too young for such a life. Finally, she had accused him of deliberate desertion, for he had every opportunity to transfer to another regiment in England in order to remain by her side. His last word had been that he had a strong sense of duty toward his men and Forrester's Light Dragoons, which demanded his going wherever they were sent.

So William and his precious regiment had sailed and she had tried to console herself with the hope of greater peace of mind, to say nothing of the freedom his absence would give her. The hope had been a false one. The dreary Delacourt routine had made her almost crazy with boredom, and William's going had given her no freedom whatsoever. His ring was on her finger; she bore his name. He controlled her in his absence. The fact was particularly depressing when she considered that he would be enjoying life to the full, with his troublesome wife out of sight and, therefore, out of mind.

After enduring a second season in which she had felt neither spinster, wife, nor widow, the frustration and sense of injustice she had nursed for so long had burst into open revolt. Telling the long-suffering Delacourts that she needed a change of scene, she had hastened to Wellford for an indefinite holiday, knowing that Lavinia Mount would cosset her and lend a sympathetic ear.

As Marny emerged through the trees to tread across broken fencing in to the overgrown park comprising part of Wellford Manor estate, Elizabeth owned that her unhappiness was not due to William's absence but to being denied the opportunity to visit India. All she had heard and read about the country appealed to her love of variety, richness and colour. In her heart she sensed that her own love of the exotic would find true fulfilment in that distant continent.

Lost in images conjured up by her thoughts, Elizabeth gained the open hillside to be startled from her reverie by the sight of another rider thundering toward her in the belief that he had the morning to himself. Her heartbeat increased alarmingly as she reined in. The other horse, a huge brute with wild eyes, took exception to her presence, however, and gave a frenzied display of temperament which should have unseated even the most skilled of riders. Elizabeth watched with awed admiration as the horseman controlled his mount with a firm hand and soothing commands until the beast stood, lathered and snorting, but reassured.

'Bravo, sir. Bravo indeed!' Her words were instinctive and genuinely warm with praise but the recipient, although hardly a huge brute with wild eyes, clearly also took as great an exception to her presence as his black stallion.

'This is private property, madam. You are trespassing.'

Her fiery defence stuck in Elizabeth's throat as the man urged his animal toward her. Dark tumbled hair, blue eyes vivid with annoyance, a square face as dark as that of any rajah, and an air of implacability made the stranger disturbingly exciting in the aftermath of shock from the near collision.

'You ride superbly,' she murmured. 'By rights, you should be at my feet with a broken neck.'

'It would serve me well if I were. Only a fool mounts a horse he cannot control.' Scrutinizing her closely from the coils of dark hair at each ear right down to the hem of her elegant blue skirt, he then asked roughly, 'Have you lost your way?'

She shook her head. 'No. I will admit to your charge of trespassing but I challenge your right to levy it. You have no more right to be here than I. The Squire died recently in a hunting accident caused by liberal indulgence in the stirrup-cup rather than bad horsemanship.'

'Oh, indeed! How do you know this?' he demanded aggressively.

'My dear friend Lavinia Mount wrote to tell me of it,' Elizabeth said with matching directness. 'It was no secret that Tom Stavenham was as big a libertine as his father. Sir Francis killed himself in almost identical fashion only two years ago.'

'By too liberal indulgence in the stirrup-cup? So your dear friend Lavinia Mount wrote to acquaint you with the news of my father's death, also, did she?'

'She writes to me of all village gossip whenever . . .' The full import of his words filtered through her bemused senses. 'Your *father!*'

'I have the doubtful honour of being another of the breed; John Stavenham, captain of Chetwynde's Hussars, at your service.'

Her cheeks grew warm as she realized she had unwittingly insulted this man's family. She hastened to apologize. 'You must think me disgustingly ill-mannered. I had no notion that Sir Francis had another son. I came here only yesterday evening, so had not heard of your presence at the manor.'

'Lavinia Mount is shockingly behindhand with the latest gossip, it seems.'

The colour in her cheeks deepened. 'You have every right to order me off your property, Captain Stavenham.'

'Yes, but you apparently felt you had every right to be on it.' He was silent for a moment as if trying to reach a decision. When he spoke again he surprised her. 'Perhaps we should continue our ride. Kasper is growing restless and we shall be overtaken by this deceptive chill unless we move on. I suggest a brisk trot to the trees at the far end. Do you agree?'

Elizabeth nodded, accepting his olive-branch gladly. He intrigued her, despite all she had heard of his family — or because of it. It would have been disappointing if he had insisted that she leave when fortune had decreed that their paths should cross in such a dramatic manner. They set off side by side, their horses' hooves falling in muffled beat on the springy turf. She had ridden here whenever she had visited her former companion, for Tom Stavenham had never repaired fences or protected his property with any vigilance. Yet she had never before noticed the soft haze, blue against the green valley, or the way the sun shimmered on the dew which clothed the sloping hillside. The very air this morning seemed sweeter and more exhilarating than Sussex usually produced.

'You will be accustomed to the gentle aspect of mornings like this,' her companion remarked as they neared the trees and slowed to a walking pace, 'to a man recently arrived from India it is more a matter of rediscovery.'

The sensation of disturbing excitement which this man had initially aroused, now doubled to the extent of making Elizabeth breathless as she reined in. 'You are from India! I can scarce believe it.'

13

He gently drew the stallion to a halt facing her, and again studied her intently as he asked, with a return to coolness, 'Is it so unbelievable that a military officer should serve in India?'

Too enthusiastic to be discouraged by his reversal of manner, Elizabeth explained. 'When I emerged from the copse into your path I was lost in speculation about the very land you claim to have left so short a time ago. Is that not an amazing coincidence?'

'Amazing,' he agreed dryly. 'Shall we now retrace our way back to the copse?'

Sensing that he had decided to see her off his property after all, Elizabeth sighed with regret. 'Forgive me. I have trespassed on your good nature as well as your acres. You are here for the sad task of settling your late brother's affairs and I have shown great insensitivity this morning.'

They had covered more than fifty yards at a walking pace before he spoke again. 'You will doubtless think *me* insensitive if I tell you that the only sadness my brother's demise arouses in me is the fact that he also killed a good horse in the fall. What a man chooses to do with his own life is his privilege, but it is a sin wilfully to ruin a beast who has no choice in the matter. His grey had to be destroyed on the field.'

Moved by this unexpected frankness, so at variance with his cool manner, Elizabeth ventured to take the subject a step further. 'I did not know Mr Stavenham, but it was impossible not to hear of his exploits with the Wellford Vale Hunt.'

'There is a body of men who will mourn his passing,' he commented in harsh tones, gazing at the distance as if seeing into the past. 'Tom was a generous, hospitable man toward anyone who would take a drink with him. With his death they have lost an endless fount of ale.'

Casting a swift glance at his set features, Elizabeth decided that here was a Stavenham of vastly different mould. She could now understand the complexion darkened by the Indian sun, the erect bearing found in many military men, and the quality of his horsemanship. Clearly, he was a person of some principle, unlike his dissolute kinsmen. He intrigued her and, seeing the copse looming ahead, she hastened to recapture his attention before they reached it and had to part.

'I have ridden in the grounds of Wellford Manor many times, sir. The estate possesses potential beauty. You must despair at being faced with a house and acres which have been allowed to decline so badly. You have a difficult task ahead.'

He turned to her. 'That's the least of my worries.'

Probing the enigmatic statement, she asked, 'Is your wife happy to settle at Wellford after so long in India?'

The characteristic change in manner, which she had found so disconcerting, was so swift and intense this time, it was almost a rebuke when he said coldly, 'I have no wife, ma'am, and there is no question of my ever settling at Wellford.'

Elizabeth drew Marny to a halt at the edge of the copse, bristling beneath his brusqueness which she felt was unwarranted. She had merely been making polite enquiries, such as any stranger might.

'Your authoritative manner towards my trespassing naturally suggested to me that you were jealous of your inherited property,' she said deliberately. 'So you are not to take up residence?'

He circled to face her on the tall stallion, ready to ride back to the home he apparently did not want. 'I have taken a furlough in order to settle everything in the hands of my cousin. He has the soul of a countryman and will run Wellford better than any Stavenham. His brood of six children will thrive in this soft county, and the flower garden cannot fail to flourish in the tender care of his wife who has magic in her fingers when handling plants.'

'You plan to rejoin your regiment abroad?' she asked enviously.

He nodded. 'Next month. I was not born to play the squire. The army is in my blood . . . and so is India,' he added, as if telling himself the fact.

Feeling that he had almost forgotten her presence, she studied him during the curious hiatus. This man was clearly too full of burning energy, too restless for a rustic life. Military service in a land as restless as he would suit him admirably. She felt immense envy of his freedom to leave responsibility behind and return to the one place she yearned to see. It drove her to say, 'I wish you would give me your personal account of the colony. I have read all I can on the subject, but one cannot ask questions of a book when its pages do not provide the right information. Printed words are often cold and unfeeling, do you not find? Yours would contain human warmth inspired by experience.'

He frowned at her. 'You wish to ask questions of me in the hope of becoming an expert on the subject in just a few minutes? To tell even the little I know of so complex a country would take a very long time, I fear.'

It sounded like another rebuke, and she sighed. 'I have been told that inquisitiveness is my greatest failing. I beg your pardon. You have been remarkably tolerant with your trespasser.'

15

Just as he seemed on the brink of bringing the encounter to an end, he hesitated. Then, still frowning, he asked, 'Why are you so interested in hearing my opinion of India?'

Eager to coax it from him when he appeared to be relenting, she said, 'I lost my husband to the country over a year ago, so I long to acquire an accurate impression of it.'

This time the change in him took her totally by surprise. The rigid lines of his features softened dramatically and warmth crept into his vivid blue eyes.

'Forgive me, I did not mean to pry. My condolences on your sad loss. Of course I shall endeavour to give you a brief word picture while I accompany you back to the village, ma'am.'

Elizabeth underwent a shattering sense of embarrassment as she realized how he had misconstrued her words. Confused thoughts raced through her head as he turned to escort her through the copse. To attempt to correct his mistake now would be uncomfortable for them both. Caught in a web of her own spinning, she moved off alongside him, telling herself that here was a perfect example of William's charge of precocious behaviour with gentlemen. The moment for truth was irrevocably lost as he began to describe the land she had been denied by her unyielding husband, but guilt soon vanished as her imagination flew on the wings of longing while she listened avidly.

'India is a land of great contrasts,' he began, as the trees closed around them to provide enticing dimness. 'It is baffling yet simple, heat-ridden and snow-bound, in rags and magnificent riches. The gilded rulers live in vast palaces, clothing themselves and their favourites in jewels, yet caste laws put ordinary men and their descendants into social categories from which they can never escape. India is beautiful and it is tawdry. Rain falls for weeks on end at certain times of the year. For the rest it is parched, dusty and plagued with fever. Its people worship a variety of gods; value individual cultures. Distances are vast; journeying is slow and difficult. Conflict occurs frequently; often blowing up without warning over some minor point of race, caste or religion. Our rule is made uneasy by dint of the impossibility to match the European and Asian mind.' He frowned at the twisting path ahead. 'One either hates India or is totally spellbound.'

'And you are spellbound?' she asked gently.

Turning to her swiftly, he said, 'Not exactly. I simply sense that my destiny lies in that sweet and savage land.'

Elizabeth allowed several moments to pass before she ventured to say, 'As an Englishman and a soldier is that not a somewhat disturbing premonition?'

He considered her momentarily with narrowed eyes. 'How very perceptive you are. I had never before seen it in that light.'

'Perhaps the mystique of the country has taken possession of you. That would explain the sensation of fate awaiting you there.'

He shook his head. 'I am not a fanciful man. Soldiers rarely are.'

'Then I can only express my sincere hope that your destiny will lie in the sweet and not the savage aspects of India, Captain Stavenham.'

They rode on without speaking until they reached the fifteenth-century church. There she drew rein and turned to smile up at him. 'Miss Mount's cottage is now in clear view. You have been very civil, sir. I appreciate your concise but remarkably vivid reply to my request for knowledge. I'll now leave you free to continue the ride which I so dangerously interrupted.'

He circled to face her, clearly now in no hurry to leave. 'You must understand that one can no more divine India in a few years than a child can learn all his lessons in one day. I am familiar with just two areas, which makes me no more qualified to extend your knowledge than the books which disappointed you with their shortcomings. On your next morning ride you should endeavour to cross the path of a maharajah,' he added, with a hesitant smile which softened his austere expression dramatically.

'When I hear of one in the neighbourhood I shall certainly do so,' she murmured, struck by a volatile personality which caused unwelcome confusion in her. She was normally so assured in company.

'May I know your name before bidding you good day?' he asked. 'I have no Lavinia Mount to relate such facts to me.'

Colouring at his gentle reminder of her earlier free words, she told him what he wanted to know. He then touched his forehead with his whip in a salute of farewell.

'Please trespass on my land whenever you wish, Mrs Delacourt. I promise never to charge down upon you again.'

His departure spared Elizabeth the need to reply. She walked Marny back through the cobbled streets where the little cottages were now stirring with the sounds of clattering pails, runabout children and barking, morning-bright dogs. She must not ride along that hillside again during her visit to Wellford. It was unlikely that she would meet John Stavenham elsewhere, so it did not matter too much that his misunderstanding over William remained uncorrected. It was a great pity that she was obliged to avoid another meeting, however. It would have been so interesting to hear of his experiences as a military man, and to discuss all manner of social topics with him. Although he had alternated between aloofness and civility in a most bewildering fashion, he had in no way treated her questions with an attitude which suggested that he shared William's opinion of female intellect. Quite the reverse, she believed.

When she walked in to the parlour, filled with the smells of lavender and beeswax, Miss Mount was so struck by her appearance, she forgot to remonstrate. Instead, the plump figure in brown sprigged cotton studied the girl she had raised from a child.

'My dear, how very charming you look. You have the most delightful roses in your cheeks which make me wonder if you really were as pale as I thought you on your arrival. How very wise you were to come.'

Elizabeth smiled back fondly. 'Desperation not wisdom governed the decision, Vinnie. You have met the Misses Delacourt. Their wit sparkles like neglected brass, their humour is so subtle they have yet to appreciate the joke, and their intellect surpasses even that of a fish.'

Miss Mount clicked her tongue disapprovingly at such sarcasm, but she continued to set blue and white china upon the table which already bore pots of honey, strawberry jam and butter.

'Jane will be bringing breakfast in a very few minutes. If you wish to eat any of it wash your hands and tidy your disgracefully windblown hair. Go on, off with you.'

Laughing lightheartedly, Elizabeth ran up the stairs to her bedroom. There was curious comfort in Lavinia's nursemaid treatment after the admonishments of the Delacourt household. Had she thought deeply on the subject, she might have realized that the love of this doting spinster compensated for that she had never received from her parents and fault-finding husband.

Her laughter gradually subsided as she saw herself in the plain mirror on the wall. There was a delicate pink in her cheeks and a glow in eyes which had looked dull for too long. Putting cool hands up to the smudge of colour on her face she realized that there was also a surge of life inside her which had not been there before this morning. Thoughts of a dark

18

face which could be suddenly lit by a smile, and blue eyes which were shrewd, suspicious and appreciative in bewildering succession increased her sense of vitality. A flutter of something remarkably akin to fear touched her, then. Half an hour in his company had left her more intrigued than she had ever been with a new acquaintance. It would be unwise to dwell on his words, his puzzling switch from aggression to frankness and back. It would be worse than unwise to recall the timbre of his voice as he had spoken of India. She must put John Stavenham from her mind.

Miss Mount's reminder to hasten, which floated up from the parlour, broke that moment of chilling awareness, and she patted her hair into place with hands which were trembling slightly. There were coddled eggs and slices of ham on the table, but her appetite had vanished. Taking a piece of bread and butter to eat with her coffee, she instantly ignored her inner warnings by speaking of the man she had just vowed to forget.

'You should have advised me that I must not ride through Wellford estate, Vinnie. I did not know the new owner has an eye to protecting his property.'

Miss Mount glanced up from salting her egg, her myopic hazel eyes bright with indignation. 'And *I* did not know that you would rise at dawn in order to trespass, madam. From the distressed and weary state you were in when you came last night, I naturally assumed that your bed would be much occupied for your first few days with me.'

'You know me better than that,' said Elizabeth with a shake of her head. 'I have the greatest aversion to languishing between the sheets unless I am at death's door.'

'I know that is so, my dear, but pray do not tax me with failing to warn you from something I had no notion you would do.'

'I did not know Sir Francis had sired two sons, Vinnie. Why have I never heard of the fact?'

Concentrating on her egg, the other woman said, 'The younger Stavenham has been abroad for years.'

'That should not have put him from the minds of the villagers as if he did not exist.'

'No, but the exploits of Sir Francis and Mr Thomas certainly overwhelmed any interest in the Captain,' Miss Mount explained as she poured more coffee in Elizabeth's cup. 'You should take more than bread and butter at the start of the day, my dear. I cannot have you fainting away by noon.'

'Why did you not tell me yesterday of Captain Stavenham's arrival from India?' she demanded impatiently. 'You know of my passion for that country.'

With placid precision her companion continued to eat her light breakfast while countering the challenge in her normal mild manner. 'The coach deposited you at the inn at eight-thirty—more than one hour late, which is most unusual—and you did little more than regale me with your sense of injustice at being left with Mr Delacourt's dull, prosy, lacklustre family, whilst drinking hot milk, before going to your bed. I had no opportunity to acquaint you with village news.'

Giving a repentant smile, Elizabeth said, 'Dear Vinnie, how restful you are after the critical reproaches of William's family, who manage to make the slightest slip into a major misdemeanour.'

The pink-cheeked woman, whose thickening figure and few streaks of grey in her brown hair denoted contentment, forgot her breakfast as some new thought struck her. 'As I did not offer the news regarding Captain Stavenham, you must have heard it elsewhere. Not from Thompkins, surely?'

'He was also out riding this morning. I fear he accused me of trespassing on his property when I emerged from the copse right into his path.'

Miss Mount's cheeks grew even pinker. 'Well, so you were! You should not have gone there, and alone, too. What must he have thought of you? I'm sure the Delacourts have every reason to be reproachful if you behave in such a reprehensible fashion. What if he makes it known that you have so little decorum you ride carelessly across private property at the crack of dawn?'

A laugh escaped her. 'Oh Vinnie, you look so prune-faced! You speak as if he were an ogre and I a hoyden. Captain Stavenham might have initially been cool and rather reserved, but he invited me to continue my ride in his company and then escorted me in the most respectful fashion as far as the church. We parted on most amicable terms. Even the Delacourts could not take exception to my behaviour.' She paused to consider. 'Well, *they* might, I suppose, but no sensible person would.'

'Do you include your absent husband in that category?' came the sobering question.

Recalling the sympathetic condolences John Stavenham had offered on the supposed loss of her husband, a shadow crossed the sunshine of the morning. The Delacourts would definitely frown on that unwitting

20

deception. The thought silenced her, and some minutes passed before Miss Mount finished her egg, set down her spoon and fixed Elizabeth with a look she knew well.

'You must not ride in the grounds of Wellford Manor again.'

'I had no thought of doing so,' she murmured. 'The late Mr Stavenham was careless of all he owned — even his life, it seems — but his younger brother is of a different cut. There appears to have been little love lost between them, Vinnie. Do you know why?'

Settling back in her chair with a second cup of tea in her hands, Lavinia said, 'I only know what I was told by Maud Barratt, who has lived in Wellford all her life. Lady Stavenham died soon after producing her second son. Her husband took an aversion to the baby, although there is no evidence to suggest that Sir Francis was overly fond of his wife. Quite the reverse. However, there is no doubt that Thomas was pampered, favoured and encouraged to indulge in every excess, whilst young John was ignored. Maud says there was no suggestion of unkindness or undeserved punishment levied on the boy, but isolation and lack of interest can prove to be as cruel to a small child.'

'Poor John,' murmured Elizabeth from the heart.

'Thomas emulated his father in every respect, so he grew to manhood disliking his brother heartily. It was as well that young John spent little time at Wellford during his schooldays. On leaving Cambridge, where he reputedly acquitted himself very well, he asked his father to purchase for him a commission in the cavalry. Sir Francis was only too pleased to do so and get the boy off his hands.'

As her companion was now well into her favourite pastime Elizabeth made no attempt to interrupt her flow of revelations, but she heard it all with an increasing sense of affinity with the man she had met just this morning.

'Soon after joining his regiment, it was posted to India. The family parting was welcomed by all members, according to Maud, and father and elder son continued their downhill path with even more zest. You already know that Sir Francis broke his neck whilst riding a beast said to be possessed of the devil. Even a sober man had difficulty controlling it, and Sir Francis was extremely intoxicated, by all accounts. Thomas took his father's death so badly he then abandoned the few virtues he had retained and indulged in every extravagance possible. You would not credit, my dear, the kind of people he invited to the Manor. Those few of the servants who lived locally refused to go up there again. You will know there must have been strong cause for such a sacrifice, for employment is not easily come by in country districts. They were replaced by menials from London. On the few occasions that these people ventured to the village they were seen to be shifty, mean-faced creatures unwilling to pass the time of day with those they clearly considered to be their inferiors,' Miss Mount declared significantly. 'No one knows to this day what exactly went on in that house but suffice it to say that anyone who passed near heard the most disquieting sounds of revelry which were often punctuated by *pistol shots*! The Rector braved the place several times in the dread expectation of finding a corpse.'

'Vinnie, how very melodramatic,' cried Elizabeth in mirth. 'Gentlemen often indulge in ridiculous and rather dangerous antics when they have been drinking. An officer in William's regiment is reputed to have shot all the crystal drops from a priceless chandelier to win a wager.'

Lavinia looked shocked. 'How very, very wicked!'

Taking far more interest in village gossip than she had before, Elizabeth was beginning to glimpse a possible reason for John Stavenham's disconcerting attitude toward others. What a legacy to return to, especially after a long complicated journey from a distant land. Too restless to remain at the table, she got to her feet and crossed to the small window where a bowl of sweet-scented blue hyacinths stood on the sill. Gazing out at the sweep of meadows where black and white cows grazed, she said, 'Tell me more about the Captain.'

'There is little more I can tell you, dear. He was away in India but Thomas was here beneath the noses of the villagers. They are bound to be more acquainted with the doings of the older Stavenham.'

'I see,' she said in disappointment.

'There is some talk of a marriage soon after he left England,' mused the gentle voice.

Elizabeth swung round from her study of the countryside. 'A marriage? He told me he has no wife.'

'So he has not. The information is not at all reliable, you must understand, but Amy Goddard had it from her niece who is in service with a military family. One of the sons of the house was in India at the time and wrote home of the affair. It caused something of a scandal.'

'A scandal . . . why?'

'The wife simply disappeared.'

'Disappeared?' repeated Elizabeth once more, even more sharply. 'Whatever do you mean by that?'

Miss Mount's uncomplicated features took on a bewildered expression. 'Just that, my dear . . . I think. It happened eight years ago and Amy is rather vague on the subject. The pair were absurdly young, of course. According to Amy, the girl was an artist who went out very early one morning, accompanied by only a servant, to paint the Indian sunrise. Neither ever returned.' She pushed back her chair, rose, and began packing up the used china onto a tray. 'The story has been relayed through many sources. There might be no truth in it. I confess that I have doubted its veracity since first hearing it.' She glanced up from her task with a frown. 'However, after hearing your account of the disgraceful destruction of a priceless chandelier as a result of a wager, I suppose anything is possible . . . with military gentlemen.'

The sounds of breakfast being cleared from the table and taken to the adjacent kitchen by the village girl who did the cooking and heavier cleaning, faded to the background, as Elizabeth turned back to the view from the window. *I lost my husband to India just over a year ago.* Small wonder he had been instantly sympathetic. Her sense of guilt redoubled as she thought of the tragedy in his life. Eight years in which to wonder if she could possibly still be alive; almost three thousand days, each one dominated by torment over a loved one's unknown fate. Elizabeth had already sensed that he was not a man of shallow feelings, so he was unlikely to have tied himself in youthful marriage for any reason other than undeniable passion. He had declared that his destiny lay in India. Did he still hope to find his lost love there? Unbidden came swift, surprising envy of a woman who had won such a man's devotion and held it throughout all those absent years.

Chapter Two

From the gazebo at the western end of the deer park, Wellford Manor looked most impressive. Its sturdy Georgian exterior gave no sign of the deterioration at this distance, but John sighed heavily as he gazed across at the house he had hoped never to see again. Tom had taken no more pride in the place than their father had. They had both seen it merely as somewhere to entertain their dissolute friends, and a roof under which to sleep off the effects of heavy drinking. To spend money on repairs and the upkeep of a building was to waste it, in their opinion. Wealth was there to be squandered on pleasures and self-indulgence. The wealth had long gone, yet the spending had continued. The estate was now deeply in debt; Tom owed thousands in personal obligations. The pictures hanging along the walls were simply convincing copies, the originals having been sold, one by one, to finance further revels. The jewellery which Estella Stavenham had worn must have been sacrificed soon after her death. The velvet cases, still in the safe, contained no more than the imprint of what had once gleamed against the satin linings.

Urging Kasper forward, John rode slowly over the wilderness which was the park, filled with dull anger. Although Wellford held only unhappy memories for him, he thought his father and Tom should have taken more pride in their inheritance. It had once been a very beautiful house, surrounded by grounds designed by a man who had a fine eye for trees and landscapes. John had been obliged to sell the Manor to his cousin for the little it was worth today. He did not begrudge Giles the acquisition of Wellford for so small a sum — he was a man of letters earning a meagre income on which to rear his six children — but the sale of the house would only cover a percentage of the overall debts. John's bequest from an aunt on his mother's side would have to take care of the rest, for he had only his army pay in addition to that.

Kasper's hooves clattered on the cobbles as they entered the yard. The stables were empty. Tom's horses, on whom he had lavished

24

money without hesitation, had fetched a good price, and John had a buyer for Kasper when he left to rejoin his regiment. Handing the stallion over to the old man who had been head groom for many years, John exchanged a few words with him before walking across to the house where Flinders would have breakfast ready. John did not like the man but he was the only servant who had been prepared to stay on after Tom's death. Giles would bring his own with him, and Flinders was bearable enough for the short time John would be in England.

Left alone to eat a breakfast of ham, eggs, potatoes and a variety of fruits, John suddenly found himself regretting the few short weeks before his departure. This furlough had not been a pleasant one in any respect. Not only had he been faced with a crumbling estate and piled debts, he had discovered that every mama in the neighbourhood who had unmarried daughters supposed that he was looking for a wife to take back with him. He had been swamped with invitations and ogled by all manner of unblushing maidens who fancied themselves to be just whom he needed.

When a striking young woman in a very stylish riding-dress had ridden straight into his path this morning, he had believed the manoeuvre to be deliberately planned by a hopeful spinster with more impudence than the rest. The encounter had developed along puzzling lines which had made him distrust her one minute, and feel astonishingly at ease in her company the next. Elizabeth Delacourt intrigued him. Certain now that she was no scheming hoyden, despite her frank approach and very free manners, he went over the details of that extraordinary meeting. A widow of more than one year's standing, she could nevertheless be no more than twenty. Delacourt must have been mad or a fool to embark for India leaving behind a wife with such vivacity and intelligence. However, the man might have been engaged in work which entailed living in the more remote parts of India and, perhaps wisely, preferred to ensure his wife's safety by leaving her in England. Maybe Delacourt had been an elderly man who, like many others, took a young bride in the hope of continuing the line and left her in the family home with his relations to bring up the child. Was there a child in this case, he wondered. Suspicious of her motives when she had appeared so unexpectedly, causing him to fight against colliding with her, he had decided to believe her explanation for being on his land when the intelligence of her conversation persuaded him that she was sincere; a young woman who apparently had no notion of trying to

25

ensnare a husband. With a startling twinge of regret he realized that she might have succeeded.

Pushing away his empty plate, John leaned back in his chair to indulge in thoughts he had put from his mind with great resolution fourteen months ago. At the age of twenty-two he had defied all advice, military frowns, and common sense to marry a girl who had taken him by storm. Clare had been the daughter of an eccentric anthropologist studying in India, and she had been three years John's senior. Fascinating rather than beautiful, she had captured him with her intellect, her appreciation of the definitive aspects of life, and her power to entrance him with her complex personality. Perhaps his youth had appealed to her; perhaps she had revelled in dominating the emotions of another human being. Whatever her reason, she had married him and maintained the illusion of happiness for almost two years. Those months had been tortured happiness for him. Despite the joy of possessing her body, he had known in his heart that he did not possess her spirit. Throughout their brief marriage, the fear of losing her had been constant in him. When fear had become reality it was the manner of her leaving which had been cruel in the extreme. She had taken easel and paints one morning before he was awake and, with just their bearer for company, had vanished from his life and from existence itself.

Her disappearance had caused a search to be mounted on a wide scale: the uneasy relations between the British and the Indians of that region had worsened to the brink of conflict. No bodies were ever discovered, however. No reports from any natives in the pay of the British gave a single clue as to the fate of Clare Stavenham or the bearer. John had lived through hell imagining his beloved wife's last hours. Had she been attacked and eaten by tigers? Had a band of marauding tribesmen captured, raped then murdered her? Time, and a war against the Sikhs in which his regiment had been deeply involved, had eased the horror which had lived inside his breast since her disappearance. Seven years after her inexplicable departure, John had obtained a legal dissolution of his marriage. Older, more emotionally mature, toughened both physically and mentally by the savagery of war, he had believed it possible to erase the tragedy and begin again. It had proved harder than expected, then news of Tom's death had arrived to bring him home after an absence of ten years.

He glanced around the parlour where Flinders had served breakfast and saw a room which had no life in it, no invitation to linger within its walls, and it suddenly struck him why. His mother had died soon after his birth. Since then there had been no mistress of Wellford. His father had not married again; Tom had been a determined bachelor. There had been women here during the thirty years following Estella Stavenham's death, an abundance of women, but they had had no influence on the character of the house they used purely for the pursuit of pleasure. Giles and Roseanne would make the place into a real home, at last, and he would return to his bachelor quarters at Ratnapore.

This morning, the prospect did not seem at all attractive. He was happy in his profession, which offered action, good companions, and the chance of leadership. India had brought him pain in several guises, yet the undeniable conviction that in that land of bewildering contrasts lay his destiny urged him to go back. Thinking of the bare walls of the accommodation provided for single officers, seeing in his mind's eye the spartan furniture and the punkah swinging back and forth from the ceiling with rhythmic squeaks, he knew that his quarters were like this house. There was no life in them, no invitation to linger.

For the first time in several years, John allowed himself to think about those months with Clare. As a memsahib she had left all matters concerning the running of the household to the bearer and his underlings, but she had turned their large airy bungalow into a home filled with colour, music and laughter. Already a very fine pianist, she had learned to play the sitar with great skill after taking lessons from a teacher within Ratnapore city. Many British wives had then cold-shouldered the Stavenhams, because they regarded any woman who took music lessons from a low-caste Indian as very much beyond the pale, but the military officers had all adored Clare's soirées, during which she had entertained them in unconventional style. Even they, however, had begun refusing invitations when Lieutenant Stavenham's wife greeted them dressed in a sari with her dark hair hanging loose to her waist.

A frown creased John's forehead as he now saw it all with the eyes of a man back in his own country, surrounded by conventional English behaviour. He had then been dazzled by an older woman who had pumped excitement through him with everything she did. Clare had looked extremely beautiful in Indian dress: he had seen nothing wrong in her wearing it. Eight years on, he accepted that British convention had been as offended by her behaviour as Indians would have been if one of their own number had appeared before them in a crinoline and

27

bonnet to sing old English madrigals to a lute. Clare had been too charmed by the country. A number of European men succumbed to the spell of India, lived with women of the country and adopted its dress and customs. Such bewitchment touched women more rarely. Clare had been one of those few who had felt total affinity with the East.

Though her behaviour had offended the closed community in which they had lived, her talent as an artist could be denied by none. Her paintings of ethnic life and scenes were snapped up by those keen to send the canvases home to relatives. Colonel Hume had been unhappy about one of his subalterns' wives earning large sums of money for doing what well-bred ladies were taught to do as a social accomplishment. Even he could no longer show open disapproval when his own wife bought two of Clare's paintings which could in no way be compared with amateur water-colours. Consequently, when Clare one day decided to cover the plain walls of their home with vivid murals depicting Indian life, no word of reprimand was sent to John from his commanding-officer.

He was so infatuated with his uninhibited wife he had not cared that his career was certain to suffer as a result of disapproval by his superiors. What was seen by them as his folly in marrying such a woman, plus subsequent military outrage over the expensive campaign vainly mounted to discover her whereabouts, still governed the attitude of many at High Command. John was popular with the men he commanded for having proved in battle that he was ready to do anything he asked them to do. Relations with his fellow officers varied according to how stiff-necked they were, but he had one or two close friends with whom he indulged in those pastimes available to troops in cantonments abroad. Pondering on those pastimes — cards, racing, women — he felt suddenly jaded. In time, a man could become little more than a copy of Tom Stavenham unless something jolted him from that cycle of meaningless occupations.

Rising slowly to his feet, John strolled through the house towards the study where he was finalizing the accounts in order to establish what still had to be settled. Yes, he could become as carelessly ineffectual as his father and brother, before long, if he returned to Ratnapore to take up his life exactly where he had left it three months ago. Reaching the study, where sunshine was now streaming in to highlight furniture dull for want of polish and heavy curtains which had provided many a meal for moths, he had no immediate inclination to sit at the desk. Gazing, hands in pockets, at the neglect in every direction, he owned to himself that the idea of finding a wife in England had been at the back of his mind from the time he had sailed. As an idea it had had great merit. In reality he had shied from it. A single encounter this morning had brought it back to the forefront of his mind.

He was ten years older than the young widow: he had just four weeks before he sailed in which to discover whether or not his instinct was correct. An impossible notion, surely, yet she had touched in him some chords which were still vibrating. There had been an unrestrained vivacity in Elizabeth Delacourt which had reminded him of Clare; a suggestion of courage in her convictions which was refreshingly attractive when compared with the girls he had had systematically thrust before him over the past ten weeks. He did not want a partner who became his echo, or one who thought of nothing but procuring his social and military advancement. Something told him that the girl he had met three hours ago would have little patience with either attitude. He had liked her perception, her lack of coyness, her apparent interest in learning from books. He had also very much liked her feminine appeal, he admitted ruefully. Dark hair coiled over each ear, glowing eyes the colour of amber, a mobile, pointed face which was far too pale for her to be a country resident, a voice which betrayed her emotions far more vividly than any woman he knew, all these things had impressed him to the point of now considering the near impossible. Time was his great enemy, yet he sensed that she had shared his reaction to their meeting. He also sensed that Elizabeth Delacourt would know her own mind very swiftly. Time might prove no barrier where she was concerned.

Taking the sudden madness a step further, he considered what the implications would be if it reached the conclusion he had in mind. Would it be right to take a young woman back to an area which was seething with the kind of tension which would surely lead to another war with the Sikhs before long? The last conflict had been savage enough, leaving the defeated Indians burning for revenge. The next clash could be on a greater scale altogether, proving even more savage. The war against the Afghans eight years ago had resulted in British women and children being attacked without discrimination, then marched around the country as captives for nine months. He would not care to expose any woman to similar dangers, or any child. Aside from that, would it be fair to take a wife knowing that the chances of her

29

becoming a widow soon afterward were considerable? He had seen too many poor creatures forced into uncongenial relationships with any man prepared to help or protect them from sudden abandonment in a foreign country. Those with children had an even rougher time of it when widowed by war or pestilence.

Dismissing the plan as impractical, impetuous, and verging on lunacy, John applied himself to the job awaiting him on the desk. But his attention kept straying to the glorious morning outside, and to thoughts of a girl in a rich blue riding-dress, who had shown such interest in the country to which he would soon be returning. Finally, pushing aside a pile of legal papers, he began to write a short note of invitation which he sealed, then gave to Flinders to send by hand of the kitchen boy, who would surely know the exact location of Miss Mount's cottage. A second encounter under more conventional circumstances would probably dispel the wild idea which had taken hold of him. Or it would set him on a determined course; with four weeks in which to accomplish his goal.

Lavinia had strongly advised against accepting an invitation to tea from any man named Stavenham, declaring that nothing on earth would persuade her to set foot in a house where all manner of wickedness had been practised. Elizabeth immediately wrote a note expressing her own and Miss Mount's pleasure in finding themselves free at four the following afternoon, and the boy from Wellford took the reply back. After a long discussion, during which the older woman insisted that their reputations, if not their very persons, would be placed at risk, which she was not prepared to tolerate, Elizabeth told her companion firmly that she had best stay at home while she took tea alone with Captain Stavenham. Faced with that unthinkable ultimatum, Lavinia had adopted her most governessy manner to say, through stiff lips, that it would never be said of her that she had failed in her duties, even at the greatest personal sacrifice. The girl she had lovingly guided through childhood and adolescence had burst into delighted laughter, saying through it that whatever terrible fate awaited them at the house of ill repute, they would stoically see it through together.

Elizabeth privately counted the hours until they could set out on the visit. John Stavenham had been constantly in her thoughts. Despite telling herself that she must not ride along that hillside again in the hope of meeting him, their brief, stimulating encounter had instilled in her the desire to know more of a man whom, she could not deny, had taken her by storm. Lavinia's gossip concerning a wife who had vanished without trace had touched her deeply. He must have suffered profoundly over the inexplicable loss of a wife whom he had chosen with all the fervour of youthful passion. The tragedy surely explained his frequent and abrupt change of manner, and the lines of harsh experience on his face.

She had sensed an affinity with him at once; now she knew something of his past, that sense was even stronger. She longed to explore it, probe his personality, discover the man beneath his aloof exterior. If her conscience spoke to her of the deception in allowing him to believe her a widow, it spoke but softly. She might as well be husbandless for all the contact she had with a man whose existence she had almost forgotten. In the fifteen months since William's departure she had received just three stilted letters. He wrote every month to his mother, but Emily Delacourt never divulged the contents to her. All Elizabeth was told of her husband's communications was that he hoped she was profiting from the guidance of his dear family. In the three replies she had penned, Elizabeth had defiantly written of her boredom, which was only occasionally relieved at social events where she sometimes met those with wit, intelligence and a merry humour. Small wonder that it was easy to ignore ties to an uncaring husband when faced with a man who promised a glimpse of all William had denied her. John Stavenham would return to India within the month, so was it so very wrong to pursue the little happiness to be found in his company, when he so clearly wished for it too?

Anyone witnessing her preparations for the meeting would never have believed that all she craved was wit, intelligence and a merry humour from her host. She chose, then discarded, three gowns before deciding on a yellow fine-wool dress which had grey velvet frogging and epaulettes à la militaire, and a short cloak swinging from the shoulders. With it she wore a black tall-crowned bonnet bearing a yellow cockade. In London it had been considered very dashing; here, in this village, it must arouse awe in those who took their fashions from journals almost twelve months out of date. What effect it might have on a man from India, where distance from Europe prevented ladies from seeing new trends until nearly two years after their creation, Elizabeth could not tell.

Lavinia, in a dull green coat-dress and brown bonnet, made no secret

31

of her disapproval as she climbed in to the light carriage in which Thompkins was to drive them the short distance. Sitting bolt upright on the leather seat, she wore a martyred expression on her flushed face. Elizabeth could not resist teasing her as they moved off along the leafy lane which cut through the village and led to the main gates of the estate.

'Do you suppose there will be any crystal drops left on the chandeliers, Vinnie . . . and what shall we do if there should be a corpse or two lying about the place?'

'If you wish to add to my misery with behaviour more worthy of a hoyden than a well-bred female, then I suppose I must bear it as best I can,' came the stiff reply.

Taking her companion's mittened hand in an apologetic gesture, Elizabeth said gently, 'Do you truly suppose that I should be on my way to visit Captain Stavenham if he were cut from the same cloth as his disreputable relations? I assure you, dear, that you will be charmed by his gentlemanly qualities and by his quiet, sincere manner. There is really no need for you to resemble a Christian approaching the lions' den.'

Miss Mount was unwilling to be appeased, so Elizabeth gave all her attention to the passing scene as the carriage bowled through the main gateway. Neglect was immediately evident in the rusty state of the ornate gates which had once been embellished with black and gold scrolls. The long drive leading to the Manor was overgrown and pitted, making the carriage jolt so severely that the occupants received a few painful knocks before they approached their destination. Square, well-proportioned, and potentially impressive, the Georgian house had also been allowed to moulder. An air of melancholy hung about it which almost gave credibility to Lavinia's fears of finding a corpse. Almost certainly, a few ghosts flitted through the rooms.

As Thompkins turned the carriage with precision, so that it drew up beside the flight of shallow steps, Elizabeth wondered fleetingly about the small boy who had lived here, unloved by brother or parent. Her own childhood had been spent in a modest house set upon a hill in Kent. Lavinia had been teacher, nurse and substitute mother then, so life had not been too unhappy. Her parents had come and gone as their commitments dictated, and Elizabeth had been neither delighted nor disappointed with the relationship since it hardly affected her calm routine. Only when her father died had the parental influence become more apparent. The house in Kent had been sold and they had all gone to live in the London home of a man Elizabeth had been told to call Uncle Matthew. Although the young girl had hated leaving the country, there had been exciting things to do in London which had compensated for the grim, silent atmosphere of the bachelor residence. Without Lavinia to provide constant affection, life for Elizabeth would have been vastly different. John Stavenham had probably lacked even a friend in this rambling house where his brother had been given all and himself very little. All the more reason to imagine that, on reaching manhood, such a boy would be overwhelmed by the first experience of love being offered to him. What consequences would result from having that love tragically and inexplicably snatched away?

Climbing from the carriage, Elizabeth looked up to see the subject of her thoughts waiting at the top of the steps to greet them. He must have been watching for their arrival. In the rush of delight prompted by such a deduction, she mounted the steps without a word for Thompkins and forgetting the companion who had been so unwilling to come.

'You cannot accuse me of trespassing today,' she said gaily, 'for I have arrived in very respectable style.'

The strained expression he had been wearing, vanished. 'I gave you the freedom of Wellford yesterday, if you recall. You could have arrived in any fashion you chose.' He smiled then. 'I can only accuse you of being uncommonly punctual for a lady. They have a marked preference for adding as much as an hour to the time of any meeting.'

'That is for one of two reasons, you should know,' she told him with a light laugh. 'They either do not wish to keep the appointment so delay it as long as possible, or they wish to capture attention by extending the anticipation of their arrival.'

His smile faded to leave an intense expression as he said, 'I'm glad that you decided this was an appointment you wished to keep . . . and you have no need to resort to ruses in order to capture *anyone's* attention.'

Elizabeth was experienced enough to know that he was not indulging in light flirtation. She had spoken without thinking and he had read into her words a message she had been unaware of giving. Yet he was right. She had wanted to see him again, so much that a delay of even a single moment would have been too long. The arrival of Miss Mount, prim and poker-faced, broke the personal exchange and introductions were made.

John's mouth twitched slightly as he bowed at the disapproving figure regarding him. 'Ma'am, I am delighted to make the acquaintance of she who writes such informative letters on the vagaries of rural life.' Turning toward the open door, he added, 'Please allow me to escort you both inside. My man will provide refreshment which I promise will be more attractive than the interior of this neglected mansion.'

Elizabeth's first opinion of Wellford Manor was that it was dingy, unwelcoming and bleak. Their footsteps echoed eerily in the deserted chambers, giving the impression that they were the sole human presence in a place of ghosts. When lit by several hundred candles and filled with richly dressed revellers they might assume a false grandeur, she supposed, but those tawdry days were over and the rooms now revealed the ravages of former excesses. Murals had begun to flake, chandeliers had lost their lustre, and there were damp patches darkening the ceilings. The carpets over which they trod were dimmed by ingrained dust and stains; the marble of the grand staircase looked lifeless from lack of care. Elizabeth saw it all as she walked beside him through several rooms and she sensed that wickedness had reigned here once, as Lavinia had averred. She shivered involuntarily.

John broke off in the middle of a speech concerning the antiquity of several suits of armour on display, and turned to her swiftly. 'Are you cold? I'm so sorry. There is a merry fire burning in the sitting-room and you shall have a chair right beside it with a cup of tea to warm you.'

She shook her head. 'That sounds most attractive, but I fear it is my intuition rather than the temperature which makes me feel chill. One of my very distant French ancestors was reputed to be a medium, and I have frequently experienced curious sensations which make me wonder if the power has re-emerged in me. I hope I shall not offend you if I say that this house appears to me to be crying in shame.'

'*Elizabeth!*' cried Miss Mount, halting in her tracks in horror at this being said by a female guest to her gentleman host.

They all stopped in a group, but John was clearly more fascinated than angry. 'You can actually sense details of events from the past without prior knowledge of them?'

'Not details,' she confessed. 'I could not tell you of any specific occurrence at Wellford.' A smile broke through then. 'If I did, sir, it would be a case of gross deception for I would simply be reporting something overheard in the village. However, I am remarkably sensitive to atmosphere and can often divine whether good or evil, happiness or woe has prevailed in a particular place.'

'That explains your immediate understanding of my own sense of destiny awaiting in India,' he said, speaking eagerly and as if he had forgotten the presence of Miss Mount beside them. 'It was your hope yesterday morning that it lay in the sweet rather than the savage aspect of the country. Have you no further illumination on the subject?'

'I know too little of you for that,' she murmured, also disregarding her companion's proximity.

'You know little of Wellford, yet its troubled past has touched you.'

Before she knew it, Elizabeth said, 'Where your own past is concerned, I sense that it has also been troubled, but you are asking for enlightenment on the future; on something which has yet to happen.'

The effect of her words upon him was profound. Gazing at her with a mixture of shock and awareness, he said, 'Your perception is astonishing. You could not know of an event which happened half-way across the world when you would have been little more than a child.' After a short pause, he said quietly, 'You claim that you cannot predict future events, Mrs Delacourt, but you have just clarified the obscurity of *my* future quite considerably.'

A black-suited manservant with a pale, mournful face appeared in the open doorway of a room where sunlight streamed in to emphasize the faded colours of what had once been a magnificent carpet. His bored announcement that tea was awaiting them broke the moment of intimacy which had arisen between Elizabeth and this man to whom she felt strongly drawn. She longed to be rid of her disapproving chaperone, who must overhear every word. Knowing John Stavenham for just a day had brought greater fulfilment than she had known with any friend or suitor before. It needed no kinship with a reputed mystic for her to know that here was an affinity so deep it could become a rapture or a torment.

While they enjoyed the dainty tea John had arranged for them, conversation was mostly between the younger pair. John did his best to coax Lavinia into a more relaxed attitude, but soon abandoned the attempt when she made it clear that she was finding the entire afternoon a severe trial to her sense of propriety. Uncharacteristically, Elizabeth lost all patience with her: finding an outlet for her yearning spirit made her temporarily insensible to all other considerations. They talked

35

about art, literature and the theatre or, rather, Elizabeth talked while John listened avidly to her descriptions of plays, operas, exhibitions and literary sensations which had all occurred whilst he had been out of England. He, in turn, described the colour, noise and exotic pageantry of Indian festivals which held his listener spellbound, despite Miss Mount's audible coughs of disapproval. While they talked, Elizabeth was acutely aware of his square brown hands, which moved in emphasis of his words, and noticed with pleasure the way the blue of his eyes deepened when serious, or grew bright with amusement. As the afternoon lengthened to early evening, the knowledge that he must sail for India at the end of the month brought an inner chill which the warmth of the fire did nothing to dispel.

The sun had gone down and the embers were glowing seductively in the dimness of the room when the manservant entered to say that the carriage had returned for the ladies. Lavinia was on her feet instantly, but Elizabeth was swept with regret that she must leave when the desire to remain was so very strong. John looked as reluctant to part as she, saying as he rose to his feet that the time had passed far too quickly. They walked slowly back to the front entrance, the air of sadness and neglect even more apparent in the rooms they crossed. A lonely man in a lonely house, she thought with deep compassion. He did not deserve the hand fate had dealt him. Then, like a shadow passing over her, she had a premonition of further pain in store for him.

Turning swiftly as they reached the door, she said, 'Wellford could be made very comfortable and charming beneath a caring hand. Will you not reconsider your decision to go back?'

A frown accompanied his response. 'It is too late to reconsider. I have already signed the deed of sale.'

'I see,' she said slowly. 'Then your destiny must truly lie in that far off land.'

Miss Mount thanked her host in a crisp and dutiful manner for a delightful afternoon — which was a perfect example of a lie for the sake of convention — then made her way down the steps to where Thompkins was waiting on the box of her only carriage. Elizabeth offered John her hand in farewell and found it still clasped in his, even after they had both expressed pleasure in the meeting.

'I shall ride on the hillside tomorrow morning at eight. If you should decide to trespass we could continue the pursuit of an interesting acquaintance. Two short meetings have shown that it would take many more to exhaust all we could discuss together, don't you agree?' Retaining her hand when she would have drawn it away, he urged in low tones, 'Say you will come.'

Hearing the cough Lavinia always gave to gain her attention, Elizabeth drew free, murmuring, 'It may well rain.'

'If it is fine?' he asked.

Over her shoulder she said swiftly, 'If it is fine . . . I shall be there.'

Her heart was racing as she entered the carriage. When it started forward she looked back at the figure only just discernible in the gathering dusk. Parting from him now was an unbelievable wrench: how would she take the final break in four weeks' time?

The return to Walnut Tree Cottage was made without a word exchanged between the two passengers, but Lavinia was ready with a flood of them as soon as they were within her parlour. Making no attempt to unpin her brown ruched bonnet, the older woman stood before the inner door to prevent Elizabeth's escape upstairs while she gave her opinion of the afternoon.

'I never thought I would be forced to consider that I had failed in my duties,' she began in mournful tones. 'You have always been volatile and, in moderation, that can be an attractive facet to a young lady's personality. Today, however, I well perceived the reason behind Mr Delacourt's decision to leave you with his family during his absence. I have never before felt so mortified.'

Elizabeth unfastened the ribbons of her stylish hat, saying coolly, 'Then you have led a charmed life, Vinnie. To have reached your age without being upset by anything worse than taking tea with Sir Francis Stavenham's very civil younger son is a piece of good fortune you should not treat lightly. I wish I had been as lucky.'

Flushing even more rosily, Miss Mount continued in the same vein. 'I declare I cannot believe the change in you. Where is the loving, sweet, and biddable girl I have cared for since her childhood?'

Jabbing the tall crown of her bonnet with a hat-pin, Elizabeth replied, 'Ask the Delacourts. If there is a change in me they are responsible for it.'

The short silence was broken by an audible sigh as Miss Mount's bosom rose and fell in protest. 'His manner was so . . . so *free*.'

'He's a man of the world. Life in India is vastly different from the cramped gossip-ridden existence in this village, and from the over-exaggerated niceties of London society. Of course his manner is free.

37

He is free,' she cried with heat. 'If he wishes to return to India, he will; if he chooses to remain at Wellford Manor there is no one to say he must not. Oh, Vinnie,' she exclaimed, moving round to confront her companion with the fervour born of her longings, 'John Stavenham does not have to do as he is bid and live like a nun in a repressive family convent. He can sail to India, or to anywhere in the world he chooses to visit. He does not have monthly reports on his behaviour sent to someone who cares so little for their subject, he can face a parting of up to ten years with perfect equanimity; neither does he have to remain faithful to a vow which has become a mockery.' Lowering her voice, she added, 'When Captain Stavenham's marriage partner vanished suddenly, she never returned. Mine has every hope of doing so, and he will be a stranger to whom I am tied for life. Is it any wonder that I seek what little lightness I can to brighten the greyness of my unshackled imprisonment? You cannot know how much I melted in the warmth of his intellect, his sympathetic personality and his interest in my thoughts or opinions. Do you know how long it has been since I have felt able to speak without first considering my every word in case it should bring censure?'

Lavinia was clearly touched by the passionate outburst but not so much that she abandoned her lecture. 'It was certainly unfortunate that Mr Delacourt's regiment should have been sent abroad so soon after your marriage . . .'

'He could have transferred and remained at my side,' she interspersed sharply.

'. . . but you cannot expect to enjoy the opportunities which are available to a spinster, Elizabeth,' the older woman stated firmly. 'A wife must be dutiful and loyal no matter where her husband is obliged to travel. Naturally she will feel a little lonely, especially if there are no children to care for, and it is perfectly unexceptional for her to accept invitations which will take her into the company of single gentlemen when there are others present. This afternoon was quite different. I thank God we were not seen entering Wellford Manor. Thompkins will not breathe a word of the excursion to anyone, but you risked your own reputation and my standing in the village with your headstrong behaviour.'

'What nonsense,' Elizabeth declared roundly. 'There was nothing in the least questionable in Captain Stavenham sending us an invitation to tea, or in us accepting it. As the new owner of Wellford Manor he must surely have entertained numerous local families to whom his father and brother had acted as squire . . . and even you must own that there was not the least sign of an orgy, a shattered chandelier, or a corpse. Vinnie dear, you are being melodramatic once more. I am a married lady and therefore a most suitable chaperone for you, wherever you may choose to go. Your standing cannot possibly be damaged.'

That speech appeared to leave Miss Mount nonplussed. '*You* a chaperone for *me!*'

'Of course. I may be no more than twenty but this ring on my finger proclaims me a matron who is alive to the cunning ways of gentlemen. You are a spinster who must be protected from them. I think I did my duty by you this afternoon.'

'Are you gone completely mad?' cried her bewildered companion. 'I have never known you to be capricious. Are you ailing? Your cheeks are too flushed and there is an unusual urgency in your manner. Perhaps you should take a powder and lie down for a while. I will bring you some broth and a spoonful or so of egg custard at eight o'clock, although it is usual to starve a fever.'

Seeing that her companion was genuinely troubled, Elizabeth sought to soothe her. Taking her hands, she coaxed the other woman in to the chair by the fireplace, then sank down beside her as she had done on many occasions.

'Dearest Vinnie, I beg your pardon. I should not have teased you but I so enjoyed our outing this afternoon I could not bear to have my enjoyment spoiled by an admonition, from you of all people. I'm so heartily weary of being criticized for everything I do.' Gazing earnestly at the person who had been her only steadfast influence for twenty years, she asked, 'Please think carefully about Captain Stavenham. Was he not extremely civil to us both? Did he not show great consideration in seating us beside a comforting fire, and in providing a tea which was chosen with the female palate in mind? Can you truly find objections to any aspect of the visit aside from his manners which you found too direct? Did he deserve to be treated to your most severe expression, your chilliest responses throughout? Was there any evidence at all to suggest that he is of the same cut as Sir Francis and Thomas Stavenham? Answer truthfully.'

Miss Mount's bright little eyes regarded her sadly for some moments before the truth did, in fact, emerge. 'I may not be alive to the cunning ways of gentlemen, my dear, but I have eyes in my head. Captain

Stavenham is clearly very taken with you. I sincerely hope your vivacious response to him has not suggested that you return his interest.'

Turning away to gaze at the fire, Elizabeth murmured, 'He is due to sail for India at the end of the month. I am doomed to remain in England. You have no cause for anxiety, Vinnie.'

'Have you?' came the quiet question.

Still watching the shifting patterns in the embers, she said thoughtfully, 'I have been anxious for many months; dreading the thought of facing my long, lonely, grey future. However shall I endure my allotted three score years and ten? Fifty of them remain, yet any joy in living has been snatched from my grasp by the Delacourt family.'

A hand touched her dark curls in a caress. 'Hush, child. It cannot be as bad as you suggest.'

'Perhaps not . . . but I see now that it could be infinitely better.'

Chapter Three

They met at eight the following morning. The air was clear and full of promise so they galloped side by side to the trees at the far end of the level stretch. They then turned to cross the overgrown park, circle the gazebo, and race back to the spot from where they had started. Elizabeth's heart and spirits sang with the joy of freedom and with the excitement of having John beside her. Breathless, flushed from their energetic ride, they brought their horses to a halt where they could look out over the green downland typical of Sussex. Larks were rising up to the cloudless sky with that heartbreaking song which would bring a tear to anyone who had been long exiled from this gentle island, and lambs were plaintively calling in morning hunger to ewes satisfying their own on the grassy hillside. There was an atmosphere of hope, of youth with the entire universe at its feet; there was a wonderful serenity in the soft breeze and in the blue distance which marked the coast.

Elizabeth sighed with pain at the perfection of that moment. A hundred times during her restless night she had vowed not to keep the rendezvous. That she would do so had been as inevitable as the morning. Glancing at John, she caught him watching her closely.

'After winter in the city this is pure enchantment,' she explained. 'India must be wonderful indeed to persuade you to leave all this.'

'One can find beauty in every aspect of the country,' he said. 'A bizarre kind in some, I'll confess, but only the most insensitive creatures fail to see it. There is no area to compare with this soft pastel landscape, of course, but the hill stations are green, cool and invigorating. Most ladies go up to them during the hot season.'

'Not the gentlemen?'

He smiled. 'Only if they are sick . . . or very fortunate. The troops must remain on duty at all times; the civil servants have to administer the colony whatever the temperature.'

'You have survived it for a number of years?'

'For ten . . . ten and a half if I include the passage out, which was

41

undertaken during the hottest season of each area through which I travelled.'

'Tell me about it,' she urged. 'Tell me how a regiment is transported in its entirety half-way across the world.'

After a considered study of her face, he asked gently, 'Can you stand the truth?'

'Is it so bad that you need to ask?'

'Perhaps.' He dismounted and came over to her. 'Shall we walk for a while?'

It was the first time he had touched her body. His hands were firm against her waist as he lifted her from the saddle to the ground, and hers felt the strength of his upper arms as she steadied herself against him. The contact was momentary but it nevertheless silenced them during the first few yards of their stroll. Then he began to speak of the conditions his men had endured below decks in an ancient sailing ship taking the long route around the Cape.

'Many a trooper is the kind of ruffian who would fill our prisons if they had not taken the shilling. Quite a number are good loyal men with a little education and simple philosophies,' he explained as they wandered slowly over the dewy grass. 'Neither sort deserves to suffer as they do crowded together in the lower regions of a ship's hull, where fresh air is unknown and the heat insupportable. Each man is allotted sufficient space to stretch out full length, and in those few feet he lives out the greater part of six months.'

'But that's inhuman,' she declared in shocked tones.

He nodded. 'I agree. My protest was registered even before we left these shores but soldiers, ma'am, are accredited with very few human qualities by the Government and more consideration is given to cavalry horses than to the men who ride them. There is an endless supply of rogues willing to escape the penalties of justice by donning a uniform: horseflesh is costly.'

As John continued to speak of the growing hopelessness of men who, whilst prepared to offer their lives in battle, were resentful over the number of deaths caused by fever and heat suffocation on a ship, she listened with growing compassion. He described how the ship had been becalmed for days beneath the blazing sun and how, when the troopers were allowed úp to wash their clothes and refresh themselves in the sea, up to a dozen who could not swim had jumped over the side to drown rather than endure the rest of the voyage. It occurred to her at that point that William had never spoken to her of such things. He had recounted the wild exploits of his fellow officers, such as the shooting down of a chandelier, and had given her verbatim accounts of the plans for a ball, tattoo, or military pageant. William had represented army life to his wife as little more than the usual pastimes enjoyed by men of means who preferred to dress in fancy red coats and wear a sword at their sides. The only time he had ever mentioned the men he supposedly commanded was in declaring that a sense of duty demanded that he go with them to India. Had her estranged husband hidden the shocking facts of a trooper's lot because of his ridiculous premise that females must never be exposed to any but the blandest truths, or could it be that he had so little interest in his men their unhappy plight did not bother him?

'Have I distressed you?' asked John in concern at her silence.

He had certainly distressed her, but not by telling her those facts which made life more real, more comprehensible. Now was the moment to confess that she was not a widow, as he supposed, yet she returned his steady gaze and told herself that those four weeks, now down to three and a half, were too precious to forgo.

'Anyone with the least sensitivity must be disturbed by such callous treatment of human souls,' she told him. 'If I'm distressed at all it is because I can do nothing to prevent it. If you could not help the poor creatures, then who can?'

He shook his head. 'Only someone with very great influence who also has the ear of the Prince Consort and enough determination to fight until he wins.'

'Or *she* wins,' added Elizabeth thoughtfully. 'The Government and the Army are controlled by men. If they have so low an opinion of soldiers as you say, they are unlikely to change it on the voice of one male advocate. Our monarch is a woman. Perhaps it requires another to speak out on a subject which would surely persuade a multitude of females to petition the Queen once they knew the truth. It is their husbands, brothers and sons who have taken the royal shilling.'

He stopped walking and turned to her with a smile. 'How very refreshing you are! You should meet Lady Mason, the wife of the general who commands all troops in the province where my regiment serves. She is an eccentric lady who is afraid of no one. Indian rulers find her delightfully amusing, but they respect her. The memsahibs either live in awe of her if they have ambition for their husbands, or laugh behind her back if they have not. She is forever embroiling

General Mason in schemes she has launched on behalf of the common soldier. This obliges the man to offer a continual succession of official explanations to the Governor, who does not believe in females concerning themselves in military matters. I swear you would find in her a possible candidate for what you propose.'

'I think not, for she would have acted before now.'

'I believe she has. India is far from London. Communications take three or four months to travel in just one direction. A lone voice may shout in the Punjab but it is no more than a whisper when it reaches Her Majesty's ear, especially if it is a female voice. The Queen is a woman advised by a consort and ministers who are male. They are the villains who will not listen.'

'So what is to be done?'

He sighed. 'The poor wretches will continue to be treated badly until some catastrophe robs us of an entire army. Only then will each and every soldier be considered valuable enough to bring widespread reforms.'

'Bonaparte realized that only when it was too late to fulfil his ambitions,' she commented.

'Indeed, he did.' Reaching for her hand, he took it slowly to his mouth and kissed it. What was a perfectly acceptable greeting between men and women took on a more intimate nature in this instance. They were both aware of the fact as he said, 'I count it a privilege to walk and talk with you. There are few ladies of my acquaintance with whom I am able to discuss such a range of subjects; hardly any who would show great interest in military matters. You are almost unique, Mrs Delacourt.'

Trying to mask the effect his kiss had had upon her senses, she strove for lightness. 'Like Lady Mason of the Punjab?'

'Oh no, not in the least like Lady Mason,' he murmured with great warmth. 'She is a lady of some fifty years or more who wears a collection of wigs in alarming colours to cover a head deprived of hair by a debilitating illness. She is rather immodest and fond of a cigar. You are in a class of your own.'

Recognizing danger, Elizabeth had enough will-power to avert it. Turning swiftly, she said, 'I do not care for cigars, sir, but I do have a partiality for breakfast after my morning ride. Lavinia will have it ready. Will you assist me to mount?'

He did so in silence, then swung into the saddle on Kasper to ride beside her as far as the copse. There, she glanced at his troubled expression to say quietly, 'There is no need to come further. I shall be perfectly safe.'

'As you wish,' he replied heavily. 'I have delayed you unforgivably, ma'am, but I trust you will decide to ride here tomorrow at eight. If you prefer to be alone, I'll take my exercise elsewhere.'

With her will-power fast evaporating, she said, 'Of course you must not. Wellford is your property. I am the trespasser.'

'Will you come? Will you allow me to accompany you?' he asked urgently.

'It may well rain,' she replied, with the same weak excuse.

'If it does not?'

'Yes, I shall come,' she told him swiftly, then rode off through the copse, praying that the rain would hold off until the end of the month.

With two weeks to go before he must either take up the passage he had booked, or cancel it and arrange to sell his commission, John was still unsure of his best course of action. That he was irrevocably in love with Elizabeth Delacourt was in no doubt whatever. He sincerely believed that she returned his feelings. Lack of time was the great enemy, but the lady herself was also confusing his ability to make a decision. One day she spoke of how splendid Wellford could be if correctly run, which suggested that she would be happiest as the Squire's wife; on another day she spoke with such enthusiasm of her great wish to experience India, he believed she would be happy nowhere else with him. To that end he had deliberately mentioned the dangers, sickness and crushing heat to be found in that land, which also beckoned with a jewelled finger. He had related the distressing side of military life, told of the loneliness of service in outlying forts, and of the long, exhausting marches to reach them. He had given her a full account of the cruelties as well as the charm of life in an Indian city. To his immense delight she had responded to all this with absorbing interest and with an intelligence which told him she would enrich his life even beyond that elusive fulfilment he had found with Clare. Certain of Elizabeth's loyalty as he had never been with his lost wife, John needed only to see how best to handle this delicate situation.

This dark-haired vivacious widow who had crossed his path so miraculously but belatedly showed him visually that she was his, yet she grew evasive whenever he tried to hint at the depth of his feeling for her.

45

She was no coquette and there was certainly no evidence to suggest that she still mourned her late husband, so John could only believe that she had had a most unhappy experience of intimacy with the man. They had ridden together every morning, she had allowed him to drive her to local beauty spots on three afternoons, in company with Giles and Roseanne who had arrived from Norfolk to make a start on refurbishing their new home, and this evening she and Miss Mount, who had almost certainly been her former governess, had dined at Wellford with his cousins. On each occasion he had contrived to spend a while apart with her so that they could speak more freely. Elizabeth had discussed her Anglo–French family, her lonely childhood, and her passionate interest in so many subjects which also pleased him. Not once had she mentioned Delacourt.

John guessed that she had been given at a tender age to an elderly colonial, anxious for a son to continue the name. It was a common enough occurrence. Sometimes a mere child from the schoolroom succeeded a barren first wife. Often, men of wealth and position were so busy pursuing greatness they had no time for marriage until creaking joints reminded them of their duty to family and heritage. Their contemporaries were then too old to bear children, so a young bride was selected, purely as a breeding mare. These young girls were frequently brutally broken by the insensitive treatment of their aged husbands and mistrusted all men thereafter. The thought of his lovely, vivacious, compassionate girl suffering marital violation by an old man intent on siring another of his kind filled John with anger. It also posed the problem of how best to win her trust within the two weeks remaining.

He lay awake well into the night trying to reach a solution. Giles might well be prepared to tear up the deed of sale if Elizabeth really wanted to live here at Wellford. However, the value of his commission was not enough to pay for the restoration of the Manor. He would do better to buy a smaller property with less land, where he could possibly breed horses. Was that enough to offer her in place of a manor house and a large but run down estate? Turning restlessly, he told himself this girl was not the kind to crave possessions and a position in society. She would set more value on deep and lasting devotion. He could go on half-pay and extend his furlough in order to pursue a conventional courtship, but that would make the situation even more complicated. He could not remain in a house he had sold to his cousin and act as the owner, and he could not entertain Elizabeth in the local inn. Two weeks was a ridiculously short time in which to persuade any woman to pledge the rest of her life to him, but if he could only achieve it they could be married on the day before the packet sailed, or even on the high seas. Most women would probably wish to follow later, insisting that they must have all manner of items to take out with them, but he would make their wedding night so unforgettable Elizabeth would refuse to be parted from him for even a day. By morning he was resolved to advance the relationship and risk frightening her away. If he was tender and chose the right moment, she would surely respond as he hoped.

Fate had other plans. Dawn produced a storm of such magnitude neither man nor beast was safe outdoors. A hurricane settled over Wellford laying flat the copse and other trees in the district, snatching lambs from exposed hillsides to hurl them a mile or more from their mothers, and taking its toll of buildings in the village and its environs. The river swelled from the torrential rains, then burst its banks to flood meadows and young crops already green in the fields of numerous farms. The broken roof over the south wing of Wellford Manor was lifted, and dashed to pieces on the terrace around it. The deluge spoiled the contents of rooms then exposed to the elements and dampness began seeping through to the rooms on the floor below.

John was fully occupied helping his cousins to organize whatever protection could be found while the storm continued to rage, although his mind was constantly concerned with the safety of the occupants of Walnut Tree Cottage. There was no means of gaining news, for the path through the copse had been obliterated, and the road to the village was totally blocked by two enormous felled oaks. Even so, he had been set on battling his way to Elizabeth, but then the old Head Groom was found dead by one of the kitchen boys beside a wall against which he had been blown while attempting to cross from the coach house. Knowing then that it would help no one to risk the force of that wind, John had had to try and contain his fears until it died down.

The storm lasted an incredible three days before it moved toward the coast to blow itself out over the sea. It left behind a scene of devastation such as even the oldest inhabitant of Wellford had never before witnessed. On that fourth morning John set out on foot to reach Elizabeth, knowing he would never get through on Kasper. Everywhere he looked there was destruction. Huge trees which had stood for two hundred years or more had been blown over within seconds to expose roots as thick as a man's arm. Fields lay waterlogged, crops were

47

ruined. The road was a sea of mud which sucked at his boots as he trudged on. The more he saw, the greater were his fears. For three days he had been desperate with worry; for three days he had longed to see her, hear her voice, rejoice in the love shining in her eyes; which she could not hide. What if she had been injured, or worse? Urgency spurred him on, despite the obstacles in his way. The oaks blocking the road were a formidable challenge. In climbing over them, his sleeve was ripped and his palms were cut by sharp twigs. He lost his footing once and slipped, narrowly missing being blinded by a protruding, needle-sharp point of wood. Finally, torn, mud-splashed and breathless, he reached the church from where the cottage was visible. Aside from the broken walnut tree which gave the dwelling its name, no other damage was immediately apparent.

Slipping and sliding on the wet mud covering the cobbles, John increased his pace as best he could until he reached the front gate. There he saw evidence of the receding flood waters in the layer of silt stretching to the front door, and possibly right into the cottage itself. Two women alone here during the hours of darkness while that hurricane tore the heart from an entire village! How terrified they must have been. Reaching the door beneath an overhanging arch, he wielded the knocker with force to release some of his apprehension. A thin, red-faced girl in cap and apron opened the door to stare wide-eyed at him.

'I wish to see Mrs Delacourt,' he informed her brusquely, noticing the filthy state of the square flagged entrance hall.

'Who do I say is calling, sir?' she asked, still staring.

'I don't wish to be announced. This is no time for social refinements. Take me to her right away.'

'I'm not sure I should, sir.'

John stepped inside, smelled the dankness left by the receding flood water, then swung round with renewed urgency.

'Where is she?'

The girl pointed to a latched door straight ahead. Loath to walk in unannounced on two females, he knocked on it but hesitated no longer when Elizabeth's voice called, 'Yes, what is it?'

He saw nothing of the parlour, filled with an assortment of knick-knacks typical of those collected by spinsters. His gaze flew to the girl he loved. In a frilled overall which covered most of her blue cambric dress, and with her hair escaping in wisps from a large knot on top of her head, Elizabeth was busily mopping muddy water from the flagstones in the far corner of the room. Her face was very pale, despite her energetic movements. Glancing up to see who had come in, she grew even paler as her hands and body stilled. Those three days cut off from her when time was so precious, had seemed an eternity, so John instantly forgot his resolution to approach her with gentleness and understanding, to gain her trust.

'I've been half out of my mind with fear for your safety,' he said huskily.

Her clear amber eyes gazed back almost in shock at his sudden appearance. 'And I for you,' she murmured.

Moving around a small table to reach her, he took her hands in his to discover that they were shaking. No longer controlled, his arms closed around her as he bent to kiss her mouth with the fervour of relief, passion and final commitment. She responded with a matching desperation which made nonsense of his theory that she had been brutalized by her husband's intimacy. Here was a woman capable of intense passion, he realized. Had she been starved of it? Driven on by this thought, he adored her with his hands and lips until there were tears on her cheeks. Only then did he grow aware of what was happening, and, reluctantly, held her away.

'I came to give you strength, not to make you weep, my darling girl, but these past days have been empty and endless. I have missed your smile, your voice, your quick wit and your power to entrance me with everything you do. I suspected on that first day that I could love you. I know now that my life is meaningless without you. My passage is booked for the end of the month, but I can arrange to delay it . . .'

The sound of a voice outside warned him that they were about to be interrupted. He cursed softly as Elizabeth pulled free of his arms seconds before the door opened behind them.

'Captain Stavenham, it's you,' exclaimed Miss Mount as she entered. 'Is the road open again?'

In the confused aftermath of passion interrupted, John swung round to find the older woman also wearing an overall, with a cap upon her curls.

'No, ma'am, I fear it will be closed for some days,' he said, collecting his thoughts with an effort. 'Those oaks are ten feet in girth, at least. They'll be difficult to saw through and lift clear. I came on foot . . . with some formidable obstacles as you'll observe from the state I'm in.'

49

'Dear me, it is so very kind of you to take this trouble in order to visit us and offer your assistance,' she said, taking in the torn jacket and slashed palms. 'Have you had much damage up at the Manor?'

'No more than one could expect of a building left to rot,' he returned with bitterness. 'The real tragedy is the death of Robson who was with my family for most of his life. The poor fellow was too frail to attempt defiance of such a hurricane.'

'Another loss? How terrible!' Miss Mount sank into a chair where she shook her head sadly. 'The blacksmith was crushed when that great chestnut which overhung his cottage fell on the room in which he slept. Mrs Hampton has collapsed with shock. Dr Bodley is in attendance daily. Then there is the youngest Clegg child who ran from the house in fright and has not been seen again.' Giving John a dazed frown, she added, 'Martha Tildsworth told me a moment ago that some of Farmer Doyce's sheep have travelled as much as five miles through the sky, so that poor little girl might be far away from here and in the worst of conditions.'

Acutely conscious of Elizabeth's stillness and silence, John summoned a comforting smile and said, 'An exaggeration, ma'am, take my word. The child will be found sheltering somewhere quite near, I'm sure. But you have also suffered, I see. When did the flood subside?' He had turned to ask the question of the girl he had been embracing, and was troubled by the immense sadness she now radiated. Miss Mount answered into the silence, but John heard nothing of it. He could not remember how much he had said to Elizabeth before they were interrupted. That his passage was booked he had certainly told her. Had he been prevented from adding that he could delay the sailing long enough for them to sort out their future together? Surely she did not believe that he would declare his love and announce his return to India alone in the same breath, yet why else would she now look so distressed?

Further speculation or action was denied by the arrival of Mr Noble, Rector of Wellford, who had brushed aside the maid to enter the parlour on an urgent errand. A spare man of sixty-five, he had amounted to very little in his profession, but his long years of service at St Barnabas at Wellford had endeared him to his parishioners and that had been reward enough for a man who loved the country life. Today he was doing his duty with great diligence.

Casting his anxious glance around the parlour, he said, 'Forgive this unmannerly intrusion, ladies, but Ethel Thompkins told me she saw

Captain Stavenham enter your cottage. He is the very person I need.' Turning to John, he asked, 'Will you come at once? Mrs Monk slipped on the slime covering her floor and pulled a dresser down upon herself. The poor woman is screaming — whether with pain or fright is uncertain — and I cannot lift the piece of furniture without help. Most of the men are out trying to clear the road. Those who are not, are as feeble as I. Your presence here is a godsend, John.'

There was no choice but to go with this man who had known him since boyhood. Sorry for the victim, yet cursing her ill-timed accident, he looked directly at Elizabeth to say, 'I'll be back as soon as I am able.'

'Both of you must return when you have relieved poor Mrs Monk,' declared Lavinia. 'We shall have tea and cherry tartlets ready for you.'

Mrs Monk's dwelling was gloomy and unattractive after the charm of Walnut Tree Cottage. John got there ahead of the Rector and made short work of heaving the dresser up to free the hysterical woman. By the time Mr Noble arrived to pant his thanks and attempt to calm the victim, Cissie Monk had been sent by John to fetch the doctor.

'My word, you must have prodigious strength in your back to right that heavy piece without help,' marvelled his breathless companion, between soothing comments to the woman who had been pinned beneath it.

'It's the life I lead,' John replied briefly, impatient to return to Elizabeth. 'Soldiering in India can make or break men.'

'So I have heard. Ah, here is Dr Bodley, if I'm not mistaken.'

Ten minutes passed while Mrs Monk's limbs were examined for fractures and a bromide was administered. John and the doctor then helped the unsteady patient to her bed in a dingy, rather malodorous upstairs room. A further ten minutes crawled past as John waited impatiently for Cissie Monk to be given instructions on what to do for her mother. Then the doctor embarked on a conversation with Mr Noble about the funeral arrangements for the blacksmith, which delayed departure further. Only when John very obviously studied his pocket-watch for the second time did his companions take note.

'Captain Stavenham has little time to spare and I have encroached upon it, I fear,' said the Rector. 'He has much to do before his return to India, yet he was good enough to force his way through from the Manor to offer what help he could to the people in the village. We should detain him no longer with affairs we can discuss later.'

Obliged to keep the slow pace of the older man, John strolled beside him, fighting the urge to hurry.

'You mentioned just now that life in India can make or break a man, John,' said the Rector. 'You look quite unbroken and have abandoned your heritage in order to return there, so I can only suppose that the unhappy boy and youth I knew has found his correct path through life.'

'Wellford contains no nostalgia for me,' he confessed. 'My cousins will be excellent supporters of the village and its environs. Giles is a studious man much interested in the history of rural Sussex. His wife has their six children well controlled by affection, so there's no doubt in my mind that the Manor will become one of the happiest places for miles around.' He sighed. 'After thirty years of Stavenham dissolution the people will have a Squire of whom they can be proud.'

'They would have been proud of you had you chosen to remain.'

John smiled. 'You've just observed that I appear to have found my correct path through life.'

'Yes, yes.' The Rector nodded. 'Clearly it is what you want, but are you not a trifle lonely, my boy? I baptized you and my memory is sharp enough to tell me that it was all of thirty years ago. I . . . er, I attempted to guide your thoughts when you first arrived back and I believed . . . well, everyone believed, that you would do so.'

Having a strong idea what he meant, John nevertheless asked, 'What did you and everyone else think I would do, sir?'

The thin face studied him frankly, despite a slight flush of awkwardness which stained its cheeks. 'Take a wife, of course. I'm sure you were offered your pick of the region's most eligible and delightful ladies, and I have been hoping every day that you would approach me to arrange a marriage before this month was out. What is it, John? Not that tragic affair in your past, I trust. You are too young a man to go through the rest of your life alone. A good wife can be a comfort and a joy, to say nothing of the blessings that children bring. Your brother ignored his duty, but you have every chance to compensate for Tom's heedlessness by siring sons to continue the line.'

After hesitating a moment, John decided that providence was producing the solution to his problem this morning. In no further doubt of Elizabeth's love for him after her response to his declaration of deep devotion, he could approach her shortly, in the full confidence of being able to marry before they sailed.

'Is there still time enough to arrange a marriage ceremony? I am due to travel to Southampton on the thirtieth. That gives us just thirteen days.'

The Rector halted, turning a shade pinker. 'You wish to be married . . . you have chosen . . . dear me, it was generally believed that the case was hopeless. Thirteen days, eh? One normally requires . . . but under such circumstances it could doubtless be arranged. Yes, yes,' he blustered, taken completely by surprise, 'it could be arranged, but . . . but what a pity you have taken so long to reach a decision.'

John gave a slight chuckle. 'On the contrary, this is one of the swiftest decisions I've ever made. I only met the lady two weeks ago.'

'Two weeks ago? Good gracious, that *is* very swift, my boy. Are you quite certain?'

'*Quite* certain,' he returned, with some amusement over the elderly cleric's change of approach.

'Who is she, John?'

'The lady who is presently waiting to offer us tea and cherry tartlets, sir.'

'Tea and cherry . . .' he began faintly. 'You are contemplating . . . you wish to marry Miss . . . *Miss Mount?*'

John's chuckle increased to a joyous laugh. 'I fear Miss Mount would not have a Stavenham at any price. I'm speaking of Mrs Delacourt, naturally.'

Mr Noble stared at him with no trace of matching humour. 'I don't quite understand.'

'I think we both knew at our first meeting that it must come to this, but time has been so short. This storm has snatched three days from us — three most precious days — so please proceed with what must be done without further delay. In view of Elizabeth's standing, it will be a very quiet affair.'

There was a curious hiatus while Mr Noble's expression grew more and more disturbed. Then he said, 'You are not the kind of man to joke about something as sacred as matrimony, but how can you wed a lady who is already married?'

'She is a widow, sir.'

The older man shook his head. 'Mr Delacourt is with his cavalry regiment in Calcutta.'

'He was lost over a year ago,' John told him, realizing that he had been wrong to imagine an aged, brutal husband.

'He is alive and well.'

The surrounding devastation of a village began to crowd in on John as he insisted, 'You are out of date with your news. Of course you are.' The kindly face wrinkled in incomprehension. 'The whole of Wellford knew that you were entertaining Mrs Delacourt, John, and it was supposed that you were acquainted with her husband and had promised to visit his lady whilst in England. It is a usual enough practice when military husbands spend long years abroad. How came you to think . . . whatever could have fostered in you the belief that . . . however did you reach this state in such a short time, my boy? Believe me, the lady is not free to marry you.'

The voice faded beneath the thundering chorus which shouted the unacceptable in his ears. Yet he knew he must accept it. Mr Noble was honest and honourable; what he declared to be the truth must be so. Elizabeth Delacourt had been part of his life for only two and a half weeks, yet he had foolishly believed what she had wanted him to believe. The thundering inner voices grew even louder, more derisive. He turned, and walked away from words which now broke him apart, away from the village, away from a girl who had promised him that human bond which had eluded him all his life. He walked on, bombarded by that mocking chorus, through flooded meadows and over ground covered with tangles of uprooted trees until he was exhausted. Still the anger, the sense of bitter humiliation endured, so he forced his body on beyond exhaustion, until he dropped to the ground.

Lavinia had surely never chattered so continuously as she did whilst mopping the floor around the table where she would set tea when the men returned.

'I do hope Mrs Monk is not badly hurt. However will they lift that dresser from her? Having seen it a dozen or more times I would guess that it weighs several tons. How very fortunate that Captain Stavenham should have been here during the emergency. It was excessively good of him to battle his way from the manor to offer his help. Such a gentleman! You were quite right, dear. He is not in the least like Sir Francis or Mr Thomas. What a pity he does not intend to stay in Wellford. Let us hope Mr Selworthy will prove to be a fit substitute for the rightful Squire. His wife seems admirably sweet-natured, if something of a drab, and it will be wonderful for that house to ring with children's laughter rather than more sinister sounds.'

Her chattering tongue ran on as she mopped, until Elizabeth was on the point of being driven to seek peace in the garden. But her thoughts were in even greater disorder than the countryside, right now. Three days without seeing John, three violent days, during which she had been afraid for her own safety and for his, had played havoc with her emotions. His unexpected appearance, dishevelled and desperate for her, had drawn her instinctive response to his passion. In his arms, she had forgotten all else but the love which had so swiftly possessed her; body, mind, and soul. Gripping her mop so tightly her fingers ached, she knew the time had come to pay the penalty for her weakness. Aware from the start that he was caught in the same web of fatal attraction, she had foolishly believed that time would be her saviour. Later, she had not cared. The days with him had been too precious; the hours too heady; the minutes far too joyous for common-sense. John had put a glorious rainbow across the greyness of her life and, like a rainbow, her love had had no visible end. The crock of gold, always unseen, must nevertheless be there at the end of every rainbow. If she had considered the future at all over the past days, it had been as that distant treasure; out of sight but certain to be hers one day.

A storm had now destroyed the rainbow and the grey reality once more confronted her. How could she ever have believed that John would return to India without precipitating the situation now facing her? What must she do when he returned shortly? Dear heaven, how could she have lost all sense of responsibility so swiftly and willingly? What had she done to them both? They had formed a rare and precious bond few people ever experienced. Had she believed that it would sustain her throughout the coming bleak years; that to have known perfect harmony for a brief while was better than never to have experienced it? How wrong she had been. It would torment, not sustain her, for she had to inflict further pain on a man who had surely suffered enough through love.

The sound of footsteps on the flagged hall made her heart race, but Mr Noble entered the room alone and looking so grave Lavinia immediately concluded that Mrs Monk had perished beneath her own sideboard.

'No, no,' he assured her abstractedly. 'She is little worse than bruised and shaken. John had the presence of mind to send for Dr Bodley right away. She'll be up and about tomorrow.'

55

'Where is Captain Stavenham?' Miss Mount enquired as she abandoned her mop and headed for the kitchen. 'Has he stayed to offer help elsewhere? I will bring a cup for him, nevertheless. He is sure to be back by the time tea is ready.'

As her overalled figure disappeared in to the adjacent room, Elizabeth moved up to the table, mop in hand. 'Where is Captain Stavenham?' she repeated urgently.

'He is gone, ma'am,' the Rector declared in bewildered tones. 'Gone who knows where, for he walked away like a man bewitched, crossing the flooded meadow as if he could not feel or see the water lapping the tops of his boots . . . walked off in the midst of my words to him as if he were unaware of my presence.' Rounding the table, he fixed her with a damning but puzzled gaze. 'I have known John Stavenham since he was born. I baptized him. Neglected by those who should have held him in affection he still grew to manhood possessing many excellent qualities. But he is also stubborn, inclined to be suspicious of others, and is easily aroused to aggression. His greatest fault is that he finds it almost impossible to forgive those who abuse his trust.'

No longer able to meet his gaze, Elizabeth sat and stared with unseeing eyes at the polished table. 'What were you speaking of when he walked away, sir?' she asked with difficulty.

A long and heavy sigh preceded the reply. 'John had just asked me if a marriage could be arranged before he sailed. When I told him that it might be managed, and deplored the time it had taken him to reach a decision, he smiled and said his mind had been made up on first setting eyes upon the lady of his choice.' Allowing a significant pause to elapse, Mr Noble then said, 'He named *you* as the prospective bride, ma'am. Ah, I see by your expression that my news does not astonish you. Whatever have you said or done to make him believe that you are free to marry, and that you would be willing to become his wife within two weeks of your first encounter? Whatever have you been about, ma'am?'

Elizabeth looked up at him stricken, unable to answer his charge. Defence was useless. No one would reach the point of trying to arrange a swift marriage unless he had been given full encouragement to do so.

'You have near broken a good man, Mrs Delacourt, to say nothing of your disloyalty to your husband. I have seldom seen such a look of defeat as there was on John Stavenham's face as he strode away from me.'

★

56

Elizabeth's first attempts to reach John ended in failure. With the road still blocked she tried to cross country, but what had been a formidable feat for a strong, determined man proved impossible for a woman in long heavy skirts. Distraught and heartbroken, she was forced to wait until the road was opened. This delay gave John thirty-six hours in which to make his premature departure from a village where unhappiness continued to dog him.

'I hold myself to blame for this,' Miss Mount declared tearfully when Elizabeth returned from Wellford Manor with the news.

'*I* am to blame, Vinnie,' she corrected heavily. 'When I should have spoken, I remained silent.'

Her companion glanced up from the depths of her handkerchief. 'I perfectly understand how you found the situation too difficult in the face of his gentle condolences. It was a predicament any woman could find herself in. But if I had only known he believed you to be a widow I would have perceived the dangers and acted far more sternly to prevent further meetings. *Why* did you not tell me, dear?'

Gazing from the window, still dressed in her riding-habit, Elizabeth made a weary gesture. 'We have been over all that so many times.'

'Did it never occur to you that . . . ?'

She swung round in a passion. 'No, it did *not* occur to me, Vinnie, because I selfishly thought only of the present moment. I have told you that a hundred times.' Gripping the sill behind her, she said brokenly, 'He entered my life with such overwhelming impact I was helpless to resist. In three short weeks I believe I lived a whole lifetime of happiness. My soul was so perfectly attuned to his it was as if all else was unreal and easily forgotten. You could not have prevented further meetings. I would have reached him against all advice.'

Lavinia dried her eyes, saying sadly, 'No, my dear, you would not, for I would have referred to your husband's presence in Calcutta during our first visit for tea and the Captain would have ended the affair there and then. That my few references to Mr Delacourt were necessarily of past events, which easily supported the misapprehension, is to be deeply regretted . . . but I confess that I rarely think of him, for he seems to play no part in your life since he left for India. It is very easy to forget your commitment to him and so, I suppose, it must be for you.' She sighed. 'But I am to blame. *I* am. It was abundantly clear that the poor man was very taken with you and that you were so lively, so happy and glowing in his company. Yet I confess I saw no deep harm in the

57

meetings. Captain Stavenham is an honourable man and it seemed . . .
Oh dear, had I known that he believed you to be free I would have . . .'
'Do stop,' begged Elizabeth. '*I* knew it, and I fervently wished it to
be true. My deception toward you both was deliberate. You have
forgiven me. John never will. If I could have seen him but once to
explain why I behaved as I did . . . but he will believe the worst of me
until the end of his days.' Moving forward to sink into a chair, she
confessed, 'I was feeling quite desperate when I came here. You cannot
know what it is like to live with a family of precise, unimaginative critics
who disapprove of one's every action, who have no understanding of
those elements which give life colour, zest and excitement, and who pen
monthly reports to a jailer in India. Yes, Vinnie,' she insisted, 'William
is my jailer. This gold band on my finger ties me to him, restricts my life
in the way a prisoner is confined behind bars. His name proclaims to the
world that I am his until death releases me. A life sentence!' Too restless
to sit for long, she was up again and walking to the window, as if seeking
escape from imprisonment. 'Marriage is considered to be every
woman's great hope, my dear friend, but it is all too often the death of
it.' Swinging round to confront the other woman, she continued in
tremulous tones, 'Being with John revealed to me for the first time the
true cause for William's treatment of me. It is not, as he claims, that I
am too precocious, too unconventional and too preoccupied with
books; that I am an embarrassment socially and a hindrance to his
career because my behaviour offends others. John's response made me
see that the supposed precociousness is really lively interest, that
defiance of convention can be a result of clear thinking, and that
knowledge adds richness to a relationship between a man and a woman.
In short, Vinnie, I am an embarrassment and a hindrance to William's
career only because I outshine him in company. *That* is why he left me
behind in England, and that is why I am being systematically subdued
by the Delacourts. Knowing that he cannot, or will not attempt to
match my enquiring, questioning approach to life, he has put me out of
harm's way for ten years. Can you wonder that when I find the perfect
partner in understanding, intellect, and soul harmony, I swiftly reject
all thoughts of a relationship which William has brushed aside with
such ease? He wears no gold band of ownership to me; he has not taken
my name to tell the world of his obligations to Elizabeth de Rioches. He
is *free*, Vinnie, free to live as he wishes out there in a land filled with the
riches I yearn to see, but which his glance will pass over without even

noticing. He is free to mix with whomsoever he fancies, and flirt as often as the next man. No one will condemn him for it. He will take other women . . . yes, *of course* he will. Don't look at me in that disapproving fashion, for you are well enough acquainted with scandal in this village to know the habits of those who call themselves gentlemen. He will take mistresses, and society will regard the fact indulgently because it is to be expected when a man is apart from his wife for years.' Going forward again to lean on the table, she added passionately, 'Yet I am condemned by Mr Noble — and would be by anyone who knew of it — for allowing John to love and honour me so much he tried to wed me.' Dropping wearily into the chair, she put her head in her hands. 'One small deception, prompted by my own love and honour, has made John also condemn me. He will think as a man thinks, Vinnie, and he will also condemn me.'

There was no sound but the ticking of the clock for some moments, then a quiet voice said, 'I see now who is really to blame for this tragedy, poor child. It is William Delacourt.'

May ended in a blaze of sunshine. On the day that a second man sailed for India and left her behind, this time a dearly loved man, the elements should have reflected Elizabeth's misery. That they did not came as further punishment. The Delacourt family could find no fault with the behaviour of a pale, silent, lifeless girl who sat in the garden, lost in contemplation, day after day. Accepting that nothing could be done to change or alleviate the heartbreaking consequences of her visit to Wellford, Elizabeth had to face the dragging greyness of her future again.

Only when June had passed into July did she gradually come to see that there was one glimmer of hope left. Love for William, if love it had ever been, had faded soon after the wedding, but they could surely live in tolerable contentment together by attempting compromise. If an absence of one year could induce her to abandon any sense of loyalty to a man she could scarcely recall, how could she greet him after ten, and live happily as his wife thereafter? She must write to him, explain how desperately unhappy she was, and beg him to transfer to a regiment stationed in England. If she used the right submissive tone, the most persuasive feminine phrases, he would surely be convinced that she had changed into the kind of wife he expected. Only the most inhuman man would ignore an impassioned plea from a distant partner. She had called

59

her marriage a life sentence, so she must serve it under the best possible terms.

On the brink of composing a letter that William could not possibly resist, a small item in the daily news caught her eye and changed her plans in the most unexpected way. The social column stated that Major Lord Blayne would be taking up his inheritance, after the recent death of the sixth baronet, when Chetwynde's Hussars returned to England in the autumn, after ten years in India. In a state of inner turmoil, Elizabeth realized two things simultaneously. First, with John back in England there was every chance of meeting him in some military gathering, which would make her resolution to put him out of her life harder to stand by than it was now. Second, if John was leaving India, her attempt to mend her marriage would stand a better chance out there with her husband. With William's family well distant, she could really make a fresh start. He could remain with his precious Dragoons and she . . . and she would see that land which John had described so vividly. That emotive link was all she could allow herself of a love which had arrived too late and broken so tragically.

The Delacourts were horrified by her request for a passage to Calcutta. After a week of heated arguments which ended with her vow to go begging in the streets for the money if they withheld it, they sent for the doctor in the belief that she was losing her mind. However, this susceptible man came from his patient to give his opinion that she should be allowed to join their son in India. Taking Austin Delacourt aside, he made his case by explaining in terms familiar to gentlemen who owned horses that there were times when mares needed a stallion and, if denied, were liable to grow wild and uncontrollable. Elizabeth's behaviour bore this fact out.

Observing the delicacy the subject demanded, the Delacourt patriarch impressed upon his wife the fact that their lively and beautiful daughter-in-law would be over thirty when their dear son came back from India. Did they not desire grandchildren? Would William not wish for sons to succeed him? Rosy with blushes, Emily agreed with all he said, as she invariably did. Austin wrote to inform his son of his decision, and took up a cancelled passage on a steamer leaving on the first day of November, because Canon and Mrs Hall, old friends of Emily's family, would be aboard to chaperon the young matron. Elizabeth's hasty departure would not allow sufficient time to receive a reply from William on the wisdom of their decision, but her extraordinary fervour to join her husband was proving an embarrassment to a family anxious to return to the peace they valued. Preparations for the journey began and everyone concerned breathed in relief.

Having achieved her desire, Elizabeth faced it with an aching heart despite her great determination. India lay within her sphere at last. John sensed that his destiny lay in that land. What awaited her there would surely be more fulfilling than incarceration with William's family for nine more years.

John leaned on the rail as the steamer made its slow passage along the River Hooghly. He saw little of the banks covered with thick jungle, broken here and there by ghats and giving way to open parkland; where pleasant villas created an air of elegance to take the excited, thronging passengers' attention from the garbage in the water. The stench of this port returned to his nostrils with unwelcome familiarity as the great bulk of Fort William came into sight behind the harbour. It would not be long before he stepped back onto Indian soil.

The knowledge left him unmoved. It had taken but a week to accept that time, not distance, was his only hope of easing the fierce, throbbing anger which had mastered him since that day in Sussex. He moved from the ship's side as a flash of renewed despair ran through him like the blade of a sabre. Women of all kinds had crossed his path since Clare had vanished. He should have known enough to recognize Elizabeth Delacourt for what she was, yet he had shown no more sense than a gullible youth. He and his brother officers had jeered at many an inexperienced cornet who had been mortified by a precocious female in much the same way, and treated them to the usual humiliating horseplay in the hope of making them wiser. What would be their verdict on his adult folly? The penance he was paying was the inability to put her out of his mind. Heat-ridden nights in his cabin had been haunted by memories of dark curls surrounding a face of great charm and vivacity; days on the sun-warmed deck had been spent in recollection of her voice, her laughter, her amber eyes which shone with enthusiasm as she listened to his words. The rocking, bumping, overland journey from Alexandria to Suez had sent the blood throbbing through him as he imagined riding beside her along that Sussex hillside.

His mouth twisted bitterly. Mr Noble had written to him at Southampton, begging him to hold on to hope and to his faith. Far from flinging himself on to the first enemy sword he faced, as the Rector had

61

feared, John had every intention of staying alive. It would take a long time to recover his integrity and peace of mind. He could only do that by fighting anything that threatened his resolution, for he would not let that sweet scheming wanton destroy him.

The heat inside his cabin was intense so he gladly collected his small bags prior to disembarkation. His first destination was Fort William, where he would report and confirm that he would be joining his regiment as soon as he could travel north. It was a tedious journey to the Punjab, but this time of year was best for travelling and he was desperate for action after weeks cooped up on the steamer. He eventually walked down the gangway to the quay feeling no emotion, his only thought being that somewhere in this vast city was a poor devil whose wife was deceiving him with any fool who would allow himself to fall for her charms.

Chapter Four

The first day of November was grey and cold, with a sharp wind that whipped the cheeks of passengers watching the gap widen between themselves and those who stood on the quay, waving forlornly. The Delacourt family was not among them. Only one person watched the packet leave for Calcutta and shed tears over the departure of a girl in blue velvet cloak and bonnet. Lavinia was heartbroken. Instinct told her she would never again see Elizabeth whom she loved as her own child. Blaming herself for doing so little to prevent what had happened at Wellford, she could only question the Lord's wisdom in bringing together far too late two young people clearly made for each other. If it had been to test their resistance to temptation, they had failed abysmally. If He had designed the disastrous affair as a judgement upon them, Lavinia could not think what they had done to warrant it. She did not know John Stavenham well, of course, but if the rumours concerning his youthful marriage had any foundation, he had surely been punished enough. As for Elizabeth's sin in allowing the misconception over her marital state to stand uncorrected, it would have been of little importance if there had been no further meetings between them. Miss Mount had never experienced deep feelings for a gentleman, even as a girl, and had counted the fact as her greatest misfortune. She now considered herself lucky to have escaped the affliction, although the anguish it brought could not be worse than this she suffered as the sea took her girl away to an uncertain future half-way across the world.

For the first time since the Rector had revealed the extent of what she had done to John, Elizabeth shed tears. Lavinia had played a major role in her life. She could not part easily from her, especially after the support and comfort she had offered when everything had seemed so black. Hurting those one loved was as painful as being hurt oneself, Elizabeth had discovered, but she was now full of a resolution to create nothing but happiness for William and for those around her from this time on. Nothing could undo what had occurred at Wellford, and her penance would be in knowing that she would be forever damned in John's eyes.

The steamer headed first for Falmouth to pick up the mail before it turned away from the shores of England, and passengers began drifting below to escape the bitter wind off the sea. Elizabeth did the same, but was soon driven back up for fresh air, and a comforting sight of the coastline just visible through the gloom. In her cabin she had been alarmed by the creaks and groans of the ship's timbers as the vessel rolled in the heavy swell, and she had grown queasy from the unwelcome movement. With Falmouth behind them, however, she had no choice but to descend for the night, during which she regretted having eaten dinner. By morning it was evident that her constitution did not take kindly to seafaring, so she remained in her bunk, retching and miserable, while the packet fought its way across the Bay of Biscay toward Gibraltar. In an attempt to strengthen her resolution, she recalled John's description of his own outward voyage almost ten years before and told herself this was pure luxury compared with the conditions the soldiers had endured, but a third day of constant sickness persuaded her that she would be dead within the week. What a relief it would be!

The six hour stop at Gibraltar afforded an opportunity to leave the confines of her cabin and venture up on shaky legs for fresh air. The hardier passengers who had laughed their way across the first stage of the journey all trooped ashore to see what they could of the island bastion. Elizabeth was content to sit on board and watch the bustle on the quay, now that the deck was steady. It was cold, but their anchorage was protected and she had a rug over her knees. Canon Hall had suffered a stroke a week before sailing, so Elizabeth had no companions aboard. It was a relief not to be burdened with pious chaperons. She welcomed isolation from disapproving elders during a voyage which was changing her life so drastically. Despite her resolution to put John from her mind, her presence at this harbour where his ships had docked brought him painfully near in spirit. Chetwynde's Hussars must have sailed from India now, *en route* for England. Somewhere on the high seas, perhaps in the dead of night, his steamer would pass hers and neither would know the other was so close. That was how it must be from now on. He must leave her life, much like a ship which had passed close to hers and then sailed on forever. William must occupy her

64

thoughts . . . William and the future they would forge with fresh understanding.

Lost in such thoughts, she was reminded of her surroundings by the voices of passengers returning from their excursions, carrying souvenirs over which they were loudly comparing prices. A tea tray was brought to her by a steward, and she surprised herself by discovering that her appetite had returned fully. Indeed, her sense of well-being had improved sufficiently for her to take pleasure in watching the birds which circled, then alighted, on the towering rock with sureness of wing and claw.

'One day a man will do that with as much ease as they,' said a voice to her right.

She turned to see a gentleman of about her own age dressed in trousers of the latest patterned design and a dark-red coat. He doffed his tall hat with graceful good manners, but the smile on his handsome fair- moustached face contained a trace of impudence.

'Good day, ma'am. Forgive my intrusion but I noted your interest in the gulls and was moved to confide in you. I am Rupert Carruthers, your fellow voyager. May I sit beside you for a while?'

A sudden urge for company, especially youthful company, caused Elizabeth to smile up at him. 'On a vessel as small as this we are certain to sit together at some time during the voyage, Mr Carruthers, but I warn you I am sad company.'

'You do not take kindly to the motion of the sea, eh?' he asked, with all the heartiness of one who has never suffered from it.

She shook her head. 'I promise you I would walk ashore now if I was not aware that I should have to remain in Gibraltar for the rest of my days, for there is no way off the rock save by ship.'

He sank in to the chair beside her and balanced his expensive hat on his right leg, which rested negligently across his left knee. 'Well, you could brave an extremely short crossing to the coast of Spain, ma'am, then endure an overland journey through the barbarous countryside to reach France. Another long and uncomfortable foray over the hazards to be found in the land of our late enemies would then bring you to Calais, where a short but violent crossing of the Channel would return you to the home you so recently left. You might not suffer from *mal de mer* for long, but I venture to suggest that you would be exposed to all manner of diseases and plagues along the route, so that you would eventually set foot in England

65

believing this neat little vessel to be the height of comfort and the only sensible way to travel.'

Elizabeth laughingly denied that she would ever agree with his last statement. His manner was refreshing, and his youth such that she need not take him seriously. The style of his dress reflected wealth, his confidence suggested education at the highest level, and the lightness of his approach persuaded her that he was seeking nothing more than pleasant diversion to enliven the tedious hours on board.

'I wish I shared your confidence in the sea, sir.'

'The Captain assured me that conditions will improve. You must believe him and take heart.'

'I sincerely hope he is right,' she said ruefully. 'The confines of my cabin have grown most unattractive.'

'Then it is definitely time that you left them to enjoy all there is to see along the Mediterranean, to say nothing of the overland crossing to Suez. You are making the complete journey to Calcutta, ma'am?'

'Yes. My husband's regiment is stationed there.'

'Your husband! By George, I had not taken you for a married lady.'

She was amused by his patent disappointment. Clearly, his golden hair and frank blue-grey eyes had won many a young girl to his side. 'I should not be sitting here taking tea alone, prey to any gentleman seeking shipboard dalliance, if I did not have the protection of a wedding-ring.'

A picture of youthful affront, he said, 'You surely did not take me for a . . . I am a *Carruthers*, ma'am.'

Even more amused, she hid her smile. 'To be sure you are. That is the sole reason why I allowed you to bear me company. Will you have some of this tea? The steward has provided several extra cups.'

Placated by her words, and by the offer of refreshment, the young man was soon smiling again. 'Which regiment does your husband serve, ma'am, and in what capacity?'

'Lieutenant Delacourt has been with Forrester's Light Dragoons for the past eight years.'

With a sandwich half-way to his mouth, Rupert Carruthers grew still with astonishment. 'By all that is wonderful! I am on my way to join them; have been waiting to do so for the past two years. My guardian refused to come up with the price of my commission before my twentieth birthday, so I have been kicking my heels and having a hard time of it trying to be patient.' He gave her a doleful look. 'Patience is not one of my virtues, Mrs Delacourt.'

'I can well believe that, sir,' she teased, as she poured tea for him. 'I have every sympathy. It is not one of my own. But tell me why, when you reached twenty, your guardian chose to put you in a regiment serving so far away.'

'It wasn't a question of choosing,' he told her heartily. 'My brother is a major in the Forrester's, so there could be no other regiment for me. When they received orders for foreign service, I was not then nineteen and nothing would persuade Uncle Bart to buy me in so that I could accompany them. Even Hugh himself refused to support me, despite the number of vacancies left by men transferring in order to remain in England. You have no idea how hard it was to see him go and be obliged to stay at home.'

'Oh, but I have,' she assured him. 'I suffered the same experience when my husband sailed without me.'

A wicked gleam entered his eye as he murmured, 'I find it hard to understand how any man could bring himself to do so, although there must have been excellent reasons, I'm sure. How fortunate it is that we have the same destination. As we are both going to be closely associated with Forrester's during the coming years, will you allow me to act as your escort until you are safely in your husband's care?'

She shook her head. 'If the past days are anything to go by I shall be in no need of an escort until we reach land.'

'We shall have no more talk of indisposition,' he ruled firmly. 'The Captain is confident that there will be a full complement of passengers in the saloon for dinner tonight. I have to own it has been dashed dreary with only two missionaries, an elderly scholar and a fierce female explorer for companionship all the week.'

He looked so glum that Elizabeth found herself laughing. 'Poor Mr Carruthers. Are you sure your offer to be my escort was not prompted by desperation for younger company rather than consideration for my welfare?'

'You may tease me, ma'am,' he said sternly, 'but you have been so amused over my discomfiture that you have not noticed that we have put to sea again. Can you deny that I have already been of great service to you?'

Glancing across the deck, she saw that there was a distance of some three hundred yards between ship and shore, yet the movement had been insufficient to draw her attention from her companion. Perhaps he was the ideal person to ease the tedium of the voyage. At that moment a break in the clouds allowed a pale sun through, which lit up the grey rock with a luminous sheen and turned the wings of the wheeling birds a brilliant white. Optimism rose suddenly as she turned back to him.

'I accept your offer on condition that you rule the waves flat and hang a warm sun above me until our arrival in Calcutta.'

'Done,' he agreed, leaping to his feet. 'I suggest that we take a short turn about the deck to gain an appetite for dinner. It promises to be excellent because we took on fresh provisions at Gibraltar.'

As Rupert had predicted, the saloon was full that evening, and it remained so for every meal during the voyage to Malta. There, the entire complement of passengers felt sufficiently robust to go ashore, Elizabeth and Rupert among them. She had soon guessed the reason for the young subaltern's gallantry on meeting the other females aboard — most of whom were elderly or forbidding — but he was excellent company, despite displays of bombast which emphasized his immaturity. Another sign of it was his clear hero-worship of his brother, Major Sir Hugo Carruthers. He could not understand why Elizabeth had never met this apparent paragon. She explained that she had been married for less than a year when the regiment sailed for India, which had been insufficient time for her to be acquainted with all her husband's brother officers. He then expressed great surprise that Mr Delacourt's letters had not been full of comments concerning Sir Hugo. Unwilling to reveal that there had been few letters, and those full of strictures on her behaviour, Elizabeth decided to tease him.

'You must remember, Mr Carruthers, that my husband is a mere lieutenant. An exalted person like Sir Hugo would not be much in his company.'

'Oh, Hugh is a capital fellow who will drink a glass with anyone,' came the artless reply from the youthful admirer, who then regaled her with a list of virtues the Major possessed, starting with those of his boyhood and covering schooldays, holidays and campaigning days. Sir Hugo had apparently never found the time to marry, although Elizabeth was assured that there was a multitude of females always after him. 'He is a dashed handsome fellow, you know, and he will be obliged to take a wife on his return to England because of the name. I hope very sincerely that she will be a female of the highest order . . . although Hugh could not fail to choose any but the most admirable of partners,' he added, to console himself on the matter.

By the time the steamer left Malta, Elizabeth was convinced there could be nothing more to learn about Carruthers senior, but she was wrong. The young officer had not covered his brother's superb expertise with horses, nor the marvellous way he wielded a sabre. Elizabeth had to stop him in the midst of one enthusiastic account of Sir Hugo's deadly prowess because she began to feel faint. Rupert immediately apologized. After that, a whole day passed without mention of the paragon but he began to creep back into the conversation within a few days.

Elizabeth might have been irritated by her companion's ingenuous chatter, but she was feeling so much better and the sun was gaining in strength daily so she was able to close her ears during their walks around the deck and enjoy the conviviality of other passengers without really listening. He was an engaging young man, despite his immaturity, and she feared that he would receive a hard knock when Sir Hugo fell from his pedestal, as he must eventually do.

It was a major stepping-stone in their long journey when the steamer reached Alexandria. Even though her health had improved, Elizabeth was not sorry to leave the ship. The port was an ill-favoured place which hardly recommended the East to a stranger. The stench was unpleasant enough to turn even a strong stomach, and the filthy state of the streets did little to encourage travellers to investigate them. Elizabeth had her first sight of brown people and was glad of Rupert's company, for she felt that the wild, belligerent look in their black eyes belied their whining protestations of unworthiness which accompanied their offers to be of service.

Rupert took it all in his stride, ignoring the donkey drivers and the porters who had humped his prodigious luggage up the steps of the hotel where they were to put up for several nights. At the desk he demanded instant service for himself and Mrs Delacourt in spite of the others waiting for attention. That he received priority treatment did not surprise Elizabeth, for he had an air of authority which was augmented by a loud, arrogant tone that brooked no argument. Many of their fellow passengers showed their disgust at such high-handed behaviour from so young a man, and when he threw a handful of coins on the ground for his porters to squabble over, there were several comments passed on the subject of bad manners. This disapprobation soon extended to Elizabeth, but she decided that her comfort was more important than the resentment of a few strangers, and remained at Rupert's side throughout the following days. She had reason to be thankful for that decision.

The paddle steamer which transported them down the Nile was

cramped, uncomfortable and extremely stuffy. In addition, the wind blew the black smoke from the funnel down upon the decks so it was necessary to remain below, unless one wished to be covered in soot. On arrival at Bulak, Elizabeth again had cause to be thankful for Rupert's ability to obtain the best service their hotel could provide. It was impossible not to admire the ease with which he dealt with everything, and she guessed it must stem from his background. He never boasted about anything save his marvellous brother, but his conversation unselfconsciously revealed a heritage which was considerably impressive and way above her own or the Delacourts'. Rupert Carruthers was clearly a member of the aristocracy, with an inborn notion of superiority over those less fortunate. There was true courage beneath his brashness and arrogance, however, as Elizabeth discovered when they reached Cairo.

From this fabled city all passengers travelling as far as Calcutta were obliged to cross the desert in a long caravan of horse-drawn conveyances, stopping for refreshments and rest at stations all along the route. When they reached Suez they would again embark for the last stage of their journey. This desert crossing was timed to coincide with the arrival of the India steamer, and they all went ashore at Cairo to be told that the ship was already in port at Suez and waiting for them. This meant they would have no time for sightseeing, after all.

Rupert was furious. 'To think that we have come all this distance only to be denied a visit to the pyramids,' he complained to Elizabeth, as their luggage was stowed on the back of a carriage which was to convey them to the desert terminus immediately. 'Hugh particularly instructed me to study them for, although the regiment took the long route around the Cape, he saw the wonders of Egypt when he made the Grand Tour. It really is too bad!' After a few minutes' silence, he said, 'I'm very tempted to make the excursion, you know. They would not dare to leave without me.'

Wilting in the heat and almost suffocated by the combined smells of the wharves, streets and passing humanity, Elizabeth begged him not to be foolhardy.

'You cannot make an individual stand against a shipping line,' she pointed out irritably. 'Much as it might surprise you, I tend to believe the schedule of the India steamer will hold more sway with the captain of it than the absence of one passenger . . . even though his name is Carruthers.'

When he remained mutinous she resorted to extreme measures. 'However much Sir Hugo might wish you to see the pyramids, I am sure he has too much consideration for his fellows to expect you to delay upwards of fifty others who have also been denied a sight of them.'

It did the trick. Helping her aboard the carriage, he then sat meekly, if sullenly, beside her as they left the vicinity of the Nile to head toward the glare and desolation of the desert. Elizabeth had also been hoping to see the wonders of this region, but it happened to be that time of the month when she was suffering considerable discomfort so the thought of missing a tiring excursion — when the ache in her head was as great as that in her stomach — was not too disappointing. Today, she would gladly be back with the Delacourts, in a serene household where she could take to her bed with a cool cloth on her forehead and a warm brick for her stomach until the pain eased. As it was, every jolt of the carriage, every raucous human or animal sound in the streets, every minute beneath the killing sun, was severe punishment.

Rupert took her total silence as a rebuke and eventually apologized, rather shamefaced. 'Forgive me, ma'am, I had momentarily forgotten how any thought of delay must lower your spirits, for you will be so anxious to join Mr Delacourt.'

It was easy to make no reply and allow him to believe it the truth. The initial impetus which had sent her on this course had faded slowly with each mile nearer to William. Recollection of their bitter quarrels persuaded her that he would be livid with anger over her behaviour. Hardly the best terms on which to base a reconciliation. Suppose he insisted on sending her straight home again? Whatever would she do? Small wonder she felt little despondency over missing the pyramids, for they could be visited on her return to England.

On arrival at the terminus where they would begin their overland drive to Suez, which was an inescapable part of the new shorter route to India, Elizabeth saw immediately that Rupert had been right to say that she would come to regard the packet from Southampton as the height of comfort. Drawn up in a long line was a series of open-sided vans with canopies to shade the long benches each side, on which passengers must sit facing each other for hours on end. The prospect was extremely unwelcome. There were no facilities for those who might feel unwell, or for any lady suffering as she was today. There was no choice but to alight from the carriage and wait in resignation, while Rupert pushed his way through the sea of confused passengers to demand, in what

Elizabeth privately called 'the Carruthers bawl', seats in the leading van for them both. By the time he returned to where she stood beside their baggage, the noise and pandemonium had doubled due to the arrival of a large number of Europeans planning short excursions into the desert on camels. Their appearance on the scene prompted the usual chorus of excited gesticulating and shouting as camel drivers vied with each other for custom. The animals smelt so vile, Elizabeth wondered that anyone would care to sit on their backs for a moment, much less than for an hour or two.

'The most accursed luck,' exploded Rupert, arriving beside her with a handful of tickets. 'We have been allocated places in the sixteenth of these obnoxious vehicles, which means we shall suffer the dust kicked up by all those ahead of us. I could do nothing to move the idiot to take note of my requirements,' he added with a scowl. 'His skull is fashioned from wood, in my opinion, and I told him so.'

'Then I am amazed he did not seat us in the *last* of these forty conveyances,' she told him wearily. 'Pray let us find our places so that we may at least benefit from the little relief offered by the canopy.'

Further dismay awaited them on seeing who was to share the van: two elderly couples who had stopped speaking to them in protest over Rupert's high-handedness, an eccentric lady explorer who planned to end her journey in the middle of the desert to go in search of a nomad tribe, and a middle-aged civil servant returning to India, who was constantly semi-inebriated. Rupert's scowl deepened as he handed Elizabeth up to occupy one of the two places left vacant right at the front of the van, where they would suffer the worst of the sand kicked up by their own horses. He was about to climb up after her when fighting broke out between a string of bad-tempered camels nearby. The fat overseer cursed his useless drivers and flexed his whip several times to restore order. The sharp cracks so resembled pistol shots, the lead horses of their van took fright and bolted, throwing their driver from his perch on the box. Caught with one foot on the step, Rupert managed to haul himself aboard and scramble across the alarmed ladies to reach her.

'Are you all right?' he shouted, as the van swayed from side to side on its mad progress over the desert road in pursuit of the first ten, which had already set off.

Elizabeth nodded, too overwhelmed to speak. It had all happened so swiftly. Clutching the rail behind her back, she was unaware of Rupert's intention until he began to climb up over the driver's box and, from there, started to inch his way along the shafts enclosing the racing, terrified horses. The sheer danger of what he was doing made her turn cold. It also silenced the others, who clung to the rail as Elizabeth did, staring in horror at the young man flirting with death. The hot air rushed past her face as fear for him banished all thought of her own present discomfort. Then she held her breath as he began to reach out for the reins lying along the back of one of the rear horses. Slowly, slowly, his hand stretched toward the leather straps as he squatted on the shaft and retained his hold on the metal grip fixed to the box. It was a demonstration of great courage from someone whose character was clearly more complex than he had so far revealed.

Once in possession of the reins, Rupert then clambered onto the box for a masterly demonstration of his ability to control a team of carriage horses. The threat of overturning gradually dwindled until the van came to a complete halt in full view of the advance vehicles, which had stopped to watch the drama. For a moment or two there was a hush over the vast stretch of sand as the horses' flanks heaved in the aftermath of their gallop from some imagined terror. Then an astonishing ripple of applause floated on the still air from the distant vans, and there were cries of 'Bravo!'. The elderly husbands who had formerly disapproved of Rupert's manner were now driven to their feet to express words of admiration for his heroism, and their ladies tearfully declared that he had saved all their lives by endangering his own. Elizabeth was impressed by the modest way he received lavish praise from those who had cut him earlier, and fell to wondering if all Rupert had said of Sir Hugo might be the truth. Given the same brand of courage, plus maturity, he could well be a hero without match, as his young brother claimed.

Only when they had reached the terminus again, where worse pandemonium than ever had been created by verbal and physical combat between the van drivers and those who led the camels, did Elizabeth offer praise to her companion as he leapt easily from the driving box to help her alight.

'When I accepted your offer to act as my escort I had no notion that my life might be in your hands, Mr Carruthers. Your courage is equalled only by your presence of mind.'

To her astonishment, he flushed, turning her admiration aside by saying gruffly, 'Not at all, ma'am, or I should have thought to remove my hat first and it would not now be trampled to pieces and totally unwearable, obliging me to extricate my hatbox from the baggage cart in order to replace it. Forgive me if I desert you for five minutes.' Leading her to a shaded seat alongside the terminus building, he then strode off toward the rear, where baggage was being carelessly tossed into several caged carts by porters with no interest in the fate of the contents. Despite her shaken state, Elizabeth was soon compelled to smile when she heard Rupert's imperious voice demanding his hatbox be retrieved from beneath a heap of stacked trunks; and commenting on the mental faculties of those who had placed such a vulnerable piece of baggage there. A surprising thought then struck her. She was growing very fond of Rupert, in the way she would have been fond of a brother. He might be exasperating, at times, but she was thankful that he was going all the way to Calcutta. The journey would have been sadly boring without his company, and their friendship could happily continue when they reached the regiment.

They set off again in better circumstances, their fellows keeping up a lively conversation all the way to the first station along the route. Elizabeth felt it was too grand a name for the small square building with barred windows which resembled a prison rather than a post-house. However, after being jolted and bounced over sand which reflected the sun in a vicious white glare, she welcomed the refreshment provided while the horses were changed. Back in the van, the long day grew more and more monotonous. There was no scenery save sand; no relief from the heat. Everyone dozed, the men snoring loudly, and her headache returned in full force. Sustained by liberal applications of cologne, she walked thankfully into the bedroom Rupert had acquired for her at the half-way house and sank on to the bed, her head throbbing unmercifully.

The second leg of the land crossing was as boring as the first, there being nothing but miles and miles of arid, featureless landscape enlivened only by occasional strings of camels laden with merchandise which was regularly transported between Suez and Cairo. Conversation was desultory after they had exhausted speculation on the possible fate of the lady explorer who had remained at their overnight stop to prepare for her foray in search of nomads. Elizabeth marvelled that any female would wish to risk a terrible fate at the hands of such people, but envied the woman's comfort in her loose flowing robe fashioned in the style of the desert dwellers. John's words concerning a person either hating or being spellbound by India also applied here, surely. The explorer had

74

fallen for the aura of the desert; Elizabeth was certain she hated it, even after this short time.

Suez was another dirty, malodorous port swarming with guides, pedlars, and the usual mass of labourers necessary to load and refurbish ships. The steamer was ready to leave. Once they had boarded, found their cabins, and ensured that their personal baggage was stowed there, the vessel slipped away from the quay and out to the gulf which led to the Red Sea. It was pleasantly familiar to return to shipboard life, but although the sea was calm, the heat was such that even Rupert grew too lethargic to do more than sit on deck, hoping to find a slight breeze. During that section of their journey, Elizabeth heard more about her companion's childhood on a large estate in Cumberland, and about the deaths of both parents from an epidemic whilst travelling in Portugal, where his father had served with Forrester's Light Dragoons under Wellington.

When he asked her for details of her life, she gave them frankly and happily, thus marking another step in the warm relationship between them. The days passed in pleasant companionship, which grew so easy Elizabeth began to call him by his first name, as she would a brother, and invited him to do the same. Doubtful about the propriety of it as she was married, he soon surrendered to her pleas and this completed the happy state of that somnolent period.

Once the steamer entered the Indian Ocean, however, the long heavy swell around the tip of the continent drove Elizabeth back to her cabin to suffer the misery of seasickness again. Not until they reached the long approaches to Calcutta was she able to venture up to sit beside Rupert as the ship made its slow way up the estuary. This moment she had dreamed of caused little excitement. The past week or so had exhausted her beyond caring very much what awaited her here. Her companion was just the reverse. He had been dashing from side to side of the upper deck exclaiming on all he saw, making no secret of his exaltation over the approaching reunion with his brother.

Calcutta finally came into view. Cypress trees and green lawns surrounding tasteful villas gave an impression of sedate tranquillity. The mass of ships from all over the world which crowded the harbour were indicative of the commerce and trade associated with this port, despite the backdrop of classical pillars and spires of the ancient and beautiful city. As Elizabeth gazed at the garbage in the river, at the clutter of dirty merchant-shipping, and at the armies of black labourers in scant clothing which swarmed over the wharves, her visions of golden palaces, tigers, and ethnic ceremonial all seemed far from this first sight of India. Then she recalled John saying that there was beauty in every aspect of this land, and saw it all with different eyes. There was a stark attraction in the forest of masts against the rich blue sky, and in the constantly swinging cranes. The bodies of the native workmen were lithe and surefooted as they scrambled about the vessels, their dark skins gleaming in the sunlight. Even the river produced pleasant aspects; if one looked beyond the areas of floating rubbish. Suddenly, emotion set a lump in her throat. He knew all this; he had tried to make it real for her with his words. Now she was here and could see how vivid they had been.

The signal for disembarkation was given. The gangplank was lowered. Those who waited on the quay, some to meet passengers, others merely to watch the steamer arrive because they felt an echo of their homeland in its presence, began to rush aboard. Rupert stood beside Elizabeth while they scanned the crowd for a sight of a Forrester's uniform. He looked very splendid in his own thick scarlet jacket, and dark blue overalls strapped beneath his boots. It was the first time he had worn his uniform, and Elizabeth had to own that he looked every inch the aristocrat, despite the boyish eagerness on what could be seen of his face between the thick chain strap and the brim of his plumed head-dress. However, although there was quite a number of military men in the welcoming throng, she could not immediately recognize William's sturdy frame. In fact, she could see no member of Forrester's Light Dragoons, and said as much to Rupert. After scanning the shakos and helmets below, he had to agree.

'They may have urgent duties,' he said earnestly. 'But they will have sent someone in their stead, rest assured.'

Only when the majority of passengers had been claimed and led ashore, leaving several jovial young men still celebrating their reunion, and a family who had mislaid an item of baggage, did an officer appear in a carriage; jump from it; and hasten up the gangplank. He made straight for them and arrived with an apology offered in jerky sentences.

'Sorry. Excessively sorry. Held up at the last moment. You must be Carruthers. Forrester's uniform. Can't mistake it. Here now and completely at your service, old fellow.' He grinned. 'Name's Chaplin . . . of the Artillery.'

Rupert sized him up in true Carruthers style. 'My brother sent you, did he?'

'Yes. No. Not exactly. Well, yes, I expect he did. Came through Headquarters, d'you see? No knowing the source, but if you've a brother, daresay he's behind it.'

'Behind what?' demanded Rupert very coolly.

'Instructions to meet the steamer, tell you the situation, offer any assistance.' Unable to keep his attention from Elizabeth any longer, he feasted his eyes on her pale yellow muslin gown, crisp bonnet and matching sunshade, finally allowing his admiring gaze to rest on her face. 'Wasn't told about Mrs Carruthers. Should have been. Forgive me, ma'am. Never would have been late.' He frowned and pursed his lips. 'Must have a hotel room. Can't stay at Fort William now. Wish I'd been told. Dashed awkward, but daresay we'll find a room somewhere.'

In tones grown even cooler Rupert said, 'This lady is Mrs Delacourt. Her husband is with Forrester's and she has come out to join him.'

Lieutenant Chaplin's eyes began to goggle. '*Not* your wife? By George! No message from Delacourt. What's to do now?'

Elizabeth was growing very irritated by this young man in impressive uniform, especially after his embarrassing conclusion that she was Rupert's wife. If Sir Hugo was unable to meet the ship and had sent someone to find his young brother, it did not follow that William could not be here. However angry he might have been on receiving the Delacourts' letter, he would not ignore her arrival so callously.

'Mr Chaplin,' she began firmly, 'why should there be any message from my husband and why must I have a hotel room? Nothing you have said makes any sense to me. Why is an Artillery officer here to meet Mr Carruthers instead of one of Sir Hugo's regimental colleagues?'

Flushing painfully, the gangling, dark-moustached young man drew in a deep breath before answering. 'Forrester's Light Dragoons marched out of Calcutta two months ago, heading for the Punjab. They should be arriving at Ratnapore any day now. Excessively sorry, ma'am.'

The news came as a double shock. Firstly, William must have left Calcutta before his parents' letter reached him; secondly, Ratnapore was the military station at which John's regiment had served. He had spoken of it so expressively she felt she already knew every building and tree.

'Marched out!' exlaimed Rupert in acute disappointment. 'How do we reach them?'

Chaplin appeared to take great pleasure in disconcerting this pair, who had shown little gratitude for the trouble he had been put to in meeting them. 'By budgerow, palki-garee and palanquin. It will take all of two months, even if nothing goes wrong.'

'*Two months*,' cried Elizabeth in dismay. 'How can we undertake such a journey in this heat?'

'You had best set off immediately,' added Chaplin slyly. 'Hot season is almost upon us.'

'The hot season! It surely cannot grow hotter than it is now.' She turned to her companion with a sense of despair. 'Rupert, what are we to do?'

'Why has the regiment gone north?' he demanded of Chaplin in his most imperious manner. 'Is there trouble brewing?'

Chaplin shook his head. 'No more than one expects at a frontier station. Gone to relieve Chetwynde's Hussars who left on the monthly ship from Bombay.'

Turning away from the two young men, Elizabeth gazed across at the land she had come so far to reach. She had gathered all her courage for this moment of reunion with her estranged husband. Now she must wait a further two months at least, and he would learn too late that she was coming to join him. However great her determination, destiny clearly had no intention of smoothing her path. Yet, as she ran her gaze over the minarets and domes of this city famed throughout the world, she felt new strength invade her. Of what use were her bold words and vows if she weakened at the first hurdle? Rupert would be there to provide assistance and jolly company, and she would have an unforeseen opportunity to see the colour and atmosphere of this land she had yearned to visit. Turning back to blind Lieutenant Chaplin with a wide smile she said, 'Let us go ashore, sir. We have spent more time than any sensible person would wish within this vessel and it is madness to prolong it. If the hot season is truly almost with us we must set out upon our journey without delay. Will you give me your arm, Mr Chaplin?'

Led down the gangplank by a young man reduced to awed silence by her sudden resolution, Elizabeth set foot on the soil of India for the first time.

Chapter Five

Forrester's Light Dragoons rode wearily in to Ratnapore garrison to be given a warm reception by those troops already in occupation. They had been lucky to strike the cold weather season, but the long journey had not been without accidents, hardship and loss of life so everyone from colonel to groom was glad to reach this unsettled area of India.

Calcutta had been very agreeable for the officers, who spent the minimum time in their quarters and were able to take part in the city's social life whenever they pleased. The rank and file had found it sheer hell, especially during May and June when the heat had taken seven of them with apoplexy and the barracks had resembled an oven from which there was no escape. They had drilled beneath the copper sun in the heavy uniforms they had brought from home until each had thought he would drop from giddiness and nausea, then they had been told to carry out stabling duties with no hope of a drink in between. The unbearable heat had made the NCOs irritable and vicious, meting out punishments for the slightest misdemeanour, and the troops themselves had fought as a result of easily inflamed tempers and an over-indulgence in liquor purchased from native pedlars, who knew the vices of British soldiers.

The first week of July had heralded the wet season. It had grown slightly cooler, but rain brought its attendant ills. The men had found that their boots turned mouldy overnight, their clothes were nibbled by cockroaches and attacked by rust. They slept on damp mattresses while water constantly dripped through every conceivable crack in the barrack building, and turned the floor into a quagmire. The worst aspect of this period had been the annual visit of cholera which ran through the cantonment unchecked and was claimed as the worst for a decade. It had seemed like a message of deliverance when marching orders were received, and the number of deaths had diminished daily as the column moved out of Calcutta and left the epidemic behind.

Their relief on leaving that pestilential city had been replaced by

79

sinking spirits when they saw the kind of country they were forced to cross, and additional irritations such as the desertion of camp followers without warning, mix ups with the contractors hired to provide stores which resulted in basic foods being in short supply, and a short but severe attack of malarial fever did not make their lives any easier during that first section of the long march. Only by telling themselves that Ratnapore could not be worse than Calcutta, despite the desolation of the plain on which it stood, did they push on with a glimmer of hope.

It proved a stirring sight early one morning as the troops leading the column caught a first sight of their destination. Across miles of flat, thorn-covered landscape, the walled city of Ratnapore materialized from the mauve-tinted horizon like a lost civilization rising from the sea. It remained a distant vision for an incredibly long period, although the men were on the move the whole time. To the right of the city and several miles away, the cantonments spread across a slight slope in a neat regimental pattern, commanding an unhindered view of the entire area.

From the verandah of his bungalow John Stavenham watched the military column winding its way nearer. His request to remain in India had been favourably received by Headquarters. This relieving regiment had spent little more than a year in Calcutta with no experience of the frontier and its dangers. None of its officers were proficient in native dialects yet and they had lost two of them plus fifty-one men through sickness. John had been in India for ten years; he knew the customs and the terrain reasonably well. In addition, he was fluent in the local dialect and had been acting as interpreter between the European garrison and the local sirdar, whose life and subjects they were there to protect. John's request had enabled General Mason to retain his valuable services and also fill one of the vacancies in the incoming regiment.

John's thoughts as he stood in the shade, watching through eyes half-closed against the glare, were anything but serene. His old regiment could not have been sent home at a worse time, in his opinion. They had fought in a war against the Sikhs of the Punjab in an attempt to stabilize the leadership of these proud people, so Chetwynde's would have been the best men to control the growing unrest which could explode into a second war at any time. These troops marching in were straight from garrison duty in Calcutta, where the only enemies had been heat and sickness. Their colonel was reputed to be ailing. How would they fare against the kind of savage warrior he had faced at

Moodki; men who gave no quarter, nor expected any from their enemies, and who saw a wounded soldier as a live foe, so killed him?

That battle had been John's first experience of brutal fighting. All his life he would remember the sight of dark eyes burning with relentless hatred, in faces full of pride and fanaticism, as the turbanned enemy had fought with a ferocity and a lack of fear which compensated for erratic command. They had attacked unexpectedly, when the British had just completed an exhausting march and were engrossed in making camp. The resultant battle had been violent and confused, fought over ground covered with thorn-bush and overhung by a pall of smoke and dust. The noise of it all had been indescribable, at first. Curiously, sound had faded to no more than a background murmur as John had found himself cutting and slashing at the bearded men surrounding . him, knowing that death hung between them waiting for a victim. He had not been afraid. Fear had only invaded him when it was all over, when the dead and dying covering the battleground showed the awesome truth of what had happened there; what simple men could do to each other on the word of a commander. Only when evidence of the enemies' murder and mutilation of wounded who had had every chance of survival became apparent, had his sense of professional unease faded.

Since Moodki, there had been occasional skirmishes against bands of brigands, and a minor action to put down an insurrection precipitated by the harshness of a local chief, who had been killed by his own people during the fighting. John viewed combat more philosophically now. Slaughter and treachery between rival factions so often set Indian against Indian. British intervention was usually the only hope of maintaining relative peace.

The first ranks of Forrester's Light Dragoons were now entering the gates of the station and John felt the usual thrill on seeing them automatically straighten in their saddles, hold up their drooping heads, and tighten their ranks on approaching a regimental garrison. No matter how exhausted or dispirited, British troops made a point of displaying traditional pomp and swagger when occasion demanded it. His own men had ridden back thus after Moodki, tattered, bloodstained, and with their ranks sadly depleted, but showing the garrison that they were still masters of themselves. He had been proud to ride with them, and they with an officer who had earned their respect in battle. He would soon be commanding a new company of strangers who would be as eager to size him up as he would them. He was battle-hardened;

they were untried. It was important to strike the right attitude from the start. If they had had a good relationship with the dead officer he was replacing, there might be resentment to overcome, not only toward a stranger but because he was from another regiment. For many a trooper loyalty to his colours was a creed; in many officers 'the regiment' came next in loyalty only to monarch and country. Men who transferred frequently had to overcome suspicion, lack of respect, and closed ranks. John had done it just this once, but he would still be like a new boy at school. There was a subtle difference, however. Ratnapore was familiar to him; strange to them. It was more like the school arriving to join the new boy.

Even so, he felt the coming weeks might be difficult. He knew how to command men in cantonments, he was experienced at leading them into battle, yet how could he expect others to respect him when he did not do so himself? Until he could recall that morning in Wellford — when he had tried to arrange a marriage to another officer's wife — and feel no sense of shock and humiliation, he would not be entitled to anyone's esteem. The members of his new regiment might well have heard of the wife who had vanished so mysteriously, and pity him. Thank God they would never know about Elizabeth, and be filled with derision for a man who would rather abandon his regimental loyalty and his friends than return to England and risk meeting her again.

It was late afternoon when John rode slowly toward the white-washed offices. There were still signs of the muddle and confusion which always accompanied arrival at a new garrison, and he smiled faintly at snatches of overheard conversation between weary and irate men who were trying to bring order out of chaos. From all John had heard of the commanding-officer of Forrester's, it seemed he must be vastly different from the colonel of Chetwynde's. Justin Lakeland was reputed to be a man of sixty-five who had distinguished himself in the Peninsular War, but whose temper and constitution had suffered from the Indian climate. Famed for a pig-headedness which made him tenacious in battle, his relations with his officers suffered from that same trait. Never one to listen to the advice of a subordinate, he consistently refused to give credit where it was due on eventually acting upon it. John should have taken more heed of what he had been told of the man, for Lakeland's attitude when the adjutant ushered him in to his new colonel's presence hinted that he did not appreciate this courtesy accorded him by a Hussar who had no wish to go home.

Looking up from his task of arranging a series of English hunting prints on walls which would be better occupied by maps and charts, Justin Lakeland greeted John testily.

'There was really no need to present yourself so promptly, Captain Stavenham. We only marched in six hours ago. I imagine even Chetwynde's take a few hours to settle in before commencing their duties.'

John studied the tall thin man whose greying hair curled on the back of his high collar. He was not impressed by his narrow sunburnt face and weak watery eyes. A mouth that drooped at the corners suggested a fault-finding personality, bearing out the reputation for impatience with his subordinates. This immediate resentment of a man from a rival regiment hardly augured well for John's future.

'I merely came to see if I could offer you any assistance, sir, not to report for duty,' he said quietly. 'As I know Ratnapore and the people here I thought you might welcome information on either matter. However, I'll return to my quarters and await your summons.'

'Oh, come back, man,' Lakeland snapped, as John turned smartly about. 'We might as well get the preliminaries over now that you're here.' His glance flicked over John's pale-blue Hussar uniform as he turned back again. 'The first thing you can do is to visit the tailor so that you can put aside that pretty suit and dress like an officer of this regiment. Now tell me,' he went on as he sat heavily at his desk, 'why did you choose to extend your long service in this benighted country? Is it in the hope of swift promotion into dead men's shoes, or are you tangled up with a young woman?'

Affronted by this extremely boorish attitude, John refused to answer, standing to attention and gazing at the sporting prints in growing anger. Lakeland gave him extra time to reply then, realizing that he was avoiding the issue, studied him through narrowed eyes.

'I have not had time to read Colonel Howarth's report on your ability and value as a junior officer, but Headquarters recommended you in very flowery phrases. That being the case, I would suspect that advancement by any means would not be abhorrent to you, but from the evidence of that red colour rising up around your neck it seems there is a female behind your extraordinary decision to leave a regiment you have served for twelve years or more in order to stay in Ratnapore. I must inform you that I have no time for subordinates who spend their time dallying after the ladies. Their attention to duty suffers, and they are cautious in battle for fear of returning mutilated and being rejected thereafter.' He sighed heavily. 'Now we have that straight I will confess I am glad to have you. I lost two very good officers to cholera in Calcutta. Another was devilish ill with malaria a few weeks ago and shows little sign of shaking it off. I couldn't rely on him if trouble started. Not that it is likely.'

'I would advise you that it is, sir,' John told him tonelessly, still smarting over the comment which had touched a sensitive spot and caused him to colour up like a boy. 'Ganda Singh is complaining of a plot by his half-brother to overthrow, then murder him. What's more, the bands of hostile tribesmen who swoop on his supply caravans are growing bigger, despite the presence of our protective patrols.'

'There is never a shortage of brigands in this country, Captain Stavenham,' Lakeland remarked dryly. 'They are mere cut-throats who are no match for trained soldiers.'

'We had to double our patrols after one of our officers was killed and two troopers wounded,' John pointed out immediately. 'The men who lay in wait in the hills are better trained than roaming cut-throats, sir.'

Justin Lakeland gave a thin smile. 'Your regiment was about to go home after ten years in this land of heat and fevers. How many of those who came out in '37 were still in the ranks? The white man suffers out here. His health deteriorates; he grows exhausted and dispirited. After ten years continuous service in India it is not surprising if trained troops are less alert; less efficient under sudden attack.'

John could hardly believe that this man was suggesting his former regiment had been unequal to its duty at the end of a long period of service. He found it insulting to men he knew and respected, so he fired up in their defence.

'Our patrols were alert and highly efficient, I assure you. They were outnumbered by hill fighters who were certainly part of a trained army masquerading as robbers, whose objective was to reduce our numbers rather than to steal the Sirdar's supplies.' At the other's expression of disbelief, he added forcibly, 'Ganda Singh has no love for us, in spite of our protection of his realm. It's my belief that he sends out his own troops against us while crying treachery from his numerous relatives.'

'Mmm,' mused Lakeland with a hint of derision. 'Well, *you* have been in India for ten years, too. Don't let your weary mind create duplicity where there is none, or let your sun-dazed eyes see an army in place of a handful of ragged thieves. Ganda Singh is merely behaving true to his kind by imagining plots against him. Most native rulers have come to power by bringing about the downfall of their predecessors. It's instinctive to feel insecure. You should know that simple truth by now.'

Seeing that he was failing to impress this unlikeable man with details of the volatile situation, John decided not to pursue the subject further. Lakeland would hear the same facts from the other regiments at the garrison. Unless he thought they too were suffering the effects of long service beneath the killing sun, he might take note of what they said and be prepared for events to move fast and without warning. Taking his silence as acceptance of a more common sense attitude, the older man then brought the interview to an end by saying that A Troop was without a commander, so John could take up his duties the next day.

Outside the office, John walked the verandah pensively. Lakeland had done well as a junior officer in Portugal, so it could not be that he had no understanding of battle or campaigning. Nor did it seem likely that his aggressive attitude was merely directed at a transferred officer. On setting out from England eighteen months ago he must have suffered many changes due to officers selling their commissions or changing regiments to avoid going to India. Was the man more seriously ill than anyone supposed, or was he simply a tyrant who enjoyed humiliating and dominating those juniors obliged by rank to submit to such treatment? Swinging into the saddle, John recalled that flush of mortification which had betrayed him and suggested that he was so in thrall to a woman he had abandoned regiment and homeland in order to remain with her. The reverse was the case, but the guess was near enough to the truth to make him curse that lively face and sweet, captivating persuasion which had forced him into his present situation. Maybe Lakeland's contempt was justified.

Forcing his thoughts in to a professional channel, he decided to make a point of meeting the officers of A Troop in the Mess tonight. It would be an advantage to find out a little about them before taking command in the morning. He hoped they were more likeable than their CO. Reaching his bungalow, he found a great deal of baggage littering the verandah. It told him that the officer who would be sharing this quarter with him was in the process of moving in. A strong voice reciting to his servants the punishments they would suffer unless they put some ginger into their efforts, suggested that the Dragoon officer was a man of impatience, and John crossed to the door of the central sitting-room to find a big blond captain of around twenty-eight with light eyes and profuse side-whiskers. He was handsome, despite the redness of a face which was too fair to withstand bombardment from the sun during a lengthy march.

Impressed by the oaths with which he was regaling four unheeding servants, John leaned against the door-jamb to say, 'They have an inborn talent for doing things their way and in their own time. Over the years I have found the least exhausting practice is to quit the place and leave them to it. When I return everything is orderly and to my complete satisfaction.'

The new arrival studied John for a moment or two. 'I guess from the beauty of that Hussar uniform that you must be John Stavenham, our replacement officer. Sorry about the mess on the verandah. I've had the deuce of a job trying to locate all my belongings. Some of our pack animals died on the march. Baggage was redistributed, some between the remaining beasts and some on the wagons. Mine appears to have fared worse than any other. My collapsible bath and several cases of decent wine have vanished. When I catch up with the villain who has filched them, there'll be the devil to pay.'

'You have my sympathies,' John said. 'Somewhere in India is the unscrupulous fellow who is enjoying the benefits of my writing desk.' Establishing friendly relations with this man, who would be under the same roof in the coming months, he added, 'Why not take my advice and leave them to settle you in? Come and have a drink in my rooms. I don't keep a very selective cellar, but I daresay I'll have something to suit you.'

'That's a very decent offer,' the other responded. 'There's time enough for a glass before dinner. Is the Mess comfortable?'

'As good as any,' John replied, straightening up to lead the way in to the large airy room containing his bed, a double wardrobe, a dressing-chest, a desk and two easy chairs; one each side of a cabinet containing a limited selection of bottles. 'After a number of meals cooked in the field I daresay you'll welcome what is on offer here. It's a gruelling march up from Calcutta, isn't it? We did it in the hot season and paid the penalty.' Shouting for his bearer, John then asked his guest what he fancied from the cabinet. The servant came from a side door which led from the rear regions of the spacious bungalow. He carried a tray bearing a jug of water and ice in a small silver bucket. While the two officers settled back in the chairs, unhooking their high collars for comfort, the Indian poured the drinks.

The blond man said, 'You must know the area well. What's the city like?'

'Like any other city in this region of India, except that it's seething with treachery and unrest. If you're looking for action, this is the right place.'

'Really, how splendid!' Drinking deeply, he then nodded at his glass. 'This is excellent. French, isn't it? You're too modest over your cellar, Stavenham. If I ever recover those missing cases, I'll offer you a claret which is second to none.'

'I'll look forward to it,' John murmured, slightly disappointed that his companion had dismissed the subject of possible action so immediately to discuss wines instead. 'You haven't introduced yourself yet, by the way. I've been given command of A Troop by your commanding-officer.'

'He's your commanding-officer now,' the other pointed out dryly. 'I'm William Delacourt, captain of D Troop.'

The wine turned to liquid fire as it coursed through John's body, and he stared at the handsome reddened face as his thoughts raced along shocking lines. There could be any number of Delacourts in India, he reasoned. Yet Forrester's Light Dragoons had come from Calcutta, the place mentioned by Mr Noble when locating the young cavalry husband of the girl he claimed could not be a widow, and the regiment had been in India for the right length of time. Dear God, was this the poor devil he had pitied on arriving back in Calcutta; the man whose wife he had desired and kissed with great passion whilst declaring his eternal love?

'I say, are you all right, Stavenham?'

'Yes . . . quite all right.'

'You look remarkably shaken up.'

'I . . . knew someone called Delacourt. It was . . . well, it came as a shock when you told me,' he invented wildly, hoping to explain his behaviour to someone who had the right to challenge him.

'Not dead, is he?' came the sympathetic query.

John shook his head. 'Lost touch, that's all.'

'Oh,' said Delacourt, losing interest. 'What kind of social life can a man expect here? Bit of a far cry from the elegance of Calcutta, isn't it?'

'Care for another drink?' asked John, signalling the bearer to pour it then leave them. The pause allowed him pull himself together and answer with outward calm, despite the shaking of his hand as he

87

downed a rare second drink. 'If you have a number of ladies with you there'll be frequent dinner parties and soirées. Each regiment mounts a ball or two at appropriate times of the year, in addition to those given by the civilian element on the station. You can depend on card parties, musical evenings and amateur theatricals. Every month there is racing on the course. You must have seen it as you came in this morning. The Resident takes a pride in it, claiming it to be the best in India. Do you compete?'

'I'll say. How about you?'

He nodded. 'I've a temperamental thoroughbred who shows up very well against any competition.'

'You haven't yet matched him against a bay owned by one of our majors. Sir Hugo Carruthers is an aristocrat with a string of beasts unlikely to find equals in the whole of India. He's also a damned handsome fellow liable to win the ballroom stakes, although there's not much pleasure to be had when most of the ladies are other men's wives. Point of honour not to fish in forbidden waters, eh?'

That innocent comment thrust the sword of guilt even deeper and John found it impossible to meet the man's eyes as he reverted to a safer topic. 'I heard you're still under strength after that cholera outbreak.'

'A very severe attack,' agreed the other leaning back at his ease after emptying his glass. 'We managed to replace most of our losses from other regiments, but you'll find your troop is still undermanned by about ten.' He grinned lazily. 'We all ensured that we had very nearly full ranks in our own commands. Sorry, old fellow, but you'd have done the same in our place.'

John nodded. He was the new boy so must expect it. 'What about officers?'

'You've just joined us, and the young brother of Sir Hugo — the aristo with the horse which'll beat yours easily — is due to join us from England. Poor devil will have a setback when he arrives in Calcutta to find he must straightway follow us up here. We shall still be short of a subaltern — in A Troop, I fear — until someone buys my lieutenancy. I gained promotion through the death of my superior several months ago. One always feels uneasy about dead men's shoes, especially when it is sickness, not battle, which has carried him off. It's a stroke of luck so far as money goes, and who is sufficiently well off to refuse it?'

'Few enough, especially if a man is married.'

'You are not?'

'No,' he said brusquely.

'Ah, then I suspect you will be off to the hills at the first chance, where a fresh crop of daughters, nieces and cousins are sure to be searching for a handsome officer to snare.'

Clutching at a last straw of hope that he could be wrong about this Delacourt, John asked, 'Will you be off to the hills, also?'

'It's too late for me, Stavenham. I have a wife in England,' said Elizabeth's husband with a gusty sigh. 'She is safely with my family, so I have no worries on that score.'

The Mess was noisy that evening. Officers who had been on the march for several months celebrated their arrival by drinking heavily. It was an informal occasion. The married men were still settling wives and children in new quarters so were absent, Colonel Lakeland included. It was said that Charlotte Lakeland was in awe of her husband to the point of being wholly ineffectual and had turned to religion for strength. Her habit of offering words from the scriptures rather than any practical assistance to the women in her husband's regiment was well known and ridiculed. How she would fare when introduced to the campaigning Lady Mason was a source of great anticipation to those already at Ratnapore. The cantonments supported a regiment of Native Infantry, a company of Artillery and a small detachment of Engineers under the command of a British officer, in addition to the cavalry regiment. Outside the military lines were the usual establishments manned by civil servants: several stores and coffee-houses; a native quarter; and the Resident's mansion. The relationship between the troops and the civilians depended upon the behaviour of the soldiers, and on whatever scandal was currently circulating. Chetwynde's Hussars had found general favour with the resident civilians. The incoming cavalrymen had yet to be introduced.

Aside from being the stranger in their midst, John had the additional disadvantage of knowing that he must live, eat, drink and — by the way things were developing — *fight* beside a man whose wife he had practically seduced. He had certainly done so in thought many times over. In consequence, he was quiet and made no attempt to force his company on the rowdy strangers. William Delacourt appeared popular enough with his fellows, his *bonhomie* increasing with his steady consumption of wine. In spite of everything, John could not stop himself imagining this large amiable man being with Elizabeth, and

89

finding the thought unacceptable. The mind of the girl he had met was surely too lively and complex to find communion with a husband who appeared to have more brawn than brain; a husband interested in social frippery and this kind of rowdy camaraderie, rather than the deeper aspects of this land he was here to defend. Then he reminded himself that Elizabeth Delacourt was clever; an exceptional actress who probably played a different role to suit each man she charmed.

Making a point of seeking out the officers who would be under his command, John spoke briefly to three cornets, all of them little more than boys. Only one impressed him as promising. The other pair were like many of their kind; younger sons who were given the choice of the Church or the Army as a choice of career. These two would have been blasphemous clerics, he decided. One of the senior subalterns was in bed with a fever and Lieutenant Humphrey, who would be John's second-in-command, was married and busily unpacking tonight.

He was on the point of leaving his new colleagues to go to the devil their own way, so that he could do so himself by thinking about Wellford, when he was approached by a tall, distinguished major who introduced himself as Sir Hugo Carruthers. A quiet, thoughtful man who could hold his wine while others were losing control, he was apparently the owner of the horse which could beat any other in India, according to Delacourt. He welcomed John to the regiment with genuine sincerity.

'We count ourselves very fortunate to acquire a man whose reputation is so highly valued at Headquarters,' he said. 'You fought against the Sikhs of this area at Moodki, I heard. Care to tell me about it?'

An instinctive liking for someone who struck him as a truly professional soldier caused John to abandon his plan to retire. He spoke frankly about an experience which was still vivid in his memory, and his companion listened attentively. Finally, John gave his opinion that the war had brought only temporary settlement of Sikh resentment against the British.

Sir Hugo nodded. 'So I believe, also. I've studied the issues involved and, as usual in this country, they are extraordinarily complicated. A single throne and too many hopeful heirs apparent.'

John smiled. 'They're all related in one way or another. Half brothers, stepsons, cousins, great-grandchildren, nephews and favourite bastards.'

'To say nothing of ambitious viziers, murderous generals and steel-hearted widows,' he added with an answering smile. 'That's merely the complex problem at the very top of the Sikh ladder. Each rung has its own complications which affect the struggle for overall power almost monthly. With each minor plot, murder, or kidnapping, the chances of the main contenders change, according to whether or not the new sirdar is a friend or a foe.' Pausing as some of the rowdier members, including William Delacourt, roared with laughter and encouragement over the antics of a lieutenant who was attempting to walk on his hands holding two bottles by their necks, he went on, 'There is a highly explosive situation developing at Ratnapore, I should tell you.'

'I have heard rumours to that effect, Stavenham. Several officers I spoke to at stations *en route* mentioned a seething cauldron, but none knew the details.' He glanced at the noisy younger element with irritation. 'Shall we find a quieter spot while you enlighten me?'

Glad to escape the tomfoolery of men relieving the hardships of the past few months, John took Sir Hugo to the smoking-room of the building he knew so well which had been invaded by strangers. They sat in facing chairs beneath the swaying punkah while John outlined his theory to an avid listener, enjoying a cigar.

'Ganda Singh came to us to ask for an escort for his supply caravans. He claimed to know of a plot against him, hatched by a half brother who has begun by sending raiding parties to attack the regular consignments of goods to Ratnapore. This move is supposedly intended to starve the populace into being willing to sell the life of their sirdar in return for food. For the past six months we've been sending a cavalry patrol out to meet the camel trains on the far side of Mashni Pass, where the raiders usually strike. Each time I have been detailed to lead the patrol, I've studied the direction from which these so-called brigands appear. I've also adjudged their strength. There's no doubt that not only are these bands swelling in size, they are coming from directions covering a wide area.'

Sir Hugo raised his thick blond eyebrows. 'Ganda Singh is right to worry, then?'

'Oh yes, but not necessarily over a plot to starve his subjects into treachery against him. I've acted as interpreter for several years and I'm certain he's not as simple as he makes out. In my opinion, the men raiding his caravans are doing so on his own orders.'

91

Studying him through eyes narrowed by cigar smoke, the senior man asked, 'Why would he steal supplies vital to his city?'

'He doesn't. Our patrols normally stop the raiders before they make away with anything. The attacks are carefully staged so that the camel trains arrive safely but we risk losing troopers, whilst leaving the cantonment short of cavalrymen.'

'You're suggesting that Ganda Singh is lying about the hostile half brother and is, instead, planning to attack us here?'

John nodded. 'If you study the background of the man you'll discover that he has little cause to like the British. His grandfather was defeated and driven into exile by a rival, with our full approval, fifty years ago. Although subsequent treachery killed off the man we supported and left Ganda Singh free to claim power for himself, we received the cold shoulder from him initially. Relations have grown more cordial since the end of the war in which we happened to kill one of his most committed enemies, but the desire for revenge burns long in the breasts of these people.'

'Doesn't it in all of us?' asked Sir Hugo with a wry smile. 'I look forward to meeting this gentleman in view of what you have told me. I value your assessment of the situation.'

'I'm glad. Colonel Lakeland tended to regard it as the fanciful thinking of a man who has spent too many years in India.'

'He's a sick man, Stavenham. Give him time to settle in and he'll see the evidence of his own eyes.' He rose, pipe in hand. 'I'm for my bed. This is the first night for weeks that we haven't to march, so I intend to savour it.'

They strolled out together into the chilly darkness. Neither spoke for a moment or two as they took pleasure in the still, starry night. The silence was only disturbed by the sound of horses stamping restlessly and snorting to each other in the clear air, the subdued voices of the guards as they patrolled the cantonment, and the sound of their own boots crunching the hard earth. On parting at the far end of the single officers' quarters, Sir Hugo clapped John on the shoulder.

'You're a shrewd fellow, Stavenham. It's the regiment's good fortune that you decided to stay on and join us. We need a few really sharp officers to tighten up the ranks. Some of our subalterns are little more than handsome fools. You'll find out. Goodnight.'

John went to bed feeling that he had discovered a potential ally in Carruthers. He liked the man already; felt he would respect any opinion he held. He was also impressed by his frankness concerning the regiment. If it really lacked discipline in the junior ranks, something should be done swiftly to remedy it. A slack regiment would be the very element Ganda Singh required to make his move. He had spies in the native quarter who would soon divulge the information. The cantonment could be at risk of attack. Lying awake for some time assessing the problem, his concentration was then broken by the noisy return of William Delacourt, very drunk and cursing his servants in a voice loud enough to waken every occupant of that row of bungalows. John immediately thought of Elizabeth, and all hope of sleep fled.

Forrester's Light Dragoons had been at Ratnapore a little over two months when their first evidence of unrest materialized.

Aside from Hugo, none of the officers sought John's friendship during those early days. They were not hostile, they simply tended to regard him as an outsider. He had quickly realized the truth of his friend's statement concerning the laxity in junior ranks. There was little evidence of regimental interest or ability in the dissipated boys who pursued pleasure to the detriment of duty. John identified the basis for Lakeland's contempt for such subalterns, but wondered why the man did nothing to discipline them. Was the Colonel a man of words rather than action? So far as the rank and file were concerned, those comprising A Troop were difficult to read. Captain Johnstone, whose death from cholera had left the vacancy, had reputedly been well liked for his easy manner and fondness for a joke. A new commander from a Hussar regiment who rarely smiled, and whose manner was curt, was seen as no fair replacement. Not taking kindly to John's criticisms and his instructions to take their duties more seriously now they were at a frontier station, they were surly in their compliance.

As he rode out one morning at the head of a patrol, John nevertheless sensed that they held him in some respect, even if they disliked him personally. The same could not be said of Cornet Phipps, riding at the rear of the column. Twenty years old, rather effete, the boy had suffered badly from malaria since arriving in India. Homesick, hopelessly unsuited to the military life, a natural butt of his more robust colleagues, Matthew Phipps did mutely as John ordered, finding evident masochistic pleasure in being dominated by him and thereby spared the sly insubordination of shilling-a-day soldiers. Like all responsible commanders, John dealt out in private the reprimands he withheld in public. To his dismay, young Phipps seemed further excited by individual punishment from him, and John knew he had a problem on his hands. The boy was useless to him and to the regiment.

Glancing now at the red-haired man riding beside him as they crossed the plain, John admitted that George Humphrey constituted a vastly different problem. His second-in-command was an excellent officer who would pursue a distinguished career if sickness and battle spared him for old age, yet he resembled an automaton. After nine weeks, John was still unable to break through the abstraction ruling the young lieutenant and had asked Hugo's opinion on the matter. His friend had thrown light on it, but John could not possibly intervene in a marriage between a pair who were devoted, yet who were slowly destroying one another over his refusal to give her the child she was desperate to mother. It was a great pity that marital unhappiness was preventing the rapport John felt was so important between men whose lives often depended on it. In battle, personal enmity could endanger not only those concerned, but a great many others who were dependent on them. Similarly, a complete lack of understanding between commanders sometimes led to fatal hesitations. He sighed as the silent ranks rode on across the vast plain while the sun gradually climbed in a sky of milky yellow. The only sounds were the jingle of harnesses, the squeak of saddles and the muffled plodding of hooves; the usual quiet conversation between men on such occasions was missing. John's mouth tightened. He might be wearing the correct scarlet jacket but he was no more a member of Forrester's Light Dragoons now than he had ever been.

After three hours in the saddle, they reached the rock-strewn approaches to the hills where the Mashni Pass gave access to the region beyond. The patrol must ride through the defile to reach their rendezvous with the camel-train, then escort it back along the dangerous, narrow way, and up to the gates of Ratnapore. John looked up at the sun-baked hills ahead. Behind any jutting edge, crouching in some crevice, peering through those sparse patches of growth, could be men with rifles; watching their progress, counting their ranks, picking out the officers as their main targets. The silence might be broken by a sudden crack and he would feel a red hot ball of lead enter a limb, his chest, his back. Or he would feel nothing . . . nothing more throughout eternity. John narrowed his eyes against the glare coming off the rearing walls of rock. Were they alone out here or was there a small army hidden waiting to attack?

'Watch for the glint of sun on a rifle,' he said quietly to the man beside him. 'Look out for a moving bush, a rock which changes shape. Listen for the rattle of stones loosened by a man's feet.'

They entered the shadows at a walking pace. The noise of their progress echoed louder and louder as the confining walls of rock rose high on either side. John tensed. The palms of his hands were wet inside his white gloves; the twists in the defile blurred as perspiration slid from his forehead to his eyelashes. There had been no sign of human presence in the hills, yet his body tingled with the expectation of hearing that crack and feeling the searing pain of a bullet tearing his flesh. His nerves jumped, therefore, when a human cry magnified by the confines broke the silence. It was followed by vocal confusion at the rear of the single mounted file. He twisted in his saddle, rising in the stirrups as he did so in order to gain some idea of what had happened. The patrol had split in two with the rear half halted in disarray. Telling George Humphrey to carry on, John circled in the narrow space and picked his way back over the rocky floor as fast as he could to where the stationary men were concerned with something lying on the ground.

'Why have you halted, Corporal Gates?' he demanded sharply as he neared them. 'Get these men on the move at once.'

The dismounted NCO looked up at him defiantly. 'It's Trooper Donegal, sir. Passed out, 'e 'as. Jest dropped from the saddle sudden like. Piper says 'e was took bad with a belly ache 'arfway acrowse the plain.'

'Then why the devil didn't he report the fact and turn back?' fumed John, knowing they were extremely vulnerable in this situation. 'Put the man over his horse and secure him. The rest of you move on double quick. NOW!' Glancing over his shoulder at the wilting cornet whose face was whiter than usual, he snapped, 'Go with your men, Mr Phipps. I'll bring up the rear instead.'

The boy had moved no more than a yard when he gave a terrible scream; a sound which filled the ravine with ghastly echoes to chill John's blood. Phipps toppled from his saddle, clutching the spear which had entered his breast and gone clear through his body to project a foot or so beyond his back. His cry of anguish frightened two horses which reared and plunged, causing further confusion among those who had not yet obeyed the order to ride on. Jumping to the ground, John bellowed at them with a voice magnified by fear and anger.

'Move, you villains, or you'll all be spiked from above!'

95

They fled!

Striding across to haul up the body of the dead cornet, John then yelled at Gates to mount and lead away Trooper Donegal's horse with the sick man lashed to it. Even as he prepared to do the same with Phipps, a curious whirring sound passed close to his ear and a second spear embedded itself in the boy's corpse. Guessing that he was the real target, John swung into his saddle. Next minute, the whirring flight of a third weapon brought a savage cry from the Corporal as he was hit in the side by a spear which entered so deeply it remained like a skewer projecting from his scarlet coat. John rode forward swiftly. Gates was a lightweight man who had fortunately fallen across his mount's neck. This made it easier for John to transfer from one saddle to the other on the move. He had done it before — it could be a life-saving trick in battle when a man's horse was shot from under him — but this was in a confined area where the ground was slippery and uneven.

Expecting all the time to hear the sinister rush of flight, he did not flinch when another spear passed close enough for him to feel the slight breeze on his cheek. Mounted up behind Gates and holding the man secure, he held his own horse back to ensure that the other three were clear ahead of him. Then he drew his pistol and fired one shot. No starting gun at a race track had ever been more effective. The animals could go no way but forward, so they were off in a bid to escape. John brought up the rear, holding on to a man who was either unconscious or dead.

The flight through the tortuous zigzags resembled the kind of nightmare common to troubled minds. He was hardly aware of sound or sensation. The total concentration needed to avoid collision with jutting rocks, or from taking a toss through the several sections where melting snows crossed the defile in grooves before disappearing into underground catchments, drove all awareness from him, so that the morning seemed silent and unreal. Then, with a rush, he was suddenly out from between the high walls and facing a valley green from the irrigation of a river. A quarter of a mile distant, the patrol was drawn up, awaiting him. Three figures detached themselves from the group to chase and secure the uncontrolled horses ahead of him. None other of the men moved as John came up level with them and drew rein. They all looked shaken, including George Humphrey. The officer had them under control, however, and, more importantly, had resisted the temptation to go to John's assistance leaving his men without a commander. He would be a valuable second-in-command in the coming days.

In crisp sentences, John outlined to his lieutenant what had occurred. Young Phipps had been killed instantly, ending the short span of a boy whose death had been more spectacular than his life would ever have been. A reprieve from misery, perhaps? Trooper Donegal's face resembled parchment. He was clearly very ill. They had no dhoolie with them, only several canvas slings which could be lashed between two horses. His chances of survival during the return would depend on how tough he was. Corporal Gates was moaning in anguish as John debated whether or not to draw out the spear. They were cruel weapons which tore the flesh further on being removed, and usually caused the wound to bleed profusely. On the other hand, the sight of their NCO resembling a pig on a spit all the way back to Ratnapore would be very demoralizing for the rest of the men. Whatever he decided to do, John knew the poor devil would never hold on until they reached the cantonment. With that in mind he slowly unhooked the fastenings of his own jacket, then stripped off his white cotton shirt. Stepping forward, he resolutely seized the end of the spear. It was a hard thing for any man to do. John sensed the aggression of those around him as he tortured their comrade until his screams of pain were silenced by unconsciousness, which coincided with a great surge of blood from the wound. Throwing the spear to the ground, John knelt beside the man to stuff his shirt into the gaping hole. The sun began to burn his bared back; the sight and smell of the bleeding flesh increased the nausea rising in him as his hands grew red and slimy. Perspiration ran freely over his face so that he had to clear his vision by wiping his forearm across his eyes. Just as he faced the fact that the wound would not be staunched and that he had probably made the wrong decision, someone arrived beside him to hold out a bundle of white cloth. He glanced around to find George Humphrey also stripped to the waist.

'This should do the trick,' the man said quietly.

'Thank you,' John murmured, taking the other shirt. 'We'll bind them in place with my riding-cloak and spare leathers. It's all we can do for him, I'm afraid.'

Together they secured the pad in place, then stood up to shrug into their jackets while several men lifted Gates to lie in one of the slings.

'He'll die before we reach the hospital, I suppose,' said the red-haired man in an undertone.

'Yes, and possibly the sick trooper. Did you know that Donegal was unfit this morning?'

The other shook his head. 'He hid the fact well. They were all so keen to come on this patrol.' Busy with the hooks on his coat, he added, 'I owe you an apology. Along with most of our officers, I believed you were exaggerating the situation here. Now I see how right you are to be suspicious. If the supply caravan really was the target, the attack would have been made *after* we meet up with it this morning and escort it through the pass. It's pretty clear that we constituted no threat or challenge to these tribesmen, and the attack was quite deliberate. I'll give my full support to any report you care to write on our return, sir.'

John nodded. 'Thanks, but neither of us may be in a position to give a report to Colonel Lakeland. We have to negotiate the pass again later today, hemmed in by a hundred or so laden camels. I suggest that we move on to the banks of the river to await the caravan. While the men rest and water their horses, you and I had better confer on the best way to ensure that someone gets safely back to warn Lakeland and put the station on alert.'

Chapter Six

The journey from Calcutta took so long Elizabeth was almost lulled into forgetting her final destination, where a confrontation with a husband she could hardly remember awaited her. Everything she saw and heard along the way drew her closer in spirit to the man who had described it so vividly and so faithfully, yet John was on his way to England, unaware that she was sharing this land with him on a spiritual plane.

Rupert was invaluable as an escort and as a friend. Organizing everything in that unconsciously arrogant fashion which officials and servants alike recognized as a sahib not to be thwarted, he had even engaged as their personal servants a husband and wife anxious to return to the Punjab. As the couple knew exactly how to look after British travellers, even he was satisfied with them.

They went from Calcutta to Cawnpore by water. Rupert declared that they were lucky to obtain passages on a budgerow towed by a steamer along the tortuous reaches of the river, but any suggestion of cabins in vessels filled Elizabeth with dismay, and being told that there was no comparison between the tediously slow passage of a river barge and the heaving and pitching of an ocean-going ship did nothing to ease it. It turned out to be a relatively pleasant mode of travel, if one were not in a hurry, and it was as well not to be when undertaking any journey in India, where speed was unknown. There were a number of British people going to Cawnpore. These all made the initial mistake of thinking them husband and wife, so Elizabeth was the subject of great interest when the truth came out. It was certainly not rare for a military man to accompany a brother officer's wife on a journey up-country, but they usually did so because the husband was prevented from doing so by sickness or duty. In this instance, the girl was particularly young and attractive, the pair were on most familiar terms, and the husband was apparently unaware that his wife had ever left England. Fellow travellers sensed a mystery, maybe even a scandal.

Elizabeth felt helpless to combat the growing interest she aroused.

Had she fully understood the society she was joining, she would have known that gossip was the only means most women had of relieving their boredom. They did not seem overly interested in books or painting, or even in the country they had adopted; and she was driven to recall that morning when John had said only the most insensitive creatures failed to see the fascination all around them. Her own defiance of convention seemed more fascinating to these people.

Despite this, she appreciated the sights along the riverbank as their vessel made its way up to Cawnpore. It was just as John had described it to her: women pounding their washing with flat stones, bare brown children splashing in play, oxen and other beasts of burden wallowing and drinking the brown mottled water. There were also stretches of dark jungle which threw shadows and coolness over the river. Tigers were said to stalk these areas but none obliged the voyagers by showing themselves.

At various stopping places on the river small boats put out to meet them, their owners offering boxes, bric-à-brac, baskets and even live birds. Trade was brisk, but Elizabeth bought nothing. She knew it would be enough to confront William with her own presence; if she were hung about with talking birds, necklets or sewing boxes his wrath would surely explode.

When they reached Cawnpore, Rupert was invited to lodge in the Officers' Mess while he went about the tedious task of acquiring palanquins. Elizabeth was swamped with invitations and eventually accepted that from the surgeon and his wife. It was her first experience of a cantonment bungalow. She thought it very spartan, but her hosts were kind and tried to prepare her for life in a military station by explaining the unofficial rules by which they were governed. It seemed to her that these were far more strict and exaggerated than any in civilian society, and her sense of foreboding over her arrival in Ratnapore increased. Had she left one form of invisible imprisonment only to enter another, far worse?

The second stage of the journey was made in elaborate curtained boxes uncomfortably similar to coffins. These palanquins had to be bought outright, but Rupert was assured of a quick return on his outlay on completion of his journey because they were much in demand. There had been the opportunity for him to buy cheaper second-hand ones but while Rupert was prepared to sell his own to any prospective buyer, he had no intention of occupying anything as personal as a palanquin if it were not new. One never knew who might have lain in it previously, he declared to Elizabeth. For herself, once she had succeeded in banishing the unpleasant notion that her carriers were pall-bearers, she found it possible to relax in the curious conveyance, although she preferred to keep the curtains apart so that she could see the country through which they were passing and also assure herself that Rupert was still being borne along beside her. The up and down motion of the jogging bearers raised serious misgivings in her mind, at first, but the dreaded sickness did not occur.

Their own party consisted of two palanquins and six camels, which Rupert had hired to carry their baggage, but they were frequently joined by other similar parties for certain stretches of the route before they stopped off at another destination. Most of the travelling was done before ten in the morning and after the sun had set, the hottest part of the day being spent resting in the shade. The travellers stopped at the chain of *dak* bungalows provided by the government all along the way. There, the weary folk sampled the indifferent meals which hardly varied from place to place and tried to pass the stifling hours on makeshift beds in the tiny square cubicles.

During this slow lethargic section of their journey, their friendship was severely tested as a consequence of Elizabeth's desire to visit beauty spots or places of especial interest, when Rupert would not consider the slightest delay. They argued heatedly until he finally, and very ungraciously, agreed to halt for two days in order to join a small mounted group setting out to view a 'hanging temple' built on a hillside which was being eroded by a waterfall. He was only persuaded by Elizabeth's conviction that Sir Hugo would wish his brother to see the phenomenon before it plunged into the valley. He marvelled over the sight when they reached the spot, declaring that he would not have missed it for the world. Even so, his eagerness to reach Ratnapore and take his place with the family regiment overrode everything else, and made him chafe against the inevitably slow pace of their progress. Whilst Elizabeth found the peculiar limbo of travelling by palanquin very welcome, it made Rupert irritable.

At every bungalow he complained of the food. He complained even more bitterly about the wine and ale, which was unchilled. He also continued his eulogy of the virtues of his brother, whom he doubted he would ever join at this interminable pace. At one such stop Elizabeth felt she could stand no more, and told him so.

'Rupert, I must confess to you that I am so weary of hearing the impossible list of Sir Hugo's qualities, I fear I have a dislike of your brother before I have even met him. There is not a virtue he does not possess in abundance, nor an accomplishment he cannot perform with more skill than any other living person. As for his handsome appearance, I cannot understand why we have not witnessed a solid stream of ladies heading for Ratnapore in the hope of catching his interest which, being the incomparable gentleman he is, he would never be cruel enough to withhold.'

Rupert looked thunderstruck as he stared at her across yet another fly-blown table on which they had been served with, and consequently rejected, the usual greasy, ill-cooked meal.

'Are you feeling ill?' he asked eventually.

Drawing in a deep breath, she let it out in a long calming sigh. 'Not ill, just incredibly fatigued and more than a little hungry. I think I have eaten just enough to keep a hen alive and only that because it will not do for me to arrive at Ratnapore and faint at William's feet.' Brushing away another fly which persisted in settling on her perspiring forehead, she was driven to add, 'Although I have not confided the fact to you, you must be aware by now that I do not enjoy the best of relations with my husband. We have had enough evidence from those along the way that the circumstances of my coming to India are regarded as unconventional, almost shocking. In truth, I suppose they are. Have you never pondered that?'

'Of course, but I have all along admired your resolution,' he replied, surprising her considerably before going on to reveal his misconception of her actions. 'When a female bears such devotion for her absent husband that she is driven to defy anything in order to join him, the fact cannot fail to inspire the utmost support from any true gentleman. I believe I once said to you that I did not understand how any man could bring himself to leave you. As we have progressed, I have understood it less. You have spoken freely of your feelings for Hugh. I must tell you now that my opinion of William Delacourt is not in the least favourable. In fact, I do not like him one jot.'

Touched by his loyalty, she smiled. 'It's very likely that William will not like you, either, my dear. Even if gossip has not travelled ahead of us, our arrival is sure to cause raised eyebrows and a deal of speculation. You will be forgiven: gentlemen are indulgently excused their tendency to dally with any female who crosses their path. It is only to be expected of them. For me it will be different. If I were older or plainer they might be charitable enough to dub me an eccentric and laugh fondly. As it is, I shall attract sideways glances from the ladies of the cantonment, and disrespect from the regiment we are joining.'

'Not from Hugh,' he declared stoutly. 'And he will soon crush any fellow who does not behave toward you as he should.'

'Ah, Sir Hugo will have the truth of the matter from you.'

'He'll need no explanation from me. His judgment is unerring.'

Warmed by his welcome reassurance she summoned a smile. 'What a friend you are! I apologize for my unwarranted comments about your brother.'

He smiled back incorrigibly. 'Hugh would forgive you instantly. He's the most wonderfully understanding person in the world.'

Elizabeth stayed silent. If she could only say the same of William she would not now be wishing that this limbo of leaving, but not yet arriving, could go on and on.

Dawn was breaking over the plain when they had their first sight of their goal. It was now March of the year 1848; four and a half months from that chilly grey day when the packet had set sail from Southampton. The air was deliciously fresh and, in the pale enchantment of a new day, the fortified walls of the old city represented a glimpse of the romantic India of Elizabeth's imagination. The cantonments stretching along the rise showed white and orderly in the dawn glow. *Ratnapore*. The final destination.

Rupert was shouting to her in delight from his palanquin, but she lay back silently against her cushions as a curious sensation of excitement, a certain foreknowledge of unhappiness mingled with pain began to burn in her breast to spread until her limbs ached with it. Recognizing her ability to sense atmospheric qualities in her surroundings, she could not understand this reaction to Ratnapore. John had certainly been here, yet he had also been in Calcutta, Cawnpore and a hundred other places she had visited *en route* where she had not known this sense of his spiritual presence reaching out to her.

The palanquins, followed by a team of camels bearing their baggage, progressed through the environs of the station to the area occupied by the military. Elizabeth saw none of it. She was in a world apart; perhaps a world beyond this one. The rush of apprehension which assailed her could be explained only one way. From this place John's wife must surely have vanished so mysteriously: why else would she feel such aching kinship with a man gone from her own life with matching drama? Only when the bearers halted, and Rupert arrived alongside to help her alight, did she see his famililar face and return from her distant realm to find that they were in a broad avenue containing a line of beehive bungalows washed white, each surrounded by a fenced compound.

'The officers' quarters,' explained Rupert, his eyes sparkling with the boyish thrill of being where he had yearned to be for so many years. 'We've been noticed already. Some fellow is approaching from what I imagine to be the Mess. The Officer of the Day, no doubt. He'll soon fetch your husband then direct me to Hugh's abode.'

Captain Barstowe of the Native Infantry was, indeed, the man on duty expecting to be relieved at any moment by his successor. A plump perspiring man with thinning hair and profuse side whiskers, he goggled at Elizabeth with undisguised fascination. Sir Hugo had been expecting his brother to arrive at any day, but no provision had been made for *Mrs* Carruthers, he told Rupert cheerfully.

'Pleased to welcome you, ma'am,' he added. 'Always delighted at the addition of a lady to make the place more lively, you know.'

Rupert adopted his haughtiest manner toward a man who was not only in the East India Company's army, which was looked down upon by the Queen's soldiers, but had also clearly been promoted from the rank and file and was therefore not counted as a true gentleman by those who were.

'You may tell Major Sir Hugo Carruthers that I shall join him just as soon as I have delivered this lady into the protection of her husband. Seek Lieutenant Delacourt out immediately.'

Bristling at the insolent tone of this very young man, the yellow-jacketed captain's face grew red with anger. 'There's a *Captain* Delacourt here, but he ain't expecting any lady, you young sprig. His wife's in England. I don't know what game you're playing, sonny, but you can try it on Cornet Helderman who's just rounding the corner to take over my duty.'

He saluted Elizabeth in offhand manner and walked away to where a tall gangling figure in what looked like a Forrester's uniform was now leaning negligently against a pillar of the Officers' Mess verandah. Elizabeth had seen Rupert in a temper before, but never one equal in ferocity to that which overtook him now.

'By God, I'll have his apology for that! I'll seize him by his fancy yellow coat and shake it out of him. How *dare* he behave in such insulting fashion?'

So great was his fury, he strode off to confront the pair who were conversing and giving intermittent glances in their direction. Elizabeth was left standing in her loose travelling robe in the middle of the dust road. The unwelcome news that William still had not received notification of her presence in India did not affect her much, for she was still enveloped in the inexplicable sensation of breathlessness which had touched her on first sighting Ratnapore. The heated scene fifty yards away seemed like part of a dream; the certainty of imminent revelation was her only reality. It still dominated her when Rupert marched Cornet Helderman toward her. He was scowling, but was in no way the loser of the contretemps, she felt.

'This fellow says he will fetch Captain Delacourt to you, but there might be some delay. There was a celebration of some kind last night. Your husband was . . . he did not reach his bed until an hour ago,' Rupert explained awkwardly, a comparative stranger to tact. 'It's the deuce of a situation. Hugh would offer you the seclusion of his quarters except that he is a bachelor. It wouldn't do . . . and a lady cannot be permitted to use the Mess.' Turning to the boy subaltern who was gazing at Elizabeth like a hungry horse being shown a beautiful juicy apple, he said sharply, 'Get about the business of advising Captain Delacourt that his wife is here, then come back to hear from me what arrangements I've made for her.'

Still bewitched, Elizabeth had enough of her wits about her to appreciate her friend's feelings at this unexpected turn of events. 'Rupert, you've waited so long to see your brother. Do please go to him. I shall wait in my palanquin for William to come.'

He made an uneasy gesture with his hands. 'I can't leave you here like this. No gentleman could.'

'You have done more than enough for me, my dear. But please do this last thing, if you will,' she begged, putting her hand on his sleeve. 'Delay your reunion with Sir Hugo no longer. I know how precious the thought of it has been to you all these past weeks.'

'No, Elizabeth,' he argued with a sigh of determination. 'It's unthinkable for me to leave you in the street like . . . like so much baggage to be collected by your husband, when he is in a fit condition to do so. Delacourt would not thank me for it.'

'May I be of help?' asked a voice to their right.

They both swung round to see a young woman in a blue muslin morning-gown standing at the gate of a nearby bungalow. She wore her brown hair in ringlets around a face of surprising sadness, yet there was a gentle friendliness in her manner which did not resemble the curiosity of the gossip mongers they had encountered *en route*.

'I fear I overheard your dilemma,' she confessed. 'It might be some while before your husband arrives, Mrs Delacourt. He is not expecting you, I regret to say. The letter informing him of your imminent arrival will probably come long after you have settled in. It is always happening. Would you care to wait inside my bungalow? My husband is out on patrol so I'm eating a solitary breakfast. Perhaps you would welcome a cup of tea while Mr Carruthers seeks out his brother.'

Seeing the way for Rupert to leave her without feeling guilty, Elizabeth smiled and said, 'Thank you very much. I should appreciate some tea and the coolness of your home.'

Within a short time she was walking with the woman, who introduced herself as Fanny Humphrey, in to a small parlour. Rupert went off with a promise to tell Helderman where she could be found. He looked relieved and excited.

'I apologize for my dress,' Elizabeth told her hostess. 'It's quite unsuitable for a morning call.'

'It's the only sort of garment one can reasonably wear in a palanquin. Please sit down and make yourself comfortable while I arrange for extra china to be brought. It will take no more than a minute.'

The normal thing for a woman to do when left alone in a strange room would be to look around it and gain some impression of its owner from the contents. Elizabeth sat quietly, lost in that continuing sense of superlative awareness of an imminent revelation which would explain her inner foreboding that had increased to almost uncontainable proportions. Her hostess returned and sat beside a small table bearing a tray, while a servant set out china for the guest.

'I had not known when today dawned that it would prove to be so very interesting,' she said with a smile, as she poured tea for Elizabeth then handed it to her. 'I warn you, you will have little time to yourself until we have all heard the latest news from our beloved England.'

'What news I have will hardly be the latest,' she responded, wondering why her hands were shaking so much the cup rattled in its saucer. 'I left Southampton as long ago as the first day of November.'

'Yet you are here so soon,' marvelled the other woman. 'I came out with the regiment. We spent six months at sea and toiled around the Cape in a storm which blew us two days' sailing too far south. I confess I thought I might never survive it.' She gave an apologetic smile. 'Dear me, you will not wish to hear all that right now. It's so unfortunate that your letter to Captain Delacourt did not precede you when it is plain from your anxious expression that you cannot wait to be with him again. He will not be far away, rest assured. I know he is not taking the patrol because my husband is out with Mr Phipps and Captain Stavenham.'

Elizabeth felt the room spin, taking her in dizzying turns with it. It was impossible: his regiment was on the high seas heading for England. Yet John's presence here would explain the sense of foreboding, the breathless awareness that had told her Ratnapore held unhappiness in store.

Hardly able to form the words, she murmured, 'I do not recall a Captain Stavenham with the regiment.'

'He transferred from Chetwynde's Hussars two months ago. It seems he had no desire to return home. I thought it very strange, but there are rumours concerning a wife who disappeared without trace in India, so one must suppose that he cannot bear to leave the country where she was lost. The tragedy would explain his reserved manner and rather grim expression. George says he is looking for trouble with the Sikhs, which no one else thinks likely, but he clearly bears a personal grudge against those he holds responsible for whatever happened to his wife. Poor man! One must sympathize, naturally, but the only cure for such a loss is to marry again. There are more than enough females in India willing to . . .' She broke off in remorse. 'Oh dear, I have allowed my tongue to run away with me. I'm so sorry. You have come all the way from England and cannot wish to be regaled with station gossip the minute you arrive. This unfortunate delay must suggest to you that your reunion will never come.'

'On the contrary,' said Elizabeth from the depths of her shock, 'I had not dreamed it would ever take place.'

The sound of loud voices broke into her chaotic thoughts of why John had elected to remain in India, and of how she could possibly seek reconciliation with William when the subject of her spiritual unfaithfulness would be there as a constant reminder. On top of everything she must face this morning, this was a cruel blow. How would John treat her; how could she hide the truth from William and behave as if John were a stranger? So overwhelmed was she by what must be the hand of destiny, that only a small part of her mind registered the import of a loud argument as heavy footsteps approached the bungalow. Mrs

Humphrey had stopped chattering and was looking rather startled. The gist of what was being said by two male voices was clearly audible in that parlour.

'It's some damn fool jest by you, or by this *female*,' roared William. 'By God, you'll both get the length of my tongue for it.'

'She said . . . Mr Carruthers said . . . said she was your wife, sir,' panted the more youthful voice. 'He told me just a few minutes ago that she was with Mrs Humphrey.'

'How *dare* you plant some doxy of mine in the home of a respectable woman? I'll have you broken, I swear I will.'

Fanny Humphrey rose to her feet looking even more startled, and made for the front entrance. Elizabeth was rooted to her seat. The sound of that familiar voice berating someone brought back the way she had felt when the victim of it. The person she had chosen to forget, because remembering made her unhappy, suddenly became clear in her mind's eye once more. Then William was reality bursting into the room, driving her to her feet to face him. She saw a large blond man whose scarlet jacket was unevenly hooked, with the collar left open to reveal that he wore no shirt beneath. His blue overalls were crumpled and stained dark in places; his hair tumbled in dishevelled fashion over eyes which looked bloodshot and drooping with sleeplessness. His handsome looks had coarsened in the two years they had been apart; they now blanched with shock as he stared at her speechlessly. As Elizabeth gazed back, her determination faltered. Why had she believed resolution alone was needed to mend her marriage? She had no love for this man. She did not even like him.

Shaken by the realization, she nevertheless managed to say with tolerable composure, 'Your father wrote to advise you that I was coming. The letter must be sitting neglected within Fort William, or in some *dak* office in Calcutta. The fact has inconvenienced us both. I have been obliged to travel up country without the benefit of arrangements usually made for their wives by men who are prevented from escorting them. You have had no opportunity to prepare for my arrival.'

'Who gave you permission . . . who was foolish and weak enough . . . my father must have taken leave of his senses. How *dare* you do this to me?' he choked, grasping the back of a chair as he swayed and almost fell.

Thinking it strange that she had dreaded this moment for so long, yet was not in the least afraid of his anger now that she was facing it, she replied calmly, 'I did it because I did not care to live as I was forced to by your absence. I survived the journey you claimed was too rigorous for me; I met enough ladies *en route* to make nonsense of the reasons you gave for leaving me at home. William, you once spoke of your duty toward the regiment, which required you to go wherever it was sent,' she continued firmly. 'As your wife I have that same duty. Your parents finally saw the truth of that and sent me to join you. I am certain you will also see it in a little while.'

He continued to clutch the chair, while staring at what he plainly believed to be a vision conjured up by his wine-inflamed senses. Elizabeth began to grow angry. She was not responsible for the failure of the Delacourts' letter to reach him; it was not her fault that she had arrived on the very morning after a wild celebration of some kind. Although Mrs Humphrey and Cornet Helderman had tactfully left them alone, they would certainly be within earshot of this reunion. That much she had learned whilst travelling through India.

'Might we now go to your quarters? I feel we have prevailed upon Mrs Humphrey's hospitality long enough.'

'My quarters?' he repeated loudly. '*My quarters?*' His harsh laugh must have been heard by the pair outside. 'I live as a bachelor with a fellow called Stavenham. We share the place. I cannot have a woman there.'

She could take no more shocks. Dear heaven, John had been suffering the ignominy of living beside a man whose wife he had loved enough to try to marry. Destiny had been cruel to him, also.

'I am not "a woman", William, I'm your wife,' she told him in a voice that shook. 'Where *can* we go so that we may be private, and you can . . .' Remembering the eavesdroppers, she changed what she had been about to say. 'You can explain to me what arrangements must be made to obtain a married officer's bungalow.'

Pushing a hand across his brow to sweep his hair from his eyes, he then clutched at the blond tangle in desperation. 'Go? There is nowhere we can go. Nothing like this ever happens. Nothing like this ever . . . dear God, Elizabeth, is it your design to ruin me?'

She stepped toward him swiftly to say in an undertone, 'You will ruin yourself, if you continue to announce to the entire cantonment that you have no respect or consideration for a wife who has come half a world's journey to join you. Pull yourself together. I would sooner continue this out on the plain than here, where every word we say will be generally discussed for days to come.'

His bleary, bloodshot gaze bore into hers as he heaved a long deep sigh, but her words had made sense to him, at last.

'Just remembered, Stavenham's taken today's patrol. Won't be back until late tonight.'

'Then take me there, for pity's sake,' she urged. 'I have been subjected to enough malicious curiosity from fellow travellers. Be so good as to spare me more.'

Somehow William managed to sound reasonably composed when they left, but the damage had been done. Fanny Humphrey was too effusive; the boy officer was smug. Dressed as she was, Elizabeth had no choice but to be carried the short distance by palanquin. William strode off, doubtless to ensure that all traces of his inebriation were removed from sight. Feeling taut with emotion, her physical perception of John's presence reached a new intensity as she stepped onto the verandah of his present home. He had slept here last night; he would return tonight. Within twelve hours she would see him again.

William had brushed his hair and fastened his jacket correctly, although the high collar was still undone, but his efforts had not banished his general air of dissipation. A tray of coffee had been placed on a table between two easy chairs in a tidy sitting-room. Beyond it, through the crack in the door, she saw a servant stripping sheets from a bed.

Her husband did not ask her to sit down. He was too worked up for social niceties. 'Why the devil have you disobeyed me in this manner? Was my family so dreadfully unkind to you that you were driven to desperate means?'

'No,' she told him calmly.

'Had you been so indiscreet that it was necessary for you to leave England for a while?'

It was uncomfortably close to the truth. 'I don't know what you mean by that, William.'

He gave a grim smile. 'Then you soon will, for they will be hinting at it from Calcutta to Ratnapore. When I left you I did not expect you to enter a nunnery — you are young and romantic enough to enjoy flirtations in the conventional manner — but I trusted you to be sensible to your duty, both to myself and to my family. You've not made a fool of yourself over some young idiot, have you?'

Attack was her best answer. 'Has it not occurred to you that I might have missed you beyond endurance; that I wanted to be with my husband as other officers' wives are?'

'No, my dear, that excuse will not do,' he told her savagely. 'No one can say we were ideally suited and, unless my absence built up a false image in your mind, I cannot believe that you made this journey for love of me. The very fact that you have tells me you are no more conventional than before. It was your waywardness I hoped to cure by leaving you with my mother and sisters. That, and your tendency to chatter in the most uninhibited manner to distinguished gentlemen on subjects no junior officer's wife should presume to offer an opinion on, much less demand one from them. If we were at odds in England, how much more we shall differ in this bedevilled country!' He clutched his hair once more in a gesture of despair. 'How could you do this to me? Have you no consideration for my future? What connivance on your part bemused my father into allowing you your way?' His voice rose further. 'Have you any notion of how you will set this place by the ears? I shall be the laughing-stock of the whole station: a man who leaves his wife safely with his family only to have her turn up on his doorstep unannounced! I tell you, ma'am, this is the worst harm you could have done me.'

'Indeed, I now see that it is,' she retaliated furiously. 'A wife turning up on your doorstep will oblige you to leave all future celebrations in the Mess long before you grow too drunk . . . and your . . . your *doxies* will have to be paid off.'

'*Elizabeth!*' he cried on a note of outrage.

'Have you no consideration for *me?*' she demanded in return. 'Was I not the laughing-stock of the regiment when you placed me with your good, pious, unbearably dull family as if I were a recalcitrant child, while other wives sailed with their husbands? What do you think it has been like for me these past two years, neither wife nor widow? How dared you be so patronizing as to concede that I might indulge in conventional flirtations in your absence, so long as I was sensible to my duty toward you. What of your duty toward me? Have you kept it in mind when indulging in *your* flirtations, William? Or have the women on this station pitied the poor wife who must be such a little drab she had to be left behind so that her husband can console himself wherever he chooses?'

Either the shock of this challenge from a female or the physical inability to stay on his feet any longer made William sink into a nearby chair, lost for words. Elizabeth also sat, looking across at him in resignation.

'I did not intend to fly at you the moment we met, but we have both been disconcerted by the absence of your father's letter which would have eased this meeting.' She sighed. 'I think you have no notion of how unhappy I have been since you deserted me. Yes, William, it was desertion,' she added hastily as he made to protest. 'I have proof of many women living safely and contentedly with their husbands during long years of service out here . . . and Mrs Humphrey spoke of her voyage taken with her husband and the regiment, which makes nonsense of your claim that no female could endure such hardship. I did try to accept the life you forced on me, but there came a point when I felt I should go mad rather than face another London season. Yes, we were at odds in England but I came here with the express intention of making our marriage more agreeable. After spending ten years or more apart, you must acknowledge that we would be strangers and a great deal more at odds, William. I am your wife until death parts us. Can we not make the very best of that fact, instead of your turning your back on it?' she ended on a plea.

William poured black coffee and downed two cups of it in quick succession. A third he left to send up a spiral of steam while he studied her morosely over his clasped hands until reaching a decision. Ignoring her plea, he said heavily, 'Well, you are here and we must put a brave face on it. You can be quite captivating when you choose to be, and your youth will encourage an attitude of indulgence over this escapade. So long as your behaviour is completely blameless from now on, we might rub through this tolerably well. For your own sake, pray that my father's letter arrives soon as proof that you undertook the journey in the belief that I had been appraised of the fact. Who acted as your chaperon as far as Calcutta?'

'Mr Carruthers. Canon and Mrs Hall could not sail, due to illness,' she added hastily. 'Rupert has been magnificent throughout.'

'*Rupert!*' he yelled, then winced and held his head momentarily.

'We became very good friends.'

'My God, I'll wager you did,' he said bitterly.

'He is a Carruthers,' she pointed out calmly, pouring herself some of the coffee. 'You should know better than to question his integrity. I do not know what I should have done without his help and protection. In the desert he saved eight people when our horses bolted. You are indebted to him for the life of your youthful, sometimes captivating, wife . . . and for the cost of my journey from Calcutta. I assured him you would settle with him immediately.'

'You *what*? It may interest you to know that I'm up to my . . .' He broke off to put his head back in his hands.

After a pause, she said quietly, 'For someone who does not wish his wife to concern herself with subjects his mother and sisters are certainly ignorant of, you are being remarkably honest with me. How deeply are you in debt, William?' He made no answer, so she went on pointedly, 'Well, we must put a brave face on this, also. *You* can be quite captivating when you choose, I must allow. For your own sake, pray that my standing with Rupert is high enough to allow him to take your note of hand.'

With a swift movement, William stood up and made for the adjoining room. 'This is intolerable,' he swore. 'How is it possible to make the best of the situation when you have become such a virago?' Turning at the doorway, he added savagely, 'I cannot order you back to England yet for fear of creating even more damage to my career than your arrival here will cause, but I will tell you this, ma'am. You came of your own will. If there is any part of your life here with me that you do not like, you will have to submit to it with good grace. You came to be my wife, and be my wife you will, until I can reasonably rid myself of you. I shall now take a tub and dress myself ready to face the Adjutant with a request to move quarters by nightfall, when Stavenham is due back. They say his wife disappeared one day without trace. He should count himself a lucky fellow.'

The returning patrol was spotted just as night was falling and it was soon apparent that something was wrong. The forward piquet sent a man for the Sergeant of the Guard. He arrived too late to see anything clearly. The light had faded too much to make out distinct shapes on that plain. The dust raised by a moving column blended into the general obscurity of oncoming night, and sun-dazzled eyes could easily imagine movement in a hundred different places. All the guard could report was that they were approaching at a slower pace than usual, and the ranks seemed broken and uneven. The sergeant interpreted this as meaning that they had suffered casualties. He sent an immediate message to the hospital to prepare stretchers for the wounded. Word flew around the cantonment, bringing troopers and officers to their doors. Could there have been some real action? Each man envied those who had gone out today, even though pain or death might have been awaiting them. Peacetime soldiering was conducive to madness; much better to die in battle than from some dirty disease or other, they agreed.

As darkness fell, lights began to flare all over the station, dramatizing the scene as stretcher-bearers moved forward and Indian grooms swarmed to the gates, anxious to learn the fate of their horses. There was a general air of excited apprehension as they waited for the first shout to go up from the lookouts. It was not long in coming. Within minutes, the patrol, or what remained of it, entered the gates of the cantonment with only the sound of soft hoof-beats to herald their presence until they came beneath the light thrown from the flares.

The exhausted men rode along the side of the Native Bazaar, past the cluster of huts housing the grooms and grass-cutters and circled the horse lines to reach the parade ground in front of the regimental offices. Those who pressed forward were both appalled and impressed by the disciplined manner in which Captain Stavenham brought the tattered and bloody men to the scheduled end of their patrol. The watchers fell silent so that his quiet commands could be heard against the jingle of harness and the squeak of leather, as the troopers lined up in formation behind him. The normal odour of sweating men and horses was augmented by the stench of open wounds which had had to bleed freely over victims and their mounts until they had baked dry beneath the sun.

Eyes grew rounder as they counted the number lying motionless across their saddles, and saw the white faces of those who had stayed upright only because their leader had. The men of Forrester's Light Dragoons had not seen anything like this before. Cholera was a dirty killer which had swept through the regiment, giving men no hope of survival. Battle wounds were different. What stories lay behind those lifeless figures? The night chill was already turning the breath from weary horses into vapour, but most of the riders seemed hardly to be breathing at all. The harsh lights of the garrison cast shadows on the men's faces as Captain Stavenham gave the order to dismiss the patrol. When he dismounted and handed his charger over to the care of his groom, he was seen to stagger, but his first concern was to check that all the wounded were helped from their horses and put on dhoolies to be carried to the hospital. The dead were taken on stretchers behind them.

The surrounding troopers muttered amongst themselves as new evidence came to light. The Captain had a sabre-cut across his shoulders. Blood had dried and encrusted the slashed jacket with a ridge of brown matter. Lieutenant Humphrey had had the top of his shako sliced right off. An inch lower, and the blow would have removed his scalp! Cornet Phipps was finished: so was Tom Donegal and Corporal Gates. There was Billy Martin, poor devil, or what was left of him. Lance-Corporal Haynes had a foot missing. One by one they noted the condition of the occupants of the stretchers as they moved off, but still they knew nothing of what had happened out there today. Those who were not injured were too exhausted to do more than push through the crowd and head for the barrack room, and the officers would say nothing until a report had been handed to the CO. Within a matter of minutes a shock of excitement had run through the lines, transforming the lacklustre atmosphere of this sweltering frontier station to one of eager anticipation. Were they going to be lucky enough to prove their worth and be covered in glory, at last?

Having ensured that his men received the attention they needed, John turned to his lieutenant, who had also been directing orderlies from the hospital.

'So we came through it, George,' he said quietly.

'Thanks to you.'

He shook his head. 'No man could have got us safely back without luck being on his side. Get along home now and put your wife's fears at rest . . . and for God's sake remove that hat before you go in. If she sees what a sabre can do she'll have no further peace.'

George demurred instantly. 'That wound of yours is deep, sir. I'll see you into the hands of the surgeon first.'

'No, I must report to Lakeland without delay.'

'But . . . I can put in an interim account which will suffice until you are made more comfortable.'

Gripping the man's arm, John said, 'I don't mistrust your ability to deputize. My flesh will suffer no more in the next twenty minutes than it has all afternoon, but Mrs Humphrey will die a thousand deaths in that time. Do as I say, if you will.'

George did so reluctantly. John then turned to the Officer of the Day, who had arrived on the scene disgracefully late. Cornet Helderman looked pale and apprehensive as John wearily told him to ride up to the Commanding-Officer's bungalow to warn him that Captain Stavenham was on his way to inform him of an engagement resulting in severe casualties. Then, knowing he would never stand the pain of attempting to mount again, John told his groom to take the animal back to the stable attached to the bungalow he shared with William Delacourt. He took a last look at the procession of dead and wounded being carried or wheeled off into the darkness beyond the flickering flares, then set out on foot for the largest bungalow in the officers' lines. Although he was in considerable anguish he was determined to give the facts in person to a man who had suggested that ten years in India had made him see trained troops where there were only undisciplined bandits. He was not triumphant over this proof of his own suspicions, but Lakeland could not ignore such concerted aggression against the patrol. Ratnapore and its outlying forts were ridiculously undermanned to counter an attack. Lakeland must take action to get reinforcements before it was too late.

As he walked stoically toward his objective, John was passed by many hurrying down to see if what they had heard was true. He brushed aside their eager questions in exhausted fashion, saying that they would know the truth soon enough. If he stopped now he knew he might never reach the CO's bungalow. It did not bode well for his determination, however, to be met by the Adjutant as he reached the foot of the three steps leading up to a verandah illuminated by tallow flares.

Frederick Ashburton-Smythe, slimly elegant in Mess Dress, expressed horror at the sight of a cavalry officer *walking* through the cantonment. Then he announced that Colonel Lakeland was dressing for dinner and invited John to enjoy a drink while he waited. When he took John's arm to aid his ascent of the steps, the pull of the blood-encrusted flesh on his back caused John to gasp in agony.

'Sorry, old fellow,' enthused the Adjutant. 'Bit tender, are you?'

'*Tender?* Yes, you could say that,' he snapped, furious at being told that his colonel was continuing with his toilet as if there were no urgency attached to his visit. 'Is Lakeland aware that we tangled with tribesmen and lost half our number?

'I . . . well, not exactly,' Ashburton-Smythe confessed weakly. 'Young Helderman came up to say you'd met with an accident of some kind and would be coming along later with the details.' The long face, made comical by side whiskers of varying shades, now registered the import of John's words. '*Lost half your number?* How did that come about?'

By now they were standing in the centre of a spacious white-walled room, enlivened by yet another set of sporting prints, some equestrian trophies, and a painting of the Duke of Wellington. John studied the other man through eyelids drooping with fatigue.

'You'll hear the details just as soon as our commanding-officer is pleased enough with his appearance. He clearly considers the choice of shirt studs more important than a field report.'

'I am sure he does not, Captain Stavenham,' said a reproving voice from behind him.

John turned too swiftly and gave a loud grunt of pain. Charlotte Lakeland came up to him swiftly. 'You are wounded? Why are you not at the hospital receiving attention, sir?'

There was deep concern on a face which she had long ago refrained from pampering with oils and lotions, and which was not enhanced by a plain grey gown with brown trimming. However, her eyes were luminous with distress and her voice was sweet on his ears after the frenzied masculine sounds of the day.

'I will see the surgeon just as soon as I have told your husband news I feel he should know without delay, ma'am,' John murmured.

'But surely it is unwise to leave wounds unattended for too long.'

'It is my hope that they will not be,' he replied significantly.

She took his hint and went off promising to acquaint her husband with the situation, leaving the Adjutant examining the back of John's jacket with morbid interest.

'So *that's* why you were walking,' he mused. 'Thought it strange.'

Colonel Lakeland bustled in to the room, wearing a long silk dressing-gown over his uniform trousers. He looked highly annoyed. 'Helderman said nothing of wounds, just that you had met with an accident. Thought you'd taken a toss, or some such thing. What are you doing here in that state, man? Humphrey and Phipps are perfectly competent officers.'

'Phipps is dead, sir. Humphrey has a wife to reassure,' he said stonily.

'And you look dead on your feet!' Turning to the Adjutant, he snapped, 'Send for a dhoolie, Freddie. He cannot be expected to ride to the hospital.' As the man went out, Lakeland swung round on John once more. 'Right, give me a concise account of what happened, then have that wound sewn up. There's no indication that Ratnapore is under imminent attack, is there?'

John was startled. 'Good God, no, sir.'

'As I thought. The details can wait until tomorrow. The bare facts, if you please.'

Fatigue resulted in John doing merely as he was told. 'We rode straight into an ambush in the pass. Tribesmen had been seen lurking there before, sir, but never in such numbers. Knowing that we had to return through the pass, they reserved their main attack and I was able to bring out the bodies.'

'Was that wise? If you had been killed, who would have led the patrol on its return?'

'The tribes in this area have a habit of mutilating the dead in a most grotesque fashion, and of torturing the wounded so as to inflict indescribable pain. It is my practice to prevent them from carrying out their obscene rituals, if at all possible.'

'I see. Go on.'

'Once clear of the pass, I left Humphrey with half the patrol and rode on to meet the caravan. It never came.'

Lakeland frowned. 'It had already been attacked?'

'No, sir. It's my belief there was no caravan. The merchants knew what was planned for us and stayed well clear. This must prove my theory that the attacks are not aimed at Ganda Singh's supply camels but at us . . . as they always have been.'

'Now, look here . . .'

John had no intention of being silenced now he had the bit between his teeth. 'I think we should have a meeting with the Sirdar, sir. The entire patrol could have been massacred.'

'How many did you lose?'

'Six, and fourteen wounded. Two of them will be dead before morning, and four others will be lucky to last the week out. When I realized that the caravan was non-existent, I roped the horses in threes and sent in one man with each group with orders to race through as fast as possible to raise the dust. I took the remaining men up the rock face so that we came up behind the tribesmen and took them by surprise. We were outnumbered, but they fortunately hadn't the skill to match ours. They fled up the incline and vanished over the top. Sir, I have made this request many times, but today's engagement surely supports my demand for the patrol to be armed with carbines.'

'I thought I had made it clear to you that there are none to be had, at the moment,' barked Lakeland. 'I'm glad to hear that you took the obvious action under such circumstances. Pity you lost so many.'

John's mouth tightened at this suggestion of a reprimand. 'They lost a great many more than we did. Our men fought very well. Cavalrymen are not at their best on foot in hilly country, but I have to say I was proud of them.'

'I'm glad of it,' Lakeland said shortly, 'even though you used a tone of surprise that you could ever be proud of them. Hussar regiments are not unique in producing first-class mounted troops, you know.'

Knowing his past service still rankled with this testy man, John determinedly returned to the point at issue. 'I can arrange a meeting with Ganda Singh before we agree to provide another escort for his caravans, sir.'

The other man was not to be pushed, however. 'We can discuss that at another time. It is more important that you should have that wound dressed and have a meal. Ah, yes,' he added as he made to turn away, 'I must tell you that you have been moved to a single bungalow. I'm sorry that it was necessary to shift your belongings in your absence, but Delacourt had to fix up something before dark and their baggage was in the compound.'

'Delacourt's baggage in the compound?' repeated John in bewilderment. 'I don't understand.'

'Well, I am amazed that you have retained command of your wits this long. Hallo, that sounds like the dhoolie arriving now. Cut along to the surgeon right away.' Dismissing John with a wave of his hand, he said, 'Freddie will tell you where to find your new quarters.'

The Adjutant was full of consideration now, shouting at the bearers to stand ready and taking John's arm as they went out into the night and started down the steps.

'What's this about Delacourt's baggage being in the compound?' he asked, to take his mind from the pain in his shoulders. 'Why am I obliged to quit the place?'

'New arrivals from Calcutta,' said Ashburton-Smythe breezily. 'Sir Hugo's young brother finally reached us. Brought with him a most stylish and attractive young woman. Not his wife, it transpired, but Delacourt's. Ticklish situation. Letter never reached William so he had no idea she was even in India. No time to arrange anything. Only thing to do was move you out and put the lovely lady in with her husband.'

John felt the night swirling around him as he asked, 'Was she . . . is she . . . did you say Delacourt's *wife*?'

'Deuce of a business turning up with young Carruthers without warning. Gave Delacourt no end of a problem to solve. Word is going around that she was indiscreet and had to leave England, and whatever the truth of that, she is a damned fine looking lady who should never have been left at home to seek consolation from some poor besotted fool. *Look out, man*,' he said sharply, as John missed his footing and almost pitched head-first into the dhoolie. 'Gad, that wound must be deeper than I imagined.'

Hugo arrived at the hospital to see how his friend was faring and was shocked to find John lying face down in a filthy wooden cot covered with four coarse blankets; his back covered with a bloodstained bandage. He appeared to be in a delirious state.

'What in God's name are you thinking of, Cockerford?' he demanded of the Surgeon in the Carruthers' bawl. 'Why hasn't Stavenham been returned to his own quarters? Get him off this . . . this *bier* and into the fresh air at once! The stench in this place is enough to finish him off even if your grisly ministrations do not.'

Hugo did not care for the Surgeon. He was no more than a butcher — of persons rather than animals — but it made him a *tradesman* in his eyes. Having for a long time supported those who maintained that surgeons and vets were not gentlemen, he opposed their admission to the Officers' Mess. They were given commissioned rank only because the Army did not know what else to do with them, in his opinion, and he did not see why the Mess should be saddled with them.

Captain Cockerford knew that this opinion generally prevailed and was only at ease when in the hospital. It was all very well for an aristocrat like Sir Hugo to look down his nose but let him try being a superior cavalry officer while riding a donkey and armed with a meat knife. In the Surgeon's opinion, that would be a comparable situation to his own. Medical skill was no use whatever if the military authorities took so little interest in it. He had long since given up the attempt to impress upon them that more soldiers died in hospitals than on battlefields, and since the regiment had arrived in India, he had resigned himself to an early death from cholera. As it was his duty to attend all the victims of the disease, he must surely succumb himself. With that in mind, he had set out to make his last years as pleasant as possible in this hellish country. He had found an Indian crone who supplied him with cheap liquor and girls. Now he was suffering from a thick head; thanks to an afternoon spent in her establishment, and it was that, plus the fact that he did not wish his patients to hear any more of Sir Hugo's insufferable condescension, that brought about his rapid surrender.

'Captain Stavenham has a fever. I find it worrying given the slightness of his injury,' he explained weakly.

'*The slightness of his injury!*' roared Hugo. 'Let me give *you* a damned sabre cut across the shoulders and see how slight you think it then.'

Cockerford stiffened. 'I have just amputated a leg below the knee, and sewn up another man's stomach to prevent the guts from spilling out. I consider a flesh wound slight.'

'Really? This man has served in India for ten years. He almost died from cholera in '42, received a swordthrust in the stomach during the Sikh war, and contracted malarial fever just two months before going home on furlough to bury his brother. Today, he has been riding for five hours under the blazing sun after hand-to-hand fighting during which he received the wound you call slight.' His voice rose to full power once more. '*No wonder he has a fever, man!*'

The Surgeon flushed. 'If you remove him from the hospital his safety will be on my conscience.'

'Damn your conscience! Get a dhoolie here and I will escort him to his quarters. If he is in a fever let him ride it out decently, not in a charnel-house with the common troopers.'

Hugo made a night of it with young Rupert, whom he was very moved at seeing again after so long. The brothers celebrated their reunion in the usual fashion, with their reminiscences growing more colourful and untruthful as time passed. But Hugo did not omit to look in on John as he made his way to bed. The fever was subsiding fast as a result of the careful ministrations of his loyal bearer, but he was still muttering wildly. Hugo nodded, well satisfied with himself. He was certain John would not have wanted all and sundry to hear his ramblings, particularly those concerning a temptress named Elizabeth.

Chapter Seven

It was the custom for European residents to ride in the cool of early morning, much as they had in England. In his determination to put a brave face on the situation, William insisted that Elizabeth should accompany him on that first morning after her arrival, so that they could put on a show of married harmony before the other riders. She went submissively, despite a headache and very low spirits. The events of yesterday had piled up to torment her during a night when there had been little chance of sleep to offer her relief. It had been enough to discover that John was here when she had believed him to be on his way home, without being obliged to occupy the room from which he had been ejected in his absence. Rumours concerning the ill-fated patrol had circulated fast. That John had been wounded seemed certain, but on how badly and in what way, no two reports agreed. Elizabeth could not ask, which was the worst aspect of the affair. Any suggestion of unusual interest in him would arouse speculation. The full penalties of her position at Ratnapore had struck her during a night spent between walls so vibrant with his presence, it was as if he were there with her.

That same curious awareness of him had prevented her from seeing much of her surroundings on entering yesterday, so she tried to concentrate on all she saw as she rode beside her husband. Officers of the various resident regiments were returning from the morning exercise on the plain. They all showed interest in the woman beside Captain Delacourt but knew better than to stop and speak. Until Elizabeth had been formally presented at an evening function, no one would do more than salute or raise a hat in passing. She thought the habit ludicrous but made no attempt to say so to the man she had come to join in the hope of reconciliation. She now knew that this was impossible. He had slipped into a life of bachelor dissipation, that much was already clear. She could not recall that he had been a particularly heavy drinker in England nor, so far as she had been aware, had he played for such high stakes as to plunge himself deeply into debt. She had had no knowledge of his finances, of course, but she now had her first suspicion that her dowry might have been as attractive to him as the bride he was gaining. As for women, nothing much had changed; she had suspected his infidelity soon after their first quarrel. Add to all that the facts that he saw her as the ruin of his pleasant habits, and that she was deeply in love with someone else, and any hope of making an acceptable marriage together was doomed. William vowed he would send her home again as soon as he could decently do so. What would life be like for her if she stayed? One thing of which she was certain was that she could never live with the Delacourts again. After the intensive experience of travelling to Ratnapore, life with William's parents would be more intolerable than ever. The only acceptable prospect would be to go to Wellford and take up residence in Walnut Tree Cottage with the one person who truly loved her. If William had abandoned any sense of responsibility for her, then she would do as she pleased.

They had no sooner broken out onto the plain than she saw Rupert riding toward them. He looked extremely dashing on a glossy chestnut horse which he spurred to a trot on spotting Elizabeth.

'Good morning,' he cried, saluting smartly. 'Isn't it a splendid one?'

She reined in, immensely glad to see him. 'My goodness, Rupert, you have the air of having settled in already.'

'Well, not quite, you know, but Hugh has sent me out to secure my bearings while he takes breakfast.' He grinned. 'We made a night of it and he is not overkeen to show himself to the world just yet.'

'Yet you are?'

'Two months of rising at dawn form a habit not easily broken, as you must have also discovered,' he said.

Elizabeth turned to the grim-faced man beside her. 'William, may I present Mr Carruthers who rendered me invaluable assistance during my journey? I do not know what I would have done if he had not been travelling to join the regiment also.'

'It was certainly a fortuitous circumstance,' agreed William through tight lips. 'My thanks, Carruthers.'

All Rupert's *bonhomie* vanished as he gave silent acknowledgement of the words, and Elizabeth hastily added, 'If you could have seen the splendid piece of heroism which resulted in him saving eight people from being dashed to the sands beneath an overturned vehicle, you would offer more than your thanks, William.'

'An exaggeration, I assure you,' Rupert told him with true Carruthers hauteur.

'I hope not. I understand you are to be my second-in-command. Heroism might compensate for total lack of military experience if the situation here is worsening. You doubtless heard of the attack on our patrol yesterday.'

'I did, sir.' His eyes regained some of their sparkle. 'It seems I arrived just in time.'

'I daresay the regiment could have coped if you had not,' William drawled. Then, before anything more could be said, he went on, 'Sir Hugo is very much respected. We are all glad to have his brother in our ranks.'

The grudging welcome went unnoticed as Rupert looked beyond them with an expression of growing incredulity. Then a small figure on a grey mare drew level as he uttered a loud exclamation.

'*Lucy!* Lucy Belmont! By all that's wonderful, what are you doing here?'

Elizabeth turned her head to study a girl of little more than seventeen, who was dressed in a severe black habit far too sophisticated for her youth. She was blonde, blue-eyed and as pretty as a doll with rosebud cheeks and long curling lashes. Her expression registered confusion then blushed beguilingly as she drew rein.

'I'm sorry, sir,' she mumbled. 'Should I know you?'

Rupert laughed joyously. 'Lord, my dear girl, how very prissy you have become. It won't do. I well remember you with tangles in your hair and a muddy dress whenever we went rabbiting, so do not put on those airs with me.'

The blush deepened as her face grew animated. '*Rupert!* I cannot believe my eyes! So your guardian bought you a commission at last, and a lieutenancy, at that. I am *so* glad for you. Are you with Forrester's? Why haven't I seen you these past three months? How is your brother? You look so splendid sitting there, and you have grown so tall. Is it any wonder that I did not recognize you behind that profuse moustache?'

He grinned. 'Still the same chatterbox you always were. You have asked at least half a dozen questions without giving me a chance to answer . . . and is that hat meant to be crooked? It's in great danger of falling off.'

Her confusion returned at his description of the saucy angle she had tried to achieve with her hat. 'I see you have not lost your delight in teasing me.'

'It is crooked, word of honour. Let me straighten it for you.' He edged his horse against hers and put out both hands.

'No,' she said quickly. 'Henry would not like it.'

Rupert lowered his hands again. 'Who is Henry?'

'Captain Nicholson of the Native Infantry. My . . . my husband.'

'Your *what?*' bawled Rupert. 'You're just a girl. You can't possibly have a husband.'

'I am nearly eighteen,' she told him defensively. 'It is four years since we left Buckinghamshire, you know. You have forgotten how time passes.'

The young officer was still stupefied. 'But you look no different than you did then.'

A flush darkened her face again as she told him he was extremely uncivil, which was one respect in which *he* had not changed. Being Rupert he was completely unrepentant, however, and went on to tell her she should stop turning as red as his coat if she wished to pose as a lady, for it completely gave her away.

'I daresay you have altered a little,' he conceded grudgingly. 'That habit is vastly different from your cousin's outsize breeches, and your curls are more neatly arranged than when they used to fall all over your face.'

This curious compliment appeared to delight the girl, for she exclaimed, 'I *am* so glad to see you, Rupert. I cannot think how we failed to meet up at sometime during the past three months.'

'I only arrived yesterday, that's why. I came up from Calcutta to join Hugh.'

'Your brother is here too? I had no idea. I wouldn't know him, I suspect, for I only saw him when he was down from university and he always seemed more like your father. Twelve years is a big gap in age.'

'Yes,' said Rupert bitterly. 'I wish I had been my father's second son instead of the third. I have had to wait all this time to join Hugh, but we had a splendid reunion yesterday. He has his majority already, you know, which is good going for a man of only thirty-two. He'll have a colonelcy soon. I always knew he would acquire top rank very young. You must meet him, Lucy, and I know you'll be lost in admiration of his modesty although, lord knows, he has enough to brag about. He has won the last six main events at the regimental race meetings on Garth —

do you remember his famous grey? — and no one can touch him on the hunting-field. He out-targeted every other man in the shooting contest, but could not take the cup for he presented it to the regiment himself. You should see the trophies he has in his quarters — tiger skins, stag heads and some truly splendid elephant tusks. He has promised to let me accompany him on his next trip and give me the chance of first shot at the quarry. You must agree that he is an absolutely first-class brother.'

Not for the first time did Elizabeth feel that Sir Hugo could afford to be admirably modest with Rupert shouting his praises. She thought it was time to remind him that others were present. He seemed completely absorbed in his reunion with this married child, and William was visbily annoyed with the behaviour of his new subaltern. The military relationship was unfortunate enough without Rupert's flagrant lack of interest in his new superior.

'Rupert, are we to have the pleasure of meeting your friend?' she called to him softly.

The young man turned still full of enthusiasm. 'Beg pardon, Elizabeth. So amazing a coincidence has made me forget my manners. Miss Belmont is a very old and dear friend. Her father owned the neighbouring estate and it is incredible that she should be riding in Ratnapore this morning, instead of in Lincolnshire whence her family removed.'

William inched his horse forward, saying in bored tones, 'My dear, may I present Mrs Nicholson whose husband has more than twenty years of soldiering in India to his credit, I believe.'

Elizabeth smiled at the girl whilst working out the fact that Henry Nicholson must be at least thirty-eight, and old enough to be her father.

'How do you do, Mrs Nicholson. I also only arrived in Ratnapore yesterday. Mr Carruthers travelled all the way from England in my company and, besides being of immense service to me, he became my friend. I hope that we shall be friends, also.'

Lucy Nicholson gazed in envy at Elizabeth's dashing habit of yellow and sage-green whose matching hat was set at the saucy angle she had tried to achieve and failed. She seemed eager for a female friend, but nevertheless recited a conventional greeting which contrasted badly with the fresh youthfulness of her interchange with Rupert moments before.

'How do you do, Mrs Delacourt. I trust that you will find Ratnapore to your liking. Did you have a pleasant journey?'

'As far as any journey can be pleasant in such heat,' Elizabeth replied. 'Without the consideration of our friend in finding shady spots for me to rest in *en route* I do not know how I should have survived without melting away.'

Rupert cast her a sly glance. 'I suggest there were times when you would have given a great deal to be rid of me, ma'am.'

She laughed. 'I grant I could not always see why you felt the need to send back the stew at every *dak* bungalow when there was no alternative but another plateful of the same concoction.'

William had clearly had enough. He spurred his charger forward, saying over his shoulder, 'Unless we ride soon the day will be too far advanced.'

In an attempt to cover his brusqueness, Elizabeth said, 'Will you accompany me, Mrs Nicholson? Having been here barely one day there are so many things on which I should like to ask your opinion.'

Lucy flushed again. 'I shall be delighted to accompany you, but I have been here no more than six months myself. There is so much I still have to learn.'

They formed pairs and set their mounts off at a gentle trot. Elizabeth addressed herself to the task of discovering a little more about the sweet young girl beside her who plainly idolized Rupert in much the same way he did his brother.

'Where did you live before your husband was stationed here, Mrs Nicholson?'

'With my aunt in Delhi. She invited me to come on a visit, you know,' came the sad reply. 'Mama held that it was very generous of her elder sister to offer to launch me in Anglo–Indian society, which I daresay it was, but I would so much rather have remained with my twin sisters in Lincolnshire.'

'But you would not then have met your husband.'

'No.'

It was such a sighing negative Elizabeth decided to leave that subject. 'So you have known Rupert for years.'

The pretty face began to glow as it was turned toward her. 'Oh, *yes*. He was always up to some escapade or other which made life so exciting, and he was generous enough to allow me to go with him sometimes, providing I did exactly as he said. I always tried very hard to do so, but he was exceedingly impatient over my mistakes. Then he would vow never to include me in an adventure again.' A shy smile broke out. 'But he usually did if I pleaded with him and promised to bring some of Cook's apple cake.' She broke off to acknowledge the greeting of an officer in a colourful uniform of yellow and green much embellished with gold. 'That is Mr Calhoun, Henry's second-in-command,' she confided softly. 'He is quite pleasant but very occupied with such things as astronomy and Aristotle. One cannot really be friends with a man like that, can one?'

'A man who counts books as his friends can certainly be diffident in social discourse,' Elizabeth agreed. 'Rupert does not concern himself with dull, learned subjects?'

'Yes, of course he does. When little Edward died, the place reserved for him at Eton was given to Rupert, so it goes without saying that he is extremely clever and knowledgeable on every subject . . . but he does not prattle on about all he has learned. Rupert is full of energy and ideas. He is a most exciting person to know but Mr Calhoun is, I'm afraid, exceedingly prosy.'

Warming to this girl more by the minute, Elizabeth saw a slight echo of her younger self in Lucy Nicholson. Yet their situations were vastly different. It was easy to guess that the aunt in Delhi had been charged with finding a match for a younger daughter whose twin sisters had still to be settled in marriage. Thus, Lucy had been given to an older man seeking a companion for his extended sojourn away from his motherland. Now an adored childhood friend had entered the scene. Hero worship could soon turn to love in someone just entering womanhood. Elizabeth might soon find there was another wife in Ratnapore who was faced with a love she could not claim. Poor Lucy! Rupert clearly still saw her as the tangle-haired child who had dogged him so faithfully. He could easily inflame the situation with thoughtless actions. She must try to alert him to the danger of being too free with someone who was now legally bound to another man. William was touchy enough over her own innocent friendship with a fellow traveller. Henry Nicholson might react more violently over the revival of a childhood bond.

When they all reached the end of their ride and bade each other good-day before going their separate ways, William revealed that he had been thinking along the same lines, only in masculine fashion.

'I shall have to intervene there,' he announced, watching the young pair ride off deep in conversation. 'Carruthers sees her as a child he once bullied, but she is a married woman despite looking like a schoolroom chit. He seems over fond of making friends with other men's wives. I think I shall read him a lesson on the qualities required in an officer and a gentleman, which demand that he never dishonours the reputation of a fellow officer's lady. It is the worst sin imaginable in the eyes of military men.'

John awoke at first light with a raging thirst and a headache fit for an elephant. The bellow intended to frighten his bearer into action came out as little more than a rusty croak, frightening no one but himself. The fear of illness was always with a man in India. It was very easy to die out here. Turning his head in the direction of the doorway, he attempted to call again, but the movement brought such a stabbing pain in his shoulders a groan was forced from his lips instead. The haze in his mind then began to clear a little, enough to enable him to recall that same agony caused by a sabre slicing across his back while he was desperately slitting another man's throat. He had swung round and dispatched his attacker with one thrust, before the weapon could finish him off. As many as he could lay hands on had tasted cold steel as anger had driven him on. Young Phipps had been skewered with no hope of fighting back, and John had held the memory of that boy's expression of shock in death as he had settled the debt. It was not yet paid in full. The ambush had set the seal on his determination to get to the bottom of Ganda Singh's duplicity before there was a full-scale insurrection. If that happened, the entire garrison could be put under siege before reinforcements could arrive.

The sound of bugles on the still, dawn air heralded another day in the routine of the cantonment, so he again made an attempt to summon his bearer. His hoarse shout brought the man, who expressed his delight over his master's return to clarity. Then he hurried away to fetch tea and another dose of quinine. Its curative qualities were infallible in cases of fever, but there was no remedy for the sort which possessed John as full memory returned. Dear God, Elizabeth was here in Ratnapore! It was incredible . . . unacceptable. Delacourt could not have known she was on her way out to India. He had declared that his wife was safely in England with his family. Why, *why* had she come? Surely not because he, himself, was here. No, of course not. Forrester's had been in Calcutta and news of their transfer to the frontier region could never have reached her before she had left England. Had she grown tired of the sport at home and decided to try her luck out here where men were more lonely and therefore more susceptible? Certainly her husband would be on hand, but she might derive more excitement from leading poor devils on in the most subtle manner, only to torture them with a pose of marital devotion. It then dawned on him that he could suffer similarly at her hands. How would he face her without giving himself away? How could he pretend they were strangers? He would be powerless while she employed the cruellest weapons used by women, knowing he dare not betray the truth and be branded by Delacourt as well as his brother officers.

The bearer arrived at that point, so he struggled into a sitting position. The tea was more than welcome to his parched throat, and a bowl of warm water to wash with did much to alleviate his general discomfort. Across the still, frosty air of daybreak John could hear the sharp commands of the NCOs as they disciplined the men on morning parade. There were the usual sounds of soldiers drilling, horses signalling the end of their tethered hours with soft whinneys and neighing, and Indians shouting across to each other in excited tumbling sentences. John did not understand them all because they came from different parts of India. He was proficient only in the dialect of this region. That thought recalled his determination to speak to Ganda Singh as soon as possible. He must make Colonel Lakeland hear him out this time.

Sleep must have overtaken him soon afterward because it was full daylight and already hot when he awoke to find Hugo standing at the end of the bed. His friend looked him over wryly.

'So you lived through the night after all. Three foolish men have lost their wagers.'

'From the way I feel now it could have been three nights rolled into one,' he responded. 'That fellow Cockerford needs some lessons in sewing. There is a great ridge along my back where he joined me together.'

'Damme, you were fortunate that he was able to do so at all, however painful the result.' His face curved in a knowing smile. 'Last night you were more concerned about how the ladies might ill-treat you. What a good thing I didn't leave you in the hospital, where ears were cocked enquiringly.'

John struggled up on one elbow. 'What in God's name does that mean?'

His tormentor laughed. 'My dear fellow, your libidinous secrets are

130

safe with me. I never concern myself with a man's ramblings when he is drunk or in a fever. It is much safer not to. Have you breakfasted?'

He shook his head. 'Fever always leaves me with no desire for food.'

'So, tell me of the affair. Had you no suspicion of what was to happen when you entered that pass?'

'None at all. The first indication we had of our enemies' presence was when young Phipps was transfixed with a monstrosity of a weapon. Corporal Gates suffered the same fate minutes later. I had to tear his chest to ribbons in order to remove it.' He sighed. 'Have you any knowledge of how the casualties are faring?'

'Three troopers died during the night. I enquired of Cockerford on your behalf at breakfast. You may judge the depth of my regard for you by that, for I cannot stand the man on any account.' He paused to cast a questioning look at John. 'Phipps and eight others dead; eleven wounded. This is what you have been forecasting since we arrived in Ratnapore. How did Lakeland take the news?'

'To tell the truth, man, I am hard put to remember much of what went on last night. I reported straight away but I have a faint recollection that he thought the matter not at all urgent. I believe I made a fool of myself in front of the Colonel's lady before the dhoolie arrived.'

'Mmmm! You might have done better to leave it until today. A wounded man bleeding all over the furniture would hardly gladden the heart of Mrs Lakeland, and the old man was being dined last night by the infantry. Not the best of times for you to burst in with vindication of your warnings.'

Making up his mind swiftly, John threw back the sheet. 'Hugo, give me fifteen minutes to shave and dress, then come with me to see him. I know he regards me as a prophet of doom and the fact that I am a transferred officer does my case no good. He has a distinct distaste for Hussars who decide to become Dragoons, it seems. He's been given no proof of my worth, as yet, but he knows you for the excellent fellow you are. He'll listen to you. Well, what do you say to my request?'

Hugo nodded. 'Of course I'll come with you. I always accept the word of a man who has superior knowledge on any subject, and you know far more about Ganda Singh and his troublesome relatives than the regiment does. What's more, we now have proof that your suspicions are correct. Lakeland will be a fool if he remains indifferent to your warnings. In any case, as you seem set on committing suicide by leaving your bed too soon, I am honour bound to walk beside you to

131

keep you upright all the way there and back. Get moving while you're still rational.'

They emerged from John's new bungalow a short while later and turned toward the office, where they hoped to find their commanding-officer. Hugo began telling John about his young brother's enthusiasm which had led him to rise at dawn to witness the morning parade, after having been put to bed only two hours earlier, decidedly the worse for liquor.

'I'll wager that is the only morning parade he will attend voluntarily in the whole of his career,' he added with a laugh. 'I'm anxious for you to meet him, John. He is rather embarrassingly influenced by fondness for me, but he has the makings of a first-rate officer once he realizes I am only mortal. I am impressed by his competence in arranging to travel up from Calcutta, especially as he had the additional responsibility of a lady to escort. We have a capital mystery in hand, John. Young Rupert accompanied Delacourt's wife all the way from England and it is perfectly obvious that she came without his consent, or even his knowledge. He is making the best of the situation by claiming that several letters from England went astray, but not one person in Ratnapore is convinced of the truth of it. There are hints that an indiscretion may have obliged the lady to leave England for a while, but he is doing all he should for her with every outward sign of a devotion which challenges further speculation on the matter. Of one thing there is no doubt. She is the most compellingly vital young woman the regiment has seen for a long time. There will either be a stampede of officers to the hills seeking consolation, or a bullet through the brain during the lonely night hours for more than one lovelorn subaltern. My brother will hear no word against her character, although he does not appear to have succumbed to her charms as yet.'

Hugo appeared not to expect any comment in reply, which was just as well. The muscles of John's stomach had tightened dramatically and so had his jaw. The effect was that when he entered the Regimental Office the Adjutant took one look at him and advised him to go straight back to bed.

'Colonel Lakeland is not expecting to see you for several days,' he explained. 'As a matter of fact, he is feeling a trifle frail himself this morning. The officers of the Native Infantry wined and dined him rather well last night. He is hoping to clear the routine work then call it a day.'

'We feel that it is essential that we see him without delay,' John insisted.

Ashburton-Smythe shook his head. 'Much better leave it until tomorrow . . . or the day after that.'

Hugo walked round behind the desk and grabbed him by the collar to march him across the room. 'Freddie, old fellow, go in and tell Lakeland we are here.'

The Adjutant recognized the note in his voice and surrendered. Straightening his bunched tunic, he flashed him a look of resignation. 'I'll tell him, but you must accept the consequences.'

While they waited, Hugo cast an eye over John. 'You do look dreadfully unfit, as he says. Will you stay the course?'

John gave a faint smile. 'You worry too much, Hugo. It's your one big fault.'

His friend grinned. 'Tell my brother that. He thinks I'm perfect.'

Colonel Lakeland gave them no smile of greeting. He looked extremely irritable and very much like a man who had over-indulged last night, so his opening remark was testy and very much to the point.

'I had not expected to see you on your feet so soon, Stavenham. Your devotion to duty is commendable, but my regiment will be best served by your complete recovery before you resume it.'

'I agree, sir,' said John firmly. 'It's my intention to give the reins to Lieutenant Humphrey for the next day or two. However, Major Carruthers and I felt that you would wish to be made aware of facts which might affect the safety of the cantonment.'

The Colonel looked at their determined faces and sighed heavily. He could hardly refuse to listen. 'Very well. You had better sit down. You look devilish sick. I advise you to make this as brief as you can. Freddie told me we lost three more men during the night.' He sighed again. 'Bad business about young Phipps. His father campaigned with me in the Peninsula.'

'The manner of his death was infamous,' said John, seizing that personal link to drive home his point. 'He was transfixed by a spear thrown from above. He had no chance to fight back. These tribesmen hide in the hills and pick off their enemies without exposing themselves, then melt away before an attack can be mounted.'

'Very cowardly,' said Lakeland, 'but that proves they cannot be trained troops, as you once suggested.'

133

'But they are, sir. They are trained in a type of warfare which has us at a disadvantage because we use conventional methods. These people are not conventional enemies and their numbers are growing. When they decide to attack in force . . .'

'You surely mean *if* they decide to attack,' snapped the Colonel.

John glanced swiftly at Hugo before returning to his theme. 'Sir, it is imperative that we make Ganda Singh aware that we are not deceived by his request for a military escort for his caravans. It's my belief that this army of tribesmen is actually in his pay, while he pretends to be threatened by them. The only way to avert a local uprising is to let him know we see through his game and will stand for it no longer. He is laughing behind our backs at our gullibility.'

'I have orders to keep the peace in Ratnapore Province,' the CO declared harshly. 'It is hardly wise to antagonize the ruler of it by accusing him of treachery. I believe you are making too much of this regrettable incident. When you have recovered from the weakness induced by your wounds, I think you will see that it would be more politic to keep the situation as calm as possible. It might be a wise move to double the strength of the patrols for a few weeks to discourage these bandits.'

Just as John was preparing an explosive retort, Hugo decided to intervene. 'It has crossed my mind, sir, that there might be questions asked at Headquarters about the deaths of nine men and the wounding of eleven others,' he pointed out in reasonable tones. 'John is familiar with this area, and it's not the first time patrols have been attacked while he has been at Ratnapore. Ganda Singh has not always been friendly toward the British, and if John considers him to be a wily old rascal I am very ready to believe him. As the only member of the regiment who can speak to the man in his own tongue, I would suggest that he must have a better notion of the man's true character than those of us who cannot. No harm can come from a meeting with the Sirdar, and it might be prudent to make it clear that we are not prepared to have our men slain when the merchants' caravans do not even set out on their journey. I don't think John is suggesting that we accuse Ganda Singh of treachery, simply that we hint to him that it is dangerous for anyone to defy the might of our army and let him make what he will of it. As the representation would be made by you, sir, John would simply translate the conversation, sentence by sentence, so that you would have full command over what was said. While we are not afraid to ride into the

134

hills and risk attack, we will surely be regarded as fools to suffer them and do nothing in retaliation.'

The older man began yielding ground. 'Nobody could call us fools for using diplomacy, Hugo. It is the most essential quality when dealing with these people. I had no intention of letting this incident go completely unremarked, but I prefer to wait a little before meeting Ganda Singh. He will think us in a cowardly panic if we rush to present an instant ultimatum.' He looked pointedly at John. 'An officer cannot afford to be impetuous. Time allows a man to clear his head of confusing emotions and leaves cold reason behind.' He stood, to signify that the meeting was over. 'I will mention this to General Mason when he visits the cantonment. You can ride over next week to fix a meeting with the Sirdar, Stavenham. There should be time enough for you to get back on your feet by then, eh?' He grew hearty as he ushered them from his office, a certain sign that he believed the matter had been satisfactorily solved by his own initiative.

No sooner were they out of earshot than John expressed his thanks for his friend's support. 'I swear he would never have agreed to a meeting on my recommendation. What has he against me? It cannot be only because I transferred from a regiment he has no love for.'

Hugo shook his head thoughtfully. 'I think it might be because you are a damned sight too good to be true. As a Troop Captain you are invaluable, no one can doubt your courage after the commendation you received on your action at Moodki, you speak the local tongue, and also cut a fine dash in your new uniform. On top of that, you are the only member of the Mess who is not in debt to the liquor store, and there is no evidence that you maintain a *bibee* in your quarters. Such virtuousness is a little hard for any commanding-officer to swallow. It makes him extremely wary. Before Lakeland will look kindly upon you, you will have to commit a few sins, John. I have some suggestions you might like to consider,' he ended with a laugh.

Dear God, thought John, if Hugo knew I'd committed the sin of chasing another man's wife he might not sound so light-hearted. If he only knew how perceptive he had been when suggesting there would be a great many lovelorn subalterns now Elizabeth had arrived. What would Hugo's opinion be of a captain of thirty-two who ought to have known better than to be duped by a girl of twenty looking for an easy conquest? He fell silent until they reached the officers' compounds. There, they were hailed by a young lieutenant sporting a fine cavalry moustache.

135

'How goes it, Rupert?' called Hugo as they approached. 'John, this fresh-faced youth is my brother. He has waited God knows how long to join us so I pray he might not regret it.'

'I would say that he couldn't have arrived at a more opportune moment if he is looking for action and a chance to distinguish himself. I wish you a long and noble career with the regiment, Carruthers.'

The young man smiled enthusiastically. 'Thank you, sir. If I can emulate Hugh in even the smallest degree I shall be more than happy.'

John raised an eyebrow at his friend. 'Who was speaking about committing a few sins a moment ago?'

Hugo grimaced. 'I did warn you that the boy imagines I am perfection itself. I rely on you to disillusion him on that subject. Rupert, this is John Stavenham, late of Chetwynde's Hussars. He is the one expert among us, having been ten years in India. He fought in the Sikh war of '45 earning several commendations. Heed him or you are not the person I took you for.'

'Was it a very bloody business yesterday?' Rupert asked eagerly, as they stood in the shade of a tree to escape the worst of the sun.

'Bloody enough, but that style of fighting is not to my taste. Cavalrymen are not at their best in such country. It is more suited to Gurkhas, or to the men of our Native Infantry here in Ratnapore.'

'Speaking of that regiment reminds me to tell you of a most wonderful encounter I had this morning, Hugh,' the boy said with continued enthusiasm. 'You never knew her as well as I did but I'm sure you'll recall Lucy Belmont.'

'Belmont,' murmured Hugo, creasing his brow in thought. 'Not that girl of Clarence Belmont's? What the blazes is she doing in Ratnapore?'

'She's Lucy Nicholson now, although I can scarcely believe it. Her husband is in the Native Infantry. Do you know the fellow?'

'No,' said his brother immediately. 'I have very little to do with officers of native regiments.'

This tendency to regard officers of the East India Company regiments as inferior was one subject on which John and Hugo did not see eye to eye, and he now gave the Major a deliberate look before saying, 'I know him . . . and his wife.'

'He must be either a most handsome fellow or a damned fortune-seeker,' declared Rupert hotly.

John shook his head. 'I believe he is neither, but we were all somewhat surprised when he returned from Simla with such a young

136

bride. I have every sympathy with Mrs Nicholson. It cannot be easy for her with no older relative to advise her how to go on. The ladies of the station "frighten her into a jelly" she once confided to me.'

A faint smile flitted across his face at the memory of the girl's artless confession during a quadrille at one of the station balls. He had been greatly amused to be told that she wished her husband had been a hussar for 'you look so very dashing in pale blue with a swinging pelisse at your shoulders'. Since that evening John had gone out of his way to speak kindly to her on the few occasions when they had met. He disliked her husband intensely for ruining a mere child. They all disliked him. Henry Nicholson's penchant for mingling too freely with his young Indian soldiers was known by the entire male population of the station and, when news of his activities had eventually reached the ears of those at Headquarters, it was only the benefit of having friends in the right places which had let him off lightly. Several handsome youths in his company were transferred to other regiments, and he was given several months' leave at a hill station with instructions to find himself an English wife before he returned. All those who'd had a hand in arranging the match were to blame for chaining such a young girl to a perverted man of forty-three, but Nicholson's fellow officers thought very poorly of him for using such an innocent victim for his outward show of respectability. In the strange way of military men abroad, they had taken young Lucy under their protection and tolerated the husband for her sake. Some of the most junior officers imagined themselves in love with her but, while Nicholson was suspected of continuing his activities with Indian boys, he was rigidly correct where his wife was concerned. They strolled together around the bandstand on Sunday mornings, they attended church parade like every married couple on the station, he sat beside her at race-meetings or at theatricals in the small playhouse. Dinner parties at their bungalow were as dull and proper as any others, and at the various balls Henry Nicholson was meticulous in his attentions to the girl. All the same, she had aroused a protective instinct in officers both married and single which had ensured her a number of friends, and if the women were not as warm in their approach it might be that Lucy Nicholson had an ingenuous charm most of them had long since lost.

Rupert Carruthers clearly did not know the situation, but John was not going to be the person to tell him. He would probably soon join the ranks of those pining for the girl, unless he knew her so well her appeal was lost on him.

'You'll meet Nicholson at the race-meeting this Saturday,' he said to the young man. 'What odds do you put on your brother winning the main stakes?'

Rupert grew immediately enthusiastic again. 'There is not a doubt of it. The Gold Cup is already his, for he's unbeatable.'

'Who says he is unbeatable?' asked a voice behind them. William Delacourt joined the group. 'Just wait until you see the new nag I have laid hands on.' He turned to John. 'You will have to scratch, I take it? I have only just heard of your part in the affair yesterday, and must apologize for turning you out of your quarters under such circumstances. I was so confoundedly busy settling my dear wife here with the minimum fuss I did not witness the return of the patrol. I am the last fellow to kick a man from his room when he is ill, but I did not know of the fact.' He put a hand on John's shoulder. 'Forgive me for saying so, but you look like a walking corpse.'

'I am sure he won't forgive your saying it,' murmured Hugo dryly. 'Lakeland and I have already pointed out the fact, and my brother has only refrained from doing so because he has never seen John when he looks in health.'

John glanced around at them all. 'Is this a conspiracy to rid yourselves of my company?'

'Yes,' said Hugo and William together. The Major added, 'We don't fancy the burdensome task of carrying your inert form, so go back to bed while you can get there on your own feet, there's a good fellow.'

John gave a knowing nod. 'Just beware that the rest does not do me so much good I find I am able to race on Saturday after all. You would have to look to your laurels, both of you, for you'd be totally outclassed beside me.'

Hugo laughed. 'An empty threat! You'll be fit for nothing more strenuous than keeping the ladies company. Delacourt will be pleased to leave his wife in the care of such a modest fellow.'

John felt his stomach knot up as the smile froze on his face. Through the buzzing in his head he heard William say, 'Elizabeth will certainly wish to express her regret at being the cause of your obligation to change quarters. She was extremely distressed when I told her you had been wounded yesterday, but I assured her you were a reasonable sort of fellow who would bear her no ill will. I say, Stavenham, you do look deuced groggy,' he exclaimed. 'Perhaps you should get to your bed right now.'

138

'Yes, I will,' John mumbled, feeling dangerously exposed to scrutiny from this man he had unwittingly insulted. He opened the white gate in his compound, then walked heavily up the path to his verandah, demanding once more of destiny why she had sent Elizabeth Delacourt out here. A tense masquerade between himself and the woman who had beguiled him was about to begin. He would never know from day to day what kind of dance she intended to lead him, what form her torment would take.

Chapter Eight

Elizabeth had been at Ratnapore for four days. Already it seemed natural to rise at seven, to ride on the plain before the sun turned the whole area into a shimmering griddle, then return to take a bath before breakfast. After that, her Indian servant would return from the native bazaar with the shopping, and present the accounts for Elizabeth to check. Next, she had to decide on a menu for tiffin and dinner. As the choice was very limited, the task should not have taxed Elizabeth too much, but she was determined to avoid the attitude of indifference she had encountered in so many of the women in stations all the way up to the frontier region. It did not occur to her that these women might all have been as determined as she at the outset until, fighting an enemy which has no conquerors, they had been neutralized by time and the unending heat.

Tiffin was a light meal taken at any time between one and two, after which she and William retired to their respective rooms to lie comatose on their beds until a servant brought tea to herald the hour to dress for dinner. After the meal, the great excitement of the day took place: a walk around the bandstand if there was a concert, or even if there was not. Sometimes there were theatricals, William had told her, which varied the routine somewhat. Or there was a ball at which fifty men competed with each other to dance with a dozen or so ladies, all married, while they sweated in their thick confining uniform and did their duty with true British tenacity.

Today, Saturday, had been eagerly awaited by every resident of the station. At the race-meeting this morning the Gold Cup event was to take place and tremendous stakes had been set. The rank and file had their own betting system, and the men's spirits were high at the prospect of cheering on their own particular officer. Race days were always good for the general morale, even if they ended in excessive drinking and the incurring of crippling debts. It was not uncommon for a cornet to shoot himself when the outcome of a race indicated certain ruin, but the excitement and thrill of British officers indulging their natural pursuits far outweighed the risk of dismal repercussions. The manly nature of this sporting activity was looked upon with approval by even that very moral lady, Mrs Lakeland, who strongly felt that the fabric of English country life should not be allowed to fade in this heathen country. She obligingly turned a blind eye to the sins committed after the races.

The ladies of the station had ridden unescorted this morning in groups of two or three, because their husbands had been too involved in inspecting their horses prior to the races. Elizabeth found William had already departed for the stables when she returned to bathe and take breakfast. She was glad of his absence. His anger over her arrival had not lessened, despite the semblance of marital harmony he assumed for the sake of his career. Charlotte Lakeland had made it clear that she disapproved of Elizabeth when William had presented her to his colonel and his lady at a band concert. The fact that Colonel Lakeland had been uncharacteristically flattering, whilst holding her hand for longer than was necessary, did nothing to improve his wife's mood, nor did it help Elizabeth's cause with the residents of Ratnapore.

Following the example set by their senior lady, the regimental wives were correspondingly cool in their treatment of the new arrival. The fact that she had brought with her the most ravishing fashions, and in colours none of them would dare to wear or at least not combine in one ensemble, added to their resentment of the interest she aroused in the male population of the station. They were also aware that no matter how much the Delacourts might pretend to be a loving couple, they occupied separate rooms and 'the sahib paid no visits to his lady' as the servants gleefully informed each other and their mistresses. The general opinion was that Elizabeth had embarked on an *affaire* in England which had led her to flee censure and join her disillusioned husband. Only Fanny Humphrey and Lucy Nicholson were pleased to be her friends. The remainder would have been very put out had they known that Elizabeth did not in the least care about their approval — or lack of it.

As she ate breakfast in blessed seclusion, Elizabeth reminded herself that she would see John within the hour. Fanny had provided the news that he was recovering from his wounds but not swiftly enough to allow him to race this morning. He would be in the stand to watch what was certain to be a thrilling meeting. They would come face to face surrounded by sharp-tongued women, and men who were wide awake to any hint of intrigue. How would John handle the confrontation? He must have heard of her arrival in Ratnapore so he would be prepared in advance. He could not ignore her without causing speculation, yet how would they both contrive to give the impression that they were strangers? As she dressed in a gown of blush pink with gauze water lilies tumbling down the skirt, she caught herself trembling with distress. Why had destiny played this cruel trick upon them both? Surely they had been punished enough in Wellford on the day following the hurricane without fate now destroying their attempts to escape each other. It was just as impossible for her to leave Ratnapore immediately as it was for him to exchange from a regiment he had just joined. They were prisoners here; prisoners of her heedless belief that happiness could be held for the brief life of a rainbow and leave a cloudless sky at the end of that time.

There was a festive air around the racecourse which had been bedecked with flags and bunting. The scarlet of the Dragoons stood out bravely against the green and yellow of the Native Infantry, the blue of Kingsford's Horse, and the tiny contingent of Artillerymen in grey uniforms as the troops thronged the rails. Over by the starting gate was a cluster of officers who would be the jockeys, and others nominated as race officials. These last were indulging in the mild madness such responsibility induces in those thus appointed. The enclosure which was reserved for officers and their ladies was decorated with garlands of fresh flowers and furnished with rows of chairs set out neatly beneath the striped awning. The women of the regiments were expected to withstand hours squashed between sweating, blaspheming soldiers, and they looked happy enough about the prospect since it took them away from the squalid conditions in the barrack blocks. For all it was a gala to be enjoyed in the way one was accustomed to do in England.

Despite her nervousness, even Elizabeth was caught up in the excitement generated by those trying to retain their national identity in alien surroundings. She had driven the short distance to the course with Fanny Humphrey and now sat beside her, giving automatic answers whenever a pause in her friend's chattering suggested that one was expected. Fanny was agog with anticipation of the arrival of General Sir Francis and Lady Mason, and regaled Elizabeth with all she knew of the pair.

'He is adept at timing his inspections of a station under his command so that it coincides with the regimental races. George says he places vast sums on his favourites having once been a neck-or-nothing competitor himself. Rumour has it that he is under the thumb of his eccentric wife, but I believe it is merely that she indulges in activities which oblige him to explain, then apologize, to those she offends. He is a very kind, intelligent man whom the soldiers all love and respect, but there is little chance of his being dominated by Amelia Mason. He tolerates her exceptional behaviour with commendable restraint due, so I have heard, to the fact that theirs was the great love match of the day. The daughter of Lord Grievey, she was a famous beauty — although one can hardly believe it now — and he was the impossibly handsome son of an apothecary. He is still most striking in appearance.'

There was a silence, so Elizabeth asked, 'Why not Lady Mason?'

A curiously intense expression clouded Fanny's face and even her voice sounded bleak as she said, 'She lost all three of her children when they were infants. One was carried off by cholera, another simply pined away for the brother she had lost. The third was kicked to death after straying from his ayah's care to wander in the horse-lines. Their mother lost her reason for a while, they say, then emerged from the state to indulge in a frenzy of good works.' Twisting her hands in her lap she added, 'George finds her experience a vindication of his belief that children should not be born or brought into a foreign land and exposed to fevers, disease and the danger of conflict. He insists that any man should be alive enough to his responsibilities not to sire infants unless they can be cared for in the bosom of his family in England.'

Having already guessed from her previous conversations that the Humphreys were not blissfully happy, despite their evident devotion toward each other, Elizabeth now had the reason for it: Fanny was eager for children.

'Your husband is probably right,' she said gently. 'I met so many women on the way up from Calcutta who had been forced to make a choice between sending their children to be reared by relatives at home, or leaving their husbands in order to stay with the young ones. I should not care to produce a child only to give it away, which is what one must do, in truth. Nor should I wish to part from my husband for untold years so that I might be with children whom he would not know when he eventually returned.'

She had been speaking of Fanny's dilemma, but her friend took it to be her personal view. Candid eyes looked into hers. 'You have no wish for motherhood?'

Colouring slightly at the misapprehension, Elizabeth was thankful that a stir of activity beside the stand heralded the arrival of the principal guests. Then her heart began to hammer and her cheeks grew warmer still, because the Masons headed a retinue of those officers not competing today. Somewhere among them was a man who had thundered toward her across a Sussex hillside and stolen her happiness. What would he do when they met? She would surely know from his eyes whether or not contempt had replaced love.

The lengthy business of conducting to their front seats the erect white-haired general and a tall slim woman dressed in a green crinoline of astonishing vividness, who wore on her head a purple Marie Antoinette wig, gave Elizabeth time to regain an element of composure. It was not until the senior officers and their wives had taken their places in a cluster around the Masons that the last few men entered to search out any vacant seats. Henry Nicholson made his way to where one of his subalterns was escorting Lucy this morning. The Surgeon, the Paymaster, the Quartermaster and the Veterinary Officer, all considered to be less than true gentlemen by the regular officers, clustered together at the rear of the stand. Then, pushing his way through this group in unceremonious fashion came Rupert. He had John in tow as he made straight for two empty seats behind Elizabeth and Fanny, greeting the former exuberantly.

'Good morning. What a perfectly splendid day for racing, although Hugh rides superbly whatever the weather.'

Fanny turned to smile at him. 'Good morning, Mr Carruthers. We shall doubtless have the pleasure of watching you emulate your brother at our next meeting.'

'I intend to enter into cantonment life with the greatest zest, ma'am,' he responded jovially, 'but I shall never emulate Hugh successfully. He is unbeatable on the flat. I cannot wait to see him carry off the Gold Cup this morning.'

'You have not yet seen my husband or Captain Delacourt in competition,' she teased gently. 'They will offer a formidable challenge.' As the men edged along the row to come up behind them, she greeted John with a curious touch of reserve before adding in formal tones, 'I am sorry you were obliged to withdraw your entry due to injury, Captain Stavenham. Are you fully recovered yet, sir?'

'Yes, indeed. It was a very slight wound, ma'am,' he told her in the cool tone he had used toward Elizabeth when he had first met her in England. The sound of his familiar voice accelerated her heartbeat even further. She had not dared to look at him yet, but she must within

144

the next few moments and be compelled to act as a stranger. How would he respond?

Rupert touched her lightly on the shoulder. 'Elizabeth, may I present Captain Stavenham who has risen from his sickbed only this morning in order to watch Hugh race and win?'

Their glances finally met across the three feet separating them. She turned cold. His eyes were dark with shock and a muscle moved convulsively in his tight jaw as he gave the barest nod of greeting. He looked so different in a scarlet Dragoon jacket and tall black shako, so utterly unapproachable.

Rupert continued with gusto, unaware of the constraint between them. 'Hugh says he is a capital fellow who knows a great deal about India, having served for more than ten years out here. I hope to learn all I can from him, Elizabeth. Hugh says . . .'

Elizabeth could stand the strain no longer, and broke into Rupert's report on his brother's excellent advice to say to the man she had last seen walking from the kitchen of Walnut Tree Cottage, 'Please accept my apology for turning you out of your quarters, Captain Stavenham. The matter was taken out of my hands, I fear.'

'I was happy to vacate them, ma'am.' His tone was impersonal, the words stilted and icy. Having said them he looked away, across the track to where the officers were assembling at the starting post in readiness for the first race. Elizabeth's heart pounded so heavily she felt sick. This, then, was how it would be in the days, weeks, years to come. How long would it take before she could face him without feeling this present pain? How much time would pass before she could hold a conversation with this hostile stranger and forget that she had ever known him as a beloved friend? Destiny had much to answer for.

The jockeys' silk shirts in vivid colour combinations brightened the scene further. It was a morning of thrills, free spirits, and friendly but intense rivalry: it was a pretence, a conjuring trick to bring England close enough to blot out for just a few hours a barren plain with an ancient city which signified an alien culture. The Indians danced up and down with the excitement of it all, and old soldiers bawled encouragement to their own commanders whilst attempting to drown the shouts of their rivals. The spectacle of thoroughbreds thundering around a course, close on each other's heels, created general elation. Soldiers' wives or mistresses squealed with delight; the officers' ladies simply gripped the handles of their sunshades tightly as they leaned forward with shining eyes to watch the progress of a husband, or any other jockey who had taken their fancy.

Elizabeth sat erect and still throughout. She heard none of the cheering; saw little but a blur of colour as race succeeded race. That foreknowledge of unhappiness mixed with pain, which had overwhelmed her on first seeing Ratnapore, was fully explained, for both sensations filled her now.

Hugo won the Gold Cup with ease on his prime racing thoroughbred, Garth. William came third, behind a young officer of Kingsford's Horse. George Humphrey won a crystal bowl in another race, and two other Forrester's competitors carried off prizes at the end of the meeting. The track lay empty beneath the midday sun; the spectators were drifting away in funds or in debt. Troops were brawling abusively. Women in torn and grubby dresses were kicking and screaming in a vindictive tussle while their menfolk looked on and placed bets on the outcome of *that*. The Indians who had managed to win a few rupees on the races hurried off to the Native Bazaar. The stand began to empty slowly after the guests of honour had been conducted from their seats.

A large marquee had been placed beside the course where the officers and their wives could supplement an early breakfast with tea and a selection of tempting items such as wafer-thin ham on scones, Cambridge sausages, slices of pie, eggs and dainty squares of buttered toast. It was here that they all gathered to await the competitors, who had gone to their quarters to change before returning. As William, and George Humphrey were among them, Rupert very naturally fell in beside Elizabeth to offer her his arm, and John had no choice but to offer the same courtesy to Fanny. Over the sound of Rupert's eager post-mortem on the result of the Gold Cup race, Elizabeth occasionally caught snatches of conversation between the pair behind them. Fanny's light, jerky comments appeared to meet with very brief replies from her escort. The men found seats for them then departed to fetch tea.

'A very dour sort of person,' confided Fanny, once they were out of earshot. 'You will recall I said much the same of him at our first meeting. Yet George is full of admiration since he led them safely home from the patrol and will hear no criticism of the man from anyone.' She leaned closer as John and Rupert turned their way with cups in their hands. 'Mrs Merrybanks has a niece married to a cornet in Chetwynde's.' Her lace-mittened hand rested on Elizabeth's sleeve as she leaned even closer, so that her words would not be heard by the subject of them as he approached. 'There was a wife eight years ago. The niece mentioned an awkward political and military rumpus over her curious disappearance. The mystery remains. The affair blighted his career and made him bitter. I heard this only a month ago and tried just now to make allowances for his curt manner, but he really does not help one to be civil. I thought him almost rude toward you when Mr Carruthers presented him. It is too bad of him. We cannot be blamed for his unhappiness.'

The last sentence was made in almost a whisper, for the men had practically reached them. But as both Fanny and she were looking right at John, he must have known that he was under discussion. His mouth tightened further as he handed Fanny her tea and she coloured beneath his silent reproach.

'There is a most imaginative selection of things to eat,' declared Rupert happily. 'I promise you I shall make no complaint here, Elizabeth.'

Somehow she forced a smile. 'I am pleased to hear it.' Turning to Fanny, she said, 'You should know that Mr Carruthers and I fell out more than once during our tedious journey over his habit of telling the managers of various establishments that he would not offer their food to his dogs, much less eat it himself. It was not that I did not appreciate his discerning palate — the meals really were quite inedible — but there was no alternative dish and we did not endear ourselves to those who could make or mar our comfort in the middle of the desert.'

Fanny looked up at Rupert. 'Dear me, how courageous of you to offend such people.'

'That was nothing to his courage when the horses bolted,' she continued, conscious of John's scrutiny but carefully avoiding his gaze as she related to Fanny the story of the runaway van.

Rupert cut her short in diffident manner. 'No, really, it was the merest effort, not in the least to be compared with the deeds of Captain Stavenham and his patrol four days ago.'

Risking a deliberate confrontation, Elizabeth turned her face up to John. 'You have been alert to growing aggression for some time, I believe, sir.'

He appeared to struggle with himself as he looked back at her with growing contempt. Covering her gaffe in speaking of something he had told her at Wellford, she made the situation even more uncomfortable by lying. 'My husband told me of your views after hearing of the attack you suffered on the day of my arrival.'

'Indeed,' he murmured, in a manner which effectively closed the subject.

A waiter arrived before them, carrying a selection of dainty items to eat with their tea. Fanny took a biscuit and some toast. Elizabeth declined. She would never succeed in swallowing anything through her tight throat. The arrival of some of the competitors, very spruce in their fresh uniforms, caused a distraction and some regrouping of the noisy crowd within the marquee. George Humphrey spotted his wife as he entered and crossed to the refreshment table. She excused herself in order to go to him with her congratulations and, almost immediately, Rupert's brother appeared. Hailed by him and beckoned to join them, Sir Hugo charmingly escaped those flocking to his side and made his way across. Elizabeth was forced to admit that he cut a very dashing, impressive figure, as handsome as Rupert but in a more mature style.

'You were splendid,' cried Rupert catching at his hand and pumping it up and down. 'The masterly way in which you held Garth around that final bend, then gave him his head along the winning stretch.'

'Thank you, dear boy, but your praise is far too fulsome, as usual.' Blue eyes turned toward Elizabeth. 'Ma'am, my rascal of a brother has spoken with such admiration of your many qualities and cursed the circumstances which have prevented him from presenting me to you, but now the opportunity to do so has arrived all he can do is prattle of racing.' With an elegant bow he went on, 'I present myself to you, Mrs Delacourt, and venture to express my real admiration of any lady who could withstand Rupert's company day in, day out, without being laid low by exhaustion.'

Elizabeth was totally charmed by the mischievous twinkle in his eyes and the absence of any hauteur in his voice, as there often was in Rupert's. 'Exhaustion was never a threat, sir,' she told him with an answering smile. 'It was the prospect of meeting such a paragon as Sir Hugo Carruthers which frequently gave me palpitations.'

Hugo laughed delightedly. 'Ma'am, I am sure you very soon divined that the boy is prone to the worst excesses of exaggeration. I confess I have shrunk from this meeting for fear of seeing the greatest disappointment in your expression on discovering the truth. However, I find my brother did not exaggerate in the least when speaking of you. May I hope the friendship you extended toward him might also be offered to me?'

148

'Nothing would give me greater pleasure,' she said sincerely, conscious of Rupert's fatuous pride over her response to this man he revered above all others.

There was a movement beside her as John said, 'If you'll excuse me.'

'Don't go,' instructed Hugo as he turned away. 'I think we might seize our chance this morning, don't you? I hear General Mason is deeply concerned over the events of last Tuesday and has expressed a desire to hear the details from you. It's too good an opportunity to miss, I feel.'

John nodded rather stiffly, and the other man looked surprised. 'I expected more enthusiasm from you on the subject. It's what you've been waiting for, isn't it?' Looking closely at him, Hugo then asked, 'Are you all right? I must say you look very groggy still.'

At that moment a young officer on the General's staff approached to tell Hugo that the Masons wished him to present his young brother. The summons could not be ignored, so they went off with a promise to return as soon as possible. John was unable to walk away, leaving Elizabeth so obviously deserted, which meant they had to maintain a pretence of politeness in order to avoid the curious glances which a silent pair in the midst of social jollity would have attracted. As John made no attempt to open a conversation, Elizabeth was forced to speak first.

'This is an intolerable situation for us both. The only redeeming facet of it is that I have the opportunity to give you the explanation you deserve.'

He looked right through her as he replied harshly, 'I believe there is nothing whatever that you could say which would interest me, ma'am.'

Restricted by their public situation, and wounded by his contemptuous attitude, she begged, 'Please don't condemn me unheard.'

'Why should any man but your husband condemn you?' he returned.

Trying not to betray her feelings to those around her, she struggled to assume a bland expression as she said painfully, 'I know what you must think of me now but . . .'

'You are right, ma'am,' he interjected icily, 'and I must tell you that your presence in Ratnapore bears out my poor opinion of you. Haven't you caused Delacourt enough harm without coming here to ruin what is left of his honour?'

Fighting for control, she cried softly, 'I don't understand.'

'I think you understand well enough,' he snapped. 'It was easy to betray him when he was six thousand miles away, but it will be dangerous to do so here. Having snared that boy on your journey, I see you are now starting your game with Sir Hugo. Have a care what you are about, or his career, along with Delacourt's and any others concerned, will be over.'

Appalled by his inferences, she cried softly, 'I can't believe you mean what you say; can't believe you are the same person.'

'I am not. Thank God, I am not,' he retorted savagely. 'So if you plan to dangle me on a string once more, you must think again. Gossiping of your conquests to Mrs Humphrey — oh yes, it was all too clear what you were doing a while ago — is liable to be dangerous. The slightest misjudgement on your part will lead to Delacourt's downfall as well as mine. There are some rules which should never be broken. Every man knows that. Being unaware of breaking them is no excuse; censure is equally severe.'

His departure from Sussex had caused her infinite pain. What he inflicted on her now was far worse. She hit out.

'You were right to call this a sweet and savage land. Arriving here and seeing all those things you had described to me was sweet indeed, John. You have just shown me the savage aspect.'

For an instant she glimpsed a hint of uncertainty in his grim expression, a faint questioning in his eyes, but an instant was all she was allowed before their intimacy was broken.

'My dear, I apologize for being so tardy in joining you,' said William as he came up to them. 'Norseland had begun to cast a shoe. I had to see the Farrier. Good-day, Stavenham. You missed some capital sport this morning, especially in that third race when Danby was unseated. Damme if I've ever seen a fellow roll clear so swiftly.' He frowned. 'You still look fearfully rough, if I may say so. Is the heat in this confounded marquee affecting you?'

John shook his head. 'No, it's the shock of seeing you come third in the Gold Cup race. Forgive me, I must congratulate Humphrey on his success.'

With a stiff bow in Elizabeth's direction, he walked off. After watching his progress for a moment or two, William turned to her to say, 'Strange fellow. Never quite certain how to take him. Hadn't upset him, had you? You both looked rather strained as I approached.'

'As you remarked, the heat in this "confounded marquee" is affecting us all,' she managed in reply. 'Must we stay?'

'Of course we must stay. I've only just arrived, and you must be presented to General and Lady Mason. I'll fetch some more tea. It'll revive you a little.' Any suggestion of solicitousness was destroyed by his next remark. 'Bear in mind that I have yet to live down the embarrassment of your sudden arrival. It will be of no help to me if I have to present to them a wilting, lifeless wife.'

It was half an hour later before William was given the nod to come forward. By then, Elizabeth had conquered the worst of her distress and no longer felt that those surrounding her must have heard John's every word. She approached Lady Mason with a semblance of composure, though she could not help recalling his laughing comment in Wellford that she would find an ally in this eccentric campaigner for the rights of the common soldier. The General was still extremely handsome, she discovered. He smiled winningly as he bowed to Elizabeth and declared that officers were choosing younger and younger wives to charm the jaded eyes of those who had been too long away from home. Then Amelia Mason looked her over critically, taking so long over her scrutiny, William grew visibly uncomfortable.

'You are the young woman who arrived on your husband's doorstep without warning, are you not?' she asked in a surprisingly quiet voice.

The astonishing purple wig and the bright green dress, coupled with a reputation for braving even the Governor without standing on ceremony, had led Elizabeth to expect a vibrant, overwhelming tone and an aggressive manner. However, despite the unconventional frankness of the question, it was delivered in purely conversational tones. It was what William had dreaded, but it was useless to avoid the truth.

'Yes, ma'am. The regiment had departed from Calcutta before the letter written by my husband's father could reach him. I appear to have travelled faster than the mail for it still has not arrived.'

'It most probably never will. Many of my own letters fail to reach the intended recipients . . . so I am informed,' she added with a twitch of her lips. 'How commendable of you to decide that your place is out here by your husband's side. I made that same resolution as a young wife and have kept it all these years. It must have taken a deal of courage to set out for India alone, and then to embark on the unique but deplorably slow additional journey up to the Punjab. I have written to the Queen about the building of a railway through India — it would save those poor men from covering every mile on foot — but it must be another of those letters which have gone astray.' She gave a wry smile. 'I would write to her on the subject of the extremely unreliable mail service except that I should have to take the letter by my own hand to be certain of it reaching her.'

Warming to her, and feeling that her only eccentricity, apart from her appearance, was to say what she thought, Elizabeth smiled back. 'Mr Carruthers believes that man will fly one day. Until that miracle occurs, perhaps you should try attaching your messages to the leg of a bird trained to return to the Governor, or to Her Majesty. Birds, ma'am, are rarely mislaid.'

Amelia Mason turned to her husband. 'Don't you think that a splendid notion, my dear? Hawks might be a great deal more reliable than your military gallopers.' Without waiting for a reply, and clearly expecting none from him, she turned back to William. 'I like your wife, Captain Delacourt. How fortunate you are to have chosen one who is resourceful and intelligent, beside being delightfully pretty. I wonder that you could have been so foolish as to leave her in England.' Rendering him acutely embarrassed, she addressed herself to Elizabeth again. 'You are just the person I need to help in my campaign to improve conditions for the miserable wretches who are expected to fight on our behalf. There are so many problems to overcome and your lively young mind will offer fresh solutions.'

She then embarked on a long monologue concerning one of her most favoured good causes, oblivious of William's fatuous and dazed expression and of the resentment such prolonged discussion with the new arrival instilled in those who had received no more than an uninterested nod from the General's lady. The miseries endured by the rank and file had for a long time been the basis of Lady Mason's campaign to improve the worst aspects of regimental life, in particular that of the wives, who were forced to conduct their married lives behind a curtain which divided a small section of the long barrack room from the living space of the single men. There, they begat and gave birth to their children, and there they were forced to bring them up, amidst the profane and drunken troops.

The General's wife was not one of the short-sighted people who condemned the soldier, then forgot him; she had taken the trouble to discover that he was never given the opportunity to be much more than a calculating drunkard, and had set about installing a few decent facilities for the rank and file. These in no way satisfied her, but she was dealing with bigoted officials and, for the time being, had had to content herself with the good response the troops had made to her new canteens, which served non-alcoholic drinks and nourishing snacks.

The next projects on her list were the station hospital which was disgracefully ill-equipped, and the provision of separate living quarters for the married men. Medical supplies would be difficult to obtain and she envisaged a long struggle before they were forthcoming, she confided to Elizabeth, but she had her eye on some store huts which could easily be cleared for use as quarters for the six families in Forrester's Light Dragoons. She had heard that Trooper Donegal had died this week leaving a widow and two small boys, but the woman had already married the first man who offered to take her on, and thus kept her place on the station. There was no hope for her, or her children, otherwise.

At the end of this long speech, Lady Mason gave Elizabeth a radiant smile which supported Fanny's claim that she had been the reigning beauty of her day. The tragic deaths of her three children might have robbed the woman of her looks and tampered with her sanity, but she was full of a compassion and awareness which made most of the residents of Ratnapore seem artificial in comparison. How right John was to admire her, and how perceptive he had been to realize that Elizabeth would find a kindred spirit in her. At that thought, she could no longer resist turning to where he stood with several other officers. For a moment, understanding trembled on the brink of their intercepting glances, then Elizabeth's attention was drawn back to her companion by a deliberate question which demanded an answer.

'Mrs Lakeland has promised to come to my bungalow tomorrow to hear my plans. Will you accompany her? May I depend upon your support, Mrs Delacourt?'

'Of course, ma'am. When I was first told of the deplorable conditions the men of the regiment are expected to endure I protested that something should be done. It seemed likely that only a female voice might be heeded. Naturally I shall give you my wholehearted support.'

William was satisfaction personified for the rest of the morning; the evident resentment of some ladies whose ambitions for their husbands were all too obvious only added to his state. They returned to their bungalow soon after midday and went to their separate rooms for their usual afternoon rest. Elizabeth lay for a long time chasing temporary escape from the strain of the morning, but could see nothing but John's bitter expression, hear nothing but his icy words of contempt. Yet there had been an instant when . . .

Her tormented thoughts were interrupted by the sound of her door opening gently to admit William in almost stealthy manner. His naked body was wrapped in a sheet toga-wise, his bare feet made no sound above

153

the squeak of the swaying punkah above her head. The very mode of his entry suggested the reason for it, and everything within her cried a protest. Not now; not on this particular morning.

'I have a bad headache, William,' she told him clearly and firmly. 'I must ask you to let me rest quietly.'

He was beside the bed now and looking down with a determination she well recalled. 'Of course you have a headache, my dear. I have neglected you since you arrived, but only through a misunderstanding. That damned missing letter! I did not realize the true reason for your actions until Amelia Mason made it clear. I maligned you, Elizabeth. You really did come all this way out of devotion to your husband. Now I must reward you for it.'

The hint of mockery in his voice was enough to tell her that his satisfaction over Lady Mason's interest in her was overlaid with resentment of her ability to arouse it when he could not.

'I am pleased that the misunderstanding is at an end,' she told him in impersonal tones, 'but the heat and noise this morning has taken its toll on my constitution, so I must ask you to reward me with sleep and solitude. I have only recently concluded a most exhausting journey to reach you, don't forget.'

Sitting on the side of the bed, he allowed the sheet to drop away, as he said, 'Young Carruthers is full of praise for your sturdy constitution, which apparently allowed you to keep him fully entertained for four and a half months. Your devotion to me should surely overcome a mere headache.' Putting a hand on the ribbons at her throat, he added seductively, 'You were always very beguiling in a lace wrap.'

She put her hand over his fingers which pulled at the satin bow and tried once more to avoid something which she could not welcome right now.

'Please, William, I have asked you to let me rest.'

His mouth tightened. 'And I told you at the outset that you must submit to the demands of life by my side. I did not ask you to come, but now you are here I am making the best of the fact. You played your part of dutiful wife very well this morning. Now you will continue to play it to please me.'

Before she could move or speak, he rolled across her and began to drag the flimsy wrap from her shoulders. He had always been very swift in passion. A large man and very strong, it was impossible to fight him. Silent and selfish during the ritual, he had never aroused in her more

154

than acquiescence. But neither had he hurt or disgusted her. Today, however, she lay enduring his grunts and thrusts, humiliated by his impersonal use of her body. William probably thought her tears were a result of joy at their union, but they continued long after he lay satisfied and snoring beside her.

John and Hugo rode out at seven a.m. with half a troop of men behind them and headed across the plain toward the city of Ratnapore. Once they had left the vicinity of the cantonments, the two officers relaxed and chatted about the weekend just passed. Hugo's suggestion that they should tackle General Mason about a confrontation with Ganda Singh had brought a positive response, in that he had told Lakeland that strong words in the Sirdar's ear would be timely. He ruled that two officers, backed by a contingent of their largest, most aggressive-looking troopers, should be sent to arrange a meeting without delay. Hugo's social consequence plus John's linguistic ability to communicate with a man he already knew were considered to be the ideal combination. The men with them today were as fearsome a bunch as General Mason could wish.

Sunday had been quiet after the thrills and excesses of the races, but it was of the Saturday night that Hugo spoke as he glanced slyly across at John.

'When I told you four days ago that Lakeland would like you better if you committed a few sins, I did not mean that you should rise from your sick bed and immediately break your own rule of drinking only in moderation. I have seldom seen a man go to the devil as speedily as you did in the Mess after the race-meeting.'

John groaned. 'I would sooner have Lakeland hate me for life than go through that experience again. Throughout yesterday I had four heads which swayed about trying to match up into one. They didn't succeed until evening. A fine friend you were!'

Hugo looked hurt. 'My dear fellow, you came in looking like a man who had been cut down from the gallows and asked for a full bottle of brandy. As you couldn't join in the general fun and games without splitting open that wound in your back, the kindest thing I could do was to help put you away as speedily as possible. I might remind you that I made myself responsible for putting you safely to bed.'

'Thank you for that, at least.'

They rode for a minute in silence, then Hugo said pointedly, 'She is a damned attractive woman. You will not be the only man on this station who suddenly finds his single state unbearable. But I would recommend drink as the better of the two evils. I don't relish scraping your brains from the floor at dawn one day.'

John looked straight ahead as his throat began to tighten up. 'You are incredibly observant, Hugo . . . more than others, I trust.' He paused for a time, then said, 'There is another alternative you haven't mentioned. I could train a horse to be faster than Garth. I should then be perfectly willing to scrape *your* brains from the floor after I have taken the Gold Cup off you.'

His friend laughed. 'What an incorrigible fellow you are. I offer advice and it's met with a challenge. The day you beat me in a race I shall be glad to put a pistol to my head, for I shall be infirm.'

John rode on silently, watching the distant domes of the city which shimmered in the early heat rising from the plain. But the vision soon faded beneath that of a girl in a delicate pink crinoline which had put all others in the shade. She had been even more vivid and exciting than he had remembered, and it had come as a shock to see her in a soft filmy romantic dress. Eleven months of bitterness had built in his mind the picture of a harlot in shiny satin, with bold eyes and an upthrusting voluptuous body. Instead, she had looked fragile and deeply moved by their encounter. For a while he had been deceived into forgetting that she had been so treacherous, but had collected himself in time to prevent a fatal betrayal of his feelings. He was still irrevocably drawn to her; still possessed by the deep sense of rapport which had sprung instantly between them in Wellford. Seeing her with Delacourt who claimed her as his wife, with Rupert Carruthers who claimed her as his dear friend, and with Hugo who had swiftly succumbed to her talent for charming men, he had burned with jealousy. It made no difference that she had very obviously been discussing him with Fanny Humphrey —God only knew what she had been whispering in that woman's ear — or that she had attempted to continue the game she had played with him in Wellford. Try as he might, the passion which had ruled him in England was as strong as it had ever been, and he had willingly tortured himself by watching her covertly throughout that morning. Hugo was astute and had reached a perceptive conclusion within a dismayingly short time. John hoped to God he could hide the truth more successfully during the coming ordeal of weeks, months and years in her company.

His introspection ended when they reached the dry, wide nullah which split the ground so that the track to the city curved in a long detour around it. Hugo mopped the perspiration from his face with a silk handkerchief as he nodded toward the deep gash.

'What a cursed country this is. If those things were filled in, it would cut the journey to Ratnapore by an hour, at least.'

'Then the plain would flood during the rains so that we couldn't cross at all,' John retorted with a grin. 'You could always jump it. Such a feat would be a mere nothing for the winner of the Gold Cup.'

Hugo scowled. 'I might call your bluff and try it if this beast I'm riding were a jumper. I chose the most showy piece of flesh in my stable to impress the natives this morning, but he is faint of heart when it comes to hurdles, John. I'll bring my champion steeplechaser next time and confound you by clearing the nullah with feet to spare.'

'You'll confound everyone, man. That watercourse is wider than it looks and a man would have to be desperate to risk his life by attempting to clear it.'

Hugo cast him a sidelong glance. 'When the Divine Delacourt teases your senses too unbearably, there is another alternative I had not thought of, dear boy.'

Two hours after setting out, they reached the gates of Ratnapore and passed beneath the low arch to enter. The daily life of the inhabitants was well under way so the British contingent negotiated the narrow streets with difficulty, pushing through the throng on their tall horses which inspired more interest and admiration than did the scarlet-coated Dragoons. The palace was situated on the eastern side of the city, by the river which flowed alongside the main thoroughfare. To call any of the baked mud lanes 'a thoroughfare' was elevating it beyond the truth, but the way to Ganda Singh's stronghold lay along one wider than the rest, which was lined by the houses of the council members. This made it the principal road of the city.

To reach it, the Dragoons had to ride through long stretches of bazaars which rang with vendors' cries, forcing their way past mules so heavily laden that the route was almost blocked from wall to wall. Small offshoots from these paths led to houses of mud-sealed stone with flat roofs. If the eye was quick enough, it was possible to catch a glimpse of dark-eyed women who ducked down after a swift peep at the soldiers who rode so proudly through their city.

John had seen it all many times. Hugo had paid just one visit to a place he afterward vowed would not interest anyone save a starving man, and then only if he were blind. The troopers had never seen inside the city, which was out of bounds to them, and were open-mouthed as they rode through it. The patrol had only ever escorted the caravans as far as the gates before wheeling to the north for the long winding road back to the cantonments. It was therefore fascinating to see finally what lay behind the thick stone walls which enclosed the people their regiment was there to defend. There had been stalls and bazaars and dark-eyed women in Calcutta, but it was six months since they had left that first barracks. It did them good to see a bit of life outside the restrictions of the station.

The entrance to the palace was through yet another gateway into a courtyard where the small party came to a halt in regimental fashion. With some thought for his men, who must wait while negotiations were conducted, Hugo chose a shady part of the courtyard, before relinquishing his mount to a waiting native groom. His consideration did not go unappreciated by those who wished they could also go inside the palace to witness the treasures reputed to be there.

The two officers trod through an archway to where the poverty, drabness and din of the streets were replaced by extensive gardens filled with blossoms, sun-ripened fruits which tempted the visitors to pick and enjoy them, and a dazzle of crystal waterfalls, fountains and ornamental pools. Exotic fowl strutted the mosaic paths through the gardens, and cages filled with a rainbow of small birds provided sweet and harsh songs to break the incredible tranquillity enclosed by the walls of the Sirdar's palace. They had entered a paradise within a festering sprawl of human habitation.

'The man has taste, you must allow,' murmured Hugo, as he took in the pure beauty of successive formal gardens and courtyards where marble ornaments and beasts abounded between gigantic jars from Persia and beyond.

'Wait until we go inside,' John told him. 'The halls grow in magnificence as one progresses, until it seems nothing could be more ornate and splendid, but they are certain to be nothing in comparison with the Sirdar's private chambers. Only his vizier and bodyguards can enter those hallowed walls.'

'To say nothing of his ladies, eh?'

John nodded. 'Of course. No one knows how many he has.'

'No danger of Ganda Singh blowing his brains out over just one, in that case,' came the sly thrust from a man who could not know how much pain his teasing caused.

They reached latticed doors which swung open at their approach. Their progress through the five halls was marked only by the ring of their spurred boots on the magnificent inlaid floors, for even officers of Queen Victoria's army must be awed into silence by the gold, amber, quartz and lapis lazuli decorations which stunned the beholder with their vivid patterns of colour. Finally, they reached an audience chamber hung with rich silks, satins and brocades from Samarkand and filled with the fragrance of many spices. John knew this room well and had warned Hugo that the heavy scents were opiates which not only dulled a man's wits but induced a sensation of great goodwill toward others.

A robed official appeared as if from nowhere and an elaborate ritual of greetings and introductions then had to be followed. Once that was completed, John stated that he wished for a short meeting with his old friend the Vizier. The man departed and the two officers waited silently. The waiting time varied according to the rank or importance of the visitors. John and Hugo came very low on the scale so were obliged to stand for some minutes, inhaling the pungent aromas designed to turn enemies into involuntary friends before the talks began. His head starting to swim, John found himself thinking of Hugo's remark concerning Elizabeth. He pictured her in that lovely soft pink gown, then imagined how she would respond when he began to remove it with gentle caressing hands. His body grew hotter than ever in his skintight uniform as his imagination pursued the mental seduction further. His throat began to move convulsively as it grew dry, and his hands clenched at his sides.

The draperies parted at that moment to show the Vizier resplendent in flowing silks which exceeded the hangings in brilliance and quality, and John found himself using the most elaborate words of greeting to this man he knew of old as a cunning, clever and manipulative advisor to Ganda Singh. Now he hailed him as a cherished friend on whom he bestowed the greatest affection and respect. The Vizier did likewise. Only after a great many words in the same vein, which followed the gushing greetings, did John broach the subject about which he had come. Half an hour after entering the palace gates, he received the information that His Excellency would be honoured to receive Colonel Lakeland on the following Thursday morning. Highly affectionate

159

farewells were expressed, and John turned, almost dreamily, to walk back beside a lethargic Hugo through a paradise he was now reluctant to leave. The delights induced by Ratnapore seemed irresistible when compared with the loneliness of his plain-walled, spartan bungalow which Elizabeth could never enter.

When they emerged through the inner gates, the waiting troopers gave a united sigh of relief and eased their stiff muscles as they prepared to move off. The two officers mounted in an almost trance-like state, and gently pulled their horses into a right wheel. The small procession turned smartly through the arched entrance and prepared to push its way back through the dusty, clamorous city. The din seemed doubly distressing to John's amorous thoughts. He found his feelings of goodwill turning to fury towards those who were breaking up his inner peace. Blaspheming loudly, he allowed his charger to nudge individuals from his path in very rough manner, and he even kicked at one deliberately unheeding merchant who was blocking his path. Bad temper came on the heels of affection, causing him to loathe every single inhabitant of Ratnapore as he rode through it. Only when the city was well behind them, and the silence of the plains descended to replace the raucous sounds of the streets, did John feel able to glance across at Hugo in something approaching his normal mood.

'How do you feel, friend of mine?' he asked somnolently.

'Damn thirsty,' came Hugo's heavy reply. 'Do they never offer visitors a drink?'

'Oh yes, but one has to make a prolonged visit to warrant one. By their standards we were simply making a passing call.' He rode on for a moment or two, then asked, 'How did that room affect you, by the way?'

Hugo moved his head lethargically and gave a slow wink. 'That is something I intend to keep to myself, friend of mine.'

The sun was boring down on their backs now that it had risen fully, and John felt the sweat running from beneath the rim of his shako to mist his eyes. Atmospheric mirages made the plain move and dance, so that it was possible to imagine that the stunted trees and the boulders were spinning around like skaters on a shimmering, frozen lake. Still heavy-headed from the effects of the perfumes, he was unaware, at first, of a dark shadow which really was on the move. It was some time before his aching eyes saw that the shadow was really a large body of horsemen approaching across the plain from the west. Their paths would cross some four miles from the cantonments.

'Tribesmen,' he said to Hugo, nodding toward the riders. 'They must be heading for the pass on their way to Peshawar.'

'For a durbar, or something of that nature. There must be about fifty of them.'

'All of that,' agreed John.

They rode on, swaying in their saddles as the horses made their slow and steady way along the dust road. John felt no sense of alarm, but he kept watch on the other travellers of the plain through half-closed lids. Their own small party had been seen, it was evident from the behaviour of the riders. Only when half the distant group broke away and began circling on a course which would bring them up behind the military contingent did he say quietly to Hugo, 'I don't like the look of what's happening out there. When we reach the horseshoe bend we shall be covered in front and in the rear by those two bands.'

Hugo gave him a look of surprise. 'Why would they want that? You're not suggesting that they have any notion of attacking us, are you? It must be perfectly plain we are not on any kind of active duty. Why, we haven't even a full troop behind us.'

'Just so,' said John under his breath so that the men would not hear. 'We are twelve, which makes us hopelessly outnumbered by them. If they are armed with guns we should all be killed before drawing near enough to attack with our sabres. We haven't a carbine between us.'

The tribesmen had broken into a gallop, but the two officers continued at a walk, leading their column while they studied the situation a little longer. It was abundantly clear that the galloping men were not heading for the pass, but for them.

'Do you still believe they have no intention of attacking?' asked John urgently. 'I know these people well enough to recognize this approach as aggressive. They do not charge forward in such manner to welcome fellow travellers, believe me. We stand no chance out here, but if we could lure them nearer to the cantonments we should be seen by the piquets who would send out reinforcements. We could then make a decent fight of it.'

'How do you propose to achieve that?' asked Hugo. 'If you are right, we shall be caught on that horseshoe bend with no hope of running for home.'

'I agree. There's only one way of avoiding their trap,' said John quietly, 'and that is to risk the jump across the nullah.'

Hugo studied him hard for a moment or two. 'It would be a

tremendous risk, you know. However, I think they *are* going to attack at that bend — why they should and who they are is a complete mystery to me — so I'll agree with your plan to attempt the nullah as the lesser of two certain dangers.' Gathering up his reins, he said urgently, 'You lead, John. You know the lie of the land better than any of us. I'll bring up the rear in case we are forced to stand and make a fight of it.'

So saying, he wheeled, leaving John to tell the astonished men the situation and how they planned to deal with it. Speed being the priority, John wasted no time in giving the order to gallop and spurred his horse forward at the start of the desperate dash. Bending low over the beast which went like the wind, he watched to see how the tribesmen would react. However, having left the defined track, clouds of dust flew up, coating his damp face and blinding his eyes. Blinking made the irritation worse, so he dashed a hand across them to clear his vision. It was essential to see the nullah in time to warn the men and to gather his own horse for the jump. With his eyes watering, he tried to rake the ground ahead as best he could whilst careering over the soft loose dust. All at once he saw the place where the level ground dropped away into a deep gash formed by racing water, but which was now a dry rocky ravine.

Yelling a warning over his shoulder as he raised his hand in a signal, he thundered on, trying to assess the exact moment when he should gather his horse into the most exacting jump it had ever attempted. Rubbing at his eyes in a desperate last bid to clear his vision, he realized that he was upon the nullah and it was wider than he had remembered. There was no time to think or be fearful. The ground dropped away as he urged the beast literally to fly. The far bank seemed an eternity away.

They landed short, the horse's hind legs hitting the ground several feet below the rim. Momentum and much valiant scrambling prevented them from slipping to the bottom, then the animal raced on for a hundred yards or more until John reined in, to look over his shoulder for a sight of how the others were faring. His heart was pounding with effort and the urge to reach the cantonment, but he must ensure that all was well before resuming the dash. Through the pall stirred up by their progress he saw three or four troopers emerge like centaurs on Pegasus as they successfully crossed the deep ravine. Others scrambled frantically over the edge after a jump which had fallen short, as John's had. Some had leapt off and were urging their mounts up the remaining few feet with husky commands, fearful that the creatures would fall back. Two men were now on foot, begging a ride from their friends. One by one, the Dragoons drew level with John as his horse danced restlessly. Their faces were coated with dust, but they were clearly elated over what they had done as they witnessed the last two of their number, clawing their way to safety with one horse between them. Some beasts had been abandoned and might be safely dragged out of the nullah later, but they had all done the next to impossible and could not wait to signal the piquets for reinforcements to help them teach the tribesmen a lesson.

Only as he made to turn and resume the race for home did John realize Hugo was no longer with them. 'Where's Major Carruthers?' he demanded hoarsely.

No one seemed to know and the dust was clearing enough to enable them to see there was no sign of life on their side of the nullah. The far side was still obscured by a layer of dust hanging in the air. It seemed ominously quiet now the drum of hoofbeats had ceased. Winging in on a shaft of dread came the recollection of Hugo saying laughingly that he would attempt to jump the nullah if his horse had been capable of it. Why had he not reminded John of the fact when they had discussed the problem of getting home for reinforcements? Had Hugo taken up the rear so that he would hinder no one? John's dread deepened into fear as he swiftly told Corporal Manx to ride as fast as possible to the cantonment, then ordered the other nine men to remain where they were ready to charge, if necessary, while he investigated the nullah. Cantering back to the lip of the ravine, he prayed he would see Hugo at the bottom, pinned beneath his horse or in some other way unable to climb out without assistance. All he saw were three animals lying injured. Dry-throated, his body now pounding with his heavy heart-beat, he had to accept that Hugo was somewhere on the far side at the mercy of the advancing tribesmen.

'Dear God,' he breathed. 'He won't stand a chance alone.'

Turning once more with savage haste, he raced back for fifty yards before pulling so violently on the reins his horse turned on its hind legs. Then, digging in his spurs with cruel force, he dashed toward the nullah once again. The animal had been heroic enough and was not prepared to jump again. It plunged down the steep side until it slipped on shale and fell, pinning John beneath its chestnut flanks. As he lay winded, he heard shouts on the far bank. Driven by fear, he slowly and painfully struggled free, then began to claw his way up the opposite slope.

Reaching the top, he peered through the thinning dust without exposing himself to the sight of anyone who might be there.

His heartbeat almost stilled when he saw Hugo lying where he had been thrown, his right leg almost certainly broken, judging by the angle it formed against his body. As John watched helplessly, the tribesmen reached the spot and began to dismount beside the scarlet-coated officer on the ground. Their leader approached in menacing fashion and shouted at Hugo. When he received no reply, he kicked at the broken leg to bring a cry from the injured man. Struggling into a sitting position, Hugo drew his pistol aggressively, but he never fired it. The Indian drew his sabre with a lightning movement. There was a flash of steel and the gun with Hugo's hand still holding it lay on the ground, while blood pumped from the stump of his arm. A loud cry rose up from the gathered tribesmen and they began to close in.

John felt sick. They were ten against more than fifty: they could only attack on foot from the depths of the nullah with not a single carbine between them. By the time he returned to his men and planned some kind of strategy, his friend would have died a thousand deaths. These people had got torture down to a fine art, so that a victim could be completely mutilated before merciful death. When another frenzied yell arose from the tight circle surrounding the captive, the blood began to thunder in John's head. There was no hope of saving Hugo; no hope of putting an end to his suffering save one. A red mist swam before his eyes as he drew his pistol from its holster and attempted to take aim at the turbanned head of the leader. Desperately steadying the weapon with both hands, he pulled the trigger. The man dropped to the ground and lay still. The remainder swung round in alarm, shouting in the local dialect that reserves must have arrived from the garrison. They began to mount ready for flight, but they were not to be cheated of revenge. Hugo's body was hauled up by two of the horsemen, who clearly planned to tie him with a rope to be dragged behind their galloping animals as they crossed the thorn-covered plain.

Shaking with suppressed sobs, John took aim once more. But, with the barrel pointing at Hugo's head, he found it impossible to pull the trigger. The rope was tied and secured to the saddle of a black stallion. Then, when the owner was about to mount, John's pistol discharged its only other shot. The horse jerked, then crumpled to the dry dusty earth beside the scarlet figure to which it was fastened. A moment of silence followed, but only a moment. The tribesmen began a chorus of fury as they surrounded the body of their captive and leaned from their saddles to slash at it with their long blades until it was no more than a heap of red on the brown earth. When they wheeled to race off, a pall arose to obscure all sign of their retreat.

The nine troopers heard the shots and disobeyed John's orders by returning to the nullah to discover what had happened to their officers. The dust settled in time for them to see Captain Stavenham walking out toward the carcase of a black stallion. He led Major Carruthers' riderless mount. They watched in consternation as he reached the dead animal, unsheathed his sabre, and cut a rope attached to the beast. Then he bent to take up a heavy red bundle, placing it carefully across the Major's saddle before removing his own jacket to cover it. The men's throats constricted as they watched him lead Sir Hugo's thoroughbred back in an almost reverential manner, and their eyes darkened with shock as he drew near enough for them to see his expression. In growing, disbelieving horror, each man began to realize that the red bundle was all that remained of the one person who had failed to jump the nullah.

Chapter Nine

John stumbled in to his quarters, went to the bathroom and was violently sick. He was a soldier by profession, hardened to the sights of a battlefield, but the torture of a helpless victim was a different kind of horror. Somehow he had collected up the dismembered body, strapped it to the horse which had taken fright at the sight of the nullah and brought it back. Somehow he had dismissed the men, reported to General Mason, and handed over the remains of a valued friend. Somehow he had mounted and ridden through the cantonment, minus the jacket still wrapped around the gruesome bundle. Now he began to shake, and the continued retching merely produced pain in his stomach. Heading desperately for his small drinks cabinet, he grabbed the nearest bottle, and pulled out the cork with his teeth before putting the neck of it to his mouth. He drank until the pulsebeat in his head thudded like cannonfire, then his legs buckled to pitch him into a chair where he sat, intending to finish off the contents.

It seemed that nothing would banish the terrible visions, however. They continued to torment his closed eyes until the sound of running footsteps penetrated his shattered senses. The unwelcome visitor ran the length of the verandah and across the hall, and John forced his eyes open in time to see a hand push aside the curtain as someone practically fell into the room. Rupert pulled up, swaying. His chest heaved beneath a shirt drenched with sweat. His face was ashen and working with uncontainable emotion. John sat forward, staring at the boy whom he had forgotten in his own grief. Then he rose, holding the empty bottle by its neck as the low, unsteady voice of insupportable shock accused him.

'You killed him! *You* killed my brother!'

'*No!*' he managed through stiff lips. 'Do you know what happened?'

'I know what you *said* happened,' cried the anguished boy. 'He was the fastest man in the regiment. It's inconceivable that he could have been left behind. Inconceivable!'

John saw it all anew and felt sick to the heart. 'There was nothing I could do. Nothing any of us could do. He was thrown when his horse baulked at the jump.'

'*And no one saw him fall?*' came the incredulous question.

'He was bringing up the rear. By the time we realized . . .'

'Hugh was the senior officer. He would lead. *He would lead,*' Rupert repeated on a sob as tears began to spill down his cheeks. 'You're covering your guilt with lies. I've seen the dust kicked up by a dozen galloping men and I suggest that *anything* could have happened while those with you were blinded by it.'

John stood silent beneath this accusation as the first doubts assailed his chaotic senses. Spectres of self-condemnation rose up on all sides of this demented young man as the savage words continued.

'Everyone knows you're spoiling for a war and will do anything to precipitate it, even this. I won't be the only one to ask why it is that whenever *you* are outside these cantonments, someone with you is killed. But it's never you, is it?' His next words were almost incomprehensible as he added brokenly, 'Hugh was worth more than you can ever be. You should be the obscene pile of flesh I was shown a moment ago. I'll ensure that you pay for this. My chance will come . . . one day. Carry that thought with you from now on.'

With that threat, he flung himself round and stumbled out into the melting pot of noon. John heard a horse departing at the gallop which was forbidden within the confines of the station aside from an emergency. Clear thought was impossible, so it must have been instinct which sent John stumbling across the avenue to the bungalow he had once occupied. Delacourt was Rupert's captain; he was the best person to deal with this. He went directly to the central sitting-room, calling the man's name sharply. William was at home and rose to his feet quickly.

'Good God, man, what's amiss?' he asked, in astonishment at John's unmannerly entrance.

'Hugo . . . Hugo was hideously slaughtered. This morning,' he said with bare control. 'Young Carruthers has just been told. He left me in a state of near insanity. Catch him before he commits some folly.'

'Hugo slaughtered? I don't understand,' exclaimed William in shocked manner, still staring at John as if he were an apparition.

'Go after that boy,' he reiterated desperately. 'I imagine he's making for the nullah . . . where it happened. For God's sake find him.'

Tugging on his discarded shako and jacket, the other man said, 'I still don't understand. *Hugo dead!*'

A movement to his left caught John's attention. A small figure in a cream gown and bonnet stood just inside the doorway. Her expression showed that she must have heard those last words. Taking in John's dishevelled and bloody appearance she asked faintly, 'Can Sir Hugo truly be dead?'

William brushed past her saying, 'Stavenham will tell you.' He left the bungalow, shouting for his horse.

Alone with Elizabeth, John found it impossible to speak. Lucid thought had fled, chased away by words which now came at him in waves of echoing magnitude. *He was the fastest man in the regiment . . . the senior officer . . . would lead . . . spoiling for a war with these people . . . anything to precipitate it. Even this . . . when you are outside . . . someone happens to be killed.* He stood swaying as the images of this terrible morning returned to obscure his present surroundings. He saw that vast open space where heat deceived the eye with thorn bushes which appeared to dance and swirl. Had his eye been deceived by other sights? He saw Hugo's handsome smiling face as he winked while refusing to divulge the thoughts induced by the aromatic drugs they had inhaled. Had his own senses still been influenced by the narcotics to persuade him that something he subconsciously wished for was true? He saw the dust clearing to reveal that just one was no longer with them; just one had been left behind on the far side of a wide and dangerous jump.

'Is it your blood you are wearing, or his?'

The quiet voice broke through the clamouring chorus of guilt like a glide of calm water in the midst of a torrent. He now saw only a blurred vision of a young girl whose amber eyes were bright with unshed tears and who wore an expression of deepest compassion on a face which haunted him. He had to clear his throat in order to speak.

'He was slaughtered by tribesmen. I . . . I brought him in . . . from the plain.'

'Oh, my dear, how very terrible! He was your friend.' Her eyes widened further in distress. '*Rupert!* Dear heaven, this will break him.'

'It has.' He was forced to clear his throat again. 'Delacourt has gone after him.'

'Gone after him . . . where?'

The room was shifting and spinning like the thorn bushes on the plain, and his voice sounded like a distant echo when he said, 'He holds me to blame for his brother's death.'

'How infamous! You could not possibly be to blame,' she cried, putting a gloved hand on his arm. 'John, you are mistaken.'

'I think not,' he mumbled, feeling himself spinning with the room. 'His horse could . . . could not jump. I am . . . I am as guilty as he . . . he claims.'

'No, oh no!' said the beloved voice, with a curious mounting resonance which began to ring in his ears as he fell into blackness.

The savage mutilation and murder of a British officer who had been engaged in carrying a message of friendship between the sirdar and the army pledged to protect him and his people had serious repercussions. General Mason moved swiftly to demand of Ganda Singh the apprehension and punishment of those of his subjects responsible for such barbarism, making it clear that to maintain that the murderers were not from Ratnapore Province would not be deemed an excuse. The attack on the patrol had been seen by the British as the fortunes of war, for the men had been on armed escort duty but the slaughter of an eminent senior officer acting as a diplomatic courier was regarded as an outrage. A staff officer was immediately sent to Headquarters with an urgent dispatch concerning the volatile situation, and the Political Officer was called in from the out-station he was presently visiting.

News of the atrocity raced through the station to create deep burning anger, even in the breasts of those who had been victims of Sir Hugo's aristocratic contempt. In the lines occupied by Forrester's Light Dragoons the men were shocked, aggressive, and roused from their normal apathy. Despite Major Carruthers' view that the rank and file were little more than scarlet-coated machines, he had been much admired by them for his sporting prowess. No one could outride or outshoot him, and his skill with a blade had been known throughout military circles. Sir Hugo had been a true gentleman; his title had brought distinction to the regiment. Each man had been proud to serve under him. So what if he rode at the head of a column as if he were God Almighty. It had only served to make those who followed square their shoulders and straighten in the saddle too. He might be a baronet but the sun was equally hot on his back, the dust choked his throat the same as it did theirs, and cholera threatened him as it did any man. They had admired him more than they did their colonel, for Sir Hugo had had an air about him which commanded respect. Now he was gone, and not one of them could accept the manner of his going.

The ten troopers who had been with him could not tell their comrades exactly what had happened, however. In the dust and confusion nothing had seemed very clear. How the Major had been left behind they could not figure out, nor at what point the Captain had ended his suffering. When they had been drawn back to the nullah by the sound of shots, the tribesmen were away in the distance and the terrible deed had been done. Opinions differed on the sequence of events. One minute they had been riding at an easy pace along the track, the next minute Captain Stavenham had taken command and astonished them all with an order to dash for the cantonments by jumping the nullah. Why the Major had dropped back and allowed a transferred officer to lead them in a highly dangerous manoeuvre was a mystery. It would remain so.

Some men maintained that the Captain had saved them from total massacre, for the tribesmen had surely proved they were bent on killing. Others angrily declared that the Indians had been riding quite peacefully across the plain until their own sudden and astonishing dash for the cantonments and reinforcements had suggested aggression. It was generally known that John Stavenham was spoiling for a fight — men who had earned laurels in one war often urged another to gain more — and it was a sinister coincidence that the only two attacks on the regiment since its arrival in Ratnapore had occurred when that man was riding with them. Gradually, the grudging admiration earned by their ex-Hussar officer over his leadership during the attack on the patrol faded to leave suspicion in some, outright hostility in others. When, as the most senior captain now in the regiment, he was given promotion to major without having to purchase the rank, attitudes toward him hardened further.

Colonel Lakeland's indiscriminate resentment of his officer now found full justification. In a blistering interview which took no account of John's personal stress, the CO spoke his mind over the fact that Sir Hugo's death had been reported direct to General Mason. Beside himself with rage, he had bellowed that any matter concerning his regiment was his concern and his only. How dared John go over his head to the GOC? After five minutes of insults and accusations, John's nerves had snapped. He observed that it was previous incidents which had persuaded him that it was useless to bring any report to a commanding-officer who thought his long service in India made him imagine things. It had seemed vital to save time by going straight to someone who would act on what he reported. Lakeland all but ordered a court martial, but confined himself to vowing to rid the regiment of his insubordinate and opinionated officer as soon as an opportunity for secondment occurred. Meanwhile, there was no alternative but to offer John the vacant majority left by Forrester's most distinguished and highly regarded officer; one whose family had served them honourably back through five generations.

The officers in the cantonment reserved their judgement on the new major, although what was actually known of what had happened out by the nullah suggested a damned odd affair. They held aloof, the only one among them who did not share their doubts being George Humphrey. He had been on that ill-fated patrol and had seen Stavenham in action. No one would persuade him that the man was anything but a brilliant, levelheaded officer; the best the regiment now had.

The funeral was held at five a.m. the following morning with full military honours. Rupert stood as white and still as a corpse himself during the stirring service. He had been given laudanum after William had brought him back from the plain with the aid of Surgeon-Captain Cockerford, and he could well still be under its influence for he stared right through those who ventured to offer condolences at the graveside. The rank and file respected his grief. Sir Hugo's title had passed to the youthful lieutenant and, to a man, they were prepared to offer him the same awed admiration his dead brother had earned. No one spoke to John save George Humphrey. Such public loyalty was considered surprising in view of the fact that the new vacant captaincy had been filled by a junior man who had the purchase price Humphrey could not afford. That alone should have rankled if not the debatable aspects of Sir Hugo's murder.

Elizabeth was deeply disturbed. She had been in Ratnapore for a mere week and had encountered only the savage side of India here. Too close to John in spiritual harmony, she could not forget his chilling acceptance of blame as he had stood in her room, daubed with Hugo's blood. Whatever had occurred on the plain, she was certain he would never have endangered life needlessly. The general belief that he had done so through his personal drive for aggression against an old adversary was as mistaken as it was cruel. When he had collapsed at her feet the day before she had instinctively called her bearer and told him to carry John to the bedroom before bringing water and towels. Giving her a respectful but significant look the Indian had said that he would fetch the Captain-Sahib's bearer, who would carry the sick man to his own bed and tend him there. Only then had she fully realized the penalties of their present situation. She had been forced to watch him carried off to comfortless isolation because a gold band on her finger dictated that she must. It took no account of common compassion for a man in the grip of deep shock, or of the feminine urge to comfort in the way only a woman could. She was another man's wife and must do nothing to tarnish his honour. John himself had told her that. Even so, she was haunted by the evidence of a strong, assured man who had lost heart and hope. That he could have been induced into such self-doubt was indicative of his shattered confidence. For that she held herself fully to blame.

After the funeral, she was so moved by the almost inhuman aspect of both John and Rupert, she confronted William the moment they returned home.

'Do you not consider this business tragic enough without joining the totally unfounded condemnation of a man who must be suffering deeply after witnessing the savage murder of a friend? Rupert blames him only because he must blame someone or go mad, but it is quite unforgivable for the entire station to turn cool toward Captain Stavenham in this manner.'

'*Major* Stavenham,' corrected William dryly. 'He stepped into higher rank very nicely without having to lay out one penny. Very convenient for a man who is known to be frowned upon by the military hierarchy over that business of his disappearing wife, and who has nothing whatever in his pocket.'

'His fortune was absorbed by his late brother's crippling debts, not through gambling or any other dissolute pursuits.'

William coloured angrily, taking the comment as an oblique reference to his failure to settle with Rupert for her travelling costs. Studying her from the hem of her black gown to the jet ornament at her throat, he seized upon the revelation she had let slip.

'You seem remarkably in touch with the man's affairs to speak of his brother's debts. What can you know of them?'

Turning away to remove her bonnet and hide her own giveaway colour, she murmured, 'How does anyone know anything in Ratnapore? They have been talked about, of course.' Swinging back to face him

172

again, she added, 'To suggest that he had an eye to promotion when Sir Hugo was brutally attacked is outrageous, William. I cannot believe that you subscribe to such a wicked notion.'

'It has been known.' he scowled. 'Poor Humphrey should have taken the vacant captaincy, but that jester Philpott has come up with the ready and bought it over his head. I tell you, Elizabeth, I might well have remained a lieutenant forever if Pellamore had not died at Christmas to make me a gift of his rank.'

'Well, I trust you did not stand beside his sick-bed refusing him medicines in order to benefit from his gift.'

'*Elizabeth!*'

'You are naturally shocked . . . and yet you suggest such callous behaviour in a man who once shared these quarters with you. Do you not consider that infamous?'

He was confounded by her argument. It perfectly illustrated his complaint that she had not the admirable qualities of his acquiescent mother and sisters, and he was intensely resentful of being in the position he now found himself. His usual solution at such times was to walk away. He did so now.

'It's growing damnably hot,' he growled, turning toward his bedroom and unfastening his jacket. 'I shall take a sluice before breakfast.'

Going to her own room, she was assisted out of her black bombazine dress and mourning jewellery by her young, serene Indian maid before washing herself in scented water and donning a soft lawn breakfast-gown with apple-green ribbons. Throughout, her thoughts were on that rigid figure beside the grave this morning. It was never possible to see much of a man's face when he was wearing a shako, but Rupert's had resembled a death mask. Her heart ached for him but she knew consolation was not possible. Only time would ease his sense of shock and loss; the boy was young enough to recover quite fully, eventually. However, his claim against John had caused universal condemnation. His dearly beloved brother was lost, but breaking another man would not bring Hugo back or ease the anguish. Someone must make him see that before it was too late. The obvious person to do so was his own captain.

They sat beneath the swaying punkah where their bearer served breakfast. Elizabeth felt unable to eat her usual slice of mango, and could not even face bread and butter this morning. William's appetite

173

seemed unaffected by the sombre event they had just attended. He made inroads into sausages, ham, eggs, a slice of pie, flat scones and marmalade besides several pieces of fruit. All this he washed down with tankards of ale. She watched him eat and grew progressively more angry. This husband of hers had no soul. Why had she allowed Uncle Matthew to marry her off to him? Sipping her coffee, she forced herself to recollect that she had been very taken with the extrovert gaiety of a handsome young suitor, who had introduced her to the simple delights of picnics, military revues and other outdoor pastimes. Foolishly, she had not perceived that there was no deeper side to his personality.

Looking at him now as he devoured his usual large meal, she guessed he had no awareness whatever of what John and Rupert were now suffering. The shock and anger over the affair had been real enough, but William was concerned only with his own feelings. Right now he felt hunger, so he satisfied it. When lust plagued him, he would satisfy that, regardless of her wishes or emotions.

'I would approach Rupert myself except that I'm sure you will do so now that the funeral is over,' she said quietly.

He glanced up from peeling a grape. 'Approach him? Approach him how?'

'On the subject of his damaging charge against Major Stavenham. He must be made to retract.'

Glowering he said, 'I thought we had closed that subject.'

'I have not closed it, William. Will you speak to him?'

'Certainly not,' he declared, throwing down his knife and dipping his fingers in the bowl containing water scented by floating petals. 'What the fellow chooses to believe is his own concern. What *anyone* chooses to believe is his own concern.'

'I choose to believe that Major Stavenham is innocent of any culpability. I know you will count that as of no importance. By *anyone* you meant any *gentleman*, of course. Females are not created to hold opinions, are they?'

Wiping his fingers on the small towel beside his plate, William rose in annoyance. 'You drive a man to the limit of his patience. Is it too much to be expected to be allowed to eat breakfast without being bothered by *conversation*? By God, life was enjoyable before you came out here.'

'Mine was not,' she told him swiftly. 'Now that I am here, I am trying to be of help to you. You were not displeased when Lady Mason requested my assistance with her good work, were you?' Allowing time

174

for him to light a cheroot, she then continued. 'As part of that work for the benefit of the troops it does seem to me to be in their interests to maintain harmony in the regiment. The soldiers take their lead from the officers. If you are all seen to condemn Major Stavenham, they will do so too.'

'Ha, you are mistaken, ma'am,' he declared, puffing smoke into the air. 'The blackguards are too concerned with their own grievances to care what the officers do or think. A major is too top-lofty to be taken into their account at all, believe me.'

'He is not when danger threatens and they look to him for command,' she returned passionately. 'They have to trust him or go to pieces . . . and so must his subordinate officers. What will you do when John Stavenham gives you an order, William? Is a battle likely to be lost because you and the others believe the man will needlessly sacrifice your lives for the sake of promotion or glory?'

'No, that is too much,' he cried in a fury. 'I will not have my wife attempting to run the regiment and asking me damned impertinent questions.'

'You only consider them impertinent because you don't wish to answer,' she said, rising to face him determinedly. 'I suspect that Sir Francis Mason has become a popular and successful general through answering Amelia's questions with total honesty. She is an extremely astute woman, as many wives are, and he has the sense to see it. Those old die-hards at headquarters will not tolerate her because they are afraid of admitting that a female is capable of grasping the meaning of subjects they guard so jealously as a masculine province. William, can't you see that this charge of Rupert's has created potential danger if the Sikhs really mean to rise against us soon? You *must* speak to him, make him listen to reason. Reason dictates that Sir Hugo's death was a tragedy no one could have prevented, least of all a close friend. John maintains that it is essential for men to trust each other in battle, or they could succumb to a weaker foe through their own disunity.'

No sooner had she finished speaking, Elizabeth spotted the trap into which she had fallen. William's wit was not so dulled that he missed it. He studied her suspiciously through eyes narrowed by cigar smoke.

'You are a little too free with the use of a man's first name. After spending four and a half months with young Carruthers your ready familiarity was difficult to curb, but since when have you been calling that man John? I think you have only spoken to him once.'

Against the emphatic beat of her heart, she said, 'Fanny Humphrey repeats verbatim all her husband says. You know what a chatterbox she is. I was merely quoting her.'

Still suspicious, he mused, 'I did not know that you had seen Mrs Humphrey since the tragedy yesterday.'

'It was something she mentioned at the races. I thought the view very sound.'

'How can you possibly decide whether or not a comment about conduct in battle is sound? The subject is beyond your comprehension.'

'As is your attitude, William. If you will do nothing, I must approach Rupert as a friend.'

'You'll do nothing of the kind,' he shouted, crushing his cheroot in the ashtray. 'I forbid you to interfere in this.'

'Then act yourself! It is your clear duty to do so before some disaster results.'

He stood irresolute and still very angry. Then he drew in his breath and let it out on a heavy sigh. 'It will blow over in a day or so. That boy is upset and Stavenham is too damned deep. Always said he was. Your concern over him verges on the indiscreet, my dear. What's your interest in Stavenham?'

'My interest is in any man — be he even a lowly trooper — who may be broken by an unjust charge concerning a friend whose murder he was forced to witness. My concern is for compassion, William, that is all. As you just now said, I have only spoken to Major Stavenham once.'

'Mmm,' he mused slowly, his wits sharpened by anger. 'Let me witness such championing of a lowly trooper and I shall be mollified. But mark my words, and do not interfere in regimental matters. They are best left to those who understand them. Do I make myself clear?'

'You have always made clear your dislike of my intelligence, but I possess it and will use it. Nothing will make me play the simpering, mindless wife any more than you will play the thoughtful, considerate husband, so let us both accept the facts and make the best of them.'

Giving another scowl, he turned on his heel to walk away from yet another challenge. 'I shall repair to the Mess. Thank God there is one place in Ratnapore where there are no females to spoil a man's tranquillity.'

On the third morning after Sir Hugo's funeral, a number of horses were found to be sick or dying. Each regiment suffered, but the cavalry lost up to a quarter of their animals. Those who had lived in India for some time knew it was a favourite trick of the Sikhs to creep in at night and administer poison, although how they had done it so successfully was distinctly worrying. The piquets were doubled and an urgent commission to purchase replacements was mounted. Few people then doubted that troubled days lay ahead, despite the dictum that order must be maintained peacefully, wherever possible. For Forrester's Light Dragoons, the poisoning of their horses was the last straw. Not only were cavalrymen dependent on their chargers, they often formed attachments to their animals which equalled and sometimes exceeded the bonds with their comrades. Large, brutish troopers wept openly at the pitiful sight of an equine friend's carcase, and anger flourished. United in aggression, the men decided that if it was a fight the bastards wanted, they could have it . . . and Forrester's were more than ready to oblige them. The officers were told by the NCOs that there was unrest verging on insubordination in the ranks. They then told Justin Lakeland. Being the man he was, he assured them that he had been keeping a sharp eye on the situation and measures were already under way to implement his recommendations. All the regiment could do was to wait. Aggression mounted and tempers grew shorter than ever, even in the commissioned ranks, as the hot season approached.

William spent more and more of his time in the Mess, as did most of the officers. Elizabeth felt it was probably a good thing. Hopes of making her marriage succeed had faded. As much to blame as William, she welcomed his absence from the bungalow. At breakfast this morning, she had again attempted to draw from him an explanation of why the Sikhs were launching attacks on those who were there to protect them. It had not been the best time to press him on such an issue. He had come to her last night only to be denied his pleasure by reason of her monthly indisposition, which she now welcomed as a reprieve from attentions she found distasteful. All she had received in answer to her question had been a testy comment that 'the damned natives are never happy unless they're causing trouble'. With that she had to be content . . . but she was not.

She sat now in the cool of her sitting-room, writing a letter to Lavinia. It was one of many she had written since leaving England, although none would yet have reached its destination, and she was finding it difficult to explain her growing sense of even greater drama to come. Her pen stilled after only a few lines and she gazed across the room to where John had collapsed at her feet. The killing of Sir Hugo and the poisoning of the horses surely bore out his conviction that a war was inevitable, yet she did not know the deeper issues behind the accelerating hostility. If she asked Amelia Mason she would probably be given a partial answer, but she longed to know and understand the causes for continuing conflict between foes who had already been locked in martial combat several years before. Had that war solved nothing?

Her introspection was broken by the arrival of Lucy Nicholson, who had never crossed the cantonment to visit her before. The girl's neat figure was swamped by a gown of heavy figured silk in cream and purple. It was ideal for a mature matron but not for this pretty child. The severe lines of her bonnet emphasized her pallor and the dark smudges beneath red and swollen eyes. When Elizabeth went to her to take her hands in sympathy, she found the girl was trembling.

'My dear Mrs Nicholson, you look quite exhausted,' she said gently. 'Do sit and take a cup of tea with me. I was about to ring for it.'

The visitor promptly burst into tears and covered her face with her hands as she stood swaying in the centre of the room. With her heart going out to someone life had treated very harshly, Elizabeth led her to one of the high-backed settees, settled the girl upon it, then sat beside her, wisely allowing the tears to flow unchecked. It was not hard to guess the cause of her distress. If her childhood worship had not yet turned to love it was well on the way to doing so. The clock ticked on while Lucy sobbed into the handkerchief she clutched. Only when she showed signs of recovering did Elizabeth reach up to untie her ribbons and remove the ugly bonnet. Then she smoothed her golden hair back from a damp forehead, murmuring, 'We have had enough tears, Lucy. Shall we now talk about how I can help you?'

A face full of desperation and fearfulness turned up from the sodden handkerchief beseechingly. 'Henry will be so very angry if he hears of this.'

She smiled. 'He will not hear of it from me. Besides, as most gentlemen have retired to the bastion no female can penetrate, what is more natural than for us to enjoy each other's company? Captain Nicholson can have no objection to a morning visit to a friend.'

'If he knew why I had come.'

'How can he know, unless you tell him?'

Lucy gave a shuddering sigh. 'How sensible you are. You must think me a very poor kind of creature.'

'I think you are very much as I used once to be,' she confessed in reassuring tones. 'I was not always sensible; sometimes I am not even now. My dear, we cannot be everything we should be. None of us is superhuman.' After a moment's hesitation she went straight to the heart of the matter. 'You have come to consult me about Rupert, have you not?'

The girl looked astonished as she dabbed as her red eyes. 'How could you possibly know that?'

Elizabeth smiled as she rang the small bell on the table beside her, which would tell the bearer to bring tea. 'I have already asked William to do what he can, and I believe he has, but gentlemen tend to regard depth of feeling as a sign of weakness and treat it accordingly. My husband consoles himself with the thought that grief soon lessens, and Rupert does so by directing his anguish into hatred for Major Stavenham. There the matter rests, I fear.'

'I hoped . . . I have come to ask you to . . . speak to him.'

'I regret William will hear no more on the subject.'

The bearer brought tea and poured it before retiring with a bow. As soon as he had gone, Lucy said, 'I need you to speak to Rupert. You are his confidante. You travelled out here in his company, earning his admiration and trust, Mrs Delacourt. He will listen to you.'

This was something she had longed to do, yet she calmly sipped her tea and said, 'I think you could call me Elizabeth, don't you?'

Ignoring the tea, Lucy stared at her lap where her restless hands plucked at the lace handkerchief. 'I wrote a letter. I know I should not have done so, but Rupert's misery at the funeral so distressed me. I could not bear it. He . . . he passed me yesterday without acknowledgement and I fear I have caused him to dislike me because of it. I dare not go to him, but you could.'

Elizabeth set down her cup carefully. 'I'm also married.'

The face turned upward again full of pleading. 'You are so sensible, so assured. You are not afraid of what anyone might say. It is well known that you and Rupert are friends, no more. It's quite acceptable for you to approach him.'

'And it is unacceptable for you to do so because you are more than friends?' she asked probingly.

Lucy flushed scarlet, a picture of guilt, as she stared back. Then she resorted to tears again. 'I will not believe it is wicked to feel such fondness for someone I have known all my life. He is so splendid, so good and kind. Rupert makes me feel warm and . . . safe. I am . . .' she stuffed her handkerchief in her mouth to muffle her words, 'I am frightened of Henry.'

Elizabeth could well believe it. The man was mean-mouthed, saturnine and unprepossessing. Any woman, much less an inexperienced girl, might fear him.

'Hush now,' she soothed. 'You will make yourself ill.'

'He does not harm me in any way,' Lucy hastened to explain, and she dried her eyes on the starched napkin in her lap. 'He is very seldom in my company at home, but when he is, he is so silent and forbidding I am afraid to speak for fear of offending him.'

Memories of her repressed life with the Delacourts led Elizabeth to say, 'Then you are better off remaining as silent as he.'

Lucy managed a watery smile. 'I wager you would not. I wish I were as wise as you.'

'Ah, if I were so wise I would not now be . . .' she broke off, knowing she could not exchange confidences with this girl. Instead, she said something she had been telling herself for over a year. 'There is nothing wicked in loving someone; only in hating. What you feel for a young man who puts such warmth into your life is very natural. Don't be ashamed of loving Rupert . . . but you must not write him letters which are not also from your husband. It will embarrass both gentlemen and could lead to misunderstandings.' Drawing the napkin from Lucy's hot clasp, she offered her the cup of tea. 'Drink this while you compose yourself.' She smiled. 'Now that we are on such good terms, please call on me whenever you wish. We could talk of many things, including mutual friends. There is no need for you to feel lonely, you know.'

'How good you are,' sighed Lucy.

'Dear me, first wise and now good. You will soon have me as great a paragon as Sir Hu . . . how terrible, I had forgotten momentarily,' she declared sadly. 'I wish I had had longer acquaintance with someone who will surely be a great loss to anyone who knew him well.'

'Will you speak to Rupert, Elizabeth? Please, will you?' urged Lucy, prompted by the return to the subject upon which she had come. 'I know him and I fear for his sanity. Do something, I beg you.'

Elizabeth heard herself agree. Someone had to intervene in the matter, she told her conscience, and the men had all avoided responsibility. Not only Rupert's sanity but John's peace of mind was at stake. That was surely reason enough for her.

Knowing that Rupert shunned company, Elizabeth acted on her resolution the moment Lucy left. He would not be in the Mess with his fellow officers. It was inviting speculation for a married woman to visit the bungalow of a single officer, but she knew he would not accept an invitation to come to hers. Only the most determined scandalmonger could imagine sexual intrigue when the young man was in deep mourning for a murdered brother. All the same, she imagined eyes watching her from every residence in the avenue as she walked quickly to the far end of it, where Rupert occupied quarters with a subaltern named Calthorpe. That young blade was certain to be in the Mess. He rarely left it unless it was to be carried out, dead to the world.

The red earth of the avenue shimmered with the heat of noon as she walked, which made her dread the oncoming 'hot' season. The temperature was one aspect of India which did not charm her. Opening the gate in the white fence surrounding the compound, she found the still atmosphere of the beehive bungalow rather disconcerting, but resolved not to turn back until she had seen Rupert and said what she must. Stepping inside the hall, where it was usual to ring a bell to summon the bearer, she immediately caught sight of her quarry through the open doors leading to the sitting-room. He saw her at the same time and rose from the chair where he had been sprawling.

Ignoring the bell, she moved forward a few paces to ask quietly, 'Will you allow me to come in?'

There was no response, so she continued in to the sitting-room which was so like every other in the bungalows. She was deeply shocked by his appearance. It was as if he had become aged overnight. His impudent blue eyes were lifeless; the handsome lines of his features had hardened into bitterness. Even his skin had taken on the grey hue of a dying man. His breath smelled overpoweringly of spirits and Elizabeth realized that he had got to his feet only through tremendous strength of will. He was dressed in no more than shirt and breeches, his boots having been cast several yards across the room. Yet he seemed astonishingly well in command of himself for someone so inebriated.

Putting her sunshade on a chair she went to him, hands outstretched. 'I am so deeply sorry, my dear.'

His mouth twisted. 'So you wrote in your letter of condolence. Everyone is deeply sorry.'

'Sincerely so,' she told him, her arms returning to her sides in the face of his aloofness. 'My intrusion is prompted by the warmest friendship,

Rupert. More than most people here, I understand how great a blow this has been. Let me help you to bear it. Talk to me of him.'

'You are weary of hearing me speak of his impossible virtues, you told me.'

Aching with sympathy for his jealously guarded grief, she gave a sad smile. 'A single meeting with him revealed the truth of your words.' The rhythmic squeak of the punkah punctuated the silence in that room reeking with alcoholic fumes, but she tried again to break through his self-imposed isolation.

'Friends can offer great comfort at times like this. Please allow them to do so.'

'Can they bring him back?'

'No, Rupert. Nothing will bring your brother back . . . but your rejection of those who held him in respect or affection banishes him more surely than death. Can you not see that?'

He turned from her and stood isolated and unyielding; his broad back signifying dismissal. Elizabeth did not know how to reach him. She had never encountered grief of this magnitude before, and those months of pleasant friendship during the journey did not help in this situation. He was an entirely different person from the engaging, enthusiastic young man who had rejoiced at finally achieving his heart's desire. Accepting that he was beyond her compassion, she took courage and said what she had really come to say.

'You are also dishonouring your brother's memory with this unfounded condemnation of John Stavenham. Do you not consider that he is suffering enough over the affair without this?'

Rupert swung round on her, suddenly blazingly alive with a burst of vitriolic anger. 'What is any man's suffering compared to that of one who was fiendishly mutilated and dismembered?' he choked, his face working. 'Hugh was in command that morning; he was the fastest man in the regiment. How could he have been at the rear? *How could he?*'

Taken aback by his untamed aggression, she tried to remain calm. 'Have you listened to John's explanation?'

'He took command and allowed Hugh to be massacred. That is the only explanation. Revenge is all I have left. *All I have left,*' he repeated in a whisper, as his shoulders began to heave and he put his face in his hands.

Swept by sadness, Elizabeth took up her sunshade and quietly left. Losing John had been painful enough, but this boy had lost all hope and that was far more painful for anyone to bear.

Chapter Ten

The execution of those held responsible for the attack in which Sir Hugo Carruthers was killed took place at eight a.m. The officers of Ratnapore garrison were invited to witness the ceremony, but no more than a representative dozen attended. No general in his right mind would send all his officers into the metaphorical lions' den leaving troops without commanders. Indeed, so deep was the garrison's distrust now, there was initial hesitation over the early hour, which meant setting out across the plain in darkness. However, it was deemed highly unlikely that Ganda Singh would betray his real intentions by mounting another attack on this deputation, so a group containing Colonel Lakeland, John, William, Rupert, George Humphrey, and seven others rode through the city gates in full ceremonial dress to observe something they knew would be a macabre farce.

Greeted with much courteous panache by the Vizier, the visitors were conducted to a stand decked with silk hangings which looked out over a market square. Into this were dragged a collection of wretches almost certainly taken from the dungeons where they had been incarcerated for theft, assault or any trumped up charge which was convenient. Clothed in garb similar to that worn by the tribesmen on that fatal day, these substitute victims were subjected to various public tortures before having their heads and limbs severed. The bloody torsos were then hung as a deterrent to others who might dare to humiliate the Sirdar by attacking his much valued British friends. After the grisly business was concluded, the officers were invited to a silken tent to partake of refreshment. Their lack of appetite went unremarked by their host, whose stomach had apparently been unaffected by what he had just witnessed, and so did the peculiar shade of green which had crept into their white Western faces. To their discomfort, two young subalterns threw up behind the tent, but the remainder stoically endured the next hour or so until Justin Lakeland judged that they could leave with honour — and stomachs — intact. He was not looking too robust himself, his subordinates noted thankfully. It was a quiet procession which rode back to the military camp spread on the slope facing the city.

For John, the morning revived that other occasion too strongly. He had almost been driven to join the retching subalterns, and he rode back sick at heart as well as physically nauseated, recalling each stage of that earlier return from the city. On that morning, the danger had developed so suddenly he could not now recall the exact words he and Hugo had exchanged, but he surely had not snatched command from his friend and set off for the nullah without mutual agreement. Hugo could not say and the troopers did not know, yet John could not deny that Hugo had told him that his horse was no jumper. He had given the fact no thought in his eagerness to out-ride those he saw as enemies. Doubts so beset him now he even questioned whether he had mistaken the entire situation. Had the tribesmen been harmless enough until the soldiers made a dash for home and reinforcements? Had they approached the injured Hugo with sympathy until he had drawn his pistol? Had he really seen intrigue where there was none?

They were approaching that section of the road which ran alongside the nullah, and he stared across at the place where he had gathered up Hugo's remains. His actions had cost the man his life. If he had been right, the outcome could be judged a tragedy. If he had been mistaken, he had killed a man needlessly. An instinctive glance over his right shoulder encountered that of the boy who meant to avenge that terrible death. Rupert's face was still ashen and reshaped by shock, but there was awareness in his eyes as he stared back in a cold calculating manner. It was difficult to look away from that optical threat of retribution. He did so knowing that if he was ever engaged in battle as a member of this regiment, he could expect attack from the rear as well as from the enemy ahead.

'Do you think they believe we have been taken in by that business this morning, sir?' asked the man who had come alongside.

He looked at George Humphrey and shook his head. 'They were playing a game and so were we. It is called diplomacy. Each move is designed to mollify the other player and allow for the development of deeper and more significant strategy.'

'So what will happen now?'

He sighed and surveyed the dust road ahead which now curved in the familiar horseshoe bend. 'I think destiny will play the next hand, George.'

They rode in silence for a while as John sunk into further retrospection on what had been the real intention of the tribesmen when they had split into two groups that day. Could there be a harmless reason for wishing to sandwich a small group of soldiers at a vulnerable section of the road?

'My wife has been asked by Mrs Delacourt to join Lady Mason's Welfare Committee,' said the red-haired man then. 'They are engaged this morning in inspecting some likely quarters for the regimental families. Fanny has taken a great interest in the scheme.'

Guessing that this efficient and loyal young man was talking to take his attention from the scene of the tragedy, John forced a smile. 'Lady Mason is a shrewd woman. Her committee not only helps the rank and file, it happily occupies its members in useful work. The ladies of the station should be grateful for her initiative.'

'I agree. There is so much they can do that is worthwhile, aside from rearing a clutch of children.'

'I suppose that is what most of them prefer to do,' he commented.

George sighed. 'I see those brown infants swarming everywhere in the Native Quarter. How they are ever fed and cared for I cannot guess, but they are children of India and born to the rigours of the country. The puny little wretches we have in our regiment are pitiful to see. To bring them into the world only to watch them succumb to fevers and infection seems to me to be a sin.'

'Maybe, but while there are women travelling with a regiment I suppose there are certain to be children,' he reasoned, then suddenly wondered why Clare had never conceived. He had not avoided the issue, as George evidently did, so why had two years of loving his wife never made her pregnant? Would she have changed with motherhood; abandoned her art and impenetrable independence? Would she be with him now if they had had children? Viewing it after eight years, he conceded that nothing would have altered that self-absorbed personality. He would have lost her sooner or later. Perhaps he had never really possessed her . . . like Elizabeth. At the thought of this second love in his life, which had deceived him as surely as the first, he grew hot with renewed humiliation. His recollections of the hours following Hugo's murder were highly confused, but he was vaguely aware of having blurted out some confession of guilt in the desperate need for

185

reassurance, before collapsing at Elizabeth's feet. Inebriation must have made him see again the girl he had known at Wellford; shock and grief for young Rupert had overcome his mistrust of her in a bid for understanding and support. If she had seen him as weak and manipulative before what must her opinion be now? The same as that of everyone at Ratnapore, no doubt.

He had never been the breezy, highly popular kind of officer William Delacourt was, but he presently felt totally isolated in this frontier community. Perhaps he was destined to be alone all his life . . . and, if the Punjab really was on the brink of war, his life might end shortly. A turbanned Sikh or a vengeful boy might make an end of him before the year was through. It would be no tragedy. No one would grieve for him.

The ladies of the Welfare Committee were busy with the task of arranging suitable accommodation for the married soldiers, who presently occupied a small area behind a blanket strung across a wire at the end of the barrack bungalows. Lady Mason had spotted three store huts which she felt could be adapted to suit her requirements by the orderly rearrangement of the stores into a single hut, leaving the other two empty.

It was not ideal — there would still be three couples to each hut — but there the children would not be subjected to foul language and the general coarseness of the troopers. The boys did not fare quite so badly, although many a rough soldier had taken a lad up on his knee and taught him to repeat the most disgusting words for the amusement of his comrades. The girls suffered more from this unhealthy communal living. For the most part they were fish-wives before reaching puberty, even if their mothers had any heart left to try to teach them the graces of womanhood. They invariably married, or otherwise, into the regiment because they seldom met other men, and became copies of generations of women who had washed and cooked for the troops for a few pence to help provide for the babies which soon arrived, and often just as swiftly departed from life. There were nine children remaining of the fifteen which had sailed with the regiment in an old sailing ship, and five of the ten subsequently born in India still survived. These, together with their mothers (two of them adoptive parents after the deaths of the true mothers from cholera in Calcutta), lived in unhealthy, unpleasant conditions with the men who had taken them on for various reasons and on whom they were totally dependent.

Elizabeth had recruited Fanny Humphrey after her first meeting with Amelia Mason, and she had since persuaded Lucy Nicholson to occupy some of her long empty hours in useful occupation. Together with Charlotte Lakeland and the wife of an Artillery officer named Benedict, they went first to Lady Mason's bungalow where they met the Quartermaster who was to accompany them on their tour. Having dressed in sober manner, in a gown of dull green lawn, Elizabeth was startled when their leader sallied forth in a vast crinoline of acid-yellow silk and a plum-coloured Pompadour wig topped by a gauze bonnet. Her manner was quite the reverse of her appearance, however. She made it clear from the start that her intentions were serious and that she would brook no argument in her determination to move the families from their present squalor.

This morning's visitors had never before been inside the long single-storey buildings which housed the troopers. They were not expected to do so. Their husbands, who commanded the men, had a duty to inspect the premises frequently, but most did so only when they could not avoid it. The Quartermaster did his best to dissuade the ladies from going inside, but the General's campaigning wife told him her stomach was quite strong enough to withstand anything the women of the regiment had to endure. She stepped through the doorway at the end of the building with great resolution. The ladies followed with less eagerness, for the stench wafting from the place was quite terrible. Like the others, Elizabeth hastily put her scented handkerchief to her nose as she moved from the excessive glare into the dim, stifling interior. When her eyes had grown accustomed to the darkness, she stared in appalled disbelief at the long mud-floored area, lined with beds on both sides. The straw mattresses had one coarse brown blanket folded neatly upon them. Above the beds hung the troopers' accoutrements and items of spare uniform. Saddles and horse-leathers hung there, also, adding to the foul odours in this place where fresh air never circulated. The strong smell of some greasy putrefying concoction which had been served as breakfast mingled with that rising from a huge wooden tub in the centre which served as a communal toilet. These officers' wives had never beheld anything like it before. Lady Mason had, so moved forward unhesitatingly to where a group of silent creatures stood watching this curious cavalcade approach.

Overcome by a sense of helplessness, Elizabeth saw this evidence of all John had said about the plight of those who had virtually given over their lives for a shilling. What could they ever make of themselves; what hope had they of escape? Shocked by what she saw, it occurred to her that William had never spoken of this, had never once mentioned the living conditions of those to whom he claimed a loyalty so strong he must always go where they went. Once more she wondered if his silence on the subject was due to his belief that such things should not concern females, or to his personal indifference to the problem. She suspected the latter.

Her attention was fully taken again when they reached those they had come to help. Six unkempt creatures in rags of gowns with split slippers on their brown feet, stood with an assortment of stunted children with pinched, knowing faces in a small area festooned with laundry which hung like so much dingy bunting over their heads. The army provided no beds for wives and children, so straw lay scattered wherever there was space on the floor between two large laundry tubs and a cooking stove. A few meagre possessions stood on upturned jars which could be used for no other purpose because they were cracked or too badly broken. Despair was in the evidence before them; resignation was in the eyes of the women. The children were open-mouthed at the sight of a curious creature in a bright yellow bell-tent with a head of profuse purplish hair.

The wives appeared to be struck dumb when they were told that their visitors were concerned about their living quarters, and proposed moving them away from the barrack area to somewhere more private. The mental capacity of most of the six was insufficient to understand the Quartermaster's high-flown speech. The two who did understand showed little response to something which sounded too good to be true. When they were all invited to look at their proposed new homes and hear the plans for their conversion, women and children nevertheless followed Lady Mason outside and across the grass in an obedient, bewildered crocodile. The committee members were relieved to be outside again and walked beside those they hoped to help lost for words of communication with these creatures so far from their understanding. Elizabeth was walking with Fanny when her friend suddenly accosted the woman beside her, who was cleaner than the rest and carried a baby in one arm and a toddler on her hip.

'Do allow me to carry the baby for you,' she urged. 'You cannot manage both at once.'

'No, marm, 'e might dirty your gown,' she replied earnestly. 'I couldn't let 'un do that.'

'Nonsense,' said Fanny reaching for the child. 'I am not so concerned with a gown that I would not hold the little mite because of it.' The baby was taken from the woman and clutched against her breast in an agony of eagerness. 'What is his name?'

'Arthur, marm . . . after 'is granfer. And this 'un's Mildred.'

Fanny smiled. 'You will be glad to remove them from the barrack, I am sure.'

'Yes, marm,' was the dutiful reply, but there was not much hope in the dark eyes.'

'How old are they?' asked Fanny.

'This 'un's going on two and the babby's ten weeks. My man's in your 'usband's troop,' she added with curious shyness. 'Thinks a lot of 'im, 'e does.'

Fanny was too busy looking at the baby to pay much attention to that. 'Ten weeks! He looks a little small. Do you have enough food for him? They should drink milk, you know, plenty of milk.'

Elizabeth watched the scene. Fanny glowed with delight as the baby curled his tiny fingers around one of hers, and she put her cheek against the dark down on his head in an expression of maternal gentleness. Another unhappy wife in Ratnapore!

They arrived at the store huts and clustered inside one of them. The dismal interior was half filled with a variety of crates and boxes but it was easy to see how spacious it would be when cleared. The troopers' wives must have imagined they would be moving in with the stores and showed animation only when Lady Mason explained that two of the huts would be emptied before they did so. She then spoke of putting up curtains to divide each place into three sections and of providing each family with its own washing tub and stove. The women then imagined that they had been brought there to move the stores. Two seized hold of heavy crates and struggled to lift them. The Quartermaster swiftly explained that their husbands would be detailed to do the heavy work, but that they would be expected to scrub the huts to banish vermin before they could move in. They were willing enough to do this, although they had lived cheek by jowl with vermin all their lives and thought nothing of the inconvenience. Lady Mason promised them some lime powder to put down after the scrubbing. It was clear they had no notion of the purpose of the antiseptic powder, but they showed appropriate if mystified gratitude.

This first meeting ended abruptly when one of the ten-year-olds fell from a pile of crates and knocked out a front tooth. He screamed shrilly. The mother boxed his ears for being a nuisance, then told him the black men would come and get him unless he mended his ways. The committee ladies then departed, but not before Mrs Lakeland insisted on a prayer of thankfulness to their Christian father who provided so fulsomely for them all. The regimental wives very obviously did not know who their Christian father might be and fidgeted throughout the long prayer.

Over a well earned cup of tea in Lady Mason's bungalow, they then tackled the task of allocating responsibility. The Quartermaster had departed, saying that he would organize the removal of the crates and also obtain a supply of lime powder. Amelia Mason undertook to supervise the purchase and making of attractive curtains, and the younger ladies agreed to drive to the bazaar to buy wash tubs, stoves and soap for each family. Mrs Lakeland expressed her willingness to provide texts for the walls of the huts and felt confident that her husband could prevail upon the officers of the regiment to subscribe to a fund for prayer books for the children.

'I should think that any money they give would be put to better use in supplying milk to nourish them,' said Fanny with surprising temerity. 'My husband is forever deploring the rate of sickness and death in our children. They need food, not books.'

The Colonel's wife looked astonished, and not a little affronted, at such words from the wife of a very junior officer, and was about to make a retort when Elizabeth intervened. She had seen the way Fanny had cuddled the baby in cherishing arms and the soft expression with which she had studied the infant, lost to all else but her yearning for motherhood. She had no such yearning herself, but agreed wholeheartedly that funds for the work of the committee should always be used to the greatest benefit.

'Like Mrs Humphrey I thought the children not at all robust, ma'am,' she commented to Amelia Mason, who, on entering her home, had taken off her wig and replaced it with a huge lacy cap smothered in violet ribbons. 'It is not surprising when they spend so much time in that dreadful barrack. I had no idea they endured such deplorable conditions.'

'There are very few who have, Mrs Delacourt,' Lady Mason responded dryly, 'and those few who have been made aware of it by the many letters I send, choose to pretend that I am advocating the provision of luxuries for mere animals. The ordinary soldier, ladies, is counted as nothing, you must know. That is, until he is needed to defend our lives and territories. Once he has done that with amazing courage and loyalty, he is again drilled, reviled, starved and totally disregarded as a human soul. If he should attempt to ease his lot by the only means open to him, he is flogged. When he is sick he is taken to a hospital where conditions are no better than those in the barrack, and subjected to inadequate and primitive tortures which are supposed to improve his condition. More often than not they finish him off.'

'We are all of us in the hands of God, ma'am,' ventured Mrs Lakeland. 'He decides whom He will take and who leave to the world. We must trust such decisions to His grace.'

'Fiddlesticks!' came the response from a woman who had lost all three of her children. 'God gave us intelligence which allows us to help Him by helping ourselves. And He gave us compassion to help those in need. He cannot look after the entire world on His own, Mrs Lakeland, and I'm sure He expects us to augment our hymns of praise with a little practical action.' Her gentle eyes surveyed the group. 'Well, ladies, do not sit there in silent agreement with me. Speak up!'

Lucy Nicholson surprised everyone by saying, 'The children of my husband's regiment always appear so bright and happy. They are Indian and have their homes away from the barrack area, of course, but I have often thought that our little white children do not know how to play as they do.' Her original impetus of courage began to slow. 'Forgive me, I did not mean . . . I was not suggesting . . .' Swallowing hard, she finished in a rush. 'Could we not provide the little ones with a playground?'

'What a splendid idea,' said Elizabeth warmly. 'Do let us find a small area away from the soldiers where the children can play in safety. We'll give them all a cup of milk before their mothers come to collect them.'

Fanny had been thinking further on the subject. 'It's of no use to provide a playground for children who have no idea how to use it. George says they know nothing of simple childish games. They learn from the men to play for gain with cards and other means. I believe we should teach them pastimes from our own childhood — I am very willing to devote time to it — and collect from officers' wives any dolls or toys they can spare to keep at the playground.'

Lady Mason beamed. 'What an excellent committee I have behind me. You see what can be done when ladies unite. I fear a group of gentlemen would still be humming and hawing over the advisability of moving the stores from those huts. It would take them at least three months and a deal of paperwork to reach a firm decision, and it would be negative. I declare they are past masters at wasting time.'

'I have settled on the ideal playground,' said Charlotte Lakeland. 'I know the Chaplain would have no objections to using the compound of the church for the purpose. After the games, the children could be taught the scriptures. The way to spread the word is through the mouths of babes.'

No one could think of any reasonable argument against her determined religious contribution, so she was given the task of arranging everything with the Chaplain. Fanny was asked to mount the toy collection, and agreed happily. Elizabeth offered to show the children how to do water-colours, and Lucy shyly confessed that she had a talent for sketching which she could demonstrate. Mrs Benedict claimed she would see what was in her bungalow, and those of her friends, which could be made into clothes for the regimental infants. Satisfied with the outcome of the morning, Amelia Mason announced that the next project was to use the same energy toward bringing improvement to the station hospital.

'Surgeon-Captain Cockerford has been so deeply disheartened by the total disregard of his many requests and reports he cannot raise any enthusiasm for my scheme. He believes it must come to naught.' She gave a grim smile. 'We must close ranks and see that it does not. It had entered my mind to administer some kind of mild poison to the staff at Headquarters — enough to make them feel most dreadfully ill, that's all — so that they would be compelled to seek medical help. But as they would only lie in the comfort of their own beds and be attended by the very best civilian doctors, I have had to discard the notion. We must think of some other way, although nothing alerts men to the facts of any matter more successfully than for them to suffer it themselves.'

Disconcerted, Elizabeth realized that the woman was quite serious about the poisoning. Where did unconventionality end and eccentricity take over, she wondered.

'Can they not be invited to visit the hospital, ma'am, and see the evidence of their own eyes?'

The consequent smile was charming and completely rational. 'My six invitations have all failed, like the letter to your husband, to reach their destination. Is it not amazing how cleverly the Military Postmaster manages to safely deliver all else but those letters the recipients do not wish to read?'

Elizabeth smiled back. 'Perhaps we could lure them with the promise of a ball or revue, then march them to the hospital before they are aware of our intent.'

'A ball they will avoid at all costs — elderly gentlemen cannot abide the effort it entails — but a revue is a possible solution. I'll speak to Sir Francis on the matter. How do you maintain such a wondrous shine on your hair, my dear?' she added, in one of her sudden changes of interest. 'I have been admiring it all the morning.'

The meeting ended on a social note, despite Mrs Lakeland's insistence on another prayer to ask for the strength to continue their work. Elizabeth, Fanny and Lucy strolled together in the direction of the officers' bungalows, but Fanny was significantly silent as the other pair chatted. It was easy for Elizabeth to divine the cause of her friend's introspection and, rounding a corner, they came upon the root cause of it. George Humphrey stood talking to John in the broad residential avenue. Both looked strained and weary; only one smiled his pleasure at the sight of three attractive ladies approaching. His smile faded when his wife greeted him stonily, then launched into a detailed account of what had occupied her morning.

'I have the delightful duty of collecting toys for the children from those officers' wives fortunate enough to have young ones of their own,' she added, with such pointedness his brown face darkened with embarrassment or anger, or both.

There was a short, awkward silence which Elizabeth tried to ease by smiling sympathetically at George. 'You have had a difficult morning, Mr Humphrey. Was the affair very harrowing?'

'Exceedingly so, ma'am. This is a most barbarous country.'

'As well as a stunningly beautiful one,' she could not resist saying. 'Is the affair now at an end?'

He looked at John for an answer, but it was a curiously evasive one he offered.

'In India things never really end, Mrs Delacourt.'

'But is honour now satisfied, sir?' she persisted.

'Honour is an abstract quality. Who is to know when it is offended and when assuaged?' was his response to that.

'You are speaking in riddles, sir,' protested Lucy with disarming innocence. 'I confess you are too clever for me.'

'Forgive me,' he said to her as he brushed a fly from his face. 'After the scene we have recently witnessed, I am not at my best.'

'If you will excuse us, my wife and I will retire to our bungalow where we can regale each other with the details of what has occupied our separate mornings,' put in George grimly. 'Good day, ladies. Sir.'

His salute sufficed for them all as he took Fanny's arm and marched her away. Elizabeth found herself in company with a girl disinclined to make intelligent conversation and with a man who looked to be at the limit of his endurance. To carry the silent moment into a more relaxed atmosphere she took her opportunity to broach a subject which held no personal undertones.

'Major, I am abysmally ignorant of the significance of what has been happening here since my arrival two weeks ago. Why are the Sikh people so full of vengeance against us?'

The little she could see of his expression beneath the tall black head-dress was as cold as his voice as he injected the personal undertones into his reply.

'Your husband can give you the answer to that, Mrs Delacourt.'

'I have asked him several times, but I think he does not take seriously my interest in the matter. I'm confident that you will.'

Lucy broke in to say, 'Some of the men in Henry's regiment are Sikhs. Captain Cline says it will be hard to ask them to fight their own people. Many have relations all over the Punjab. Will they be made to fight, Major?'

John had little choice but to stay and reply, but it was at Elizabeth that he looked to say, 'The situation is extremely complex, so I'll attempt to give you only the main causes for controversy. The Sikhs are bound together by a separate religion and an inborn drive to fight all-comers in order to preserve their faith and unity. The British managed to maintain an uneasy alliance with them from the time of our first expansion in India. Their greatest leader so far, Ranjit Singh, ruled his people with iron authority and a shrewdness which frequently outwitted our most wily attempts to better him. When he died, control of the Sikh empire was sought by many contenders. British conquest of areas coveted by the Sikhs did nothing to improve relations within their ranks, and the counter-claimants for power contrived to force a war with us in the partial hope of solving their own problems.' He frowned. 'If that sounds too complicated, I'll try to make it clearer. One Sikh faction wanted to drive us from our newly-acquired territories so that they could annex them themselves: the other faction encouraged the conflict in the half hope that we would kill off their rivals and look kindly upon their own claim for power.'

'How dreadful,' exclaimed Lucy.

'How clever,' mused Elizabeth. 'Were we aware of being manipulated?'

He sighed. 'Perhaps, but we took up their gauntlet and put down the army which marched against us, ridding the conspirators of those they wished to have out of their way. Our price for doing this was to gain control of half the Punjab and demand free passage over the whole of it for our troops. Many officers argued at the time that only total control would put an end to plots and intrigues which made the Punjab potentially dangerous, but the British did not have the wish nor the requisite troops to make that move. We set up a regency to guide the boy maharajah whose instigation we approved, and confidently expected peace to reign. That was two years ago.'

'After the war in which you fought,' said Elizabeth. 'Were you one of the officers who urged total control here?'

'Yes, you must know that I was,' he replied without thinking. 'Lacking a strong leader of their own, the Sikhs' only hope was to have accepted one of ours, backed by our army, until such time as the innumerable contenders killed each other off, as they invariably do.'

'But they are still active and hope to remove the regency they do not want by defeating us who support it?'

'Exactly,' he said with growing warmth. 'With us driven from the area, the maharajah and his supporters can be disposed of so that a long and bloody contest for rule can commence. They are determined upon another war. What has been happening here in Ratnapore are the pinpricks before the actual swordthrust, the design being to goad *us* into starting hostilities.'

They had forgotten the presence of Lucy, so lost had they become in a rapport which had revived suddenly and unexpectedly. Accordingly, they turned almost in guilt when the girl spoke.

'You have quite alarmed me, Major Stavenham. They sound so fearsome and inexplicable in your description. Yet Henry is forever saying how charming he finds his men. How can that be?'

Thrown off balance by the sudden return to awareness of her presence, he fiddled with the peak of his shako nervously. 'I was referring to the fanatical element, that is all, ma'am. Your husband's men are trained and loyal to their officers, naturally.'

She still looked wide-eyed. 'They have always been courtesy itself to me, and I have been perfectly comfortable in their presence. I believe I shall regard them differently now.'

'No, have I painted so black a picture?' he asked swiftly. 'You must trust your husband's judgement. He knows India far better than I. However, bear in mind that national allegiance must prevail against any other loyalty in extreme circumstances. Ask an Englishman to wage war against his own and he will think shabbily of you.'

Lucy was paying no heed to him. Her attention had been taken by the sight of a lone figure riding slowly into the avenue at the far end of it. Sir Rupert Carruthers was returning to his quarters. With her gaze fixed on this beloved friend, Lucy spoke only vaguely.

'I have to go. Henry expects me to be at home when he comes for tiffin. Goodbye.'

She walked away rapidly, a dainty, erect figure in a full crinoline of dark-blue ribbed silk with a Puritan collar of beige lace which emphasized her extreme youth.

Elizabeth watched her friend hurrying toward someone who was certain to hurt her further, and murmured, 'How sad it is that she is the only person who could break that boy's self-imposed isolation and give him comfort, yet he continues to reject her.'

'She is a married woman whose first duty is to her husband.'

The deliberate words drew her attention back to the man before her. Lines of strain had returned to his face and the rapport which had hung tantalizingly between them had vanished. Elizabeth tried to bring it back by speaking of another impersonal subject which would show him that he was wrong to believe she wished only to tempt every man in sight beneath the nose of someone he claimed she had betrayed.

'This morning I saw the conditions under which the rank and file must live, and I was filled with anger on their behalf. The barrack was empty. What it must be like when they are in occupation I dare not think. The women are so full of resignation, so lacking in hope of any kind. It was clear they cannot believe that we shall ever do as we promised.' She tried a half smile before continuing. 'Lady Mason is quite as you once described her to me, but, for all her compassionate determination, what she can achieve is but a drop in the ocean. She is fighting the obstinacy of aged, uncaring men in high office. I cannot decide whether they are totally heartless or simply blind to what should be obvious to them.'

'Which are you, Elizabeth Delacourt?'

The sudden thrust took her unawares and unprepared. For a moment she studied his shadowed face, then said quietly, 'If I am ever heartless it is unintentionally so.'

After a period of visible indecision, John asked, almost savagely, 'Why did you tell me you were a widow?'

'I did not,' she told him sadly. 'You misconstrued my words. My fault lay in allowing your mistake to stand. Initially, I thought it would not matter. I had been alone for fifteen months, neglected and abandoned by someone who thought nothing of a ten-year separation, and you were leaving Wellford within the month.'

As his blue eyes studied her face intently, she added, 'I did not allow myself to think of anything but the moment. Can you understand?'

Standing together in that wide avenue, in full view of any eyes watching from the row of bungalows, the barrier between them began to crumble. Anyone peeking from a window would have seen a tall, thickset figure, resplendent in scarlet, blue and gold, looking down at a petite woman in a green gown, whose face was turned up to his in a questioning manner. Her expression was hidden by the cluster of mimosa on the brim of her bonnet. They might hold any watcher's attention; a man and a woman alone out there on a red dust road, shimmering with noon-day heat, who were so intent on each other, they were aware of nothing else. Although they did not touch, there was an indefinable aura which defied the several feet separating them, yet onlookers would not have been able to claim they saw more than an officer's lady being polite to a man inclined to prefer solitude to socializing.

John seemed almost afraid of the truth, as if it would bring more pain than he already suffered, yet he had to ask the ultimate question. 'Why did you come to India?'

'To mend my marriage. I read in the newspaper of the autumn return of your regiment and knew that my best hope for the future was to join William here. How could I know that fortune would serve us both so ill?' When he frowned at those words, she said swiftly, 'Will you try to understand and forgive? It seems I am doomed to make men unhappy.'

'Yes, it seems that you are,' he told her with finality.

There was no alternative but to walk away from him with no more than a polite nod of her head for the benefit of anyone watching. Opening the white gate leading to the compound which surrounded a home she shared with a man she could neither love nor respect, she told herself that she must try to do both. All she could cherish now was the fact that she had explained to John why she had deceived him at Wellford. It might ease his sense of humiliation a little and give him back a modicum of pride. Perhaps they could now meet socially with less tension.

William was already indoors and in a black mood after watching the executions. He made it clear that he had witnessed her conversation with John by launching an attack on the man too complex for him to understand.

'The significance of this morning's gruesome pantomime appears to have been lost on that fellow,' he complained as he sprawled in one chair with his booted feet on another. 'It was the result of that doubtful affair which gave him his majority. And there's another thing,' he continued, after a gulp from the glass in his hand, 'he's too damned friendly with George Humphrey. It ain't the thing for field officers to be forever in the pocket of a subaltern.'

Elizabeth untied the strings of her bonnet with hands that were curiously unsteady, but her voice remained unaffected by the stress of the encounter with John as she said quietly, 'Mr Humphrey is the only officer prepared to stand by him over what you call a "doubtful affair", so it is hardly surprising that Major Stavenham shows his appreciation of such loyalty. I would do the same under those circumstances.'

William pointed at her with the hand holding his drink. 'You are too free with your championship, ma'am. Told you before I won't have my wife interfering in military affairs.'

'I am a *military* wife, William. It is absurd to rule that I may not give an opinion of what is going on all around me.'

He was on his feet so swiftly that Elizabeth was taken unawares. Walking unsteadily towards her, his face deeply florid, he roared, 'How *dare* you speak to me in that manner?'

Facing up to him, and wondering how she could ever grow to respect this man to whom she was irrevocably tied, she said with as much control as she could muster, 'I had to dare much in order to join you here, but my resolve to mend our marriage does not oblige me to remain silent when your comments are not justified. I was merely observing that it is natural enough for any person unfairly shunned by society to find peace in the company of anyone who befriends him. You must agree to that simple truth.'

Her husband's pale glance flicked over her suspiciously. 'What were you saying to him out there in full view of every prying eye? I wonder you did not bang a drum, you could not have drawn more attention to yourself.'

'That fact alone should tell you that our conversation was quite unexceptional,' she told him, realizing that he was too drunk to drop the subject easily. 'If there had been an indiscreet flavour about it, be certain I should have had more sense than to gratify prying eyes . . . and if two of them were yours, William, you will know that we were initially a group of five. The Humphreys departed on the heels of a marital squabble. Mrs Nicholson, who goes in fear of her husband, ran off to do his bidding once more. I was alone with Major Stavenham only by dint of the others' desertion.' Walking to her room, she turned at the door to add, 'We were discussing the cause of Sikh aggression toward us — military affairs again, I fear — but you have twice declined to enlighten me on the subject and I found his explanation too interesting to cut short just because prying eyes might see indiscretion where there was none.' Opening the door, she said, 'I had better take tiffin on a tray in my room. Neither of us is pleased with the other today, so we are best apart.'

Two seconds after Elizabeth had entered the unprepossessing room, the door crashed open. William stood swaying, six feet from her. 'I will not have my wife walk away from me when she stays at the side of another man in full view of the whole cantonment.'

Filled with the mixed emotions aroused a few minutes earlier, she lost patience. 'I spent this morning with the poor wretches to whom you claim inseparable loyalty. When you show it by concerning yourself with their miserable conditions rather than with imaginary intrigues and jealous rages of your own making, perhaps I shall not walk away from you . . . and there might be some hope for this marriage, at last.'

The work of the Welfare Committee was brought to a halt three days later when one of the regimental children died overnight from cholera. By the end of that week, twenty-six men had succumbed to it. Elizabeth was shocked. She had not been with the regiment in Calcutta, so had not appreciated how rapid and ruthless a killer the disease could be. An air of defeat hung over the cantonments. Cholera spread fear. It was so often fatal, many victims resigned themselves to death from the first symptoms. Surgeon-Captain Cockerford lost what little confidence he had left when he discovered that his ministrations were of no use to those who had no faith in their ability to survive. The stench and overcrowding in the hospital was a hundred times worse than usual, but the patients' tough mutton continued to be boiled in uncleaned cooking pots only a few yards away from the latrines. The heat inside the building was augmented by the temperature of the feverish men lying there, but the Surgeon and his two European assistants sweated and toiled like automatons fighting a losing battle. Driven on by long draughts from bottles of native-brewed liquor, he manfully struggled to contain the outbreak while shutting his mind to the misery, particularly when three children died in one night.

William returned to his bungalow on the eighth day to tell Elizabeth that General Mason was considering the prospect of marching out to a cholera camp until the disease loosed its grip, despite the risk of attack from tribesmen.

'He will decide within the next few days if there is then no sign of the outbreak abating.'

'He will have few men left to fight off an attack if he does not act to end these daily losses,' Elizabeth reasoned, studying the sagging lines of his face, which had once been firm and handsome. 'You look very tired, William. Are you also finding it difficult to sleep in this appalling heat?'

He sank wearily into a chair, unhooking his collar and casting his shako aside. 'Lakeland asked us to go down and speak to the men, put some heart into them, but defeat is written all over their faces. They would never show fear if ordered to combat overwhelming odds, but there is the shadow of dread in their eyes which no words will dispel. I tell you, Elizabeth, it sickens us all to see brave fellows so terrified.'

She reflected that he must be truly concerned or he would never confide in her this way. It seemed that he needed her strength, for once. 'It might appear to you that they paid no heed to your encouragement, but think how they would feel if their Troop Captain made no attempt to visit them now. I fear you are expecting too much if you hope to dispel all sense of alarm, but they would be even lower in spirits without evidence of your support. They cannot fail to be heartened by the thought that you are sharing with them the bad times as well as the good.'

He frowned at her. 'You really think so?'

Even more surprised at his attitude, she nodded. 'Certainly. I saw how their wives brightened when we showed a little understanding of their hardship. They look to their peers, William, for there is no one else to help them.'

The bearer announced tiffin at that point, and William dragged himself to his feet to go to his room to wash. When they then sat at the table, he uncharacteristically continued his theme. It was a sign of his genuine concern, she felt.

'If we do march out to camp, shall you mind sleeping under canvas?'

She smiled. 'I hope not, for there will be no alternative. Shall we be allowed to take anything with us?'

'Of course. If we are to be away some weeks we cannot manage without furniture and china. I am assured of four camels.'

'Then I had better prepare lists so that we shall be ready if the order comes.'

William looked pleased at this evidence of a normal wifely duty such as his mother would perform. 'I'd be glad if you would.' He made only a half-hearted attempt to eat; even his hearty appetite had been affected by the general gloom. Without glancing up he said, 'Old Lakeland told me this morning that his wife has gained a very good opinion of you over this committee work. She was not too happy over your unexpected arrival, as you know, so this change of attitude will be useful to us.' When she said nothing, he went on, 'I suppose Lady Mason will redouble her efforts to improve the hospital after this. Stavenham goes down there every day to visit the dying and says it is beyond belief.'

Her heart jumped with sudden fear. 'Surely it is more than dangerous and exceptionally foolhardy to wander among those who are in the grips of the sickness.'

'No more dangerous than simply being here in the cantonment. I believe he is doing it at Mason's request, in order to stop his wife going there on the same errand. Anyway, Stavenham is a robust fellow. He has survived several sabre wounds and withstands malarial fever quite regularly. I suppose he's not a bad sort, aside from his odd manner.'

Growing more and more surprised at his mellow mood, Elizabeth murmured, 'I believe any man would be a trifle uncommunicative after an experience such as he had eight years ago. Never to know the fate of his wife must be a heavy burden to bear.'

After a long pull at his ale, he put the tankard down and dabbed his mouth with the napkin, making quite a business of the small action. He seemed almost nervous as he looked her full in the eyes to say, 'By the by, my father's letter has arrived, at last. Some fool in Calcutta forwarded it to a Lieutenant de la Gaume stationed in Delhi. He returned it to Fort William and it has been travelling all over India ever since.'

Elizabeth finally understood the reason for his affability. 'Its arrival doubtless contributed toward Charlotte Lakeland's reversal of opinion. She no longer believes me to be lost to all sense of feminine obedience . . . and neither do you, William.'

For once, her sharpness did not rouse him to anger. He appeared too intent on his thoughts to notice her words. 'I found the contents of the letter rather surprising,' he continued with curious diffidence. 'My father was very frank with his account of the conditions which had persuaded him that he should buy you a passage to India, and which had suggested that he would serve me best by allowing you to sail before my permission could be sought. He is a very good man, you know, shrewd and straightforward. I should never have doubted his judgement, or his ability to guide my wife with soundness and understanding.' As he gazed at her across the table, his eyes betrayed a tenderness she had not seen there since their courtship. 'My dear, how could I guess that you so longed for me it made you ill? How should I guess that you had travelled with such eagerness to join a suspicious and ungrateful man who vowed to send you away again as soon as possible?' He left his meal to circle the table, and coaxed her to her feet by taking her hands. 'You tried to tell me on that first morning, but I was so enraged I would hear none of it. I have been a brute . . . a cold, unthinking brute. Can you forgive me, dearest?'

To Elizabeth's utter astonishment, he drew her into his arms to kiss her tenderly several times. 'My sweet adoring girl, I have the remedy for what ails you. My bed shall be moved to your room immediately and there it will stay. Our nights of pleasure will soon result in your heart's desire, I promise you, and we shall have splendid sons.'

His kisses were growing more passionate when her stunned senses recognized the sound of running footsteps and a voice calling her name. When William swiftly released her and turned to the doorway with a soft oath, she felt giddy with relief. The Delacourts must be mad! Whatever had the delayed letter contained to bring this about? To excuse their own actions, William's family had clearly told a pack of ridiculous lies suggesting that she was desperate for love and motherhood. How was she to deal with this?

The visitor was George Humphrey. He apologized for disturbing them, then said, 'I bear a message from my wife, ma'am. She is feeling a little unwell and seems almost desperate to speak to you.' Running a hand over his chin, he added with a touch of awkwardness, 'Her distress appears to concern a child. She says you will understand the situation. I felt obliged to obey her urgent request.'

Coming straight after William's promise to give her sons, Elizabeth guessed that her friend had finally obtained *her* heart's desire. The distressing sickness of pregnancy was best soothed by another female.

'I'll return with you now, sir,' she said warmly. 'I have a notion what ails Fanny, and there is no cause for alarm. I shall be glad to be of assistance.'

Telling William that she would be back soon, she then joined George outside the bungalow. He looked haggard and miserable, perhaps even guilty. Knowing his views on bringing children into an alien world, she suspected that he had upset Fanny on hearing the news. When the infant was born he would be as proud as any new father, she had no doubts. Until then, her friend would have to suffer his displeasure over something for which *he* was ultimately responsible.

Fanny was facing the window when Elizabeth tiptoed in and walked round the bed, thinking she must be asleep. The sense of gladness for her friend's happiness was replaced by shock at the sight of the girl's shrunken yellow features and her thin arms upon the sheet. This could have nothing to do with bearing a child, surely.

Fanny's dull eyes swivelled to look at Elizabeth and she mumbled. 'I have it. I have it. The baby. I cradled him in my arms and loved him right away.' The stricken face crumpled beneath the onslaught of tears. 'I could not stay away. Each day I went to see him with a gift. He was growing to know and love me, too. Then he . . . then he . . . died . . . and I . . . I.' Her dry hand reached out for Elizabeth's but there was no strength in its grip. 'Tell George . . . explain to him. He will not understand that I could not . . . not help myself. Tell him that . . . the feel of his tiny fingers . . . the little mouth . . . I could not help myself.' Beside herself with distress now, she begged Elizabeth to say what she could not to her husband. 'Tell George how a woman feels about children . . . and ask him . . . ask him to forgive . . .' Her words were ended by a bout of violent retching which left her exhausted and slavering.

Feeling ice in her veins, Elizabeth whispered to George, 'How long has she been as ill as this?'

'I have only just come in from my duties as Officer of the Day, but her servant says she has been sick since this morning. I am no use at a sickbed,' he confessed miserably. 'What is wrong with her, do you think?'

'Something which needs expert treatment,' she replied, as if by refusing to put a name to it she would refute the truth. 'You must fetch Captain Cockerford at once. Then I must talk to you very seriously.'

While she waited for George to bring back the surgeon, Elizabeth bathed Fanny's head and held her comfortingly during each spasm. All the while her mind rebelled against what was happening. It seemed too cruel that an instinctive passion for a child, which had led to Fanny making secret visits to the baby who had been cholera's first victim last week, should result in this terrible punishment. She had wanted to give love, to cherish the little creature and help it to thrive. Now it was dead, and the life was pouring from Fanny as Elizabeth watched. Her recent conversation with William returned as she recognized the look on her friend's face: Fanny Humphrey had accepted the end almost before the beginning.

The medical opinion was irrefutable. Captain Cockerford gave Elizabeth instructions to alleviate the suffering as much as possible, but his comforting clasp on the shoulder of the distraught husband told them both what he would not put into words. When he had gone, Elizabeth did her best to tell George of the instinctive need which had driven his wife to visit the ailing child of a trooper. Never having had the undeniable longing for a child of her own, she nevertheless managed to express the power of such yearning which sometimes defied all else.

'You must show her that you understand even if you do not,' she urged. 'She holds herself to blame and believes that you will not forgive her. Give her comfort, for pity's sake.'

When he went to sit beside the bed he seemed stunned. But he took Fanny's hands in his and told her that he would apply to return to England as soon as she was well enough to travel. They would raise a family in the cool greenness of their island home, he promised, and no one would be happier than he with his brood and with their loving mother.

Elizabeth stayed until sundown when Fanny died. She left George blaming himself for disregarding the importance of one of life's basic needs, and walked out to a glorious sky of orange and red which put a glow on everything in sight. Swallowing hard, she walked on through the cantonments to the perimeter, where she stood in contemplation of natural beauty. The plain lay like a deep pink sea with the minarets and cupolas rising from the distant brassy waves surrounding the old city. A sweet and savage land it truly was.

Chapter Eleven

When General Mason summoned to a meeting officers from every regiment garrisoned in Ratnapore, they concluded that he had decided to leave the cantonment to set up a cholera camp in a bid to end the outbreak which had taken so many lives. Worried about a course which would leave them exposed in open country without benefit of perimeter defences, John arrived at the meeting to discover what he considered to be a curious selection of men already waiting there. If they were to march out to cholera camp, only field officers and the most senior captains would be present. Here were a scattering of subalterns, some junior captains and just two majors — himself and a man named Galbraith of Kingsford's Horse. There was no colonel in sight.

Going straight across to Piers Galbraith, he said, 'This can't be what we expected. You and I are the senior men present. What's afoot?'

'I cannot imagine, old fellow, but it signals the probability that we two are liable to take the rub for it. There are some dashed queer things going on up here lately.' Putting a monocle to his right eye, he studied John affectedly. 'With you included in this mysterious affair we can doubtless resign ourselves to a few more.'

Before John could reply to that sly jibe, General Mason arrived with his aide and Wesley Clark, the Political Officer of Ratnapore Province, who had been called in from an out-station.

'Good morning, gentlemen, please sit,' said Sir Francis Mason. 'I shall be brief, but you might as well be comfortable while I relate several pieces of information before giving you orders.'

Once they were all settled, he announced some startling news. 'There has been an uprising of sepoys at the frontier fort of Multan. Their British officers have been overpowered and murdered. Reinforcements are now on their way, and it is considered advisable for us to strengthen the detachments at our own forts. Several weeks ago, I requested extra men to garrison Ratnapore. These regiments are presently only two days' march away.' He gave a dry smile. 'I see you are surprised, gentlemen. Contrary to the opinion held in these cantonments, we did not intend to take the recent outrages lying down. It has been our wish all along to force the issue with Ganda Singh and this affair at Multan has given us the opening we sought. It has also strengthened our suspicion of a possible Sikh uprising.

'Ordinarily, I would wait for the relieving regiments to reach us before detailing men for the out-stations but, in view of the cholera epidemic, I am sending you off immediately. Mr Clark has reported seeing large numbers of tribesmen on the move all over the province, so I feel it is essential to reinforce the frontier forts without delay. You will remain there for a considerable period and, because I am anxious to prevent further deaths from cholera, your families will be sent with you. I require you to march out at midnight tomorrow. By then the incoming regiments will be no more than several hours' march away, where I shall keep them under canvas until the epidemic ends.' His glance embraced them all. 'Your own troops or companies have been selected for frontier duty and the deployment will be as follows.'

His aide enumerated those detailed to reinforce Dhakti Fort under the command of Piers Galbraith, then announced that the remainder would strengthen Judapur Fort with Major Stavenham as their commander. When he had finished, Sir Francis took up the narrative once more.

'I am sorry that I cannot allow you any artillery but I must keep our guns here for the defence of civilians and the rest of your regiments. Each of the forts has a small battery so you will have to put it to the best use should the need arise. I want to make one thing very clear, however. There is no firm evidence that the province of Ratnapore is about to take arms against us, so this is merely a precautionary measure. My orders are still to preserve peace, if at all possible.' He smiled at the two majors. 'It will be up to you gentlemen to decide whether or not those orders can be fulfilled. The forts would be the initial targets in any attack, as you are well aware. I place complete confidence in you both to act with wisdom and circumspection in the coming weeks.'

He went on to give details of marching order, stores, pack animals and all the sundry items which must be considered when large numbers of troops are on the march. His listeners grew more and more lighthearted. Boredom, frustration, and fears of illness all dropped away at the prospect of leaving this place behind and possibly making a positive move against tribesmen who had had things their way for too long.

John sat working out which officers he would have with him. His heart sank as he realized that William's troop was among those detailed for Judapur. Not only would Elizabeth be within the claustrophobic confines of the fort, Rupert would also be under his command. Continuing with the list, he cursed the inclusion of Henry Nicholson's company. He did not like the man and would prefer not to have an officer with a penchant for young Indians in a force with a large percentage of native troops. He felt a deep sense of unease as he realized there might be more hazards inside Judapur Fort than outside its ancient walls.

The column marched out at midnight with astonishing military punctuality. It stretched for several miles because the two forts lay in the same general direction for the first twenty-five miles, so the first camp was to be set up at the parting of their ways. After that, the detachment for Judapur would travel for a further two days in a north-westerly direction. Those for Dhakti would continue for three days to the north-north-west of that camp. Kingsford's Horse provided the advance and rear guards. The British cavalry was to give flanking protection to the marching column. Major Stavenham and Major Galbraith were leading the combined force with several of their officers. The remainder were spaced along the lines of plodding men with a bevy of cornets acting as escorts for the ladies.

The rank and file were in high spirits despite the fact that they were crossing a plain shrouded by night, with only the flares spaced alongside the column to provide illumination. Sir Hugo Carruthers had been viciously done to death out here, and who could be certain that his killers were not waiting for them? They were perfectly visible by dint of their marching lights, but hidden tribesmen could ride out of the darkness before they knew it. However, there were piquets out in every direction who would sound the alarm in plenty of time, and a strong, armed force was a different prospect from the small peaceful contingent who had been driven to jump the nullah that day. They refused to be worried.

The prospect of a short march was very pleasant. Three or four days comprised a nice easy trip with none of the weary, endless dragging of feet they had experienced on other marches, and frontier forts sounded like paradise after cholera-ridden cantonments. Aside from the refreshment of being actively on the move, there was a general expectation that they were going to get the chance to show the tribesmen that they were real soldiers who meant business. It was as well they did not know that their two commanders had been given orders to maintain peace if they could.

John expressed his opinion on those orders rather forcibly to Galbraith as they headed along the dust road in the wake of the advance guard, their way lit by torch bearers holding aloft the flaming brands.

'Don't you think an uprising is inevitable, Piers? The war left things in a most unsatisfactory state. Any man with experience of that conflict will tell you that the Punjab will never be peaceful until it has been completely annexed and the warring leaders neutralized. By attempting to keep the situation calm, we are merely allowing them time to organize themselves for the war they mean to have.'

'Or time to reconsider their actions before arousing the army of a powerful British government.'

'Oh come, man, you can still say that after the events of the past week or so? They have flung down the gauntlet and are regarding us with derision because we have ignored it.'

Galbraith shook his greying head. 'Lakeland told me he thought you a hothead, and I have to agree with him. You are set on tangling with these people, come what may.'

'I shall heed our order, never fear,' John assured him with slight acidity, 'but despite my reputation for sabre-rattling, old Mason has confidence enough to give me command of Judapur.'

'In view of Lakeland's present illness he had little choice,' was the dampening reply. 'It's no doubt due to the fact that your colonel appears to have the cholera upon him that your regiment has been so badly deployed. Mason has paid no heed to the situation between you and young Carruthers. Here was the perfect opportunity to remove him from your vicinity, yet he has ignored it. He has also sent Nicholson's company with you and if what I hear about that knave is true there will be an unwelcome familiarity in the ranks of his native infantrymen . . . to say nothing of his child-bride's long-standing worship of your aristocratic enemy. Add young Humphrey's grief, which is liable to cause him to jump on to the nearest sword in battle, and you have the very deuce of an explosive collection for your very first command. Let us all hope the fort at Judapur does not come under attack.'

The sudden jogging motion as the cavalry began a period of trotting was not the only reason for added vigour in his voice as John retaliated in sarcastic vein.

'I am touched by your faith in my ability to control men under my command, especially as you had no way of knowing I successfully led four entire squadrons in the charge at Moodki after Alloway had been cut to pieces in the preliminary skirmish.'

Major Galbraith glanced across quickly but the darkness of night hid the expression on his long bewhiskered face. 'I did know, John, and I apologize. I did not mean to doubt your ability, but I do feel that you have been put in charge of a set of personal situations which might prove harder to handle at Judapur than a Sikh attack.'

'So they might,' he agreed ruefully, 'but I'm a great believer in destiny, and therefore accept whatever this command entails.'

His thoughts ran along those lines during the ensuing silence, and he caught himself wondering if Elizabeth's gift of second sight had given her knowledge of what lay ahead. He longed for her even more since that poignant conversation in which she had revealed the truth about Wellford, yet she was as unattainable as ever. Added to his helpless jealousy of Delacourt, was a new rage over that insensitive giant's treatment of his wife. The man clearly had no understanding of Elizabeth's deep longing for knowledge, of her need for passion based on intellect as well as physical desire. In order to mend her marriage she could only sublimate her own personality to what little there was of his. It would surely break her . . . and at Judapur Fort he would have to stand by and watch it happen. Cruel destiny to have placed her beneath his command and ultimate protection! Even his request to General Mason for a change in command to that of Dhakti, ostensibly because of Rupert's state of mind which might endanger others in a time of crisis, had met with a blank refusal. Sir Francis did not believe in putting personal relationships before military demands. He told John firmly, but with understanding, that a soldier must concentrate on the common foe, not on the compatibility of his comrades.

Rupert's vow of vengeance remained a threat, although John no longer doubted his own actions over the events leading to Hugo's death. He had certainly forgotten his friend's comment about the horse's reluctance to jump, but there had been no alternative to crossing the nullah to avoid the slaughter of all twelve in the detachment. The revolt at Multan, and the murder of British officers there, surely confirmed what he had been predicting, so he was vindicated on that score. Sir Francis had enough faith in him to delegate command in this emergency, and if Justin Lakeland fell victim to cholera, the man might never see his ex-Hussar prove himself as good as any Dragoon. With experience in war against the Sikhs to stand him in good stead, John had enough confidence to face any challenge in the coming months.

The women of the regiments, plus their children, travelled with the baggage at the rear of the column in hackeries; small ox-carts that shook every bone in their bodies as they lurched over the rough roads. The officers' ladies rode their own horses behind the column, escorted by the youngest subalterns, who ignored the teasing comments of their fellows and enjoyed the feminine company they rarely experienced.

Elizabeth thought she would remember this night for ever. Aware that John was way, way ahead, leading this tremendous military snake across the wide, starlit plain, the strange sounds and smells of an army on the move gave the experience a dreamlike quality which kept her silent and spellbound. For the first time, she sensed something of those intangible bonds which bound John to his profession and allowed him to forsake Wellford Manor for this life. For the first time, she felt a part of the regiment into which she had married.

The column had set off some thirty minutes before it was their turn to take up a position behind the animals needed to convey tents, food, ammunition, fodder and the personal luggage of soldiers on the move. The Delacourt baggage had been loaded onto five camels, apart from the small bandbox attached to her saddle and William's special equipment strapped to his charger. Their larger pieces of furniture had been put into hackeries with that of other officers. She had not endured the dreadful march from Calcutta with the regiment, so this was an experience which filled Elizabeth with amazement. It was a stirring moment when the regiments formed up and set off beneath the candle lamps in the cantonment, but as she watched the commissariat animals move forward behind the marching sepoys, she could hardly believe her eyes. They seemed never ending. Mules walked out, row upon resigned row, beneath their great loads; camels lurched forward on great spongy feet, belching angrily at drivers who prodded them continuously with their sticks; hackeries rumbled and creaked over the bumpy road, the paired oxen plodding in step so that their heads nodded in unison like clockwork toys. With all the baggage and stores loaded onto animals, just as many again were needed to carry fodder for the horses which carried the cavalry on their backs. And the more beasts there were conveying fodder, the more fodder was required, reasoned Elizabeth as she watched the proceedings. Therefore, there must be some animals who were, in effect, doing no more than carry the sustenance necessary for them to make the journey themselves.

It was such a provocative premise, she longed to ask John if it could possibly be true. He would either explain the complexity she had missed, or laugh in gentle teasing at her theory. William would brush her interest aside and ignore the question. When all the animals had gone, and those traders from the bazaar who had decided to accompany the column to the forts had moved off with their assortment of carts, gharries or asses, the ladies were invited by their escorts to join the column whose head was now well out across the plain. Five minutes after they had left the cantonments, the rear guard would depart, watching for signs of aggressors coming from behind.

It was a curious sensation to ride through the darkness with only the flickering brands spaced out alongside the ranks to reveal that they followed a three-mile-long procession. Elizabeth had only once before crossed this plain. On that occasion she had known an inexplicable sensation of unhappiness mingled with pain awaiting her in the station spread on the distant slope. She had spent only a month at Ratnapore; four weeks filled with drama enough to satisfy most women for a lifetime. She was crossing the plain once more, moving on beyond that place where she had anticipated John's presence so powerfully. Tonight was so full of the concerted emotions of those out here beneath the stars, and so vibrant with her own awareness of destiny playing the next hand, it did not surprise her when the fleeting sense of precognition touched her once more. Her heartbeat accelerated alarmingly as a flutter of dread deepened to one of anticipated grieving, and an abstract knowledge of pain in her own limbs lingered long enough to register before it vanished beneath a warm flow of gladness similar to that on arriving at a beloved place. It was all so momentary, yet so forceful, she sighed with the burden of such foreknowledge. What did it all mean? Pain and happiness, sweetness and savagery: the mixture of India as John had once described it on that hillside in Sussex. It lay ahead, yet near enough to tell her it would come soon, and her heartbeat had calmed until a strange lethargy overtook her to banish any sense of alarm.

She rode on through the tingling night-time aura, the regular swaying movement and the slumber song of squeaking leather, snorting animals, creaking carts and jingling harness created a soporific effect which almost made nonsense of that moment of future clarity. Just as she began to nod, she was awakened by voices. Rupert and another lieutenant had galloped the length of the column to warn everyone that they were approaching Mashni Pass, and would take a short rest while reconnaissance of the narrow defile was made by piquets.

The ladies were helped to the ground by their young escorts who spread blankets on the ground for them. Elizabeth declared that she would prefer to walk for a while and Lucy joined her, both women initially silenced by the surrounding scene. The starlit night surrounded them so that it was impossible to see the hills a mile or so ahead. It was in Mashni Pass that John's patrol had been attacked. Elizabeth wondered how he would feel riding through it in darkness with that recollection in his mind. How would she feel knowing that he had been in mortal danger there a month ago? It was comforting to be surrounded by many other souls and hundreds of beasts, all protected by armed troops. She gave a wry smile. This was one of the few times that she would have been grateful for the proximity of masculine strength and William was nowhere near!

'How strange this night seems,' she murmured to Lucy, as they walked within the area of light thrown from the torches now driven into the ground on long spiked poles. 'I cannot believe that we must be wary of attack. There was never any such fear during my long journey from Calcutta, and I did not feel the least apprehension even in the remotest areas.'

'You had Rupert with you,' came the ingenuous answer. 'I always felt perfectly safe in his company. He took me badger-hunting whenever he felt kindly disposed toward me when we were young, you know, and I was never afraid of the darkness. If he refused to include me in his plans, I would ride over the estate and wait until I saw him creep out with the sack on his back. I daresay he disliked me intensely when I threatened to scream until he promised to take me with him.'

Elizabeth walked a few paces before saying, 'I think one of us may have to resort to something like that if we are to make any impression upon his misguided refusal of our friendship.'

Lucy looked at her swiftly, her eyes bright from the glow of clustered flares. 'I couldn't. I have to be careful. Henry would not like me to . . . to draw attention to my fondness . . .'

'No more would William if I took the matter up,' she pointed out firmly, 'but I feel very strongly that we must make another attempt to reach him before arriving at the fort. If there should be an attack at any time, Rupert is liable to behave unpredictably. He could endanger us all, as well as himself.'

The girl looked indignant. 'He would never put anyone in danger. He's the most courageous person I know.'

'I know he has courage. I had evidence of it in the desert. My dear, our young friend accuses Major Stavenham of killing his brother, but he knows all too well that the actual deed was done by Indians. Put a sword in his hand and confront him with any brown-faced enemies and he will extract vengeance.'

'But isn't that . . '

'*Vengeance*, Lucy, not defence of his regiment, his queen or his country. He will kill as a means of personal retaliation and all else might be forgotten beneath that irresistible urge. His own life and the lives of those around him may count as nothing to the demon possessing him. Don't you think we should risk our husband's disapproval for such a cause?'

As they turned to walk back toward their horses, someone called that they were again on the move. It was not until they were mounted and taking up their places that Lucy resumed the subject of Rupert.

'I have no notion how to do as you suggest, Elizabeth,' she confessed unhappily. 'I am sorry to say it but he frightens me now. He's so cold and aloof, almost fearsome in manner as he salutes in passing. I wonder if he is the same person.'

'Of course he is not the same person,' Elizabeth cried in exasperation. 'He has lost a beloved brother in the most horrific manner. How can he be the same? Small wonder he is cold and aloof toward a childhood friend who clearly has no understanding of what he is suffering. Rupert is not a small boy who creeps out in the night to go badger-hunting, Lucy, he is a shattered young man . . . and you are no longer a tangle-haired child tagging along behind him with a slice of apple cake with which to please him. Good heavens, if it has not yet dawned on you that beautiful young women use different weapons toward gentlemen than children employ, you are a great deal sillier than you should be.'

Silence fell between them and continued as they neared Mashni Pass. Although piquets had declared the way to be clear of obvious danger, recollections of the return of a torn and bloody patrol were too vivid to allow anyone full confidence. They would all breathe more easily when the rocky defile was behind them. Elizabeth could now just make out the dark hills against the glittering spread of sky directly ahead. John must already be between those enclosing walls where he had been slashed with a sabre. She shivered involuntarily, as if his sensations were her own.

It was eerie within the pass when she finally entered. The twists and turns cut off vision of all but those directly ahead, so the comfort of seeing endless jogging ranks, illuminated by flares, was instantly removed. Yet the echoing sounds of the column's progress told her that they were there, albeit unseen. The additional comfort of the wide starry heavens had also been lost. The only area of sky visible to her now was that which she saw on tilting her head right back. Unfortunately, she also saw imaginary enemies in the dark jutting shapes in the rock walls, so she concentrated on the figures directly before her and counted the minutes until she would be out and free on the far side. Due to the narrowness of the pass and the uneven, difficult ground beneath feet and hooves, progress slowed drastically. Those in the rear were forced to spend long stationary periods while the various bottlenecks cleared, so tempers and nerves were sorely tried by the time the entire column had traversed the only route through the hills.

The delay meant that it was as late as nine a.m. before camp was set. To Elizabeth's tired eyes, the procedure gave an impression of chronic lack of organization. Pack animals were unloaded amid the cacophony of cries and arguments which seemed to accompany any activity of the camp followers; troops swarmed all over the site to perform those duties which must be done before taking a well-earned rest; tents rose up like white pointed flowers springing from the dry soil; cooks lit fires to prepare breakfast and yelled for pots and pans lost in the mounds of stores being taken from the backs of mules; beasts were allowed to go in relays to the narrow river to drink long and thankfully; fights broke out between native traders over the most favourable sites for stalls, and officers rode back and forth shouting orders which no one heeded. It seemed impossible for calm ever to be restored.

Elizabeth went gratefully into their tent to be served with breakfast. She had seen William briefly after halting and he had told her to carry on without him as he had his hands full trying to regulate the rush of the regiment's horses to the river.

'If they get out of hand and stampede, we shall have so much mud stirred up, the water will be undrinkable,' he had said as he rode off, shouting at some troopers who were being dragged toward the river by thirst-crazed beasts.

The tent provided shade, but little air to cool the stifling atmosphere within it. Only by securing the flaps open and sacrificing privacy could Elizabeth relieve the sense of suffocation, for there were no punkahs here to make life pleasanter. After washing her face and hands in the canvas bowl on a stand, she sat on one of the folding chairs to enjoy tea and scrambled eggs. The long ride had made her hungry. It also brought a longing for sleep. As she watched the officers riding frantically along the riverbank, shouting and waving in an attempt to head off a rush of mules intent on getting a drink, she reflected that William would also need to sleep when he joined her. Fanny's death on the day the Delacourt letter had reached him had delayed his response to it, then preparations for this journey had taken all his attention. However, his father's unexpected declaration of her supposed reason for coming to India had made a deep impression on the man who had thought nothing of leaving her behind. He had been consideration itself and full of gentle apologies for all she might endure during this march. It had not once occurred to him that she might find the experience fascinating, and the new accord between them was based on his belief that she was, after all, a submissive wife who wished for nothing more than to bear and nourish his children — all of them sons, naturally.

What was she to do? The olive branch was offered; the chance to mend her marriage was there to grasp. On leaving England she had vowed to make William and those around her happy . . . yet where was the happiness for herself? Had she truly intended to accept *any* terms and conditions in order to live with William in India? Perhaps she had believed she would; perhaps desperation had persuaded her that she must pay penance for what she had done at Wellford and make no complaint. Did that penance demand that she should endure nightly assaults by a man she could never love, and produce children who would be reared in a manner she could never approve? Must she surrender the desire for experience and learning, the hunger for colour in everything she did, the thrill she found in exploring this land and those who lived uneasily together here? Was there no alternative to

216

becoming exactly like William's mother and sisters? Everything within her cried out in protest at the prospect, yet it now seemed inescapable.

Restless, she moved to the entrance of the tent and stood watching the kaleidoscopic scene before her. *This* was life: marching through shadowy passes, over wide plains where lighted brands gave an indefinable air of mystery to the night, across undulating scrub behind rows of men and beasts whose thoughts were as wild as the land they crossed. *Here* was true fulfilment: a vast uniformed family with each member dependent on the others, some needing help and understanding, some requiring confidence, some living in a fearful world which allowed no one in to offer comfort. *Now* she had found the crock of gold at the end of that elusive rainbow . . . yet she could not hold on to it. For a moment her vision blurred as unshed tears touched her eyes. When it cleared again, there was a man on a tall black horse riding toward her through the lines between the tents. It seemed that he intended to ride on past, but suddenly drew rein beside her.

'Is your tent quite comfortable?' John asked formally.

'Very,' she replied, knowing why she found accepting William's olive branch so difficult. 'I think I have never before been so glad to be a woman. We may rest and eat breakfast; you must all attempt to bring order.' Before she could stop herself, she added lightly, 'If the chaos down by the river is any indication, you appear to be failing miserably.'

He gave one of his unexpected smiles which changed his stern expression miraculously. '*We* are doing our utmost, ma'am. It is the mules who are not.'

Responding instinctively to his smile, she gave a light laugh. 'Nevertheless, it is the beasts who earn my sympathy. *You* did not have their loads to carry throughout the day.'

Taking off his shako, he wiped his forehead with the back of his hand in a weary gesture as he scanned the scene. Seeing no one approaching, he turned back to her.

'I'm sorry we made camp so late. This was the longest leg of our journey and, in addition, the pass caused delays. Did you find the march exhausting?'

'I'm tired, yes, but it was an experience I shall always remember. You once spoke of the complications of an army on the move, if you recall. Like everything else you described to me, I found proof of your unerring verbal power to convey the truth.'

This reference to an interlude they must both forget brought

217

bleakness back to his face, and he said briefly, 'I tried to change commands so that your husband would serve under Major Galbraith. General Mason would not hear of it. My apologies.' With that he saluted and moved on through the lines, inspecting the neat row of tents as he rode.

William came in tired, angry, and very hungry. While he consumed a large breakfast, Elizabeth lay on her bed with her eyes closed. At Judapur Fort it would be impossible not to see John every day. In such a small community they would be thrown together continuously. That brief encounter outside the tent showed her how easily they could both recapture the rapport which existed between them; how easily they could re-ignite the flame which must be totally extinguished. Under these harrowing conditions, she would be obliged to embark on a new relationship with William; one which demanded that she did all the giving and he continued the path he had always taken. Surely an attempt to mend a marriage should be a compromise, not the complete capitulation of one partner. If love existed, perhaps such terms would be acceptable, but she knew indisputably that she would never love William and that his new tenderness was based only on the gratification of believing that he would be getting the submissive wife he had always wanted. Her husband had no intention of changing any aspect of his life or character in order to please her and, now that the moment of truth was there before her, she knew she could not take the olive branch. It was not an offer of peace but a demand for unconditional surrender.

Hearing William sink on to the adjacent bed with a heavy grunt, Elizabeth faced the inevitable. Marriage to this man under his inflexible terms, promised a future as grey as the one she had faced in England. Rebellion flared within her breast as it had in the early days of her marriage. She *could* not become a submissive creature with a string of subdued children; she *would* not abandon her longings for expression, discovery, and vitality when such things lay within her grasp. No, no, her inner self cried. It would be as well to enter a prison from which there was no escape. She should have made her ultimatum at Ratnapore, told William his father had mistaken her reasons for joining him. She should have made it clear that her hopes had included elements she now realized were impossible to gain, that she had believed his wider experience of travelling in India would have altered his own expectations of marriage. Yes, she should have disillusioned him at Ratnapore, yet the lure of this march and an extension of her

218

experience in this fascinating country had been too strong. Foolishly, she had deferred the inevitable. Now, a brief moment with the one man who could give her all she yearned for had shown her the height of her folly. Her presence at Judapur would torment them both, and she had done John enough harm already. Indeed, she *was* doomed to make men unhappy, for as soon as this emergency ended, she would leave William and return to Wellford to seek turbulent peace.

The Dhakti contingent got away first by half an hour and, because they had an extra day's march to make, Major Galbraith took the larger percentage of pack animals. In consequence, it was a much depleted column which headed off toward Judapur Fort, presently manned by a small contingent of sepoys under the command of British officers. Once the column joined them, the men of Forrester's Light Dragoons would form a small minority of white soldiers amid Indians. Henry Nicholson's infantrymen were all sepoys and the troopers of Kingsford's Horse were also natives of the country. This fact, along with evidence of two fresh cases of cholera in their ranks, caused a slight dampening of spirits among the scarlet-coated cavalrymen now that half their colleagues had gone off to Dhakti. The mood transferred itself to some of the officers when they made camp for the second time, and John walked in to the Mess Tent to find Nicholson's subaltern regaling those present with a tale of woe concerning the cooking arrangements for his men. There were constant problems in native regiments where the caste system ruled that a sepoy could only eat food prepared by a member of his own caste. In cantonments the difficulties were few, but confusion often reigned on the march, causing meals to be given to the wrong men. Then there was uproar, anger and near mutiny, as Lieutenant Peters had just experienced.

'Several of my most meritorious men practically came to blows over a plate of rice,' he ended with a sigh as he picked up his glass of ale.

John was helping himself to breakfast from the silver dishes set on a table at the far end of the large marquee, when he heard Rupert say coldly, 'Why ever do you pay regard to their absurd whims? If our men demanded individual attention because they did not fancy the style of their cook, they would receive very short change, I assure you. They are our own countrymen, what's more. These natives must regard you with derision for allowing them more rein than British troops.'

Jason Peters was fiercely proud of his sepoys, so rose to their defence hotly. 'We ask them to be loyal to us, so we must earn it by respecting their customs and traditions. Kick a sepoy in April and he will cut your throat in July, you fool. Anyway, you should recognize the importance of caste, Carruthers. You employ it enough yourself.'

This oblique reference to Rupert's snobbish attitude was the result of having suffered too many slights from men like him who believed that officers of native regiments were vastly inferior. Before John could intervene, however, Rupert was on his feet in a dangerously volatile state.

'Are you making a comparison between me and those damned savages of yours?'

'Sit down, for God's sake,' advised George Humphrey with unusual anger. 'You're making an issue over nothing.'

'They are not "damned savages",' roared Peters, ignoring George and others who tried to prevent a confrontation. 'I will not hear them termed as such, I tell you.'

'Will you not?' asked Rupert icily. 'I must inform you that I shall use the term whenever I choose. In addition, I begin to think those brown boys hold excessive charm for more than one of their officers.'

Peters was up and trying to seize Rupert across the table set with silver and breakfast plates. 'You will apologize for that,' he panted. 'You will take that back or I'll choke the retraction from you. You have gone too far.'

'So have you, *fellow*,' sneered Rupert. 'I tolerate bad manners from no one, especially those with whom only circumstance forces me to mingle. I suggest you remain with your own kind in future.'

John moved toward them swiftly. 'That's quite enough, gentlemen,' he told them with sharp authority. 'This is an officers' mess and you will respect it as such. You will also observe the rules while you are in it, which state that no member's integrity or honour shall be publicly questioned. We are *all* gentlemen here and must behave accordingly.' Looking directly at Rupert, he saw that the boy's face was white, his eyes blazing with unreasonable malice. 'Mr Peters has demanded an apology,' he continued. 'I hope your comment was not intended to convey what he read into it, but your attitude has been offensive throughout and I believe he is entitled to ask you to withdraw the words he found insulting.'

Turning to Jason Peters, he said, 'Your behaviour is not blameless. I must ask you and Sir Rupert to leave, taking with you Mr Calthorpe and Mr Weekes as mediators. This is not the place to settle an affair of this kind, but I want the issue dealt with by the time we march tonight. Any hint of discord between their officers has a detrimental effect on the men, and I will not have it.'

With a stiff apology, Peters and his friend Leo Weekes collected their shakos and left. Miles Calthorpe struggled to his feet, bottle in hand, already three-quarters drunk. He stood unsteadily beside Rupert as John addressed a further remark to the brother of a man he had counted his friend.

'We may soon have need of all our resources, and of trust in our fellows. This kind of thing is foolish in the extreme. If he insists on an apology, you'll give him one. Is that clear?'

Rupert's lip curled. 'If that is an order I must obey it . . . but no one can govern what I think, sir.'

'No one can govern what any of us thinks,' John replied quietly. 'Thoughts should be rational and based on wisdom acquired through experience. Bear that in mind before you allow your tongue to run away with you again.'

Rupert chose not to respond to this attempt at sympathethic advice. Treating John to a withering glance, he bowed stiffly, said 'Excuse us, gentlemen,' and sauntered out with his inebriated colleague on his heels.

When John returned to selecting his breakfast, silence ruled those left sitting at the table. When he sat with them to eat, their conversation was stilted. The greater number of them commanded Indians and therefore shared the slight dealt to Jason Peters. Doggedly working his way through his meal, John had cause to reflect that his misgivings on this command were already being justified. However, Sir Francis Mason was no fool. Vendettas within a regiment were dangerous. Keeping the principals apart only prolonged it. By sending Rupert to Judapur, the wise old campaigner was forcing the situation to a head, possibly saving a promising young officer from ruining his career before it had really begun. The move was also a compliment to John's ability to cope with difficulties during an emergency. At least, that is how he saw it.

When they struck camp for the third time, the procedure was swift and competent. Everyone had found the right and wrong way of doing things, and there was some slight regret that there would be no more travelling after today's very short march to the fort. As it was a distance of no more than nine miles, John waited until dawn broke before moving off. The terrain was much the same as they had been crossing since leaving Ratnapore, except for a stretch of thorn jungle fringing the plain on which the fort stood. This obstacle would give only minor difficulties to men and horses, but laden pack animals and hackeries required wide tracks between trees. These had to be cut before the column could penetrate the jungle, so an advance party under the command of Leo Weekes had left several hours earlier. Their success was dependent upon the density of the thorn bushes.

John was deep in thought as he swayed along beside Henry Nicholson, the senior captain present now and therefore second-in-command of the column. John had seen mules torn to ribbons on thorns when heedless drivers had tried to force them through totally unsuitable paths. That must be avoided at all costs. The animals were valuable assets to men isolated in the heart of wild country. Any losses meant less could be carried in an emergency. It might be wise to halt for breakfast after the troops had cleared the jungle, then he could personally supervise the passage of the animals and baggage.

'Dust is rising on the horizon,' said Henry suddenly. 'We are not the only men travelling this morning.'

John came from his thoughts to stare at the moving, heat-hazed distance, alert and ready to deploy his men. Despite Wesley Clark's report of large bodies of tribesmen crossing the province, this was the first time they had encountered travellers other than traders in caravans, who moved so slowly they rarely raised enough dust to be seen at a distance.

'What do you think?' he asked the saturnine man riding beside him, as they continued at a walking pace. 'I can't believe there are more than two or three riders there.'

'I agree. The most likely explanation is that one of our piquets is returning to tell us of a problem concerning the progress of our men cutting through the jungle. Thorn is the very devil to penetrate.'

A lone rider was soon discernible. With the aid of his field glasses, John could see that he wore the uniform of Kingsford's Horse, and that he was galloping flat out toward them.

'As you suspected, there is clearly a problem,' he murmured, watching the trooper's progress along the dirt road. 'We've been fortunate to come this far without one, I suppose.'

Fifteen minutes passed before the man reached them. When he reined in beside John and saluted, his face was impassive and his horse was lathered and exhausted. Taking the message he had brought, John told him to find a *bheestie* with water for himself and his charger. Then he opened the several sheets of paper sent by Lieutenant Weekes, who had been in command of the advance party. After reading the scribbled words, he looked across at Henry Nicholson with a frown.

'They have discovered a mutilated body in the thick of the jungle. Although it is dressed as a tribesman, this message hidden in his turban suggests that the poor devil was a military galloper.' He held out the second sheet of paper. 'This is dated six days ago from Lieutenant Fraser, commanding Judapur Fort. He writes that they are surrounded and under threat from their own men who are being constantly wooed by invitations to join the besiegers. This is an urgent request for reinforcements.'

Nicholson took the message and read for himself the brief plea for help. Glancing across at John, he asked, 'What else does Weekes say?'

'That he penetrated the jungle with caution, taking only two men, and came upon enemy piquets. The walls of the fort are apparently still manned by troops from the regiment stationed there . . . but the flag is no longer flying and there is a large force encamped on the plain surrounding it.'

The man who himself commanded Indian troops made no comment on this evidence of a second mutiny against British officers in a frontier fort. He knew the people of this land too well.

'Set about halting the column,' said John decisively. 'We're almost certainly too late to save Fraser and his subaltern, but we must recapture that fort. How we are possibly to do that without artillery, when they have command of the fort's cannon, only God can tell.'

Chapter Twelve

The column halted in a great sprawl of men, women and beasts all along the track. It was not a camp, nor even a bivouac, for John gave no permission for fires to be lit for brewing tea or for any other activity usual when making a halt on the march. A trooper had been sent to recall Leo Weekes's party and until those men arrived, John decreed that the column must be ready to move at a moment's notice. Without tents or trees to provide shade, the men sought it beneath cloaks draped over their rifles, beneath the bellies of laden animals, in the shadow cast by hackeries piled high with furniture. The regimental wives and children did the same, along with the camp followers. Those few officers' ladies at the rear of the column unfurled dainty sunshades which contrasted oddly with the warlike uniforms and with their own severely-tailored habits. The officers remained stoically beneath the sun, either grouped around their commander or strolling restlessly back and forth in earnest pairs, constantly searching the distance for evidence of the returning group. Over the scene hung an uneasy, sweltering hush. Although no one save the officers knew the contents of the message Weekes had sent, there was certainly some kind of emergency which could only be resolved when the Kingsford's Horse lieutenant arrived with further facts.

John stood beside the table where he had set out his map of the area. With him were Henry Nicholson, William Delacourt, and Weekes's second-in command, James Doyle; the senior officers of each regiment present. He had shown them all the messages he had been sent and credited them with the ability to assess the difficulties ahead without his outlining them. Reference to the map strengthened their belief that the force which had now taken the fort viewed the jungle as perfect protection. A wide band of thorn trees formed a very effective perimeter defence. An advancing army could not possibly rush through such deadly terrain without warning, and John was leading no army, but a small reinforcing column with cumbersome baggage. He was

understandably preoccupied, knowing that they were all in open country which offered no cover in the event of an attack. His only consolation was that the thorn was to their *own* advantage, too.

At last, the familiar cloud of dust ahead heralded the arrival of Leo Weekes, an admirable East India Company officer who surely had a brilliant future in military service. The young man's pleasing features were grim beneath the dust and sweat as he dismounted and saluted John.

'The fort is definitely in enemy hands, sir. As Fraser would never have surrendered, we have to believe that both officers and any loyal sepoys have been murdered by the mutineers,' he said, with the regret of a man who had forged strong links with the Indian people.

John nodded. 'Your message suggested as much. How large a force is on the plain?'

Taking off his shako and wiping his brow with the back of his hand, the Lieutenant pursed his lips. 'It's hard to estimate the number of actual troops. They don't set camp as we do with lines in orderly fashion. All I can tell you is that they occupy a goodly area close to the water tank, and that their camp resembles a native bazaar more than anything else. They are nevertheless an army with six light field pieces. You will be exceedingly interested to hear that their pennants are those of Ganda Singh. The old devil made his move at the same time as the mutiny at Multan, that's obvious, and our fort at Dhakti is probably in the hands of more of his troops.'

'It was always clear to me that he was awaiting the right moment,' agreed John, too worried to feel satisfied at this justification for his warnings. 'We're now in the very deuce of a situation.'

'But not a hopeless one,' came the vigorous response, accompanied by a glance which encompassed the other officers around the table. 'It's my belief that Judapur has only recently fallen. The men on that plain are in the relaxed, jubilant mood which usually follows a victory.' Fastening his gaze on John again, he added, 'They have piquets out, sir. We almost ran into them but successfully circumnavigated their positions without revealing ourselves. If we attack immediately, we shall have every advantage of surprise. They have no idea that we are here, as yet. My men went and returned silently.' He sighed. 'They are the best anyone could hope to command, Major Stavenham.'

Recognizing championship of Indian troops in the face of two mutinies, John gripped his shoulder. 'I know, Leo. You have all done

splendid service this morning. Show me on the map all you can memorize of how the enemy is deployed and the positions of their piquets.'

Weekes reached into his sabretache. 'No need for that, sir. I sketched everything on the spot.'

John smiled. 'Good man! Let's align the drawings to the map and consider the possibilities open to us.'

For some minutes, the officers bent over the table to study the symbols and lines easily translated by military men, then John glanced up at Weekes with a frown.

'Is it conceivable that we could dispose of their piquets silently, and unobserved by the encamped troops?'

The young officer in blue uniform nodded. 'They seem very confident of the obstructive capacity of those confounded thorn trees, so their vigilance is relaxed. That jungle is tiresomely thick, so the presence or absence of their piquets cannot be observed by the main force.'

'Good. If the piquets are removed will it then be possible for us to penetrate the thorn in our own time?'

Weekes's pale eyes narrowed in concentration as he nodded again. 'Perfectly possible. The jungle thins on the far side which would allow us to form up there in battle-order before breaking cover. There is a very gentle downward slope leading to the plain which would aid a surprise charge. Unfortunately, those damned cannon on the fortifications have full command of the area around the fort itself.'

John straightened from his study of the map and gave a faint smile as he addressed all four officers present. 'When I knew we were coming to Judapur, I consulted Whitechurch of the Artillery. His contempt for the fort's weapons was extremely disheartening, because my enquiry was based on the premise of having to use them myself. Those cannon are ancient, ineffective and, like the fort itself, in great need of repair. Loading the guns takes far too long and their trajectory is insufficient to do more than token damage to an advancing horde.' His smile deepened. 'Whitechurch's exact words, gentlemen.'

'Small wonder the fort fell,' observed Henry Nicholson, gazing into the distance with his usual brooding expression.

'And every chance of its falling again,' John said determinedly. 'This is how I propose to bring that about. Speed is essential if we are to take advantage of surprise attack during their present euphoria. We shall

226

advance with all haste, leaving the baggage train to move up to within two miles of the thorn at its own pace. Small parties of picked men will precede us and deal with the enemy piquets while we cut our way through to where the trees thin. Once I have seen the situation, I will deploy our own troops to the best advantage for a dusk attack. Fading light will further aid our surprise.' He looked at the four faces around him. 'Yes, gentlemen, I know that we run the risk of being overtaken by night in the midst of battle, but waiting for dawn to break might entail even greater risk. The enemy could be joined by reinforcements, the piquets will certainly be changed before then and the dead ones discovered, to say nothing of the impossibility of our pushing through the jungle in total darkness. Warfare is essentially a matter of acting to create the best possible advantage to oneself, so we must go now and pray that the element of surprise will be sufficient to ensure our success before night falls.' He began folding his map. 'Prepare to move off, leaving the usual guards to accompany stores and baggage. You must each detail a junior subaltern to remain with the column. They will prepare a field hospital and protect the ladies.' He turned to Weekes. 'I place you in command in my absence.'

'But, sir . . .'

'No, man, you performed very able service this morning but you are tired. We may have a siege ahead of us once we regain the fort. You will serve me best by substituting for me here, and using your splendid initiative should anything go wrong and the column fall under attack.'

The eager warrior still betrayed disappointment and John resolved to give him the very first opportunity to show his mettle during the coming war, for war it would certainly be now. With that prospect in mind, he could not help feeling dismayed when the armed men formed up to march at a good steady pace toward their objective. They were a very short column without pack animals and stores. Nicholson's Infantrymen, wearing green and yellow with buff turbans, stepped out bravely enough, but John would have liked at least three times their number. The Kingsford's Horse contingent bobbed along like three ranks of rippling blue water; water which ran out far too soon. The scarlet of John's adopted regiment stood out far too vividly against the faded colours of the landscape, making him wish their jackets were less conspicuous. Even so, they looked fearsome enough for any commander as they trotted at the head of this tiny force, ready to take on the unknown. John prayed they would prove as fearsome as they looked when confronting the enemy. They were untried in battle, unlike the two Native regiments, and reputed to be badly officered on the lower levels. What he was about to attempt was difficult enough for crack troops much less a contingent as uncertain of his command as he was of them.

They made good progress until the formidable jungle loomed. At that point, John detailed those who must go ahead to deal with the piquets, showing them on the map where they should be, unless their positions had been changed. Impressing upon the men the fact that the task must be done silently and unobtrusively, he sent them off with an outer assurance that disguised his inner apprehension. If the alarm should be given to Ganda Singh's troops, their own chances would be very slim.

Reaching the start of the trees, he halted and gathered all his officers together, his apprehension hardly allayed by his mental assessment of them. Whatever his sexual habits, Nicholson appeared to have total confidence in himself and his men. John hoped it was justified. The Infantry subalterns were typical examples of Company officers, from the clever, inventive professionals down to family misfits sent to India and lifelong obscurity. The Kingsford's subalterns were slightly more rakish in personality due to the regiment's preference for wild young men. There were good and bad amongst them, too, and John now regretted leaving young Weekes behind. Even a tired natural warrior was better than none. He then glanced at the Forrester's officers. William Delacourt had a splendid physique but was more of a social officer than a warlike one. Miles Calthorpe could actually prove to be a liability in battle. Cornets Minn and Petheridge cancelled each other out, one being intelligent and the other a foppish idiot. George Humphrey was another in the mould of Leo Weekes, but his wife's death had affected him so deeply John could not be as confident of the man's ability now. Then there was Sir Rupert Carruthers. The young aristocrat sat very straight in the saddle and looked every inch an officer of the Queen, but he was presently staring back with the light of battle in his blue eyes. A prickling at the back of John's neck made him wonder who would prove his greatest enemy in the coming mêlée.

Pushing such thoughts to the back of his mind, he explained the tactics he wished them to adopt when they began their push through the thorn trees, then dispatched them to repeat it to their men, so that each one was clear about what he must do. They had just finished that duty

228

when the advance party emerged from the jungle with broad smiles on their faces. One of his own corporals approached John and saluted.

'That's them dealt with nice and quiet, sir. Didn't know what happened from start to finish . . . and no one out on the plain a mite wiser. I took a quick peek. Sitting ducks they are, sir, if I might say so.'

John grinned at him. 'You may say so with my compliments, Corporal Stallard, providing it's true. Good work, man.'

A glance at the sun showed that it was lower in the sky than he cared for, so he signalled the advance without delay. If they took too long to penetrate this natural barrier, dusk would have turned to night and their chance would be lost. As the entire force fanned out to enter the jungle, he urged his charger forward in resignation. This was the very worst way to approach an enemy and, despite his strictures on making no sound, he knew man or horse was certain to give vocal response to a chance rip from the vicious thorns surrounding them. Leading the field, he picked his way through the sudden gloom of a densely wooded area, wondering what destiny had in store for him on the far side.

It took fully half an hour to cross the spiky barrier, and not as silently as he would have wished, but his deeper fears concerning the fading light were eased on breaking through to the more open section where he found that the denseness of the jungle had given a false impression of darkness. Halting in the fringes of it, John gave all his attention to the scene before him as he assessed the chances of his small force routing the enemy. Encamped across the plain, with a wild assortment of garishly coloured silk tents and draped rugs, was a formidable number of men and beasts, looking, as Leo Weekes had said, more like a native bazaar than anything else. However, the light guns were military enough in appearance, and so were the pennants and banners of Ganda Singh's warriors. John wished Justin Lakeland were here, for even he could not pretend that this was no more than a collection of untrained bandit tribesmen.

Through narrowed eyes he studied the fort which stood two miles distant. Its walls were unbroken by firing slits, but the battlements accommodated the ancient cannon derided by Whitechurch. Black smoke rose lazily from several points within the central fortifications and it looked deserted, but John knew it must be manned. No commander would occupy a tented camp while leaving a stronghold empty.

He returned to a study of the panorama of tents, where glowing fires were presently cooking the feast for relaxed, triumphant men who had no notion they were being observed. Thank God they had not. Surprise was the only real weapon John had; he must use it to the greatest advantage before darkness robbed him of it. Riding to speak to each of his sub-commanders, he outlined his overall plan. Then he gave to Kingsford's Horse the task of securing the guns and preventing them from being dragged away. The Infantry were told to cause as much confusion and panic whilst setting fire to the tents. Forrester's troopers were charged with stampeding the horses and chasing the enemy off in disorder. Unusually, he directed his cavalry to lead the attack. A full-blooded mounted swoop would cause the greatest shock and enable the Infantry to take advantage of the resulting panic as they swarmed down the slope. He impressed upon them all that total success depended on the taking of the guns.

'If they succeed in dragging them away, we shall be done for, gentlemen,' he concluded. 'Timing is of utmost importance. I want Kingsford's troopers galloping at the weapons before the enemy has the first inkling of our presence. For that reason, I shall lead them and leave Captain Delacourt to command Forrester's throughout this engagement. Are you all quite clear about your orders? We must take up position or lose the light.'

No one confessed to not understanding the general plan, so they dispersed and made ready. John rode to the right flank where the blue uniforms, dark faces and deadly lances of the Indian troopers were just visible amid the trees. They were good men, as Weekes claimed, who listened and nodded understanding of their vital task of capturing the guns. Then John turned his horse for a final scan of the coming battlefield. The sun had now dipped below the horizon so the plain lay like a dark purple cloth with sequins of camp fires twinkling in the fast-gathering gloom. Now was the moment. He prepared to give the signal for advance.

Before he could do so, the scarlet-coated Dragoons on the left flank broke ranks in undisciplined eagerness and began thundering down upon the enemy, brandishing their sabres and shouting curses at those who had killed their comrades. Subconsciously registering the fact that Miles Calthorpe was at the head of the breakaways, with William and Rupert chasing desperately behind the men they had been unable to control, John dug in his spurs and led the better disciplined and more experienced Native Cavalry in the wake of his own regiment, which had alerted the enemy too soon. Filled with fury at such disregard of orders, he bent low over the neck of his charger as it raced toward the camp. It was already in a state of confusion, yet no matter how confused they might be, gunners instinctively ran to their weapons. John could see figures scrambling and thrusting their way through the throng to where the field pieces stood unlimbered in a circle. He heard the usual medley of sounds: the shrieking of terrified horses, commands roared by men driven by fear and excitement, bloodthirsty yells as foe hacked at foe, the rattle of musketry and the clear ring of bugles which fell on ears deafened by the chorus of battle. On he rushed, toward the criss-cross of purple and yellow uniforms, scarlet silk tents and gold-trimmed banners which fluttered like exotic birds over the scene. He was only vaguely aware of the cries and rifle fire of his own infantrymen to the left and behind him, for he was afraid. His concept had failed. Confusion there certainly was, but among his own force as well as the enemy. His master card had been wasted. Destiny would now decide the winner of this day.

A hundred yards . . . seventy-five . . . fifty. It was now possible to see the proud, fierce features of Ganda Singh's men as they raced for their horses, knew that they would never reach them in time, and stood ready to fend off any blow. In the purple and yellow loose garments and dark turbans they looked warlike enough without the great curved blades they wielded. Twenty-five yards . . . fifteen! The blood began to thunder in his head as he recalled Hugo's fate at the hands of these people, and the noise around him faded to that curious, frightening silence he had experienced at Moodki as he now rode straight at three men, attempting to limber-up a gun ready to ride away with it. The sabre in his hand seemed to move of its own accord in that silent world, cutting, slashing, parrying, piercing men who died without the sound of cries, despite their open mouths. On to another gun. His blade now encountered other steel. Sparks flew on the darkening air. Enemy faces grew more difficult to see, for night was casting its early shadows. There was a pain in his thigh. A burning pain which told him he had been cut. But the whole night was burning now with a bright mass of flames which set cold steel glittering wickedly and highlighted vicious faces, both dark and pale, which passed before his eyes like a moving panorama.

His horse stumbled, fell with a scream. John crashed to the ground beside a scarlet-coated corpse which grinned at him in death. The fire continued to rage in his flesh as he stood up and searched the adjacent hell for a riderless horse. There were several, plunging and rearing in fright like burnished beasts in a nightmare, then one trotted past dragging a body whose foot was tangled in the stirrup. Cutting the poor devil free, he pulled himself into the saddle and turned back to the mute inferno which now appeared to engulf the plain and every living thing upon it.

Lieutenant Weekes had arranged for a tent to be erected for the convenience of the officers' ladies, who could not be expected to wait in the shade cast by a hackery while their husbands engaged in desperate battle on the far side of the thorn jungle. The uncertainty of the situation prevented the unpacking of chairs and a table, however, so they sat on rugs spread over the ground to be served with bread and butter and sweet cakes. None of them really wished to eat, but each did so for fear of being thought faint-hearted by the other three as they listened nervously for the sounds of conflict or galloping hooves. They insisted on fastening back the flaps to give a view of what was happening outside. Their youthful commander had refused to allow fires to be lit, so they strained their eyes against oncoming night for the first glimpse of their own forward piquets returning with news.

Lucy Nicholson, looking white and terrified, chattered incessantly. Elizabeth knew it was due to fright, but wished the girl would stop so that they could hear any distant sounds. However, they could hardly all sit in silence throughout the time it took to recapture Judapur Fort. The other two wives were women who had lived for some years with their East India Company officer husbands. Each had experienced warfare and seemed calm enough to respond to Lucy with no evidence of the irritability her chatter was provoking in Elizabeth. Her back ached from the effort of sitting gracefully on the hard ground, her head ached as a result of her fears, and her body felt uncomfortably hot and damp beneath the restrictive lines of her habit. Her mouth had become so dry, the food she chewed had lost all taste and was difficult to swallow. A cup of tea would have been very welcome, but every single person waiting there so tensely was similarly deprived and they were fortunate to have water. The men battling on the far side of the jungle did not even have that at this moment.

Elizabeth was dismayed by her own lack of fortitude in this situation. Driven to distraction by Lucy's endless and mindless chattering, and unable to sit calmly like the other pair, she got to her feet and left the tent in an attempt to ease her inner turmoil. It was hardly possible now to see the straggle of animals and hackeries ahead, yet she heard snorts, grunts and the stamp of impatient hooves and could smell the warmth of hides which had absorbed the sun for hour after weary hour. The faint laughter and conversation of camp followers and bazaar traders, who had brought their wares in the wake of the marching troops in the hope of further business, hung on the air to proclaim their presence in the dusky light. The regimental wives were somewhere along the track, doubtless as ridden with fear and anxiety for their loved ones as she and her companions. She considered seeking them out and attempting to reassure them, then told herself that Amelia Mason might do so from the depth of her experience but Elizabeth Delacourt as yet had no understanding of woman's waiting role in battle. She could hardly comfort those hardened by deprivation and squalor when she could not contain her own restlessness.

She walked along the track, past the hackeries and beasts still laden with their killing loads while her inner tumult increased. The dusk was beautiful, as usual, which seemed inconsistent with the horror of men killing each other. Stars were becoming visible as the sky darkened, and the stifling air slowly cooled to a beguiling balminess. There was never anything like this in England and she could understand why spirits yearned for it when back in that cool green isle. Yet, despite the insidious charm around her, Elizabeth finally surrendered to the sensations invading her mind and body — the undeniable foreknowledge which came to her at such times. Pain, anger, terror, mixed with a shadowy vision of a single white woman walking away across an endless plain. These sensations so possessed her, she put a fist to her mouth to stifle a cry of protest. The woman could only be herself after this battle, desolate and alone. The other afflictions must be those presently suffered by those close to her: John, whom she loved deeply and everlastingly; William, who had given her his name and sexual passion but very little else; Rupert, the friend who could have been a brother. Which of them would survive this night?

It had all happened so suddenly. One minute the column had been winding along the track as it had done for three days. Then the troops had gone in an instant, riding off to meet their fate without a backward glance. The wife of a military man knew she must always come second to duty, and never more than when danger threatened, but they had gone with no time for a word of farewell. This was her first experience of battle and it was not easy to understand. How frail was life; how soon

233

ended! Sir Hugo had departed like someone gone on a journey, for she had not been present to witness the breath in him cease: Fanny Humphrey had slipped away beneath her gaze. That had been harder to accept. This evening, some of those familiar faces which had accompanied her through a momentous month of her life would go from it as if they had never been.

A momentous month of her life! In England she had been a young girl, yearning for the reality of living, with all its mysterious facets. During the journey to India, that girl had begun to see with new eyes, assess with the dawning awareness which accompanied emergence from cloisters. In Ratnapore, the girl had become a woman. There had been no actual moment of truth, no inner glow of recognition. In Ratnapore she had encountered those things she would otherwise never have experienced, had she not been so afraid for her future that she had defied all in a bid to give it some substance. Maturity had arrived unheralded, she realized, simply by meeting, and successfully coping with, situations of which she had no previous knowledge. This present one was proving difficult to endure, but she was endeavouring to do so despite the disturbing, prophetic powers which she now cursed. Battle! When she had married William, the prospect of it had never crossed her mind. He had certainly not spoken of it at any time. Yet a soldier must surely encounter it during his career, and his wife must endure this indescribable feeling of helplessness.

As she passed the dark shapes of animals, Elizabeth considered what might have been if she had not ridden across the path of a man galloping along a Sussex hillside. Stifled and miserable in the Delacourt home, she could one day have been informed by William's mother that her son had mentioned in his monthly letter a 'slight dust-up with the natives' from which he had emerged unscathed. That would have been all she would have known of this unforgettable, harrowing side of her husband's profession. Or she could have received an official notification of William's death in a battle fought over two months earlier whilst she had possibly been painting a water-colour in the garden or accompanying the Misses Delacourt to the haberdasher to purchase bonnet ribbons.

The full significance of William's desertion on sailing to India now became clear. He had effectively excluded her from his life . . . and from his possible death. In the midst of this throbbing night Elizabeth found she could still be hurt by the knowledge, and she walked on, riding out that awareness of ultimate rejection until her attention was taken by a curious glow in the sky beyond the jungle. Her breath caught in her throat. Out there, destiny was making decisions which would overrule any she, herself, might reach. When dawn came, she would have to face them.

Another hour dragged past as the column waited, unable to unload, make fires or even seek sleep. In the tent Lucy had finally fallen silent, and now lay on the rugs as the others did, resting their bodies if not their troubled minds. Elizabeth guessed her friend's thoughts were with the childhood companion she loved with emerging power, rather than with the cold exacting husband who daunted her. Her own thoughts centred on the recurring vision of the woman walking to infinity across an Indian plain, and the accompanying sensation of unbearable loss. It frightened her because there was only one explanation for it.

The night was suddenly broken by intermittent voices, distant initially, then growing in volume and number. There was urgency in the sound. Then a thin cheer was heard. The ladies sat up swiftly, looking at each other questioningly. Before they could get to their feet, a youth's voice called to them from right outside. It was that of Cornet Jay who had been a pleasant companion all the way from Ratnapore.

'The enemy is routed, ladies. We have won the day!'

The woman nearest the entrance invited the boy inside and they all stood up in unspeakable relief. He held a lantern, and they could see brands being lit all along the road they occupied. The subaltern's face seemed almost eerie in the sudden yellow light, but his eyes glittered with excitement as his tongue raced over the news he attempted to relay.

'There's been a right royal battle. The enemy's been chased off and their camp's now ablaze. *That* was the glow we saw, of course. We've a large number of wounded and old Stavenham wants medical supplies, food and all the help he can get. We're to move off right away, Mr Weekes says.' Planting the lantern on the ground, he grinned. 'I'll have your horses ready in a trice.' With that he vanished.

Leo Weekes used his powers of organization to the full in dividing the column. The medical supplies, together with the drastically small number of orderlies to apply them, plus basic rations and cooks with their utensils, were drawn from the long stationary line to form up. Leaving a disappointed Cornet Jay and an NCO to follow with the baggage at their own pace, in company with the camp followers,

Weekes invited the ladies to join him at the head of the shortened column and arranged for the regimental wives to occupy a hackery at the rear. With a number of wounded to be tended, females were invaluable.

They moved at a vastly increased pace until reaching the band of thorn jungle. It was a silent procession. Elation had died, and each was intent on what would be discovered at the battlefield. Light from the torches illuminated the paths cut by those who had gone before them, but care had still to be taken when passing between the black tangles. Elizabeth's reflective mood was still upon her. Knowing that John was safe did not totally remove her sense of fear. If William had perished this evening, she would not walk across the plain with such depth of pain as accompanied the lone woman in her vision. What did it mean? All such mental revelations had been correct before. Was it a foreknowledge of some event further into the future? Yet the picture had been so clear, and the pain so deeply sensed, she could not believe there was no connection between it and this present conflict.

As the trees thinned to allow a first glimpse of the waiting scene, her heartbeat grew fast, and maintained its pounding as the evidence of battle lay before her eyes. Even Leo Weekes halted momentarily at the sight. The stretch between themselves and Judapor Fort was a hellish panorama lit by a multitude of small fires. Blackened circles marked the ashes of burnt tents; flapping tatters were all that remained of others. The ground between them was littered with dead and wounded men, clearly discernible in the flickering light from enduring flames, and with the carcasses of mules and horses and elephants. Half a dozen light guns were grouped together, some draped with the remains of those who would fire them no more, some overturned. Boxes of stores, and ammunition in careless mounds, now spilled their contents across the place where passions had run high. To the left of the fort lay the large tank which provided the vital water for the stronghold and an adjacent village. The weary, victorious troops were there, slaking their thirsts, as were their horses. Over the whole scene hung an awesome medley of moans, screams, equine grunts of agony, oaths, whinneys and the hoarse commands of those trying to maintain a vestige of authority in that kaleidoscope of coloured coats, staggering, stumbling troops, and poor beasts who had valiantly served without knowing why or for whom.

Pausing for only a moment or two, the whole column then moved forward, fanning out across the gentle slope to bring the means of giving relief to the suffering and food to the hungry warriors. Unfortunately, their animals, which had waited fully loaded on the road for hours without a drink, became uncontrollable when they smelled the water. Only by savage use of the whip were they prevented from stampeding to the tank before they could be off-loaded of the vital supplies. Elizabeth felt limp with the shock of it all. Lucy was crying, the tears running down her chalky cheeks unheeded, as she stared at those men she had only before seen in the ballroom, at the races, or strolling around the bandstand. The other two women with them had set expressions on faces which had seen such things before.

They reached the chaos, coaxing their reluctant horses between fires and around debris, knowing they were needed but unsure of where and in what manner. It was even more appalling now they were amongst it. Elizabeth could hardly believe the screams were human, that the bloody bundles around her had once been vital young men. She recoiled from the sight of a leg being carelessly tossed aside by a dhoolie-bearer in order to pull a moaning figure from beneath a pile of those past feeling pain. Then her gaze fastened on a groping creature in the scarlet of Forrester's whose face was a mass of blood. His cries for help grew more and more frenzied as his hands encountered only immobile bodies in every direction, and he had no means of knowing whether or not he was now in the hands of an enemy reputed to have no mercy for the wounded.

Unable to pass him, Elizabeth slipped from her saddle and began to pick her way across to the unrecognizable trooper with hesitant feet, her compassion strong enough to enable her to withstand the carnage around her.

'I'm coming,' she managed, through a constricted throat. Then louder, 'I'm coming.'

'I can't see you, lady. I can't see anything,' cried the man.

'I'm almost there. It's all right,' she called back through gathering tears. 'You're not alone.'

Next minute she was seized in a fierce grip and swung around. For an instant she was full of fright, her nerves stretched to the limit. She saw a large man in scarlet, whose fair hair was plastered to his head and whose eyes contained emotion she had never seen in them before.

'*Elizabeth!*' cried William hoarsely, clearly in the grips of something he could barely control as he stood with his mouth working convulsively. Then he clutched her hard against him and buried his face in her shoulder, as he began to shake so violently she was caught in the

237

paroxysms. Her arms went around him in a comforting gesture and her murmured words were those she had intended to offer the blinded soldier behind her. Trooper or Captain, their need was the same after the savagery of warfare.

'The men broke ranks too soon,' her husband confessed jerkily, as he lifted his head but retained his grip on her. 'We couldn't hold them. Young Calthorpe is gone. Humphrey is most dreadfully wounded. The others are whole enough, but that demented fool Carruthers refused to turn back from the chase. He has gone after the enemy on a solo tide of vengeance which gave no ear to my orders. They will slaughter him as they did his brother.'

'Oh, dear God,' she cried softly and brokenly. 'He was my friend . . . a rare friend.'

More in command of himself now, William put her away from him to say, 'Stavenham has a cut on the leg and is in the devil's own mood over an affair which our own troopers damn near lost for us. He's a man to leave well alone tonight.' He circled her with his arm and began to lead her away. 'I'll have our tent set up and a meal prepared.'

'But . . . but the wounded,' she protested. 'I am needed.'

'By me,' he asserted strongly. 'This is no place for my wife. I have always done my utmost to protect you from such things. Come away.'

Beneath the pale sheen of moonlight, the remnants of battle were thankfully muted, although the removal of the wounded, with their accompanying screams, seemed like a ghostly repeat of it at this hour of midnight. John sat gazing out at the stars, only now finding time for the luxury of private thought. The fire in his thigh would never allow him to sleep, even if his brain were drugged. The cut was not deep but the removal of his overalls so that it could be dressed had led to profuse loss of blood and a resultant dizziness which had forced him to take a short rest and eat the stew his bearer had prepared. Half-way through the meal, he had pushed away his plate. His stomach was still churning with anger and an undeniable sense of responsibility because it had been his own regiment which had run amok and alerted the enemy too soon. Because of it, the battle had raged for far longer and he had lost a great many more men than he need have done.

Young Calthorpe was slain, but those who had broken ranks and survived had received John's scathing condemnation. So much for Lakeland's insulting reservations about whether an ex-Hussar could

238

live up to his precious regiment of Dragoons! One officer had not heard his denunciation because he had waged a war this evening which had nothing to do with recapturing a fort. Rupert Carruthers had virtually deserted his men to chase after the enemy in a personal bid to continue killing. Hugo had had such high hopes for his brother's military career. This was no way in which to honour the man's memory. So a proud name and a proud tradition with the regiment had ended. The last of the line had disobeyed orders and galloped on to his ignominious end. John was immensely saddened by the knowledge. He should have tried harder to reach beyond the boy's insupportable grief; should have persisted in offering help when it was so obviously needed.

A commander should never waste time on regretting mistakes which could never be righted when there was further action to plan, he reminded himself, and turned his teeming brain to considering the actual taking of the fort tomorrow. Those who presently manned it stood no chance of holding out against them now. The wise commander would fly the white flag at dawn, but mutineers were desperate and often undisciplined, so there was a real chance of a refusal to surrender. John hoped they would see sense for there would be further needless bloodshed in the forcible capture of the stronghold. He held all the advantages, however. The six captured guns were more modern and effective than Judapur apparently contained, so a continuous bombardment could be maintained against the ponderous, spasmodic firing from the battlements. In addition, a siege would be over very soon because the water tank was in their hands. However, if there should be a bigger number inside the stronghold than he guessed, armed with accurate rifles, an immediate dawn rush by them across the plain from the fort could succeed in overwhelming his force while they were in a weak and exhausted state. He would give much to be able to see through those stout walls and count those encompassed within.

He stretched his leg to test its mobility and grunted at the pain such movement produced. Once in the saddle he would be perfectly able, he told himself, as his gaze swept the moonlit aftermath of conflict once more. It was imperative to take the fort and occupy it as soon as possible. With the captured guns to augment the defences, and a reserve of water inside the walls, he could deter any attempt by Ganda Singh's men to storm the fortress. They would not return without reinforcements and fresh guns so he had a few days in which to prepare for a possible return attack. He must act with that in mind. Those men of Nicholson's who presently stood guard over the field pieces must be relieved by double their number, and he would brief an officer and two men to be ready to ride out at dawn under a flag of truce to advise the fort to surrender in the name of humanity. If they refused, he would have no alternative but to use force.

Reaching out across the camp table, he began reluctantly to sketch a plan of action to discuss with his officers within the hour. This time Forrester's Light Dragoons would be used only in a supporting role. Once imminent danger was over, he would drill both men and officers until they were crack soldiers. They would remember Judapur for the rest of their days.

Half an hour later, John resolutely got to his feet and called for his horse. The plans were made; now he must implement them. First he would visit Nicholson's tent and tell him to double the guards on the guns. Then he must check the wounded to find how many would be fit to use in an emergency. After that he would seek out Cornet Jay who had been disappointed over being given nothing more heroic to do than to guard the ladies. The responsibility of taking out the flag of truce with a demand to surrender would compensate the boy. John tried to shut his mind to the strategical element of his choice; but he could not deny that it also ensured that he would not lose a highly valuable officer if the mutineers should disregard the flag of truce.

There was a curious quality of moving as if through a dream as he rode very slowly through the camp which had arisen beside the smoking ruin of the other. Smoke still hung on the night air, causing men to cough as they lay physically spent but too haunted by the bestiality to sleep. Some were clustered in groups, talking, because they were afraid of their private thoughts. Some sat trance-like beside the lifeless beast which had been a beloved partner for many years. John had lost his own charger, Falcon, but he had no time to mourn the animal. Too much had yet to happen.

Henry Nicholson was not in his tent, but Lucy was. She looked as near to death as those who lay mortally wounded. John guessed that it was the fate of young Carruthers which had smitten her so badly. He spoke kindly because of it.

'I'm sorry to disturb you, ma'am, but I have to speak to your husband. Where can I find him?'

'He has gone to visit the wounded,' she answered tonelessly, gazing beneath the belly of his horse as if at some distant place as she clutched a dark shawl around her shoulders.

'You are not frightened in his absence, I trust?'

Her golden curls shimmered in the light from a small lantern as she shook her head. He felt immensely sorry for the child but could do nothing to help her. She needed the company of another woman, preferably Elizabeth, but he would not go to the Delacourt tent and suggest it. He had seen his love at a distance, walking with her husband's arm around her. After battle, men grew protective of their women, often behaving with uncharacteristic emotion. He must keep his distance tonight.

Telling the horse to walk on, he guided it toward the makeshift hospital where Nicholson was certain to be visiting one or more of his 'boys'. He might prove unreliable if any of them died. John sighed in anger. The man should have been forced to retire when the truth had emerged. Instead, he had ruined a sweet little creature hardly out of the schoolroom and posed a problem at a time like this. To reach the hospital, which he had wisely sited furthest from the troops' lines so that the gory sights and chilling sounds did not undermine the general morale, he had to ride past the rough compound where the few enemy prisoners had been secured. They sat sullen and downcast, yet he felt no compassion for them as he cast his eye over men who would not have given the same quarter to their prisoners. Then he saw a face he knew — a face from the past — which sent a shock through his whole body and turned his blood cold.

Jerking the horse to a halt, he sat struggling to breathe as the Indian who had once been his bearer also recognized him and stared with wide-eyed fear. Then the man jumped to his feet and tried to run, but he could not. He was imprisoned within the stockade guarded by armed soldiers. Shaking and weakened by overpowering emotions, John marvelled at his ability to remain upright as he dismounted and made his way toward the servant who had gone off one morning with Clare Stavenham and had never returned. A storm arose within his breast, a cyclone of anger which exceeded any he had ever before known, as eight years of anguish and imagined horrors returned in a flash. This man knew what had happened to Clare; he had known all the time and had never come forward. He was alive when believed dead. Dear God, was she?

241

Reaching the side of the stockade, John gripped it with both hands. They shook so badly the palings began to rattle. His former bearer resembled a man trapped by an unleashed force as his dark eyes watched John approach.

'Where . . . where is she?' His voice was cracked and unsteady; the blood pounded in his head with a sound like thunder.

'Gone, sahib. Gone,' wailed the man.

'*Where?*' he rasped, almost afraid of the answer.

'She is too much an Indian woman, sahib. She is happy now.'

The thunder in his head grew louder. 'She's alive?'

'One year ago, yes. I served her until soldiers came to the village and took all young men away to fight in the army.' He ventured forward, cunning in his glance now. 'I will take you to her, sahib, and you will protect me from your men.'

John saw nothing but a young bride in a sari with her hair hanging loose like an Indian woman's. Clare had been so bewitched by this land she had walked away from him with no backward look and no lingering affection. She had put him out of her life so totally the thought of his subsequent suffering had been no consideration. His wife, a girl he had once madly loved, had surrendered to a passion so powerful all else had counted as nothing . . . and he had mourned for eight whole years!

The prisoner continued to cajole, to plead and to bargain for his safety, but John saw nothing save that girl who had played a sitar and painted the walls of their home with scenes of the country which had stolen her away. He was still gripping the stockade and staring sightlessly at a face he had last seen nine years ago when William Delacourt appeared beside him.

'I thought you should be told that young Carruthers has just ridden in,' he said quietly.

John lurched away into the night, unaware of anyone or anything as the thunder in his head reached unbearable proportions.

Chapter Thirteen

From her chair Elizabeth could see only the dark outline of tents, animals and the occasional moving figure now that the fires had died to embers. Midnight had passed a while ago but still she found sleep a distant prospect. George Humphrey had been only hazily aware of her presence and had called her 'Fanny' when mumbling replies through his agony. Without a surgeon to tend his wounds, his prospects looked bleak and he appeared to have lost the will to survive. She had given what comfort she could to the wounded, and it was little enough in such circumstances, so sleep would be her wisest course if she could compose herself enough to seek it.

In the adjacent tent a low light burned. She could not lie on her bed and ignore its significance. William had returned after telling John that his missing subaltern had come back, whole but exhausted and covered in the blood of other men. What he had told her about John hardly eased her troubled mind. Having apparently emerged from his initial sense of battle shock, William had gone off again to check on how many horses were likely to be available tomorrow. So she was alone again and her opportunity was here. Getting to her feet determinedly, she ducked beneath the tent opening and walked quickly across to where the lamp shining through the canvas silhouetted a seated, hunched figure.

Entering Rupert's tent without a qualm, she was immediately distressed by the gory condition of his clothes as he sat staring at the ground. He seemed in perfect control of himself even though he ignored her arrival. She knelt before him so that he could not avoid seeing her, and closed her hands around his which were loosely clasped between his knees.

'My dear, it's over. That is enough,' she said gently. 'You've done what you felt you had to do and there it must end.'

His dulled blue gaze fixed on her face. 'It was so easy. I had not realized how very easy it would be.'

'From now on it must be the most difficult thing in the world,' she said, knowing that prompted by grief, he had acted and abandoned all thought. 'What you did was wrong and you will be punished for it. Do you realize that?'

He shook his head. 'It was so easy.'

'You'll face a court martial. William is certain you will. Listen to what I'm saying, Rupert,' she ordered firmly as he continued to look right through her to something in his own mind. 'Is that how you choose to honour your brother's memory — by bringing disgrace on his name and the uniform he wore? Do you think he would be proud of what you did tonight?'

She had his attention now, so pushed home her advantage. 'I met him just once but you spoke of him with such love and admiration on so very many occasions, I feel justified in claiming to know the kind of man he was. I feel equally justified in averring that if the situation had been reversed — you slaughtered by tribesmen on the plain — he would have mourned you in decent manner and served his country today rather than his own bitter vow of revenge. It was his strength of character that you came out here to emulate, wasn't it? At the first test you have failed. Put an end to this, I beg you, before the regiment puts an end to you.'

'They cut him down without mercy,' he cried in softly vicious tones. 'He didn't stand a chance.'

'You won't give him that chance by ruining your own life. Hugo is gone for ever, Rupert. Killing a *thousand* strangers won't bring him back or deny the truth you can't begin to accept. But you can recover from this reverse by remembering your brother's hopes for you, and trying to fulfil them. For pity's sake tell me this mad vengeance is over.'

As he looked at her his face began to work. The dullness of his eyes changed to sparkling anguish as tears rose in them, and his hands slipped from hers to grip them so tightly her fingers felt crushed. Then he embarked on a torrent of words which he had forcibly dammed by will-power since learning of the tragedy.

'He was everything . . . all I had or wanted. You don't know what it meant to get here at last . . . be with him again. We had such plans. He asked me to shoot tigers with him. We were going to take a furlough and explore Tibet. He knew of a guide to lead us. His thoroughbred . . . the champion . . . he made the most splendid offer, Elizabeth. You won't believe it. Hugh said . . . he said that I could race him and as soon as I won the stakes, the beast would be mine. Was any brother ever as generous?'

'No, my dear,' she agreed, aching with sympathy for this cold killer who had become a boy again; the young brother she might have had.

'That wasn't all. He had some capital schemes for the regiment. He would have gained it, you know, when Lakeland went. Hugh would have been a splendid colonel, and Forrester's would have become one of the best cavalry regiments in the British Army under his command.'

'It can still do so one day . . . under your own command, Rupert. Hugo would want that very much. You could implement all those schemes he discussed with you.'

Still gripping her hands tightly, he explained some of them in his old eager, enthusiastic manner, which now had an added touch of desperation. Elizabeth gave him avid attention, trying to ignore the stench of blood on his clothes, as she coaxed him to talk of the brother he had mourned with such jealous solitude all this time. As the words tumbled from him with mounting anguish, she braced herself for what she was certain would come. Yet she became caught up in his terrible sense of loss as Hugo Carruthers came vividly alive again with his brother's words. Her own heart ached because she would never see that charming, intelligent, charismatic personality again; a man who possessed many virtues but tempered them with human weaknesses. Tears came without warning to run down her own cheeks as Rupert finally lost his own battle for control and began to sob. Clinging instinctively to each other in a revival of that youthful rapport which was almost kinship, they rocked back and forth in an embrace of mutual comfort which slowly eased the emotional buffeting each had encountered since they had journeyed together to this land which had promised them so much.

He finally calmed enough to break from the embrace and look at her through red-rimmed eyes. 'I feel so frighteningly lonely.'

She nodded as she dabbed her cheeks dry with a handkerchief. 'I know, but you have loving friends. I have grown so very fond of you, you must be aware of that. As an only child I have been lonely for most of my life, so may I not regard you as the brother I might have had?'

He was not yet ready to consider such a concept, but she felt that he would before too long. She tried again. 'Lucy Nicholson is a friend from your past. She knew you and your brother from those early days. She has been deeply hurt by your rejection of her condolences at a time when she also feels unhappy and alone. Speak to her about Hugo. Tell her all you have told me about his qualities and achievements. It will make her life more bearable if she has her dearest friend to cheer her.'

Although he nodded, it was clear he was still caught up in the aftermath of his breakdown. There was silence for a while as he sat the way she found him on entering. Then he looked up from contemplation of the ground to say thickly, 'I loved him so much. You don't know what it's like to lose him.'

'I do,' she told him softly. 'Oh, I do. I once loved someone very much and had to see him go out of my life. It's as if there will never be another dawn.'

They gazed at each other for several moments in growing understanding, then she said, 'You must sleep. The nightmare is over, Rupert.'

Leaving the tent, feeling very much as if she had been through a nightmare herself, Elizabeth stood for a moment in the welcome darkness. The night sky was temporarily overcast; the fires had burned so low there was a blessed obscurity over the visual aftermath of battle. William had not yet returned to their tent. It was beautifully quiet. The mood of the night matched her own. Yet, as she stood there serenely, it was broken by an inner vision of a young woman walking alone across an endless plain. It was accompanied by a brief sensation of immense despair. The sensation was gone almost before she identified it, but it left her shaken. The girl had long dark hair and was dressed in a loose white garment resembling a shroud. The same vision had come to her just before the battle and she had then been afraid of it. Why should it return now that the fighting was over . . . and why should she now feel certain that it was not herself that she saw?

In sudden need of company she went in search of Lucy, who might not yet have heard that Rupert was back and unharmed. His childhood friend could now approach him without fear of rebuff, if she could find the courage to disregard her ageing husband. Rupert could provide a modicum of warmth for her loveless youth. The ache of loving him too well would surely be nothing compared with her present fearful sense of isolation. The pair would help each other in innocent fashion . . . until the truth of their feelings could no longer be ignored. Then they would find themselves facing the same daunting dilemma she and John had to confront. Halting momentarily as the truth of her own situation returned to deal a blow to her brief serenity, she remembered her vow to leave India soon. There would be no time to enjoy a sisterly relationship with the young man she had just left to sleep off his madness. She walked on heavy-hearted. Destiny seemed determined that she should remain lonely.

The Infantry lines were on the perimeter at the nearest point to the fort. As she drew near the spot, she became aware of unexpected activity in the darkness around the neat row of tents. William had told her that Nicholson's men were mounting guard over the guns, so they must presently be changing duties. Heading for the tent where a lamp was burning, she then saw several figures silhouetted within it and hesitated. Lucy was not alone. This was no time for the glad tidings she had to relate to the girl.

Turning away, she had taken several steps before she drew up in wary disbelief. Advancing determinedly was a group of sepoys who were driving before them all six of Henry Nicholson's subordinate officers. The Englishmen's arms were bound to their sides and bayonets were held at their throats by those flanking them. Elizabeth froze in their path, eyes wide with incomprehension.

Disconcerted by her unexpected presence, the Indian troops halted and levelled their carbines at her. Jason Peters spoke swiftly.

'Don't be afraid, ma'am. They have no desire to hurt you, but pray don't speak or attempt to run.'

Rooted to the spot by another shock in a day beset by them, Elizabeth began to assess the significance of what she beheld. A hushed conversation between Lieutenant Peters and one of his men ended with an appalling statement from the captive officer which confirmed her fears.

'I've been instructed to tell you that any attempt to make known what is happening here will force them to slit our throats on the spot.' He added, with sadness rather than fear, 'They will do it, believe me, ma'am. Similarly, any attack made upon the fort will bring the same fate. You must tell your husband that as soon as the mutiny is discovered at daybreak. At the first sign of aggression we shall all be murdered.'

Elizabeth could only nod mutely, marvelling at how calmly they all accepted this fearful ultimatum from men they had commanded with such confidence. Next minute, her attention was snatched from them by sudden movement from behind the place where she stood. Henry Nicholson, not bound as the others were, was being led forward by two young sepoys whose bayonets were still attached to their carbines. Lucy's husband studied the ground as if unable to face his subordinate officers, for some reason. Even as Elizabeth wondered why this one man seemed to be under less threat than the others, she noticed that the lamp in his tent was now out. Lucy must be there facing the same ultimatum she had been given.

'Please, ma'am, not a word,' warned Jason Peters as their captors nudged them to move on toward the plain and thence to Judapur Fort.

The group had advanced no more than a few yards, however, when two sepoys appeared from the gloom and stopped in bewilderment. For several tense seconds Indian stared at Indian in a conflict of loyalties as awareness dawned. Then the pair raised their guns purposefully. A tattoo of deafening reports rent the air. Elizabeth gasped with the shock of such sounds, then covered her mouth with her hand as Jason Peters dropped to the ground, blood gushing from his throat. Seconds later, the sepoy who had killed his own officer fell beside him, a victim of retaliation from a blood brother.

The night came alive with shots, cries and bugle calls as the area filled with sleepy, stumbling men who were instantly given the choice of joining the mutineers or possibly dying at their hands. Caught in their midst, Elizabeth was too stunned to think or move. Lights began springing up in the heart of the camp, but they hardly illuminated the surrounding turmoil which appeared to surge first one way then another while the hostage officers were relentlessly marched off into the darkness beyond.

Then, through the rattle of gunfire, came a sound which finally penetrated Elizabeth's petrified thoughts. Within that dark tent Lucy was screaming with fear. It was a signal of distress which she could not ignore. Taking up her long skirt in both hands, Elizabeth began to run toward the girl who could hear but not see the substance of terror around her. In the general clamour of conflict, one shot made no recognizable sound, so the ball which flew to find its mark in the flesh of her thigh took her totally unawares. Hot agony boring into her very bones caused her to stumble, then double over to clasp the place where she had been hit. Brief recollection of that premonition of pain in her own limbs accompanied awareness that she had been wounded by crossfire. In a desperate bid to reach the relative haven where Lucy was still screaming hysterically, she dropped on all fours to crawl there. A few yards from her goal she felt a curious breeze touch her left temple. Then Elizabeth pitched into blackness and silence.

The expressions on the faces of the officers crowding around John's tent showed their awareness of the complex task confronting them. Their

248

orders had been to occupy and reinforce the frontier fort, so there was no question of retreat, yet any attempt to attack would bring the certain death of the hostages. As if that were not enough, Ganda Singh's force was out there somewhere ready to fight again, and their own infantry contingent was now reduced to the handful who had remained loyal to their colours rather than to their blood brothers. They would appear to be in a cleft stick.

John surveyed them all, feeling no more than a shell of a man. The truth about Clare had brought back all manner of memories which he had been struggling to put from his mind. Coming immediately after the shock of their revival had been the mutiny of men under his command, with the seizure of British hostages, and the tragic death of young Jason Peters who had so hotly defended to Rupert those same men who had killed him. In addition, there had been the wounding of a woman he knew he loved yet could not visualize beyond the image of his wife. He was presently empty of feeling; numb to sensation of any kind. His brain had grown correspondingly sharper, he thanked God.

'I don't know if you have ever put yourself in the position of your enemy, gentlemen, but that is what I've been doing for the past hour,' he announced. 'If I were inside Judapur Fort I would expect one of two things from a force situated as we are now. Either to retreat under cover of darkness, or to spend a long time deliberating on how best to attack without endangering the hostages and before Ganda Singh's force returns. Would you agree?'

They nodded or murmured their acceptance of such reasoning, and one cornet asked earnestly, 'They're only bluffing about killing the officers, aren't they, sir?'

'You can ask that when Lieutenant Peters is already dead by their hands?'

'So we must retreat?' the boy concluded in disappointment.

'No, Bennett, our orders are to occupy the fort and we must do so. I have thought hard and long about how to achieve our objective with the minimum risk to the hostages, and I believe I have a way.' Scanning their sceptical expressions, he said, 'I see you all have doubts. I have them myself, but it is a choice between my scheme or ignominious defeat. I have no need to ask which you would prefer, gentlemen. We can safely assume that the enemy inside the fort will be expecting a possible attack to commence with artillery bombardment, followed by an advance over the plain. The bulk of the defenders will therefore be concentrated on the eastern side. With no knowledge of their total strength I cannot judge our chance of success in such a conventional battle, so I must use our only superior weapon: surprise. It worked well enough for us during the dusk attack, despite the premature advance of the left flank. It also worked for the mutineers tonight,' he added bitterly. 'I mean to attack from the west where, according to my plan of the fort, there should be a subsidiary gate leading to the inner defences.'

There was silence until William Delacourt said caustically, 'We have no scaling-ladders or any kind of ram to force the gates.'

'No, but we have a large supply of gunpowder left by Ganda Singh's force. We shall put it to excellent use. Our contingent of Infantry is now too small to be totally effective, and those who remained loyal have been demoralized by their comrades' desertion and treatment of their officers. I have to turn to Forrester's and Kingsford's Horse — our mounted troops.'

'You can't storm a fort with cavalry, sir,' said Leo Weekes in protest.

'In conventional manner, no,' John agreed, 'but we shall enter by the back door and attack from the rear.' Clearing his throat, he went on, 'We have just under an hour to prepare, so listen carefully. I want our entire mounted force formed up in column of threes out on the plain behind the fort before dawn breaks. The Infantry will advance to the foot of the walls on each side of the gates under cover of darkness, ready to follow the cavalry in as soon as the gates are blown. Timing is vital; so is secrecy. Any hint of our presence will result in failure of the plan. You must all be in your exact positions, ready to move once the gates go. A cavalry charge into the very heart of the fort is the last thing they will expect. It will cause confusion and a sense of panic, both of which will aid us. It's my earnest prayer that they will also aid the hostages. The entire action should be so sudden and over so swiftly that no one will have the thought or time to murder our brother officers. Bennett, you will be charged with the duty of seeking them out and releasing them unharmed the moment you get inside the fort.' He sighed heavily. 'It is the only chance we can offer them, I fear. The fort *must* be taken. Do you have any questions, gentlemen?'

'Yes, sir,' said one. 'We have no Sappers and Miners with us. Who is going to blow the gates?'

'I am . . . but I warn you all that despite a knowledge of how to set charges and explode them, my notion of quantities is very vague. An explosion I promise you, but whether half the walls will collapse with the gates, or whether you will be hard put to squeeze through a gap barely large enough, remains to be seen.' Giving them all a straight look, he added, 'Whatever happens you must charge the gates the moment you hear the detonation. The only hope of survival for us and the hostages rests on your successful and unexpected entry. If you've no more questions I'll ask you to go to your men and tell them what they are expected to do.'

'Sir,' called a rather effeminate cornet from the far side of the group, 'What must we do once inside the fort?'

'You'll know the answer to that when you get in there,' he replied grimly. Then, as the officers remained where they were in distinct unhappiness over the plan, he said what he must. 'All right, gentlemen, we all know that your faith in my leadership is less than it should be, due to several tragic incidents at Ratnapore; and my faith in your ability to obey orders was badly undermined a few hours ago. However, I am not going to ask if anyone has a better plan than the one I have just outlined; a plan you would all feel much happier with because I did not hatch it. You see, I have to place my trust in all of you because there's no alternative force at my disposal, so you'll have to accept my leadership under those same conditions. We are stuck with each other, gentlemen, so for God's sake let us make the very best of our uneasy alliance and pull a brilliant victory from this impossible situation.'

The uniformed men moved off in varying attitudes of discomfiture at his frankness, some rather red in the face and others tight-lipped. When they had gone, he reached out wearily to take up his shako and began walking toward William Delacourt's tent. As the senior officer it was his duty to visit the man's wounded wife. He knew there was another reason apart from duty, yet the import of it did not touch him as he moved between empty tents until he reached his destination. Drained of all emotion, he could only consider the danger of the coming hours.

At the entrance to the tent, which was softly illuminated by lamplight, he called out, 'John Stavenham here. May I come in?'

Several moments passed before an Indian girl pushed open the flap and stepped gracefully outside to hold the canvas clear for him. Ducking his head beneath the pointed opening, he entered. A young woman with a bandage around her head was lying on a camp bed. She wore a loose travelling-gown of heavy pale-yellow cotton, and her pointed face seemed almost the same shade in that curious lamplight. Luminous amber eyes gazed at him with such yearning he knew she was

251

not in the least like Clare. He also knew instinctively that he loved her, yet he felt nothing as he returned her gaze.

'How are you?' he asked.

She took a while to answer that bald question. 'Rather faint from loss of blood when the ball was taken from my leg. I thought of Lady Mason throughout the experience. It gave me courage.' A sad smile touched her mouth. 'Do you know she once seriously considered administering a mild dose of poison to the gentlemen of the general staff so that they would be obliged to endure the horrors of a military hospital?'

He shook his head.

'She is a remarkable woman, as you averred in Wellford.'

'What of the wound in your head?' he asked then.

'The ball merely grazed my temple.'

'That was fortunate.'

Silence fell until she said in tones of increasing weariness, 'I've spoken to Rupert at some length. The storm within him has blown itself out. Please don't be too hard on him.'

'He's not under arrest. I need him. Punishment will come later . . . if it's still necessary,' he finished significantly.

Raising herself slowly and painfully on one elbow, she said, 'There will be an attack on the fort soon. Common sense tells me that. I want you to know that I shall be returning to Ratnapore as soon as the emergency is over. From there I shall go to England. Your command at Judapur will not be as irksome as you fear.'

'I see,' he murmured, hardly understanding what she was telling him. 'I have to go. There is so much to do.'

He turned away, but she halted him with his name. When he swung round she was lying flat, exhausted by the effort of raising herself. She spoke so quietly he could hardly hear her words.

'Today, I have twice had a vision of a young dark-haired woman in a pale robe walking alone across a plain. With the vision comes awareness of deep inner anguish. I know now that the woman is not me, as I first thought.' There was a slight pause before she asked, 'Who is she, John?'

This startling perception caught him unawares, slicing through his emotional hiatus to expose the depths of a despair he had endured for eight long years. This girl's face became that of someone he had long ago found and deeply loved.

'She's Clare Stavenham, my wife. I have just been told that she is not dead, as I have believed since she vanished from my life.'

Clear amber eyes mirrored his own sense of shock on hearing the news. 'So . . . so you were right. Your destiny does lie in this land . . . and in its sweetest side.'

He merely nodded before pushing his way through the canvas flaps into the waning night.

During the last half hour of darkness the men dressed for battle, and set out from their tented camp to take up the positions with mixed feelings. Having had time for reflection, the officers recognized the plan as possibly brilliant — if it succeeded — but totally dependent on that vital explosion. Those who thought John Stavenham a hothead claimed this as confirmation of it; those who knew him to be experienced in war said he was doing the only thing possible in this tricky situation. The rank and file also took opposing views. Some declared the Major was plain crazy to order a cavalry charge on a fort. The rest defended him hotly, averring that if he said it would work, it would work! On one thing they were all agreed, however: retreat was out of the question.

The subject of their speculation prepared for the coming action; worried about his lack of knowledge on explosives. He had been an interested witness to mining operations during the recent war against the Sikhs but, although he had a fair idea of where to place an explosive charge, he had little information of amounts of gunpowder in ratio to damage required. It would not matter if he over-estimated and blew up half the wall along with the gates, but too little force would result in nothing more than slight damage and a loud report which would alert the enemy. When that happened, it was essential for the cavalry to have already broken through and covered the vital areas within the fort's defences. The single detonation must blow a gap big enough to allow through it ranks of three riders abreast, or the whole plan would fail.

With this dread filling his mind, he left his tent and made his way to where a groom was holding his horse. His reserve charger, Rambler, was replacing the animal he had lost yesterday after five years of partnership. This dark-brown gelding was a valiant enough beast and John stroked its nose while murmuring words of friendship and encouragement to establish unity before they moved off. After mounting, he set off toward the dark plain, carrying in his saddle-bags the heavy, volatile gunpowder. A false dawn was lighting the sky so that the fort was faintly visible as a huge grey mass to the west. Soon, his commissariat staff and the camp followers would begin their morning duties, in order to suggest to the enemy that all was as usual in the camp. The customary bugle-calls — blown by those men too badly wounded to take part in the attack — and the glow of fires lit to cook breakfast for a waking force should deceive those within the stronghold and keep their attention on its eastern side.

It seemed immensely lonely as he rode slowly in a line parallel to the thorn jungle, then turned to approach the fort from the west. Somewhere in the surrounding obscurity a large force of cavalry was forming up, ready to perform an unusual military manoeuvre. Unhappy though he had been over his decision, the undisciplined rush of his own regiment yesterday had forced him to place them behind Kingsford's Horse for this charge. Leo Weekes had necessarily taken precedence over William Delacourt; a fact which rankled with a great many but was unavoidable. Victory was more important than personal popularity in any action. If this failed a great many things would change, the least of them being his standing with his new regiment. All their hopes rested on his shoulders, so his thoughts must be applied to what he was about to do. The future lay in the hands of destiny; he was merely the agent.

The false dawn had faded so that he was almost upon the fort before he saw the walls rearing just ahead. He reined in and dismounted silently, praying that Rambler would not betray their presence with a snort. The approach to the studded gates lay along a path bordered by low walls, and a small gate-house guarded it. John reasoned that only minimum defence would be placed here so, after picketing his horse to the spot, he drew his sabre and advanced toward the stone building which was lit by pale flickering light. Reaching it unchallenged, he edged toward the open doorway. Two voices conversing in the local dialect told him all he wished to know. This pair were the only occupants, and were completely relaxed as they waited for their comrades to relieve them at dawn after their nocturnal vigil. John gathered himself for entry, knowing the silent blade was his only means of dealing with them.

Surprise made his task easy. Two brown faces looked up in no more than astonishment when he stepped inside the small square room containing a charpoy, two chairs, and a table upon which the usual saucers of tallow provided meagre illumination. Astonishment was still on their faces as he dispatched them both swiftly and silently. Knowing the new guards were due at dawn, he then left. It was essential to place the charges beside the gates before they arrived.

Collecting Rambler, he led the beast along the path past the gate-house until they reached the studded, fortified gates which were high enough to admit elephants bearing howdahs. The animal's hooves made muffled beats on the dirt surface. He hoped there were no defenders stationed directly above the gates or, if there were, that they were also too relaxed to be aware of faint noises fifty feet below. He now cursed the darkness which hampered clear estimation of the barrier he must demolish. Time was racing past. He could not afford to waste it on further useless survey as he walked the distance between the walls.

With a sigh of determination he began lifting the bags of powder from the leather pouches attached to his saddle, and stacked them along the foot of the gates at the left side until he had emptied one of the panniers. Then he led Rambler to the right-hand gate and did the same there. It was heavy work. Perhaps he should have brought a man with him. Sweating and breathing hard, he realized that the sensation of wetness on his leg must be blood; physical exertion had split the wound open again. Blotting out such thoughts, his layman's mind reasoned that the centre of the gates would be strengthened by bolts and crossbars. It would be wiser to blow both sides. With no hinges to hold the great doors upright, the very weight of them would surely cause them to fall, possibly still bolted together. The great danger then would be that the cavalry would rush after the explosion, only to be flattened beneath an obstacle collapsing too slowly.

With the explosive material stacked up as accurately as he could guess, he took up the last bag and began running out a trail of powder from the right, then from the left, joining the two in a single line which stretched back along the path in the direction of the gate-house. When he lit this extended fuse, he would shelter behind the stone building until the whole thing blew. A grim smile touched his beaded face as he considered that he might go up with it if he had over-estimated quantities. It did not do to think of the consequences of under-estimation. Reaching the building once more, he glanced at the sky. Dawn was coming up fast. It would soon be possible for those within the fort to see the dark bulk of horsemen lined up on the plain a mere five hundred yards away; a silent, lethal force awaiting the signal to charge. He swallowed to ease his parched throat. If he was wrong, they were all likely to be slaughtered, along with the hostages who must know their comrades had no choice but to attack somehow, sometime.

Every second seemed to bring extra lightness to the sky and he swore his aching eyes could already pick out the sight of neat rows of cavalry a short distance away across the shadowy landscape. It was now or never. Taking the matchbox from his sabretache he prayed as he struck a flame, then tossed it on to the dark streak of gunpowder. Leading Rambler behind the stone building, he mounted painfully and watched the tiny glow advance along the ground. From the battlements it would be faintly discernible, but unlikely to draw the attention of some unsuspecting guard. His heart was pounding now. That glow seemed to be moving far too slowly, and he could deny his doubts no longer. Weekes was a splendid officer who would lead the men forward with perfect timing, but suppose the man led them all to eternity in response to orders from a commander who knew he was taking a tremendous risk with all their lives? His own was also at stake, of course, but if he had made a fatal decision it would be as well if he did not survive. Never had waiting been so charged with tension as he watched the infant flame run toward the gates. Then there were twin flames moving apart in a widening gap. He prepared for the moment of truth.

A tremendous thundering roar heralded a rush of hot air from the detonation which was deflected by the stone walls before John. Jabbing Rambler with his spurs, he came out from behind the gate-house like a ball from a cannon. Smoke obscured the view ahead, but surely an explosion great enough to shake the very ground beneath him had blown a passage through to the fort? From the corner of his eye as he rode, he saw ranks of blue and scarlet surging forward, accompanied by the familiar thunder of a thousand hooves beating the ground. A thrill of elation ran through him. These men were the best in the world, and his to command!

At that moment, the ground directly ahead of him rose up in a deafening cascade which reached out with burning force to knock him backward into brief blankness on hitting the ground. Before he could clear his head to understand what had happened, a silent nightmare began. From his soundless world came a herd of beasts: they appeared as if from nowhere to leap over him, or rushed past, showering him in dust as he lay helpless in their path. He heard nothing of the pounding hooves or the triumphant cries of the riders as he remained there, pinned beneath Rambler, watching the phantom cavalry fly above him as they darkened the sky with their splendid charge into the fort.

The last beast passed, and still John could hear nothing. But his thoughts were now clear enough to tell him that the explosions had been separated by some seconds; he had been caught in the blast of the delayed one, which had knocked him down and temporarily deafened him. Rambler began to struggle up now the charging horses had passed, releasing him. In his curiously silent world, John somehow managed to climb into the saddle and turn toward the gates. They were no longer there: he had blown a gap wide enough to admit an entire army. Crazy laughter began in his throat, yet he heard none of it as he headed for the fort at a gallop. If he did nothing more in this world, this was his moment of glory!

Inside the walls he found a scene he was unlikely to forget. Red and blue jackets were everywhere. Sabres flashed in the first gilded rays of sunlight as they cut down an enemy totally confused and uncoordinated; riderless horses raced past with the whites of eyes betraying fear. The green coats of the Infantry rioted with the vivid uniforms of Ganda Singh's troops as the holders of the fortress were driven backward up the steps to their death on a high ledge. Rifles cracked, blades whistled through the air, men grunted and yelled, bugles rent the bedlam with messages for men unable to obey them, but John still heard nothing. Over the entire scene hung the stench of smoke, blood and human sweat; he was very aware of that as he rode into the thick of that desperate bid for possession.

Once he began fighting for his own survival against that of his foe, the silence seemed very natural, for he always knew it in such a situation. As he cut and parried, his mind worked feverishly to tell him that his reasoning had been correct. The bulk of the defenders were on the eastern side of the stronghold. A cavalry attack from the rear had rendered them hopelessly undisciplined, and their total disorder coupled with the fearsome determination of their attackers would bring about a speedy defeat. All about him John saw the enemy now being disarmed at swordpoint. The ancient cannons were in the possession of Forrester's troopers, who had plainly gained them at some cost, and only the tussle to retain command of the tower continued. His sword arm stilled when his last adversary threw down his own weapon at the sight of several Indian sepoys advancing to John's aid, but they alone heard his words of thanks. In the silence which continued beyond the battle hush he knew well, he ran up the second flight of stone steps which led to the battlements so that he could see the general picture. The firing ledge was scattered with bodies, evidence of the fierce fighting in this well-defended sector. At the far end of the long ledge, those Infantrymen who had remained loyal were engaged in desperate

257

combat with those of their comrades who had gone over to the enemy. As he watched this last stand in a fort where the victors were now tending their wounded and rounding up prisoners, he thanked God he had made the right decision when faced with disaster. How easily he could have been wrong; how easily he could have sent three hundred men to annihilation this morning. For the first time in his career he knew the heavy weight of command and acknowledged that even the most brilliant soldier must bow to the will of destiny. Today, he had won her favour; tomorrow, she might desert him.

Feeling little true elation in the face of this slaughter, he turned wearily with the intention of seeking the fate of the hostages. There was now another living figure on that ledge of death; his scarlet jacket was bloody and torn and he stood gripping the battlements for support as he levelled his pistol at the man he held to blame for the death of his brother. The youthful face with profuse blond moustache and cold, light eyes revealed the same look of anguish which had been there on the day that he had vowed to avenge Hugo. How curious that John should suddenly see a marked resemblance to the older man who had been a valued friend; now, when vengeance was about to be realized. Rupert did not speak as he fought to remain on his feet. John stood silent, too, sensing that destiny was now about to extract her penalty for her favour today.

Their glances remained locked for a long, timeless period, yet the boy seemed unequal to pulling the trigger. With his eyes steadfastly on Rupert's, John relived that tragic morning while he waited for the one shot he would never hear. A lifetime could have passed during that wordless confrontation until Rupert's hand dropped to his side and, still holding the weapon, he turned away like a man at the point of collapse. John watched him descend the steps and knew that only iron will-power and the pride of his breed kept him upright.

When he vanished from sight below the level of the ledge, John moved across to the stone battlements and gazed out to where the sun had lifted above the dark screen of the thorn jungle to wash the tents on the plain with its golden light. He blamed the dazzle on white canvas for the moisture in his eyes.

Chapter Fourteen

Elizabeth lay in a state between dreaming and waking. Her head ached and she felt alarmingly weak. Lucy had sat with her since the men departed just before dawn; the golden-haired girl had been there each time she had opened her eyes. The sun was now high and only her Indian maid sat serenely on the small collapsible stool beside the bed. The girl offered a cup of water then cooled her mistress's face with a scented cloth before returning to her seat. For a while Elizabeth studied this beautiful young woman of India. What did she truly think of the people who had come in droves to her country and attempted to live in it as they did at home? What were her feelings toward those who had mutinied and held hostage men they had sworn to serve? Perhaps she did not concern herself with such deep issues. Her sweet, constant serenity hinted at the nature possessed by many women of this land; a demure acceptance of female subservience which was nevertheless vastly more dignified than that found in the Misses Delacourt and their ilk.

Remembering William's sisters made her remember him, and she became fully awake suddenly. There was to be an attack on the fort; an unconventional mounted attack, full of hazards, with a doubtful chance of success. John was to blow up the gates as dawn broke, William had revealed. If he failed, they would all be lost. Lucy's absence now took on a fearful aspect. Had the attack been a disaster and resulted in the murder of Henry Nicholson and his officers? Was this camp now in enemy hands? Could John possibly have failed? On the point of struggling up from the bed Elizabeth grew calm again, knowing that she would have sensed the impending tragedy as she had experienced advance awareness of everything concerned with the man she loved.

With her eyes half closed against the glare of sun on canvas, she then recalled John's fleeting, obligatory visit to enquire after her wounds. That ability to see beyond the present had even allowed her to sense his wife's survival as he was on the brink of rediscovering her. His declaration had been a blow to her, yet how much greater had been the one she had dealt him in Wellford. Although he had never mentioned the girl he had married, the facts were available from many sources, so he must have known she was acquainted with them. How had he learned the startling news that Clare Stavenham lived? Where had she been for nine years? What were his feelings for a wife who had returned from the dead? Would he now find happiness again? Would he now be able to forget Elizabeth Delacourt?

Wearied by such thoughts, she shut out the stifling interior of the tent so that the daytime brightness was no more than dull red against her closed lids. There was no gunfire, no roar of battle, no sounds of human suffering. Could she possibly be in a camp upon a plain where a fort must be wrested from the enemy, or was she again wandering in the realms of some future event? Perhaps she drifted into sleep. There was no rustle of entry, yet some impulse opened her eyes to find him there beside her bed. He had come straight from battle. The evidence was in the filthy state of his clothes and in that same smell which had been on Rupert after killing. His eyes were very dark; his expression was unreadable. A shaft of thankfulness at his survival overruled any other thought or emotion as she gazed up at him.

'So the fort is ours?'

'Yes.'

'And the hostages?'

'Safe.'

'Thank God!' Sighing with relief, she added, 'We all owe you so much, so very much.'

He was silent for a moment before asking, 'Are you feeling stronger yet?'

Only at that point did it occur to her why it should be John who had come, no one else. She drew in her breath sharply. 'You have brought news of William.'

'I have a dhoolie outside to carry you to the fort. He will not last beyond sundown.'

She heard his words with deep sadness. She had not sensed this, had not felt the abstract pain of her husband's wounds nor heard his cries in her mind. She had condemned him for leaving her in England, where she might have heard of his death only by written communication weeks afterward, yet she had been on the very threshold of his mortal suffering this morning and had known nothing of it.

'I'll come right away,' she murmured.

'Are you able to withstand the rigours of a dhoolie?'

'Of course.'

He gave a brief nod. 'I'll arrange for your tent and baggage to be brought to the fort. Everything must be within the walls by nightfall. Do you require any service from your maid before you go?'

'Not when time is vital.'

Bending swiftly, John picked her up and carried her into the brilliance of noon. The bearers lifted the dhoolie so that he could settle her on the rough blankets inside it with infinite care. When he mounted his brown gelding, the men moved off beside him. It was a silent progress toward the grey stone walls where an unknown Indian had wrought the end of William Delacourt and of a marriage which had brought little happiness. His family would be heartbroken to lose the one son among five children: they were so proud of him. Elizabeth endured the motion of the swaying box and regretted her inability to have been the partner William had desired. They had both been wrong to tie the marriage knot and had suffered the consequences in different ways. Those wasted years could never be redeemed, but William's short life would end on the erroneous belief that she had loved and wanted him so much, she had defied all to join him in India.

All her sensations of regret were swept aside when she saw the evidence of what had happened inside Judapur Fort. There was still much confusion. Dead and wounded lay in rows in the shade while *bheesties* went among them, answering the calls of those who had sufficient strength to make themselves heard. The enemy dead were piled in a far corner awaiting burial. Soldiers passed back and forth in an endless criss-cross while NCOs shouted orders which only increased the confusion. The enclosing, battlemented walls gave an immediate impression of imprisonment as they cut off any view of the plain they had just crossed. All buildings were of stone with roughly hewn doorways and window apertures, and were pitted with shot and darkened by fire . . . or blood. Elizabeth's throat constricted as she imagined the scene at dawn today.

The wounded officers had been taken to a small inner courtyard where attempts by successive occupants to create a garden had resulted in the pleasant sight of trees and an ornamental pool served by a fountain presently stilled. John directed her bearers to a cloister where two trestles had been erected side by side. On one rested William's stretcher. They set her dhoolie on the other. John dismounted and handed his horse to a waiting groom.

'Will you be all right?' he asked quietly, coming to her side.

Elizabeth looked only at her husband's drawn face. 'Yes . . . perfectly all right.'

It seemed incredible that a man so young, so large and strong could be dying. He was mercifully whole. She could write of that quite truthfully to his family. Only the death-rattle as he breathed, and the red stain which was slowly spreading over the blanket on which he lay, told her that John had tried to blunt the news. William would be gone very soon. Reaching across the space separating them, Elizabeth took up the hand lying at his right side. The slight contact forced William to open eyes whose vision was fast fading. He could not recognize the figure beside him and asked who it was. When he knew, he seemed pleased enough to manage a smile. Too spent to speak, his fingers managed to curl around hers in a message of understanding. They remained like that for about half an hour.

The moment of death was not distressing, like that of poor Fanny Humphrey, who had retched and suffered to the last. William Delacourt slipped from life as if falling asleep; only the gentle slackening of his handclasp telling her she was a widow. When Rupert and Lucy came for her as shadows began to lengthen, she was lying thoughtfully beside the man she had never entirely understood.

They found a cell-like room and ate a light meal together. It seemed a curious, unreal time for Elizabeth. She spoke without knowing what she said, she nodded agreement to words she had not heard, she ate without tasting the food. It was as if she had ceased to exist and was, instead, a creature who lived nowhere and claimed kinship to no one. William had gone; John had rediscovered his wife. Lucy was tied to an older saturnine husband and Rupert was not a true brother with the ties of blood. Maybe she *had* been the lone dark-haired woman walking across an endless plain, after all.

An officer knocked to tell her that her possessions were now safely within the fort and that her maid was in attendance outside, awaiting her call. When he withdrew, the young subaltern asked Rupert to step outside for a moment. Against the murmur of their low-toned conversation, which floated through the window aperture, Lucy asked Elizabeth if she was ready to retire.

She shook her head. 'I feel that I have slept a year during the past few hours. I can hardly believe — can you? — that just twenty-four of them have elapsed since the column first halted to watch the men ride off toward the thorn jungle.'

The young girl was visibly surprised. 'Surely it has been longer than that.'

Elizabeth managed a faint smile. 'In this country, time does not appear to rule any situation. When one is travelling it extends forever ahead so that one ceases to consider the ultimate destination . . . and yet the single month I spent at Ratnapore contained such drama, tragedy and circumstance it might be difficult to match it within a year in England.' She sighed. 'Now I have spent but a day at Judapur and my life is irrevocably altered. All our lives have been touched by what has happened here, my dear Lucy. Not one of us will be the same as those who set out in the darkness of midnight, thankful to be escaping the dread of cholera and filled with a sense of adventure. For one, thankfully, sanity has returned and he welcomes his friends once more.'

As if on cue, Rupert came back in to the room. He seemed strangely hesitant, and Elizabeth was puzzled by his serious expression which was somehow belied by a light of gladness in his eyes as he looked at his childhood friend. Crossing to Lucy, he took her hands to raise her from the chair so that she stood before him, a small slender figure whose smile gradually faded as she gazed up at him.

'Something is wrong, Rupert. I know that look so well,' she declared firmly. 'Tell me what it is.'

'It concerns Captain Nicholson,' he explained in tones more gentle than Elizabeth had ever heard him use before. 'He is dead, Lucy.'

The girl studied his face, frowning with incomprehension. 'The fighting is over; you told me so yourself. How can Henry be dead?'

'You wish me to be truthful, do you not?' he asked even more gently.

'You have always been so with me. Of course I wish it.'

The light played on their two blond heads — so close together — as Rupert broke the shattering news that Henry Nicholson had shot himself five minutes before.

'I don't understand,' cried Lucy, clearly unable to accept the bizarre notion of her husband's suicide. 'Henry was unharmed by the mutineers — I saw that he was when I came to the fort. He bore no mutilations, no unbearable suffering to turn his mind to such a thought. Why would he feel he could not live?'

The boy, who appeared to have matured overnight into a man of responsibility, slid his arm around her shoulders. 'He could not accept the burden of blame for the mutiny. They were his men who slit the throat of Lieutenant Peters and killed a number of their former comrades . . . to say nothing of wounding Elizabeth. You must accept, my dear, that a military officer can face anything with great fortitude except personal disgrace. Nicholson had lost the respect and allegiance of his men. He knew his career was finished. That was why he could not face the future.'

'But you did not stay with your men during the attack,' she countered hotly. 'Henry denounced you bitterly for leaving the field, but *you* have not put a pistol to your head.'

'I shall pay a lesser penalty for that lesser crime. I am ashamed, Lucy, but I will ensure that it never happens again. After last night, Nicholson could never have been certain of doing so.'

The scene was an extension of the feeling of unreality which had overtaken Elizabeth. She found it difficult to accept that the dour, slightly sinister, Henry Nicholson had possessed enough emotion to feel remorse of such magnitude. She felt no sense of compassion, no sadness now that the man had been driven to take his own life because some sepoys had surrendered to loyalty of blood rather than regiment. So negative a personality as his, had beckoned no one to draw close to him. Even his wife had been afraid of him, and most people would surely feel glad that the girl had been so easily set free from marital bondage to an unlikeable, ageing husband. Gladness would come to Lucy later. Now she was merely bewildered.

'What must I do, Rupert?' she asked from the circle of his arm.

'Unless you wish to see the body, and I would not advise it, you should stay with Elizabeth and try to sleep. You are both bereaved. A quiet period in which to recover your composure is essential.' Here, Rupert looked across to include Elizabeth in the next statement. 'Rest assured that you will both be accorded full protection and the greatest consideration by every officer at Judapur. You need not be anxious or frightened during the coming days and, just as soon as the situation has calmed, arrangements will be made for your safe return to Ratnapore.' Bending his full attention to Lucy once more, he added, 'I think it will be best for me to leave you now. I shall be near at hand, however. Do not hesitate to send word if you need me, no matter what the hour.'

The girl stood gazing for a long while at the door through which he had vanished. Then she turned as if in a trance and crossed slowly to

Elizabeth, her face immensely youthful with the glow of returning hope upon it.

'How odd that you should declare that we shall all change after this day,' she murmured, lost in a sense of incredulity. Sinking into the chair, she frowned at the floor. 'Henry is dead. *Henry is dead.* I cannot understand the fact.'

Elizabeth felt too weary to do more than say, 'We shall both accept our new status in time. Let's both prepare for sleep and pray that we are blessed with a little during the coming night.'

The blessing came more easily to Lucy than she, for Elizabeth heard the girl's soft breathing while she lay awake herself, considering for hour after hour what her future might be. No inner visions materialized to provide hope; no abstract sensations of gladness or even grief helped to lessen the feeling of lost identity. Of one thing she was very certain. When she returned to England, as she must, nothing would make her live with the Delacourts again. The spell of India was no longer upon her and she suddenly longed for Sussex where Lavinia would surely provide the haven she desperately needed.

The bare stone chamber looked alien and unfriendly as moonlight flooded through the high aperture to suggest incarceration in an invulnerable stronghold; a place from which she might never escape to seek the woman now released from a bond resented for so long and so instantly severed. The world lay before her yet the impulse to explore it had vanished. The one person who would make it attractive must remain here when she left.

Her thoughts were interrupted at that point by the sound of two voices on the other side of the thick stone wall; voices which carried clearly through the aperture to first mystify then shock her. The officers were either unaware of her presence in that chamber or they had taken no heed of the possibility that she might be awake.

'It's the deuce of a problem,' said one. 'If that sweet little girl were not with us he'd be buried before dawn and thankfully forgotten. But the widow has to be accorded the usual formalities, which no one save the blackguard's pretty fellows wish to observe.'

'At such times convention makes fools of us all,' the other commented. 'Consider! His fellow officers despise him, his widow will surely be overjoyed at her freedom, the generals of the East India Company will breathe an enormous sigh of relief yet the whole disgusting affair will be hidden beneath a cloak of military respectability. Death by his own hand will at least excuse the bestowing of military honours at his interment, but the convenient solution of dropping him into a hole at the dead of night and covering him swiftly with at least six feet of soil is denied us. We shall stand at the graveside with suitably solemn expressions for the sake of that pretty little creature who will never know how black a villain her husband was.'

'Thank God she won't . . . aye, and society, too. The stigma would remain for years and she'd be known as the widow of the British officer who sold his honour for love of brown-skinned boys.'

Elizabeth heard all this with growing chill. These irate men were suggesting something unacceptable concerning Henry Nicholson, but they continued, unaware that their free speaking was overheard by a woman who had no previous comprehension of such sexual irregularity. It was all the more terrible to her ears.

'Stavenham has bound us all to silence, but it's certain to be known throughout the Indies before long.'

'You're not suggesting that . . .'

'No, no, not the poor devils taken as hostages. They're bound by the rules of honour Nicholson betrayed. It'll be the sepoys who'll spread the word. Most of them have respect and regard for their officers. The fact that Bennett found them shackled and incarcerated in the dungeon containing the bodies of Fraser and Main, while Nicholson was being fed and fêted by his supposed captors, has disgusted them almost as much as it has us.'

'The fancy for boys is his unfortunate affliction, I suppose. Bad enough under ordinary circumstances, but dangerous in a profession demanding obedience to orders upon which lives depend. But to use his perversion to protect his own skin, while doing nothing to spare anguish and humiliation to his fellows, is beyond understanding. His corpse should be treated as the bad meat it is.'

They began to move away and their voices faded. 'Stavenham's too much a stickler for protocol to allow that, whatever his private thoughts on the matter. He's also too conscious of the presence of ladies here — a circumstance he regards with great regret. The situation is damnable enough without females on our hands.'

The night grew silent again, save for Lucy's gentle breathing, and Elizabeth's shattered thoughts were now all for that young girl's future. She would have to return to her mama and twin sisters in England, a widow at seventeen, with every risk of being married off to another unsuitable man as soon as the official mourning for her debauched, dishonourable husband was over. Another widow returning to her homeland, leaving the love of her life here in India!

The expected attack on Judapur Fort did not come. When a messenger arrived a week after their victorious entry through the rear gates, it became clear that events had moved fast. As they had guessed, Dhakti Fort had been similarly invested by Ganda Singh's troops. With no thorn belt there to aid surprise, the British contingent had fared badly. More than half their number had been lost in the initial clash of arms before they had been forced to retreat for some miles. There, two days later, a second bloody engagement had accounted for the rest, as the Indians vacated the fort on orders from the Sirdar and swept back to Ratnapore.

With evidence of corruption, murder, and all the usual evil which accompanied struggle for power between ruthless aspirants to the throne, the communiqué stated that an all-out war against the Sikhs of the Punjab was now inevitable if stability was to be maintained in that vital area. Aggression was reaching flashpoint in every province, so a concerted attack must now be planned. John was ordered to leave a token force of sepoys in the stronghold and return to Ratnapore to take temporary command of his regiment until a new colonel arrived to replace Justin Lakeland, whose health had finally broken after a severe attack of cholera.

After reading this message, John sat consumed with anger. Two savage and bloody engagements for control of a fort that no one really wanted now! Countless deaths and mutilations suffered during hours of anxiety, fear and deprivation — all for nothing! Anguish of spirit and body while his brain sought for solutions to situations which now counted for nothing! Within the space of a mere twenty-four hours, the strengths and weaknesses of those around him, their loyalty or fecklessness, their personal goals had been revealed under duress of the highest order. Now they were told to pack up and go back whence they had come because some greater issue was at stake. Yet what greater issue could there be than a man's life? How could he tell those who had fought alongside him that what had occurred at Judapur was of little account to their superiors, who must concentrate on the wider problem of controlling the Punjab?

His anger raged for a long while, then subsided into the rational thoughts of a man experienced in warfare. He knew commanders must act on known situations because the future was largely unpredictable. Countless soldiers had been needlessly sacrificed in this way; they would be again. Such was the uncertainty of war. Anger was futile, he knew that, but the sadness of being a survivor of a hard-earned victory, only to learn of its unimportance, now filled his heart, making it heavier than ever as he contemplated the major offensive likely to be launched in the autumn.

So, two weeks after leaving Ratnapore, the column formed up to return to the cantonments. It was a great deal shorter and contained a number of dhoolies and makeshift hospital wagons. George Humphrey was miraculously holding on to life against all expectations, although the journey could well finish him. Sir Rupert Carruthers, who, under normal circumstances, would have taken William's vacant captaincy, was prevented from doing so because he was under open arrest awaiting court martial. It was a tricky case. John could not charge him with cowardice in deserting his men during battle. There had been nothing cowardly in the way he had chased the enemy with the intention of slaughtering as many as possible. John finally charged him with disobeying orders on the field of battle. It was particularly unpleasant to enforce punishment upon the brother Hugo had held in such affection and pride, but the man himself would have done so and Rupert would be strengthened by this setback to his career. As for their confrontation on the battlements of Judapur Fort, that score was now settled, for good or ill, and neither man would allude to it again.

They left at Judapur the graves of many fine men, and one above which there was no cross or mark. Although John had pledged his officers to silence concerning Henry Nicholson, his suicide denied the man any Christian ritual at his burial, and young Cornet Bennett had been so horrified at what he had found on carrying out his order to seek the hostages on entry to the fort, he had blurted out the facts indiscriminately, thus informing the troops of the sordid truth. Nothing could be done to stop the story racing the length and breadth of India but, due to the flavour of the scandal, it would circulate in male circles only on a society level. Lucy would be spared the worst of humiliations before she left India.

The three nights spent in travelling were less jubilant, yet less watchful, than the outward journey. A temporary truce was in force to prepare for the major clash. Small contingents could move safely about

268

the country while attention was concentrated on gathering the strongest army to launch against an old adversary. The widows of the two officers shared a tent and rode together with a respectful escort. The strict demands of the obligatory mourning period made it easy for John to restrict his attentions to no more than those expected of any commander. He welcomed the excuse. He was uncertain of everything save the coming war. The sense of destiny in this land was strong, yet still elusive, despite the fact that he was returning to Ratnapore with many things changed. The successful storming of the fort had secured the trust and respect of those he commanded, and that vital vote of confidence would now be offered by others. Temporary command of his regiment would banish the resentment toward a transferred Hussar, and surely must finally eradicate the gossip over his marriage to Clare and the subsequent diplomatic furore over her mysterious disappearance. If she really was alive and living as an Indian, he would have to face the dilemma it would pose when it faced him — and that would not be until after the war, if he survived it. Apart from that possible setback, his reputation for sabre-rattling and inviting actions in which those with him were exposed to danger should be seen in the light of the present situation. In time, the blame for Hugo's death might also be lifted from his shoulders when Rupert was seen to have dropped his vendetta. John Stavenham, acting colonel of Forrester's Light Dragoons, was returning to Ratnapore as the conquering hero. His heart should be light, not weighed down by sadness and regrets.

Temporary command of the regiment occupied John fully during the next few weeks. Justin Lakeland's personality, which had demanded that he keep subordinates permanently in their place, proved the greatest problem in taking up the reins. Consigning very little to paper, so that it could be read by juniors who would then be as wise as he, the former colonel carried this knowledge in his head — a head which was now *en route* to Calcutta. John was obliged to spend much time with General Mason's aide in order to bring himself up to date with facts which would influence the coming campaign. He also took the opportunity to tighten discipline and drill the men in a new awareness of unity. With troopers and officers arriving from other regiments to bring Forrester's up to full strength, it was the perfect time to breathe new life into them all. He switched officers so that the weaker captains had highly efficient subalterns in support, and young men of the late, dissolute and reckless Calthorpe's ilk were controlled by captains who stood no nonsense. John was also adamant and delighted over the bestowing of William's vacant rank on George Humphrey, despite the fact that the man might not be back to full fighting capacity when the army was ready to move against the Sikhs. All these drastic changes from someone who was relatively junior, but whom circumstance had elevated to command very swiftly, might have been condemned by General Mason. He had known John for some years, however, and had recognized a future leader in a man whose youthful folly had blighted his early advancement. He was given a free hand with a regiment which needed reorganizing. From the men of Forrester's, who might be justified in resenting such sweeping changes from a transferred officer only briefly in command, there came no word of complaint. John Stavenham had won the admiration of distrustful, undisciplined men at Judapur. When an officer achieved that, soldiers would follow him anywhere.

All through those weeks of concentrated occupation, John was conscious of his underlying unhappiness. Professionally he was on a peak, yet his personal life was as devoid of affection as it had mostly been. His destiny did not appear to be linked with everlasting love. Long acquaintance with inner loneliness enabled him to subdue it beneath military duties, and the study of the land which had been his home for more than a decade. But it rose to the surface dramatically when he crossed the avenue from his quarter one day at sunset, ostensibly as the present colonel of William's regiment, to visit the man's widow on the eve of her departure for Calcutta. Elizabeth and Lucy, together with another woman whose husband had been lost at Dhakti, were joining a party from a nearby station which consisted of several officers whose wives were taking their children back to England to be educated. These arrangements had been made with his approval and he had detailed two of his own officers as escorts on the first leg of the journey, to the place where the entire party would gather to finalize their plans. But he had not spoken privately to Elizabeth since the day he had taken her to her dying husband. It proved impossible to watch her leave without saying what he must.

Ringing the small handbell to summon Elizabeth's bearer, John waited in the familiar bungalow, recalling the day he had returned to find a big blond man moving in to the accompaniment of loud oaths. How well he remembered the shock on discovering that his new companion was the husband of a woman he then believed to be an adventuress. Delacourt was now dead; his wife had been no heartless wanton. Yet the love he felt for her must still be denied.

The bearer departed to announce his arrival, then returned to usher him to the sitting-room. She was wearing black, as convention demanded, but John knew that the tautness of her pale, pointed face was not due to grief for her lost husband. She had intended to leave William; depart from a relationship which no amount of time or effort would enhance. The knowledge that he, himself, was the cause of her deep unhappiness intensified his own. In consequence, his opening words were stilted.

'Forgive me for neglecting you in the demands of my profession.'

She gave a slight nod. 'Duty must take precedence over all else. There is to be a war, as you have long predicted.'

They fell silent, each aware of the other's need to speak, yet almost afraid of what would be said.

'May I sit down?' he asked eventually.

'Of course.'

From his chair he studied her: hair in a neat coil over each ear, black silk dress which covered her from just beneath her chin down to her wrists and then to the floor, jet mourning jewellery. Her expressive hands now lay motionless in her lap; Delacourt's rings still on the left one. Glancing back at the face which had captured him with its vivacity at their first meeting, he saw that same desperate sadness which had shadowed her expression as he had left her in Miss Mount's parlour to go off and rescue a woman trapped beneath a dresser. That memory allowed him to approach her now.

'Elizabeth, you must have heard tales concerning my marriage. There are many versions circulating in India, none of which is entirely correct.'

A faint smile touched her mouth. 'You'll not be surprised to learn that my dear friend Lavinia Mount acquainted me with one of the vague versions on that first morning in Wellford.'

It drew a return smile from him. It was a tense smile. 'So you knew more of me than I of you during those unforgettable weeks.'

'Can you never forgive me for my deception?'

'I forgave you when you gave the reason for it. You know that I did.' There was silence again until he began the overture to what must be told. 'I should like to give you the truth about my wife.'

She nodded encouragement.

'Clare was travelling through India with her father. She was several years older than the young subaltern I was then, and a great deal more experienced in life. I married her against all advice, knowing that my career would suffer. It surely did, but more drastically than I could have imagined. The qualities in her which I found irresistible were unacceptable to the rigid rules of Anglo–Indian society, particularly the military section.'

He stared at his linked hands for a moment or two, lost in recollection of a time he had thought banished from his mind. Then he looked back at Elizabeth. 'Clare belonged to herself and no one else — something I was too immature to see. She could not endure life tied to an army officer, so she simply walked away from it early one morning. Everyone assumed, as I did, that she had met a terrible fate. Racial tension mounted to danger point while a search was mounted. The fact that no evidence of her murder was ever found rankled at High Command, where men of consequence had been made to look foolish before their Indian counterparts. I was not forgiven.' He sighed, as much with impatience at his own folly as with that of his superiors. His glance appealed to her for understanding. 'You will surely imagine something of my personal anguish during that period. I know your extraordinary powers sensed it. You told me so at Wellford.'

'My dear, I deceived you,' she confessed in her softest tones. 'It was no inherited powers but Lavinia's gossip which prompted my remark that afternoon. But I certainly found powerful understanding of what effects such cruel tragedy had wrought upon you. It enabled me to reach beyond the protective barrier you had erected at the time and find the true man.'

Her confession caused no dismay. Perhaps he was beyond such emotions now. 'You have witnessed the aftermath of battle, Elizabeth. War against the Sikhs was my first blooding. An experience of such magnitude drove all other forms of pain from me. I was able to cut Clare from my life and obtain legal dissolution of the marriage after seven years, on the grounds of her presumed demise. I therefore believed that I was free to marry you when I fell so completely beneath your spell in Wellford.'

'Please, John . . .'

He shook his head. 'Thank God you were not the widow I thought you to be. There would now be the most deplorable situation — with you the greatest sufferer.'

Shifting her position on the *chaise-longue* her face became shadowed by the tatties over the window, so he could not see her expression as she asked, 'How is it that you know of your wife's continuing existence now, when there was no clue to the fact after the official search?'

Restless, he stood up and moved across the room to where he could see her more clearly. It was important to him that they should face each other without evasion. 'I told you at Wellford that I sensed destiny awaiting in India. It can only be destiny which sent to Judapur that section of Ganda Singh's army which we attacked, and that same force which decreed that one of our captives should be the only man possessing the key to the mystery. As I rode through the camp on the night before we stormed the fort, I saw my former bearer; the man who had left my bungalow with Clare while I still slept and who had also vanished.'

Elizabeth rose to her feet to cross and take his hands in sympathy. 'A cruel move on destiny's part at such a time, my dear. A very cruel move indeed.' Her eyes were bright with threatening tears as she asked, 'This man told you where Clare is to be found?'

Her use of his wife's first name did not seem strange. There had always been such great understanding between them. 'He knows where she was a year ago.' With a sense of slight shock he found himself trying to defend the brutal desertion of a woman he had once loved so passionately. 'She was enslaved by this country, by its cults and rituals . . . and by its people. Her paintings were canvases of brilliant colour, fiery moods and Eastern symbolism. She loved to wear jewel-bright saris. She would loosen her black hair so that it hung to her waist, and touch her skin with the musky perfumes of India. I was enthralled; society was disgusted.'

'Are you trying to tell me that Clare Stavenham is living as an Indian woman?' she asked so quietly it was almost breathless.

He nodded slowly. 'In a village near the borders of Tibet. Her . . . husband . . . is a dealer in carpets. There are four brown children. She goes to the well for water and performs the normal daily duties of an obedient Indian wife, although she continues to paint. Nothing would stem the tide of her artistic fascination with her natural homeland.' He took a deep breath to steady himself before adding, 'Ramu declares that she is in the realms of eternal happiness now.'

For a long while they looked at each other with the love and understanding which had come so swiftly upon first meeting, and yet they were unable to find words to follow what he had just revealed. Finally Elizabeth broke the silence.

'The man might be lying.'

'He might. I shall only know the truth when I go to the village in search of her. There is no chance of my doing that with war threatening. The previous one lasted for two years, the next could be longer.' He gripped her hands tightly. 'If I survive it I shall then take leave and travel to Tibet.'

'Yes . . . of course,' she murmured, drawing her fingers from his and turning away. 'You must love her very deeply.'

'Once I did,' he responded quietly to her retreating back. 'Until I see her again, I shan't . . . After the horrors of war, and with a legal document severing her from my life, I believed myself free of the spell she had cast.'

'Now you're unsure of that freedom?'

'I'm unsure of my *legal* freedom. My wife is not dead. My wife is married by Indian rituals to a man who has sired four children by her. It's the very deuce of a tangle.' He strode across to stand so close behind her he could feel the tenseness of her body and smell the light perfume which would always remind him of their fleeting joy at Wellford. 'I can offer you nothing. The legal and emotional complexities of my marriage must be resolved before I can feel free again. I could disregard what I have been told and let the matter rest as it does now, but the doubt would always remain. Nothing would induce me to ask any woman to share my life under these conditions. I'm also on the brink of going to war, with all the risk to life and limb which battle entails. God knows, I can offer you *nothing*,' he finished desperately.

Still with her back to him she said, 'I understand, John. I do understand that, my dear.'

Gazing down on her shining hair and the curve of her neck, he asked through a tightening throat, 'What will you do when you reach England?'

'Go to Vinnie. I believe she will welcome me and join my campaign to improve the lot of the ordinary soldier.'

It was curious that such a prospect should cause him pain, driving him to say, 'You surely do not intend to emulate Lady Mason.'

'You disapprove? I had not expected that from you,' she declared, turning to face him to show that she had regained her composure. 'You once advocated a meeting with a like personality, if you recall.'

274

The pain intensified as he said, 'You'll not go so far as to sport bright wigs and vast gaudy crinolines.'

'I think they will be essential,' she told him with a hint of laughter in her voice despite the whiteness of her cheeks. 'How else shall I capture attention and fill stupid old gentlemen with fear and dread of an encounter with me?'

Suddenly, love was there between them as it had come at their first meeting, unexpressed but stronger than life itself. It was in their eyes, their expressions and even in the deliberate withholding of so much as a touch. He knew that Clare Stavenham had no hold over him whatever.

'Elizabeth, if I should fall in the coming campaign, remember only Wellford. If I should survive, there'll come a day when your morning ride along the hillside within the grounds of Wellford Manor will coincide with that of a man on furlough from India. He will tell you that the destiny he once sensed in this sweet and savage land was the discovery that life has no meaning without you.'

Her silence was her acceptance of the little, yet the very most, he could offer at parting. He left before that parting grew too unbearable.

Epilogue

The day on which Lucy Nicholson was to marry Captain Sir Rupert Carruthers dawned fine and warm. The villagers of Wellford were filled with excitement, for the bride, despite being a widow of nine years standing and almost twenty-six, looked no more than a golden-haired girl whose radiance encompassed everyone she met. The bridegroom was as attractive and dashing as a fairy-tale prince and if he was sometimes a trifle arrogant, his rank and consequence surely excused it.

The wedding promised to be the grandest spectacle they had witnessed since Sir Francis Stavenham had married Estella Groves, although this new alliance was vastly more romantic. The bride had apparently loved Sir Rupert since childhood. In consequence, she had refused to oblige her mama by accepting any one of the three proposals received from mature gentlemen after her husband shot himself following a military scandal in India. The bridegroom had been decorated for valour during the second Sikh War, which had resulted in the total annexation of the Punjab by the British in 1849. No sooner had he returned to England with his regiment than he was selected to join Lord Cardigan's staff in the Crimea; a great boost to his career. He had met his childhood sweetheart in the interim, however, and letters then passed between the pair throughout that terrible campaign which had changed the whole structure of the Army. These letters had led to an attachment which was to be celebrated in the village church today.

Lavinia Mount was taking credit for the match, although everyone knew it was due more to Elizabeth Stavenham's kindness; for when the bride's mama lost patience and accused the girl of spoiling the marital hopes of her unattractive twin sisters, Lucy Nicholson had come to live in the cottage her friend had bought in Wellford. The 'two Indian widows', as the pair had been known locally, had kept house together for several years after the birth of Edward Delacourt. No one in Wellford would deny that Lavinia Mount was entitled to take credit for ensuring that the child's grandparents did not win their bid to take him from his mother at birth, for it was Lavinia who implored the Rector to engage his nephew — the famous London barrister — to take on the case and settle it before it reached court. A few people were inclined to believe that she had also had a hand in bringing about the subsequent union of Elizabeth Delacourt and John Stavenham. The Postmistress had revealed that she had once forwarded a letter to the Major written in Miss Mount's copperplate script. There were even a few who slyly hinted that Master Delacourt was misnamed, but only a fool could imagine that mouse-haired, inoffensive little boy to be the offspring of any Stavenham, whatever might have occurred in India. Elizabeth's second child was proof enough of that. A sturdy two-year-old, with hair almost black and eyes as blue as the ocean, the baby was a miniature of his father.

The Rector's nephew had also handled the extraordinary affair arising from John Stavenham's first marriage. Although the facts had been kept relatively secret, stories had filtered through from various military sources suggesting that Clare Stavenham was not dead, as everyone thought. The more exaggerated versions had the woman a slave-girl in a pasha's harem, or a dancer with a travelling band of carpet merchants. Thrilling though such prospects appeared to simple Sussex country folk, no one really believed them. There was little doubt, however, that the Major had been obliged to seek legal freedom from a wife who had flagrantly ignored her marriage vows in that far off heathen country. In addition to this knowledge of a wife shed by dint of the law, the existence of the Delacourt child had robbed the quiet wedding of Elizabeth and John Stavenham of the air of romance they so loved. Yet the pair had been very evidently devoted to each other and a perfect match. Even so, the satin and lace of today's bride's antique wedding-gown with a veil which dragged the ground for twenty feet, plus the presence at the Manor of noblemen and women who would normally not even stop to change horses in this sleepy village, made the Carruthers wedding an *occasion*.

The church had been decorated with several hundred golden roses and an equal number of white carnations. The bride would be followed by eight small girls carrying long ropes of gold and white blooms. John Stavenham was to give the girl in marriage, in place of her late father. The mama and plain sisters would be there only in the hope of catching the attentions of the groom's fellow officers; according to most villagers who did not have a high opinion of any mother prepared to push her

277

beautiful daughter into the arms of yet another ageing husband, in order to make things easier for her unmarriageable sisters.

Elizabeth sat in the Stavenham pew beside Lavinia. Her dear friend and companion was looking younger and younger, she thought with affection. With so much now to occupy her time and emotions the lonely old age she had feared was driven away.

On discovering that she was carrying William's child on her return from India, Elizabeth had taken a cottage in the village and invited Lucy to share it. Thus she had gained the sister she had never had, and Lavinia had taken Lucy under her wing with suitable affection. The plump brindle-haired woman was constantly back and forth between Walnut Tree Cottage and The Briars, and so were the two widows. When Edward had been born prematurely, it had been Lavinia who had set out in the snow to fetch the doctor. Nothing could have delighted the elderly woman more than a baby to love and guide through his early years. She longed to see the family picture complete; longed for it so dearly that she went beyond the bounds of her position several years later on hearing that Forrester's Light Dragoons were returning and Major Stavenham hoped to be at the Manor by Christmas. She wrote to John in a respectful manner, expressing the hope that he would find time to visit her cottage for tea and cherry tartlets in company with the Rector. In a brief résumé of village news, she had mentioned Elizabeth and her fatherless child. Thus had John been warned of Edward's existence so that no sense of shock would spoil the lovers' reunion.

All had gone according to plan, and no one could have been prouder of personal achievement than Lavinia Mount on John and Elizabeth's wedding day. She was disappointed that marriage did not put an end to the work begun by the two widows on first coming to the village. Lucy continued to live with the pair and there was no let up in the campaign for better conditions for soldiers. Indeed, even after little Ross was born, Elizabeth determinedly travelled to London every third month to attend meetings chaired by Lady Amelia Mason — a woman who sounded as if she might be teetering on the edge of madness, in Lavinia's opinion. The disastrous losses from enemy and disease in the Crimea had brought to public attention conditions none had ever thought to consider before. Largely due to Florence Nightingale and a band of determined, influential women, the inhumane treatment of the rank and file in Britain's army became the subject of investigations and reports which caused something approaching a scandal. As many had feared, it had taken the loss of the entire Light Brigade, most of the Heavy Brigade, and a frightening percentage of the Infantry to make the authorities take notice. Reports and bands of outraged women alone would have made little difference. However, once the first cracks had appeared in general indifference, it was easy to break down the barrier altogether. Lucy and Elizabeth had marched through London with a banner held aloft in company with Lady Mason and her followers. Lavinia Mount had been highly disapproving of their behaviour and could not understand John allowing it. But he had encouraged the pair, even more so when Sir Rupert returned from the war against the Russians and confirmed the very worst atrocity stories sweeping the country. All four had then joined forces in the campaign and were waging it still. The only good thing to come from it, in Miss Mount's opinion, was that she had charge of the two boys while their parents were pursuing their cause.

Elizabeth was deep in thought on the subject of how it had taken the loss of half an army to bring about a study of the hospitals in which the sick and wounded had little chance of recovery. Recalling Surgeon-Captain Cockerford, who had been killed during the Sikh War by a crazed patient who refused to have a leg sawn off, she wished he had survived to see the reforms he had yearned for in vain. A smile touched her mouth as she recalled Lady Mason's plan to administer a light dose of poison to those at High Command because her letters never appeared to reach them. Letters were reaching every destination now — Buckingham Palace, in particular — and vast changes could not be avoided by even the most insensitive old die-hards. By the time another war began, which it surely would in a world where exploration and civilization was opening new frontiers, men need go less in fear of being taken to places formerly regarded as houses of death rather than centres of healing.

Thinking back to that morning when John had first told her of his voyage to India around the Cape, and of Lady Mason's championship of the shilling-a-day soldier, Elizabeth suddenly realized that an acute awareness of his presence was invading her. She was startled that it should do so, for she had not experienced the phenomenon since the morning of their glorious reunion. As the organ began to play and Rupert emerged with his best man to wait for his bride, inner rapport with John grew so strong she was almost fearful. What did it mean?

They had been married for three years and had a child of their own. No two people could be closer. Why, then, should his approach, with Lucy on his arm cause this breathless state? When Rupert half-turned to smile at her, she was filled with sudden inexplicable pain; a foreknowledge of immense human suffering which left her so weak she grasped her pew desperately. Brief visions accompanied the physical sensations and these brought a sense of relief — wide plains, brown faces filled with hatred, a tented camp littered with dead and dying — she had seen the past, not the future this time, she reassured herself. An emotive occasion with so many of the guests in the scarlet of Forrester's and the colours of other famous regiments could hardly fail to evoke vivid memories. Rupert and Lucy; John and herself! They had been through so much together it was not surprising that echoes of India should invade this Sussex village today.

Lucy was as beautiful as a bride should be. She had matured into a sophisticated, serene woman under the guidance of herself and Lavinia; a worthy new member of an esteemed family. Elizabeth smiled as she recalled Rupert saying in engaging, ingenuous protest, 'I am a *Carruthers*, ma'am.' Within half an hour, poor little Lucy Nicholson would be Lady Carruthers, with the world and an astonishingly adoring husband at her feet.

Elizabeth's gaze moved to the man who led the radiant girl up, to someone she had loved all her life. John was not the same person she had first encountered; suspicious, unhappy, changing moods with disconcerting speed. Their love had brought out the sunshine side of his temperament; their son had fulfilled him as a man; a decoration for gallantry in blowing the gates of Judapur Fort had removed the last reservations on his mililtary ability. The chapter on Clare Stavenham had been closed. She hoped it had also been forgotten. John had never spoken of his meeting with his former wife on the borders of Tibet, but she imagined how distressing it must have been for a man to see, under such circumstances, someone he had once loved quite madly. The divorce had been obtained, after initial difficulties which had made Elizabeth wonder if it would have been easier to leave the affair as it had stood. Only the wit and skill of the Rector's nephew had enabled the decree to be passed without proof of Clare's existence being produced in court. They had married a week afterwards and John had not mentioned Clare Stavenham since then. At forty-one, he was strong, confident, and immensely contented, in a way he had never known in his lonely life. Yet, as Elizabeth studied his broad back now, with love which had widened and deepened until it was an ocean with no limits, the sensation of overwhelming anguish swept over her once more, and filled her with apprehension. However emotionally-charged this day was, she had never suffered perception of the past in such a manner. Why should it trouble her in the midst of great happiness?

In something of a daze she watched the marriage being solemnized and kissed the happy pair, who had grown close enough to her to be the brother and sister she had never had. Fear retreated to the back of her mind during the wedding breakfast held at Wellford Manor. The old rooms rang with laughter and good nature, ending with toasts to the wedded pair and to everyone present. The most wonderful aspect of all was that Rupert had engaged a man he had encountered in the Crimea who was to make Daguerreotypes of the occasion. Even though it obliged the new husband and wife, plus attendants and principal guests, to sit absolutely motionless for long minutes while the operator dived beneath a cloth to work his equipment, everyone agreed that the new discovery of creating images on pieces of card was truly amazing.

When Lucy went off to change, Elizabeth saw Rupert momentarily isolated and went across to him, taking his hands in hers affection-ately. 'It has been a day none of us will ever forget. I have no need to beg you to make her happy, for your devotion is clear for all to see, but I have one request to make of you.'

'You had best make it quickly,' he teased, 'for my bride will be back and I shall carry her off without waiting for advice. I have had more than enough from my well-meaning brother officers over the past few days.'

'Poor Rupert,' she laughed. 'A *Carruthers* must be more than equal to such things, I'm certain. I merely mean to ask that you do not plague the poor girl with your constant complaints of the meals which are served to you on your honeymoon.'

He laughed with great fondness. 'You'll never forgive me for that, will you?'

'No,' she affirmed. 'There were times when I would have gladly slipped away into the night to escape you.'

'No, really? Was I as pompous as that?'

Growing serious, she said, 'My dear, Hugo has been here in spirit, you know. I have sensed it very strongly.'

He nodded, his eyes very blue in a face strengthened by experience. 'I too. He would approve of Lucy. Hugh was always the most amazingly discerning of fellows.'

'Still singing his praises?' she teased gently.

'I always shall, Elizabeth. He was the best brother any man could have.'

Squeezing his hands, she said, 'There's no doubt he would say that of you now, dearest Rupert. Keep that in sight as you go through life. May it be long and as happy as it is today.'

When the lovers had departed for a secret destination and the guests had dispersed, Elizabeth and John strolled through the grounds of the Manor toward the Dower House where they had lived since their marriage. They walked arm-in-arm behind Lavinia and the children. The late afternoon milkiness of sky and atmosphere cast a drowsy hush over Wellford now that the excitement was over. The sound of a song thrush, sitting high in an oak to express his joy in the day just ending, touched chords within Elizabeth which brought a return of apprehension. She said nothing of it to John, nor of the deeply felt pain on waving Rupert and Lucy off on their happy journey. Why had it seemed more like waving them goodbye for ever?

'Father and Tom must be turning in their graves,' mused John as they slowly crossed the grass, especially vivid in the pre-dusk light. 'The old house has been slowly recovering its dignity beneath the care of Giles and Roseanne, but the laughter, happiness and social goodwill filling it today must have banished the last of the depraved ghosts lingering there. It's a true home, filled with love and lightness. I never thought to see the day.'

She glanced up at him. 'You have no regrets that it is not yours, that your children will not grow up in the wonderful atmosphere it now contains?'

He did not answer immediately and something in his expression told her that the shadows which had flitted across the clear skies of today had not been echoes of the past.

'You have something to tell me,' she stated quietly. 'I sensed it from the moment you entered the church with Lucy, but I believed it must be the spell of India upon us all. You're going to reveal that it was the future I saw, aren't you?'

He stopped walking and drew her round to face him, taking her hands which had grown cold. 'What did you see?'

282

'Wide plains, savage brown warriors . . . a battlefield similar to Judapur. I felt pain, John, immense inner pain caused by anguish of the spirit rather than by wounds. What did it signify?'

'After you departed for the church with Vinnie, I received a communication from Horse Guards. The regiment is ordered to India with the greatest speed.'

Immediate recollections rose in her mind of slow brown rivers, plodding oxen, laughing children scampering freely in quiet villages; of brilliant birds, racing startled deer, rioting blossoms and purple hills standing against an evening sky tinted apricot as the sun vanished. Memories of long lines of elephants, camels and wagons; of sad-faced mules laden with guns and stores, and lines of marching men in bright coats, who carried flares to light the path through darkness, all returned so clearly to her in the midst of that green Sussex village. All this was India, the land in which she had discovered both love and fear.

'You have been home only four years. Why this return so soon?' she asked with growing apprehension.

He coaxed her to walk on as he told her of something which deepened his voice with concern. 'You already know how welcome all military men have found the new Enfield rifle. It has, however, created in India a spark of hatred which is fast turning into a flame. If fanned, that flame will become a conflagration covering the entire continent. The cause of the conflict is a new bullet for the rifle, the cap of which must be bitten off before use and which is greased to ease its insertion to the barrel for firing. Word is out that the lubricant is that of animal content, either from the cow or pig. Sepoys have refused to use the bullet on the grounds that they would be forced to swallow grease containing something offensive to their religion. Their officers assured them that their fears were groundless and ordered them to accept the cartridge. They then mutinied, killing the officers and any British troops they encountered, before setting fire to their barracks.'

Elizabeth halted again, gazing up at him with a troubled expression. 'Have they a case?'

He shrugged. 'It's an easy enough matter to change the grease so that it causes no offence, but you know as well as I that social unrest has been encouraged by racial agitators for many months and this anger within the ranks of soldiers will provide the perfect opportunity for outright revolt.' He smiled grimly. 'When planning an uprising of the people, first capture the support of the army. My dearest, this time the whole of

India is seething with mistrust. British rule itself is now endangered. Control must be restored before the whole nation is overwhelmed by an orgy of fire and bloodshed. Several regiments with Indian experience are being rushed out in case the entire East India Company force collapses.'

Calmer now that she knew the reason for her premonitions, she asked swiftly, 'What of Rupert and Lucy?'

'I made him aware of the facts and he will tell his bride at an appropriate moment. They will have to continue their honeymoon on the voyage . . . between Rupert's duties.'

Only then did the full import of this news reach her, and she turned away in agitation to walk across the lush grass to where a slight rise gave a view of the grouped cottages. Now she understood the sensation of immense inner anguish; now as she recalled a conversation she had once had with Fanny Humphrey in which she had claimed she would not care to be faced with a choice between staying in England with her children, or abandoning them in order to be with her husband. That choice faced her now, and it was one of the most painful a woman could encounter. Glancing across to where Lavinia was chatting in lively fashion to those children who had brought fresh youthfulness to her later years, Elizabeth knew the first spasm as her heart began to tear.

Edward, the boy William had sired without knowing the fact before he died, was a quiet, hesitant creature who felt very deeply that he was a cuckoo in the nest despite John's immediate and warm acceptance of him as a son. As a result, he was inordinately fond of Elizabeth. Yet all her efforts to imbue him with confidence had failed. The fact that his name was Delacourt, when the other three of his family were Stavenhams, emphasized his unwarranted sense of isolation. Without her, Edward would be lost. Her glance moved to the sturdy toddler, hopping and skipping beside someone he regarded almost as his grandmother. Little Ross was bold, full of mischief, supremely confident. He defied Edward's gentle attempts to protect him with brotherly affection — no Rupert-and-Hugo hero-worship between this pair — and was never happier than when playing soldiers. The child possessed a charm he already used to gain what he wanted from Edward, from Vinnie and even from John. Only with his mother did he recognize an authority which could not be won over with a smile and a wet childish kiss. Without her, Ross would grow wild.

John came up behind her and took her shoulders in a loving clasp. 'You must decide . . . only you, my dearest girl,' he told her softly. 'The regiment will sail two weeks from today, but you will have to give me your decision in time for me to make whatever arrangements will be necessary.'

Turning away from a scene which was beginning to blur beneath her gaze, she saw with perfect clarity the face which was dearer to her than any other. 'I shall come with you, of course.'

Only the light in his eyes betrayed his relief as he asked, 'What of the children?'

She smiled. 'They will grow and develop with determination, as we did, and will seek their own destiny. It seems we still have ours to meet in India.'